PENGUIN BOOKS
RAGE

Balaji Venkateswaran grew up in India and pursued a master's
degree in engineering in the United States. He works for a software
company in the San Francisco Bay Area, where he lives with his wife
and two children. This is his first novel.

RAGE

a novel

BALAJI VENKATESWARAN

PENGUIN BOOKS

PENGUIN BOOKS
Published by the Penguin Group
Penguin Books India Pvt. Ltd, 11 Community Centre, Panchsheel Park, New
Delhi 110 017, India
Penguin Group (USA) Inc., 375 Hudson Street, New York, NY 10014, USA
Penguin Group (Canada), 10 Alcorn Avenue, Toronto, Ontario, Canada M4V
3B2 (a division of Pearson Penguin Canada Inc.)
Penguin Books Ltd, 80 Strand, London WC2R 0RL, England
Penguin Ireland, 25 St Stephen's Green, Dublin 2, Ireland (a division of
Penguin Books Ltd)
Penguin Group (Australia), 250 Camberwell Road, Camberwell, Victoria 3124,
Australia (a division of Pearson Australia Group Pty Ltd)
Penguin Group (NZ), cnr Airborne and Rosedale Roads, Albany, Auckland
1310, New Zealand (a division of Pearson New Zealand Ltd)
Penguin Group (South Africa) (Pty) Ltd, 24 Sturdee Avenue, Rosebank,
Johannesburg 2196, South Africa

Penguin Books Ltd, Registered Offices: 80 Strand, London WC2R 0RL,
England

First published by Penguin Books India 2005

Copyright © Balaji Venkateswaran 2005

All rights reserved

10 9 8 7 6 5 4 3 2 1

Poem on p.286 is a translation from the original Tamil 'Dance of Women's
Liberation' by Subramaniam Bharati

For sale in the Indian Subcontinent only

Typeset in Sabon by InoSoft Systems, Noida
Printed at Saurabh Printers Pvt. Ltd, Noida

For Amma and Appa

Do not consider a man fortunate until you know the circumstances of his death.

—Marcus Aurelius

Do not go gentle into that good night . . .
Rage, rage against the dying of the light.

—Dylan Thomas

Prologue

When she first met her mother, Lakshmi was six years old, too old to remember her, too young to forgive her. The only mother she had known was her grey-haired grandmother who wore the nine yards of her sari with meticulous care, the thalapu wrapped carefully around her shoulder, its loose end tucked in well at the waist, and every crease kept in place by the starch that the maidservant soaked the sari in.

Her mother had appeared suddenly one evening. The lights had gone out, plunging not only the house but the entire neighbourhood into darkness on that new moon night. Nobody saw her come in, and nobody knew that she stood at the threshold peering through the darkness at the small figure in the far end of the room. When a neighbour lit a petromax lamp, a milky-white skein of light appeared through the window, throwing ghostly shadows all over the room. It was among those shadows that Lakshmi suddenly noticed one that moved in the direction opposite to all the others. She shrank in fear and stared at the nebulous form in the doorway.

'Don't be scared, Lakshmi,' her mother whispered to her, stretching out her hands, 'I'm your mother.'

In the unnatural light Lakshmi could see the stranger's skin, the colour of straw, stretched taut and diaphanous like a veil, revealing blue and purple lines that slithered over one another like earthworms. 'Amma!' Lakshmi screamed and ran into the other room where her grandmother was telling her prayer beads as well as counting the number of years since she had last seen her daughter.

'Lakshmi, my child!' her mother exclaimed and followed her.

When she got to the inner room, she smothered Lakshmi in her arms.

The lights came back on, but all Lakshmi could see was yards of sari around her, the slippery silk fabric making it difficult for her to hold on to anything. She could feel the woman's body heave and throb. She couldn't tell if the woman was crying or laughing. Scared, Lakshmi made vain attempts to reach out for her grandmother who sat impassively on the floor.

'I've come back for you,' her mother said. 'I've come to take you home.'

'Amma!' Lakshmi cried, struggling to free herself from the woman's octopus-like arms.

But her grandmother sat motionless through all this, still counting on the beads. When she finished all one hundred of them, she sighed and got up. Then she calmly walked over to them, pulled Lakshmi from her mother and said, 'Devaki, she doesn't need you any more. Don't you remember your promise?'

'It has been six years, amma.'

'That's why you should leave her alone,' her grandmother replied, her gaze meeting Devaki's eyes implacably.

'How can I?'

'You promised, Devaki. That was my condition.'

Lakshmi stood behind her grandmother and blinked with the utmost bewilderment as she watched the two women argue. She noticed the contrast between them: her grandmother—her 'mother'—speaking firmly, quietly, with such conviction that she felt safe hiding behind her; the strange woman, becoming increasingly distraught, pointing at her with her long, slender, and fashionably manicured fingers ('like those of a slut', as her grandmother would describe them years later).

Finally, after much pleading, her mother turned to her. 'You tell your grandmother that you'll come with me. To your mother!'

Lakshmi simply stared back.

'I'm your mother, Lakshmi!' she said in frustration.

Lakshmi put her hands around her grandmother, refusing to respond. And, oblivious to her pain, her grandmother said to her mother, 'Devaki, listen. I'm the only mother your daughter knows. You can never be a mother to her. That's the truth. Now leave the girl alone and go back to your man and your indecent ways.'

So saying, Lakshmi's grandmother waved Devaki towards the door. Devaki stood still for a few moments, looking at Lakshmi pleadingly once again. But Lakshmi's face remained relentlessly defiant, her expression hard like her grandmother's.

Lakshmi noticed how a few drops of tears appeared like pearls, paused momentarily at the rim of the woman's eyes before slithering down her face.

'Go away or I'll call the neighbours to throw you out!' her grandmother threatened.

Devaki knew her mother was capable of carrying out her threat. Just as she had thrown her out once before, she would do so once more. Not wishing to create a scene, Devaki retreated. She walked out of the house quietly, her shoulders crumpled.

Lakshmi's grandmother then called out, her tone ringing with finality, 'For your own daughter's sake, don't ever come back!'

And then she shut the door on the wraith-like figure who now passed out of Lakshmi's life for a very long time.

Moon-Face

As I sit at my desk and think about Lakshmi's mother I realize I cannot rely on either Lakshmi's version of the story, nor her grandmother's, for both were prejudiced in different ways. To Lakshmi's grandmother, Devaki was a daughter who had gone bad and had brought shame upon her. To the little girl, she was a stranger, an upstart who suddenly appeared on the scene trying to usurp her grandmother. And later Lakshmi, who grew up learning from her grandmother never to forgive people, could never bring herself to even look at her mother who spent the rest of her life watching Lakshmi from afar, ready to do anything for her if only she would allow her to.

To do any justice to Devaki I have to look deep beyond the stories I have heard about her from them and to reconstruct in my own words the events that led to her sudden reappearance that day to reclaim her only child whom she had foolishly given up six years before. I sometimes have to picture them in my mind's eye as they were then, go into their minds and pry out their thoughts with my pen-forceps. I'm not entirely sure if what I write about Lakshmi's mother is true or not. Perhaps my own vision is now coloured, perhaps my imagination sometimes overwhelms me, but this is the closest I'll ever get to the truth . . .

At that time, before Independence, while the country wore darkness like the brooding, black funereal garments of its foreign rulers, there existed a City under the city. This vast, cavernous underground City, buried in the bowels of the outer city, was inhabited by political activists, revolutionaries, writers, artists and all other kinds of patriots as well as some social renegades and scoundrels. It was a city as big and bustling as the outer one, but because it was underground there hung in it an even greater gloom, a pallor, like miasma emanating from the mosquito-infested coastal swamps, so thick that only the bravest and the most determined could survive its dark dungeons that suffocated with conspiracies and the smell of volatile ink and gunpowder. In this parallel City, where furtive glances replaced handshakes and the Stygian air once inhaled ironically rejuvenated passions, the inhabitants had built everything they needed to pursue their goals: printing presses, movie studios, libraries, markets, maidans where people gathered for meetings, and dungeons within dungeons where the most covert of plots were hatched. People travelled between the outer and inner cities with ease, living two seemingly contradictory lives of submission and subterfuge, transmuting themselves at whim from one form to another, from the languid city of the overlords to the furtive, invigorating City that the British had only heard of, but could never visit.

It was in the studios built somewhere in the endless maze of streets in the underground City that most of the movies made from the scripts that Lakshmi's grandfather wrote had to be screened. For all of them were subversive and would most certainly have been banned if released through normal channels. Indeed, the government had standing orders to arrest many of the members of the films' crew for seditious activities.

The only people who saw these films were the inhabitants of the City, who assembled eagerly in cramped rooms smelling of sweat and sambar, guilt and excitement. Invariably these movies ended in victory, sometimes with the melodramatically enacted death of the hero, shot through the heart by a British bullet or hanged in the gallows as he cried hoarsely, 'Long live Mother India!'

Besides working on movie scripts, Lakshmi's grandfather also published and edited, under the innocuous pseudonym of

S. Krishnaswami Aiyer, an underground newspaper in the local language as well as in English. The newspaper was not only famous for its nationalism, but also for its predilection to denounce the culture and values of the imperialists, often in such vitriolic terms that even he sometimes shuddered with glee when he read it in the staid, upright surroundings of his room at home, where quite like Frankenstein's monster he devoted his leisure hours to reading Tamil and English literary classics, and other similarly innocuous pastimes.

His articles were said to have the potential to set the City ablaze, working up the tempers and the nationalistic fervour of its readers. Hartals, arson and looting were not uncommon; randomly roving mobs wielding cycle chains, rocks, sticks, kerosene cans and broken bottles sometimes burnt down government buildings, particularly police stations, in the city above. It was increasingly difficult to control his readers. But Lakshmi's grandfather seemed to be either unconcerned or to derive pleasure from seeing the crowds go berserk. In any event, he neither altered the strident tone of his editorials nor urged his readers to keep calm.

After one serious incident in which half a dozen policemen were clubbed to death in the dead of the night in retaliation to the arrest of a freedom fighter, an all-out search was instituted for Lakshmi's grandfather. A day or two later he waited for them, sitting in an easy chair in the quadrangle downstairs after a ritual oil bath, in a freshly starched veshti, an equally bright white shirt and, a silk angavastram on his shoulder. On his forehead he had smeared sandalwood paste after prayers. He had even put on his slippers. He seemed to know when the police would come. And when they did, he serenely allowed them to lead him away.

A week later, a magistrate sentenced S. Rangachari, aka S. Krishnaswami Aiyer, to ten years in jail.

At that time Devaki was a painfully thin and shy girl of twelve. She had been unaware of her father's shadowy activities; in fact, she did not even know what he did for a living. All she knew was that a steady stream of mysterious visitors came and sat in her father's room, sometimes for a few minutes, sometimes even overnight, and then left, as silent and nervous as pall-bearers. Devaki had never been inside her father's room. Whenever she was anywhere near that room, her mother would descend upon her and chase her away in the same short, irritated manner in which she shooed away the pesky crows that sat on the terrace greedily eyeing the rows of karudams and appallams that had been left to dry in the sun.

Her father rarely spoke. And when he did, he spoke in a whisper, as though he was constantly afraid of being heard and recognized. He left home every day before dawn and returned after the street lights came on at night. The neighbours rarely saw him and knew him only as Devaki's father, the phantom figure who could recite passages from the *Thirukkural* even in his sleep. His manner of talking was so infectious that sometimes even his wife spoke in whispers.

Mostly, he remained so preoccupied with his work that he was hardly aware of what was going on in the house. It was Devaki's mother who did everything: she bought the provisions and vegetables, cooked and fed the two of them, supervised the maid-servant as she sat on her haunches washing dishes or clothes in the courtyard, enrolled Devaki in the Montessori school, bought her clothes, took her to school every day, signed her report cards, prepared for festivals, taught her songs composed by Muthuswamy Dikshitar and Thyagaraja, and took her once a month on an excursion to visit some of their many relatives who were scattered across the City.

Her mother never told her what her father did. Devaki subconsciously knew that the subject was taboo and hence never asked any questions. On the rare occasions when her father did emerge from his room other than at mealtimes and spoke to her or took her on his knee, she would glow with pride and spend the rest of the day whispering joyfully to her imaginary friends and her only toy, a wooden rocking horse she called Hari. Indeed, she grew up thinking fathers didn't talk to their children, and when, one day, she realized that other fathers in the neighbourhood not only talked to their children but also played with them—throwing them in the air and catching them as they came shrieking down—she ran home in tears and asked, 'Amma, why does appa never speak to me?'

Her mother looked up from the upma cooking on the stove and said, 'Appa is a special man. He lives in another world. It is people like him who will earn us our freedom one day.'

Devaki wiped her tears, her interest piqued. 'What is freedom, amma?'

Her mother considered the question. 'Freedom is being able to speak normally. Freedom is having your father at home more often. Freedom is being happy.' Since then Devaki associated being happy with the day her father would speak to her, and impatiently looked out through the vertical bars on the window in her room, like those of a prison cell, waiting for her father to come home running with his arms open to catch her and toss her into the air. She waited every day to hear her father knock on the front door. But he never did; when he came home late at night he just whispered to her mother through the window. Or sometimes he didn't come home the entire night.

When the policemen took him away, she cried in her mother's arms all night.

'He has gone to jail,' her mother told her proudly.

Her father did not come home for many years. By the time he did, she was too old and he was too weak to pick her up in his arms. He never did knock on the door. Even when freedom was imminent.

In the underground City, standing by S. Rangachari constantly as friend, admirer and collaborator in his different avatars of editor, scriptwriter and orator, was the handsome moplah megastar, Nasser Sharif, son of a landowner who reportedly owned half the rubber plantations in the south-western corner of the country. Known by his chiselled, perfectly proportioned features, deep dark eyes and massive frame, he was also the raging heart-throb of the day. He always played the character deeply in love with his motherland, who invariably gave his life for it at the end of the film with such panache that even the governor, a ruddy Englishman who, like Churchill, believed the Empire would never crumble, once remarked, his cheeks flushing pink with admiration and righteous indignation, 'He does seem to have the knack to whip up passions, don't you see, in a raw, native sort of way.'

It was to him that Devaki's father turned when he realized what awaited him. Sitting in his dank, gloomy room at home, inhaling the clouds of smoke his friend puffed into his face, he said to Nasser, lowering his voice further, hoping his wife and daughter could not hear him, 'I'm concerned about my family, Nasser. I know they're preparing a prison cell for me.'

Nasser Sharif shushed him. 'Don't say such inauspicious things. But if they do get you, be assured that I'll provide for your family as though it were my own. After all, your wife is like my sister.'

Devaki's father took a deep breath, his worries about his family lifting slightly from his shoulders. 'Yes, I'm glad I can depend on you. But I'm worried about Devaki. She's still young, and needs a father . . .'

'Why do you talk like that?' Nasser said. 'Devaki is my daughter also. I'll bring her up as I would bring up my own daughter. I swear that on our friendship!'

Later that day, when Nasser had gone, Devaki's mother admonished her husband. 'I heard what you said to him. You talked to him as though we're destitute. Why should he take care of us? Don't I have a brother who'll provide for me? And as far as being a father to our daughter is concerned, he's Muslim!'

Devaki's father naturally balked at the insinuation. 'So what if he's Muslim? He's closer to me than any of my real brothers. Don't go around talking like that in front of Devaki.'

Devaki's mother snorted indignantly, pulled her sari tighter around her shoulder and said tartly as she walked away, 'I don't trust that man. You're too drunk on patriotism to see it. Don't forget, he's an actor, a very good one.'

Devaki's father flew into a rage. 'Watch your tongue, Savithri!' he whispered angrily after her. 'Take that back! You don't say things like that about people who are spending every waking moment of their lives fighting for your freedom!'

But his wife was gone, confident in gait, defiant in gesture, not regretting a word she had said, somehow very sure that one day events would justify her cynicism.

Devaki, bright-eyed, was mesmerized by the milky studio lights, the star-spangled sets depicting rustic, courtroom, prison and battlefield scenes. The words of endearment that chivalrous heroes and coquettish heroines whispered into each other's ears baffled as well as excited her because they were so full of dangerous and forbidden possibilities. Nasser Sharif sent shivers through everyone's spine with his honeyed words, his insouciant manner, his daring escapes, his indomitable courage. When he lay dead on the country's map in one scene, signifying a son resting his head on his mother's lap, Devaki, teary-eyed, whispered, 'You can't die. I won't let you die!' And when the lights were turned off and the actors jumped down from their sets, she stood still, sobbing softly, drowning in the vast waters of her girlish fantasies. And Nasser Sharif came up, put his arms around her small body, comforting her as she shivered with excitement, and said, 'Now, now, child, all that was only make-believe.'

But she never listened to him. She watched his cigarette-stained lips part to produce soothing, guttural sounds while his enormous Adam's apple danced in tandem with the alternate rise and fall of his theatrical voice. Had she not seen his gallantry just moments ago with her own eyes, heard him talk of a love greater than that between two human beings? Had she not seen him sacrifice himself for a greater, nobler cause? To her the distinction between the world of the underground studios and the real world in which she lived was becoming increasingly blurred, the veil between fantasy and reality so thin that she could walk through it, as if clearing cobwebs in her path.

She was clearly stricken—by what, her mother could not tell. But her mother did not like her accompanying Nasser Sharif to the City, especially to the film studios where no decent person would ever go (she had only grudgingly tolerated her husband's activities there), least of all the daughter of a respectable family. 'I don't like the things she's being exposed to in the studios,' she once told Nasser when he came to pick her up.

He laughed. 'Chechi, my akka, why do you worry? She's my daughter. I constantly keep an eye on her even when I'm at work. She's just a child marvelling at the novelty of the studios. She'll get over it.' But he was wrong. Months and years passed by, and Devaki remained as starry-eyed as ever. She was now old enough for her mother to supervise her dress: the davani had to be just right, the skirt long enough to cover her ankles, and the only make-up she could wear was kohl.

And yet, after she finished school her visits to the underground film studios with Nasser Sharif increased so much that it became her primary home. The stars and starlets, dialogue-writers and lyricists, cameramen and sound technicians, extras and those hopeful of becoming stars themselves were all part of the larger family she now identified with. At home, her mother increasingly complained about her and Nasser Sharif, threatening her with dire consequences: 'You shameless wretch! No boy from a decent family would ever marry you!' And during her allocated visits to her incarcerated husband, she spoke of nothing else. She accused him of ruining her daughter's life and shouted at him when he tried to pacify her. 'Nasser, Nasser, Nasser! That's all you can say. Yes, he's there to take care of her. But you don't understand—that's the problem!'

Meanwhile, in the film city a thin, weakling of a boy, a year or two older than Devaki, who acted out two-bit roles for a meal and a few annas a day, was also becoming increasingly smitten. The one characteristic that people remembered of him from those days was that he constantly had a cold. He wore a sweater even when everybody else sweated copiously. He had a sickly, emaciated look. His was not a simple cold that one catches during sudden changes in the weather and then shrugs off, but a chronic malaise that affected him for many years, causing him to have a perpetually runny nose, a nasally, scratchy voice, and watery eyes that stung. And he always sniffled, inhaling large amounts of air, grunting loudly like a dissatisfied pig.

His name was K.P. Mutthukumar, but everybody called him Mutthu. He had remarkably good features. But because of his emaciated look, his rustic, clumsy ways, his constant cold, his eyelids drooping as if to protect his burning eyes from the elements, he appeared somnolent and slow-witted. Directors usually ignored him. Occasionally, when they couldn't bear having him hanging around the sets, staring at everyone morosely, they gave him roles in mob scenes where he had to stand in a crowd and shout slogans from the farthest corner of the frame.

As he spent his time with the other hangers-on, staring wistfully at the glamorous roles that the stars played, his eyes fell on Devaki, who was privileged enough to stand behind the cameraman, as though she were part of the crew. He started spending all his free time gazing at her worshipfully, trying to sneak his way close to her till he was rudely ordered out of the way by the crew. He stood in rapt attention, listening to what she said, observing what she did, hoping to anticipate her needs and jump forward to tend to them, materializing in front of her like a genie—anything just to be of assistance. But his debility slowed his reflexes, dulled his eye, and he usually ended up stumbling before her, smiling weakly and appearing confused. He would then slink away in shame, stand in a dark corner of the studio, ignore the buzz of activity around him and continue to stare at her wistfully.

But while Mutthu's eyes were on her, Devaki was conjuring up dreams and girlish fantasies of her own, awe-struck by the man she worshipped, the fire inside her burning fiercer, her determination to defy her mother's commands becoming stronger by the day. And Nasser Sharif, that man whose skin glistened like the dusk and who had the deep voice and the perfect features of a god, continued to attract a large following to his movies. His capacity to move the audience was so great that nobody left without a tear in his eye and a promise to fight on his lips. After one particularly powerful performance he was escorting Devaki home through the dark side streets and alleyways, somewhere between the underground City and the one above, between darkness and light, where nobody could see them, she threw herself into his arms, pressed her burning lips against his chest and wept hot tears with all the passion she had bottled up these past years.

Nasser Sharif reeled under the sudden impact of her body against his and by this display of forbidden passion, finally unleashed. He started to chide the young foolish girl in his arms, the girl toward whom he felt paternally disposed. And so he began to formulate the words 'Ai! What do you think you're . . .' in his mind, when suddenly he realized that the soft body sobbing against his chest was not that of the little girl in two ribboned pigtails he knew a few years ago, but that of a woman. Celibate Nasser Sharif had begun to believe in his on-screen role of a man who could not be distracted from his pursuit of a greater love. He had adamantly refused the matrimonial proposals his parents put forward and had thus far ignored the scores of female admirers who sent him all kinds of veiled and not-so-veiled love notes. At first he was repelled by Devaki's touch, but was surprised by how soft and delicate her skin felt. He had always imagined that every human body was as coarse and raw as his own. Even as he wondered how to handle Devaki, he felt his body relax involuntarily into hers.

'I cannot live without you!' Devaki sobbed.

Nasser, confused, still unable to decide whether he should give her a resounding slap or express these new emotions he was feeling, stood still, not breathing, doing nothing, finding it easier to be indecisive. At last, when Devaki had finished crying and had somewhat loosened her grip on him, he unclasped his arms and whispered to her, calling her not by her pet name—Paapa—but by her real name, Devaki. This sent a shiver down her spine, for she was finally being recognized as a person, *a woman*. But what he said was itself a little disappointingly prosaic and anti-climactic, having none of the extravagant heft of movie dialogue, none of the suave confidence with which he spoke on screen. The words that came out of his lips were so tentative that he sounded almost scared: 'Devaki, let's go home.'

A few weeks before Independence, the British, in a rush of indifference born of their impending departure, released all the prisoners from the City's jail, criminals and political activists alike. When S. Rangachari walked out of the prison he had expected a riotous reception from his supporters, but he was shocked to find only his wife waiting in the shade of a mango tree, her madisaar worn impeccably as usual, but her face grim. The first thing she said when he walked up to her almost caused his heart to fail.

'You've lost your daughter,' she said with a certain amount of perverse satisfaction.

'What happened?'

She clicked her tongue impatiently as though he should have known. 'I don't know what's got into her, but surely it is those film city friends of yours who have twisted her mind. She's not a Brahmin girl any more. She's not the daughter you and I had hoped to raise.'

'She's alive then!' he exclaimed with relief.

'Of course she is,' Devaki's mother retorted. 'But what's the use? She has brought shame on us. She spends all her time with these cinema people, running loose like an untamed horse. Who knows what she's up to?'

'Tchah! You're always exaggerating. You almost made my heart fail for no reason.' He looked around. 'Why hasn't anybody come with you?'

She looked at him askance. 'Whom did you expect? The viceroy?' They walked in silence for some moments. 'You're wondering why even Nasser Sharif has not come to receive you, aren't you?'

He nodded, his forehead creasing in a frown.

'It's been many days since I've seen him. There's only so much friends will do. I think he feels he has done enough for us. That's why he comes home only once or twice a month nowadays to find out how we are.'

He looked absently at her. 'But still, at least he should have come,' he said.

When they arrived home he heard Devaki humming a film song, standing in front of the mirror, adjusting jasmine flowers in her hair. 'Appa!' she cried and ran towards him. Joyful though he was, he remained standing in the veranda, looking at his daughter in surprise, for never had he seen her dressed so well, wearing a sari like a woman, her blouse cut in the latest fashion, cheeks pale with talcum powder, and the fragrance of the flowers in her hair wafting through the house. But more than her physical appearance what had caught his eye was the manner in which she stood in front of the mirror: boldly, with a conspiratorial smile playing on her lips, her face glowing with an inner secret. He wasn't sure if this was what he had expected from his shy, timid, daydreaming daughter.

All that evening he did not talk to anybody. He locked himself up in his room and looked around. Everything was as he had left it. The open magazine on his desk, his chair still in the same place he had pushed it back to when he had gone downstairs to wait for the police. Yet the room felt stale and unfamiliar. He opened the window to let in some fresh air. He went to the radio on the mantelpiece, his constant source of news from around the world before his incarceration. The large brass knob was lacklustre. A cloud of dust flew up at his touch. The radio crackled, but there was no news of his release. The books on the shelf were also coated with dust. He picked one at random, a thick-spined, leather-bound gift from an old friend—silverfish had dug tunnels through its pages. He put it back in despair.

He brooded. His wife's warnings somehow did not seem like the ravings of a paranoid woman any more. He sensed that not everything was well. Even as he pondered the change in his daughter, he could not help noticing that as the hours passed by, nobody came to visit him. He was sure news of his release was public knowledge by now. And, yet, nobody knocked on the door. He felt as though he had come back to a world where, like an amnesiac, he did not recognize anybody, and, worse, where nobody seemed to remember him.

That evening, after dark, he wore a white veshti, a white shirt, threw a white towel over his shoulder and said to his wife before leaving home, 'I think I need to have a long talk with Nasser.'

When he returned late that night he was cold and shivering although the weather was as hot and sweaty as ever. He went to his room and lay on the coir cot under layers of blankets. His hands and feet were clammy, his face wet with perspiration, his shirt stuck to his back, but still he shivered. As the night wore on he could feel the sweat on his burning forehead. But no matter how tightly he wrapped the blankets around him, the sensation of sleeping on a block of ice did not leave him.

He would suffer from this fever for the rest of his days; no amount of medicines, herbal concoctions, home-made tonics would cure him, for the fever was not physical, but an emotional affliction that none of the doctor's instruments, nor his years of experience, could diagnose. He had realized what nobody else had.

When he went to Nasser Sharif's house everything he had feared was reconfirmed. He noticed how evasive Nasser Sharif's responses were, how he nervously shuffled every time they talked about Devaki. He also noticed how Nasser Sharif did not call Devaki by the names he had used when she had been a baby.

It was shame that had prevented Nasser Sharif from going to welcome his friend outside the jail. S. Rangachari's visit to his place on the first night of his release caught him by surprise. 'I had entrusted my daughter in your care, and I'm indebted to you.' His friend had begun the meeting rather solemnly, sitting on the edge of the cane chair in his living room. Those words had been enough to fill Nasser with remorse, and after that he floundered, dithering like an idiot, wearing his guilt clearly on his face. But his friend, so belligerent when attacking the imperialists and very mild-mannered and non-combative in real life, spoke in his customary soft-spoken manner, as though he had observed nothing. 'Devaki has grown into a beautiful woman. Half the credit goes to you. If I had not gone to jail she may have continued to be shy and socially inept. I see that you've been a better father to her than I could ever hope to be.'

But after his friend left, bent and sighing resignedly like an old man, without having made a single accusation or having expressed any bitterness, Nasser Sharif lay awake all night, feeling wretched as he imagined his friend looking at him accusingly.

He had the same vision every night as he kept drifting between sleep and wakefulness. At such times he covered his face with his blankets, thinking of the hell he supposed he would now go to, promising himself he would not lay his eyes on Devaki again. But, inevitably, the next day when he pulled Devaki into a secluded corner of the studio to tell her that she was no more than a child, he found himself holding her in his arms, feeling his shirt drenched with her tears.

Finally, after weeks of distress, he decided he had to make some choices. He had to put an end to all this drama of teenage infatuation and his almost incestuous feelings for Devaki. He decided he would be firm with her, he would tell her in no uncertain terms that all this was nonsense, that she should hold her passions in check. But even as he made up his mind a small voice within him seemed to say, *Telling her off was all fine, but what after that? What about him?*

In the end the voices inside him turned out to be more difficult to subdue than Devaki.

And so, as the Union Jack was lowered in deference to the tricolour and the country rejoiced, Devaki's father lay in bed, ill and unhappy. At midnight, as darkness lifted and the sky burst into a vivid brightness, he kept muttering to himself,

'Nasser, you ungrateful wretch! What has become of my daughter?'

Devaki's mother heard him say this over and over again. At first she dismissed his words as deathbed hallucinations, but later his words started making sense and she sat upright in her chair as if jolted by an electric shock. Her eyes turned red with rage. She brought her face close to his, stared so deep into his half-open eyes that she could see the last vestiges of his life struggling to hold on to him. Then she looked up at the door where she imagined Nasser Sharif to be standing and spat with the kind of fury that people are capable of exhibiting only once in their lifetime. She flung out just one word, just three potent syllables that were to remain the only name by which she'd ever address Lakshmi's father for the rest of her life, a word that simply means Muslim, but when uttered by her, transformed to a vile obscenity: 'Tulukan!'

At dawn people were still rejoicing, beating drums, dancing deliriously, taking out processions all over the country. Nasser Sharif, accompanied by Devaki as usual, walked alongside Rajagopalachari, other Congress leaders and a group of well-known Theosophists. They were at the head of a procession winding its way to the beach, where the statue of the King was dismantled by a mob, and people stampeded to collect its pieces as mementoes of their final victory. Unaware of his friend's death-bed deliriums or Savithri's wrath, Nasser Sharif followed Rajaji on to the dais facing the city and surveyed the crowds around him. Devaki, who had stayed back at the foot of the dais, felt the crowd shove her up the steps. And then a line of men in Gandhi caps, holding aloft the tricolour and bearing huge garlands glittering with silver and golden strands, made its way through the parting crowds, and upon reaching the platform, garlanded all their leaders indiscriminately, piling one garland on top of another until the honourees could barely stand under the weight of the flowers. Then one of the men, eager to get things started, grabbed the microphone and shouted into it rather pompously, 'Long live our country! Long live our leaders!' He paused to survey the distinguished guests as though trying to recollect their names. 'Long live Rajaji! Long live Nasser Sharif! Long live Captain Rajeswari . . .' When he came to Devaki he stopped and held a whispered conversation with another man standing next to him. When he was done he nodded and smiled. 'And long live Nasser Sharif's beloved daughter—our sister—Miss Devaki!'

It was too late for either Nasser Sharif or Devaki to undo what had just been said, for no sooner had he uttered those words than the crowds roared. A group of photographers standing on another smaller platform a few yards away furiously clicked away at them, and a television unit from America focussed its motion-picture camera on them. Flustered by this public and erroneous acknowledgement of their relationship, Nasser Sharif and Devaki looked at each other, confused, unable to stop the surge of events around them. There was little they could do other than pretend to smile and wave to everyone. Suddenly remembering his friend, Nasser Sharif asked the self-proclaimed master of ceremonies, 'But where is Rangachari? How can he not be here at this moment of triumph?' But the man only responded, 'Who Rangachari? Go on, saar, everybody is waiting to hear you. You're next, after Rajaji.' So saying, he pushed Nasser Sharif towards the microphone with a sense of urgency. 'What do you mean? Haven't you been following our struggle?' Nasser Sharif wanted to ask the man, but the latter's attention now turned to the cameras and he smiled, baring all his teeth.

Only Nasser Sharif, the professional actor, could so quickly regain his composure a few moments later without letting either the consequences of the recent announcement or the feeling that this was an undeserved honour weigh on his mind. The crowds cheered deafeningly, the din interrupted only by the burst of fireworks. While in the north people were massacring each other based on whether they turned west to pray or not, he, the moplah who faced west five times a day, stood ramrod straight on that platform with his chest jutting out with pride, an icon of the secularism he and his fellow citizens believed in. Elsewhere the new nation was being born amid shrieks of agony and the spilling of blood, and Nasser proclaimed the free nation to the drunken masses surging toward him. 'The sun will never set on us!' his voice thundered and reverberated, 'Long live our motherland!'

Later that day, unknown to Devaki, S. Rangachari took his last breath in the presence of his frantic wife.

Not even Devaki had remembered her father the previous night or that morning. There was no celebration at their home, no garlands for the real hero, no tears of joy when the tricolour was ultimately unfurled over the country. The many years he had spent in obscurity behind prison walls were enough for the masses to plead amnesia—long enough for even his daughter to forget him.

Late that evening Devaki returned home to find her mother crying over her father's body. As soon as she stepped in, her mother, rediscovering her voice after a long time, screeched at her like a woman possessed, using all the energy she had conserved over the years by speaking in whispers. Her arms flailed about. Devaki could not understand a word of what she was saying. Bewildered, she blinked at her mother innocently when it suddenly became clear to her that her father was dead. She turned to her father, noticed for the first time in death what she had not noticed when he had been alive: the deep anguish, the sense of defeat, the shame of a failed father that creased his otherwise serene face. But surprisingly the presence of the still body did not scare or move her. She looked at her father's body intently, feeling a strange sense of detachment, noticing the fresh blue marks on his neck as though he'd put up a struggle at the very end. A few moments later she looked up at her crying mother and still felt nothing. *It's crazy,* she thought, and pinched herself. She sat still on the floor, afraid to move, afraid to admit that her father had meant nothing to her.

'You shameless tart!' she heard her mother scream. 'How could you, born from this womb, not shed a tear for your dead father? You are the cause of his death. What have I done to deserve a daughter like this? Get out of my sight!' Her mother gestured wildly, approaching her menacingly, ready to pounce on her and throw her out. Devaki shrank back towards the door. 'Get out!' her mother shouted. 'Get out of the house, you ungrateful wretch!' So saying, she pushed Devaki out of the house with both hands and bolted the door shut on her face.

Devaki found her way to the only place she could go to: she fell into Nasser Sharif's arms. When it became clear to him what had happened, he stood still and silent for a long time, his eyes clouding up. 'I must be there to carry him,' he finally said, then left hastily.

But he returned soon, his head hanging limply. 'Your mother wouldn't let me in,' he explained. After a moment's silence he continued, 'I don't blame her.'

Devaki looked at him anxiously.

'What shall we do with you, Devaki?' he asked, sighing.

'She won't let me in. Please let me stay here.'

But it was not so easy for Nasser Sharif. How could he let an unmarried woman stay with him?

To complicate matters, his secretary, a shrewd, perceptive man, appeared before him and gestured him into his office.

'Saar,' he said, 'you know how much respect I have for you, and it is not for me to question your actions. But *this*, saar? What will happen if she were to stay here? You cannot marry her because everybody thinks she's your daughter. It will be the end, saar, the end of your career. And what a career! Magnificent! A-one!' He then shook his head. 'Remember, saar, the public is very unforgiving.'

'Shankaran!' Nasser Sharif said sharply. 'This is not about my career. Now leave me alone.'

'Saar, pardon my impudence, but please give this matter a lot of thought. One bad move and you'll be finished for life.'

Nasser Sharif knew the man was right. And yet, how could he turn her away in her time of need? Besides, he wasn't exactly young at forty-two and his career would come to an end soon anyway. But what would he tell the people who looked up to him? What answer would he have for society?

He spent the rest of the day in his office alone, refusing to meet visitors. When he emerged from it late in the evening he stared at Devaki for some moments. Then he turned away from her, unable to look at her as he said, 'You can stay here for as much time as you want. But please understand that I cannot marry you.'

'Is that it? You looked as though you too were going to throw me out of your house. We don't have to marry. Just staying close to you is more than enough.' She smiled with relief.

A few days after she had arrived at his doorstep, she did go back home and knock on the door, hoping her mother would welcome her back. But the door remained tightly shut. Her mother knew it was Devaki and refused to open it. And Devaki had her answer.

So Devaki lived with Nasser Sharif, unmarried, but for all practical purposes his wife, not just for a few days but till the very end of his life. People who knew them well did frown upon their relationship privately, but nobody dared to criticize him openly because they had too much respect for him. They forgave him his social transgression; he was the icon of free India, a man who had inspired innumerable freedom fighters. Even when they saw Devaki carrying his child they chose to ignore it and carried on as though nothing were amiss.

When Devaki gave birth to a daughter, the surgeon, the nurse and the astrologer were the only outsiders who knew it was a girl, and Devaki suddenly panicked, realizing for the first time that it would not be easy to bring up a daughter hidden from the world. And the baby, with a round, glowing face, gazelle eyes that were wide open even as she came out into the world, fair, milky-skinned, hair thick and black as the night, brought gasps to everyone's lips. She was so beautiful that the astonished doctor and nurse would later recall how they thought the baby was really an apsara. With a determined, full-throated scream she announced her arrival, demanding immediate attention and fawning, for she had come with a purpose.

Nasser Sharif was ecstatic when he saw the baby. Immediately a name sprang to his lips. 'Mahtab!' he exclaimed, for he spoke Urdu (and some Farsi too, people said). 'Moon-face! That's what I shall call my daughter.'

Devaki, thrilled, yet fearful and weak after the Caesarean delivery of her daughter, looked up at Nasser Sharif's ecstatic face and hoped against hope that it would be a new beginning for them.

Only the astrologer was unimpressed. As he studied the charts spread on his vast lap, he clicked his tongue and shook his head. His pouting lips arching downwards in deep, unpleasant thought, he said peevishly, 'Bad omen! Born before her time. What do these modern doctors know? What nerve he has tearing up the mother's belly and pulling out the baby before it's ready to come out!' He paused for a moment and then pronounced without hesitation, 'The baby, having been pulled out before she was ready to face the world, will surely have her revenge. And what's more, she will make her parents, whose union was never legitimized, also pay for this!'

So saying, he stomped out of the room leaving Nasser Sharif and Devaki staring at each other anxiously. Suddenly Devaki's unfounded fears deepened and crystallized. She—who had been smitten by the world of make-believe, where tears were always made of glycerine and where once the shot was done heroes and heroines walked away with smiles into the arms of adoring fans—was once again thrown into a reality in which tears were real and the cries loud. And there were no adoring fans.

Nasser Sharif stood by silently, unable to comfort her, regretfully realizing that he could not turn back the clock now. A living, breathing baby was already here, crying at the top of its lungs, demanding his attention and due respect.

A few weeks later, when she was strong enough to walk, Devaki took the baby under the cover of darkness and knocked furiously on her mother's door. 'Amma!' she cried out softly to her mother whom she hadn't seen since the day after her father had died. 'I beg you to please open the door!'

When her mother finally opened the door, annoyed at the noise, she, too, gasped at the sight of a baby in her daughter's arms.

'Amma!' Devaki pleaded. 'Punish me all you want, spit on me, kick me out on the streets again, but please keep this baby. You can be a much better mother to her than I can ever hope to be. Amma, please don't say no.'

Her mother looked at her so severely that Devaki became scared. It was the same expression of wrath with which her mother had thrown her out of the house two years ago. Living alone without her husband and daughter seemed to have had no effect at all on her; if anything, she looked angrier than ever now.

But when Devaki's mother looked into the baby's face again she was taken aback for a moment. For in the baby's face she saw a startling resemblance, a mirror image, in fact. The same stern expression, those stubborn lips pressed tightly together, that steadfast gaze that was capable of withering even the strongest of people, all this in a face that was also fatally beautiful.

The baby put out a hand and reached for her grandmother's face. Savithri's expression softened a little. She continued to stare at the baby for a long time and Devaki alternated between hope and despair. Finally, Devaki's mother said, 'You can leave the baby here only if you promise never to come here again and never to let your daughter know who you are.' She raised her hand, indicating that that was not all. There was a further price to pay. Her face darkened remorselessly as she concluded, 'And if that tulukan ever shows his face to me again, even by mistake, your daughter will be out on the streets in an instant, like you.'

After handing over the baby to her mother and falling at her feet in gratitude, promising never to reveal her identity to her daughter, Devaki wiped the tears of joy from her cheeks and smothered her baby daughter with kisses. The baby shuddered, turned its face away and cried irritably. But Devaki didn't notice this rejection; or perhaps she did, but was happy just at the thought of being taken notice of by a daughter who would do her best to ignore her for the rest of her life.

When she melted into the darkness that night little did Devaki know that she would spend the next six years in agony, constantly chastising herself for having given up her daughter, hoping her mother would relent, forgive her, and bring her daughter over, just to assure her that she was growing up to be a fine child. For six years she kept her promise for the sake of her daughter, suppressing the ferocity of a mother's love, till the day she could not bear it any longer, when she appeared suddenly like a wraith, only to realize that six years was too long a time for a baby to remember its mother. Or to forgive her.

Growing Up

So it was that Lakshmi, born a couple of months after I was, grew up in her grandmother's house knowing no mother other than her mother's mother. Lakshmi, a piece of the moon, whose beautiful face glowed even (and especially) in the dark. Lakshmi, born out of wedlock. Lakshmi the b—.

No, I cannot use that word. No matter how egomaniacal she may have been in the eyes of the people, no matter how many people amassed godowns full of money in her name and many more died miserably in gutters and famine-parched fields, she was not that. Of course her parents never married, but I can never question their union, or the sincerity of their love for her; under the circumstances they did what was best for their daughter. Besides, Lakshmi and I were the best of friends for many years, so much so that everybody in the neighbourhood predicted that one day the two of us would get married to each other and make such a perfect couple that apsaras would dance at our wedding.

No, she was like any other child in the neighbourhood. Nobody questioned why her mother was so old. The elders somehow knew why without having to be told. The children did not think of asking. Only Lakshmi always asked this question—not to anyone but herself, her rag doll and Hari the rocking horse, none of whom had an answer. But several years later Lakshmi did divine an answer, and it shattered her world forever.

The first time I met Lakshmi was a year or so after her

mother had made her first appearance. Even at that young age it was her eyes that people first noticed; eyes that at once sparkled with intelligence and stared intensely at the world, unblinking, giving her the appearance of one perpetually searching for something. Yet it did not take people long to realize that under this veneer of vulnerability, there was a steely resolve. It was this ability to look both lost and intensely resolute that gave her eyes a power that others lacked, a mesmerizing power that would let her have her way in nearly everything she did.

The first time I witnessed the persuasive powers of her eyes was on the day I first met her. I was exploring the new neighbourhood into which my family had just moved. In one of the tiny streets a group of raucous children had gathered around a little puppy that looked frightened and lost.

'Dai! Whose dog is this?' asked an urchin in the crowd.

Nobody knew.

'So whoever it goes to can have it,' he said.

So they whistled and hooted, made monkey faces and gestured wildly to attract the puppy, and laughed delightedly when the animal shrank back in fear. I watched the crowd's inept attempts for a few moments and broke away from the ring of children by taking a step or two forward. Solemnly I carolled, 'Yooo-yooooo-yooooo-yoooo-yooooooo!' I was sure that it would come bounding to me. But the puppy shrank back further; its uncoordinated legs gave way and it sat down on its haunches against a wall, letting out a volley of frightened yelps.

The other children laughed. Just then a pair of hands pushed me aside and I saw a girl stepping towards the puppy. She crouched low and held a hand out. For a few moments both she and the puppy stared at each other and the crowd fell silent. There was something in the way she looked at the puppy, the way she commanded it gently that convinced the animal. Slowly, hesitantly, the puppy got up, still shivering with fright, and walked towards her. Each of its legs moved in a different direction, but the sum total of its movements carried it towards Lakshmi whose outstretched hands were waiting for it. The crowd cheered. 'I'm taking this puppy home,' she announced to nobody in particular, holding the puppy in her arms, and walked homewards.

The rest of the children followed her, still billing and cooing at the puppy. I too followed, sulking.

'That's not fair,' I complained from behind her. 'The puppy would have come to me if everybody hadn't made so much noise.'

Lakshmi stopped and looked back. Without a word she put the puppy down. She stood next to me and stretched her hand out towards it. I did the same. The animal did not even look at me. After a few moments of hesitation it waddled comically towards Lakshmi and the crowd roared with delight. That settled the dispute.

Lakshmi laughed and said, 'He walks like Charlie Chaplin!'

'Charlie Chaplin!' I exclaimed contemptuously, smarting from my loss, but inwardly I marvelled at her astute observation. I knew I would have said the same thing if only I'd thought of it. 'But it's a dog!'

'*He*,' Lakshmi corrected me severely. 'Yes, he does walk like Charlie Chaplin.'

'Charlie the Dog!' I taunted her as I followed her to her house. 'Charlie the Dog! Who's ever heard of a dog called Charlie?'

The puppy, in the safety of Lakshmi's arms, sensing my hostility, gave me a look of derision that only deepened my misery.

For want of anything better to do I followed Lakshmi to her house. Her grandmother, upon seeing the puppy in her arms, immediately expressed her displeasure. 'I don't want an unclean dog in my house. Take it back!'

Lakshmi looked disappointed even as I began to feel jubilant. She put the puppy down and stared at her grandmother wordlessly. No protests, no complaints, no tantrums. She simply looked at her grandmother with her large eyes, as did the puppy. For a moment I thought her grandmother would stand her ground and turn the puppy out, but she relented, as though giving in to the whims of a sick child. Lakshmi picked up the puppy and joyfully went into the courtyard.

Lakshmi's grandmother noticed me and smiled. 'I haven't seen you before,' she remarked. 'Are you new here?'

I nodded.

'What's your name?'

'Vasu,' I replied. 'Vasuki.'

Lakshmi giggled. I felt foolish. Foolish for having lost the puppy to her, foolish for having a name like that.

Just as I was about to turn around and go back home Lakshmi said, still giggling, 'You can come and play with Charlie whenever you want.'

I left without responding. I was in no mood to accept the consolation prize.

Charlie the Dog wasn't really a dog. Or so Lakshmi's grandmother said, smiling grudgingly a few days later, as he gobbled up a banana she had cut into several pieces for him. She had begun to warm to him. 'He must have been a human being in his previous birth. A muni, no less.'

He—Lakshmi admonished me every time I referred to Charlie as 'it'—became somewhat of a curiosity in our neighbourhood because he almost exclusively ate only fruit. He rarely lapped the milk that Lakshmi's grandmother poured for him in the special aluminium bowl she had set aside in a corner of the courtyard. Instead, he could smell fruit from a long way away and would dart enthusiastically towards it, yapping madly and wagging his tail furiously. When fruit sellers passed by pushing their carts or carrying baskets on their heads, he would run after them and nip at their ankles. No fruit was too exotic for him. He could eat the flesh of a mango and leave out the pit. When offered pomegranates once, he expertly chewed the flesh and spat out the seeds. He especially liked figs—the plumper and juicier, the better.

But for all his fruit eating, he was always constipated and he sneezed frequently. The tip of his nose was always wet and cold, and occasionally mucus dripped from it like the discharge from a gum tree. When Lakshmi took him for his daily walk he left a trail of small, perfectly round, black droppings that gleamed like obsidian beads.

I went to Devaki's house every day to catch a glimpse of the dog, resentful that I had to go there to see him. But her grandmother's welcoming ways slowly converted me from a reluctant visitor to an enthusiastic one. She was always in the kitchen, cooking and cleaning. She had quite a reputation in the neighbourhood for her ability to make sweets and snacks, pickles and appallams, and multicourse meals. Her kurma was legendary, as were several dishes that she reputedly concocted, using spices and vegetables that nobody had heard of. It was said that during her husband's preoccupation with the freedom struggle when he was hardly ever home she spent all her lonely hours in the kitchen dreaming, imagining that the spices, the legumes, the vegetables and the lentils all had personalities of their own. It was after years of spending most of her waking hours with them that she learnt to mould, even command them to exude new flavours that lingered on one's palate for days. It was indeed in the kitchen, that most domestic of places, that Lakshmi's grandfather and his friends sometimes plotted their next move in such soft whispers that even Lakshmi's grandmother, hardly a few feet away at the stove, could not hear them. She not only resented their secretiveness but also their presence in her kitchen because some of them were non-Brahmins, and some, like Nasser Sharif, were Muslim. In defiance she would retreat further into the dark corner of the kitchen, among her boiling cauldrons and spice cabinets, often not even aware of her daughter who was alone in her room staring at Hari, her wooden rocking horse.

Every day Savithri would pull up a little palaka for me in the kitchen and make me sit on it while she plied me with her latest offerings and asked me what I had done at school that day. In that dank kitchen—where the walls were black with layers of soot and spices held together by oil from condensing fumes, where if one were to scratch the wooden rafters one would release age-old aromas, telling long-forgotten stories of underground intrigue and days of yearning and loneliness—I sat down on the wooden plank fashioned into a squat, rectangular stool, awed, even a little scared, as though I had entered a wizard's grotto. Despite its simple construction, the house seemed mysterious and labyrinthine. Even the disused chimney was so remote that Lakshmi insisted that bats lived in it, and the large wooden cupboard containing the stainless steel utensils, having stood stolidly as witness to Lakshmi's grandmother's dreams, was so integral a part of the room that it slowly fused into the surrounding wall. Among the remnants of the echoes of her banished daughter and the now forgotten associates of her husband, Savithri still performed her magic unstintingly, untiringly, although now she warily kept an eye on her new charge, watching over Lakshmi even as she continued to conjure up her recipes.

Lakshmi sat next to me on her palaka, the one that her grandfather had used, and we ravenously ate kesaree and murukku and other delicacies. Charlie the Dog, standing outside the threshold looked on, salivating, whining, snuffling and sneezing, snapping up the occasional piece of fruit that Lakshmi's grandmother threw at him.

Lakshmi's grandmother talked to us incessantly while we ate. Sometimes she told us stories, mostly about Tenali Raman or about a sage and his doltish disciples. Often there was also idle chitchat, about our schoolwork and friends. If she paid special attention to me sometimes, Lakshmi would flash a resentful look at me, put her arms around her grandmother and silently stake a greater claim on her. Her grandmother would then run her fingers through her hair and smile, fully aware of her insecurity.

Lakshmi's grandmother was unusually gentle, even overly indulgent with Lakshmi, as though making up for the harshness with which she had treated her own daughter. Lakshmi sensed this weakness and took advantage of it with all the ruthlessness of a child. Even at that young age she had discovered the power of blackmail. If her grandmother refused her anything, instead of throwing a tantrum like other children, she would protest wordlessly, with a cold, hard stare. And her grandmother, perhaps remembering the daughter she had lost, would relent, much against her own strong will.

But for all her indulgence she kept a vigilant eye on Lakshmi. She brought her up on a strict regimen. Every morning she made Lakshmi recite shlokas after bathing. In the evening there would be no dinner before visiting the Meenakshiamman temple nearby. Sunday mornings were the only times she turned on the old radio, and that too only to listen to the sahasranamam. 'I brought up my daughter without temple and prayer,' she said to my mother once. 'I won't make the same mistake twice.'

Lakshmi also knew the price of disobeying her grandmother. After weeks and months of spoiling her, her grandmother would suddenly burst with fury over the smallest act of disobedience. Nobody could predict her outbursts. Not even Lakshmi, who normally knew innately how far to push her grandmother.

One day Lakshmi was sitting on the steps of a neighbour's house listening to film songs playing on the radio inside when her grandmother happened to walk past on her way to buy vegetables.

'What do you think you're doing?' her grandmother hissed, yanking her from the stairs by her pigtail and literally dragging her home. 'Is this how a Brahmin girl should behave?' She slapped her hard. Lakshmi began bawling.

The neighbour came out. 'Maami, she was sitting quietly,' he said.

Lakshmi's grandmother ignored him. 'How many times have I told you only indecent people watch films and listen to film music? And still you sit there on the stairs, in the open, like a street urchin, enjoying that vulgar music?' With that she gave Lakshmi two more hard slaps on her cheeks. Lakshmi was shrieking now.

The neighbour persisted, 'It's only music, maami. Why are you being so harsh with her? I'll turn off the radio if you want.'

'It's not just music,' she snarled back at him. 'It's filth. She was enjoying it. All that's left now is for her to wiggle her hips.'

With that she dragged Lakshmi in, shut the door and meted out her severest punishment: Lakshmi was not given any food for the rest of the day.

Every day after school I would go to her house, eat the snacks her grandmother offered me, and then both of us would take Charlie out for a walk. Lakshmi had improvised a leash for Charlie with a coir rope that she tied around his neck loosely, and the other end of which she fastened to a pipe in the courtyard before she left for school in the morning. Lakshmi, as possessive of the dog as she was of her grandmother, rarely allowed anybody to hold his leash; only occasionally did she grant me the honour of holding it briefly.

We walked Charlie the Dog to the rectangular tank behind the Meenakshiamman temple. Most of the year the tank was bone-dry and we descended the steps that flanked all four sides to the bottom where dead lotuses were strewn about in the sand. There Charlie the Dog would run, frisking about among the lotus stems and leaves, digging holes and retrieving useless objects like cheap necklaces, torn rubber balls and cups made of leaves.

But even when he did the things other dogs did, he had about him an air of distinction, a grave dignity that was almost human, and a bark that sounded remarkably like an attempt to speak a human language. Indeed, as Lakshmi got more and more attached to the dog she paid more attention to the sounds he made, the Morse code of snaps and barks, grunts and groans, the way he opened his mouth and seemed to laugh sometimes. She listened to him with concentration, nodding at regular intervals as though she was carrying on a conversation with him, clicked her tongue sympathetically when he whined, and patted him on the head when he gambolled up to her. So, one day, when she announced to her grandmother and me that she could understand Charlie's language I should have not been surprised.

'Charlie's language?' I retorted. 'What sort of language does Charlie *the Dog* speak?'

'A special language,' she replied, unfazed. 'Only I can understand him.'

And, as though to reaffirm this, the dog stood by her and seemed to nod approvingly. Her grandmother, having observed this without comment, pursed her lips, and gently, yet firmly, steered the topic of conversation away from Charlie's verbal abilities. She came to me a few moments later, when Lakshmi had gone out of the room, and explained, almost regretfully, 'She's a lonely child. And very imaginative too.'

It was around that time that Lakshmi's grandmother began to find every excuse to invite my parents over—whether it was for a puja even on marginally auspicious days or just for a meal. She would especially insist that my father come too. She'd make Lakshmi show my father her homework, her report card from school, her new clothes. If we planned to go out on holidays to the beach or to nearby towns, she'd ask if Lakshmi could go with us. Sometimes this annoyed my mother, but my father, ever so perceptive, explained to her, 'She's trying to knit together a family for the poor girl.'

I did not understand then or for a long time afterwards why my father referred to Lakshmi as the poor girl. But when I did, years later, unfortunately, it was too late. She did not want my sympathy any more.

The day a whole colony of kuravas camped in the open maidan nearby, there was uproar all through our neighbourhood. In the past kuravas had passed by in the course of their peripatetic life, but they had come in small groups: a family or two, sometimes just a couple and a small child sitting precariously on the woman's wide hips. They had always passed through the neighbourhood, and had never squatted or camped anywhere near us. Nobody knew where they came from or where they went, but like phantoms they would suddenly appear in the mellow light of the evening, chattering amongst themselves unintelligibly, driving their donkeys loaded with their belongings ahead of them, collecting sticks and fallen branches from the streets, and they would disappear into the darkness, never to be seen again. For the most part everyone ignored them and they ignored the residents of the neighbourhood too. Occasionally some of the residents complained that the kuravas were polluting the agraharam, the Brahmin neighbourhood, that they would steal or encroach upon their property.

But this was the first time that so many kuravas had appeared at once. Like all the kuravas before them, they appeared suddenly. It was only after they had occupied the maidan unnoticed, like an invading colony of ants, that their presence was felt.

That evening I joined my friends and we stood at a safe distance from the maidan, watching them build their houses. They had already cleared the maidan of the overgrown grass and weeds, mercilessly hacked the unruly bushes of wild berries and thorns around the edges to make more space, and flattened anthills hidden in the grass. The men, in their loose pantaloons and brightly coloured shirts, were building shacks from wooden planks retrieved from discarded crates, from tin sheets, dried coconut palms, cardboard, stones and bricks. They used clay and nails to hold these items in place and weighed down the thatched and tarpaulin roofs with bricks and rocks. They then plastered the walls with a layer of cow dung that made the dun-coloured shacks look smooth and clean.

In the meantime, the women were building small ovens with some of the bricks and had gathered dry twigs and branches to light them. As they walked briskly, carrying clanking pots and pans and fetching water in enormous copper vessels from the roadside tap, their long red embroidered skirts swished about them, the thick white and red and green bangles on their forearms jangled in a cacophony of sounds that mingled with their animated voices, their shrill laughter and their incessant chattering. Their children ran all around, chasing each other, screaming at the top of their voices, pulling at each other's clothes, snot oozing from their noses, laughing delightedly as they tackled each other to the ground and scratched each others' faces with their unkempt nails.

As the orange sun dipped into the red earth behind them the sight of the ragtag community bursting with such energy and working with perfect synchronization mesmerized me. I had not seen so many people having so much fun together. I tried my best to not show my interest because I knew that it would not be looked upon kindly by the elders. I wished I could join the raucous children, run over piles of building material, in and out of unfinished shacks, roll over heaps of garbage and have uninhibited fun like them.

Lakshmi had not come with us that evening. She gave me a horrified look when I told her where I had been. She hated the kuravas. When she was younger her grandmother had instilled a fear of kuravas in her, frightening her with stories of what they did to misbehaving children when they kidnapped them. When Lakshmi was difficult, her grandmother would warn her, 'I'll give you away to the next kuravan couple that passes by. Look at their large, black eyes. Like hawks they watch children and swoop down on them.' Lakshmi would stare at their sparkling eyes, their wild hair, the bold colours of their clothes, and shudder and bury her face in her grandmother's saree, promising that she would be a good girl.

But when she was older dislike and then hatred slowly replaced her dread of the kuravas. 'You spent all afternoon in their company!' she exclaimed with disgust. 'Leave me alone, I don't want to talk about them.'

A few days after the kuravas set up home, two young women appeared in our neighbourhood. They had copper urns resting on their hips and were on their way to a tap outside the temple. When Lakshmi saw them she grew furious. 'Get out of here, you filthy creatures!' she shouted. 'Go back to your slum before I call the police!'

The two women did not understand what Lakshmi was saying, but they understood her gestures. They shouted back at her in their language and waved their urns angrily. Lakshmi took a few steps in their direction, looking as though she would go after them. For a nine-year-old she had a lot of guts, but I was afraid. 'Leave them alone,' I hissed at her. 'Look at them, they're big. If they hit you you'll fall down unconscious.'

The two women, for some reason, contrary to all the stories I had heard about them, chose not to confront us and left, chattering angrily.

The next day as Lakshmi and I walked Charlie to the tank we saw a couple of kuravan boys playing a game of marbles with a couple of boys from the agraharam, their legs covered in a layer of dust up to their knees. Lakshmi shouted, 'There they are again! Those pigs!' She directed Charlie the Dog—who had by now grown quite impressively on the fruits he devoured—at them. Charlie growled and bared his teeth. The kuravan boys, realizing that there was little use in staying and fighting a dog, got up and ran. Charlie pursued them to the far end of the tank and stopped only when the boys turned around and threw a few marbles at him. As Charlie slowly retreated, still letting out a volley of barks as though to remind them who was in control of the situation, the kuravan boys disappeared, laughing and yelling to each other.

Lakshmi, who had been intently following the fleeing kuravas with her eyes, said to the boys from the agraharam, 'If those thieves ever come here again, just yell for me and I'll hunt them down with my Charlie.'

I couldn't fathom her bravado. What I had seen by then had given me enough reason to be concerned that she would get into trouble with the kuravas. So I warned her; but she giggled and accused me of being a sissy.

It made me wonder: Lakshmi's anger at the kuravas was not the blanket impersonal anger one might have for a despised community. Her gestures and words were ridiculous, too exaggerated even for someone with Lakshmi's excitable imagination. Her anger was personal; as though she knew them intimately like one gets to know one's sworn enemy, as though they had done her some personal harm in the past. I asked her later that day why she disliked them so much. For a moment she looked like she was going to tell me the reason, but she changed her mind and shrugged. 'I don't know. I just don't like them.' There was a sense of certainty in her voice, a belligerence that made me shudder.

Soon, Lakshmi started snooping around the maidan in search of reasons to hate the kuravas, and often in the evenings, just as the cool sea breeze was beginning to blow inland from across the maidan, carrying with it the smell of their food and refuse alike, she would sit across the road that skirted past the settlement with Charlie by her side for support and protection, though she was reluctant to admit it. There, in the lengthening shadows of the trees, holding Charlie's collar tightly she would look daggers at the settlement. The kuravas went about their work as usual, paying no attention to Lakshmi and Charlie, cooking their evening meal, smoking in the shade of their shacks and waiting for it to grow dark when, after a hearty meal, they made bonfires of their daily garbage and drank, sang and danced around them till they dropped off to sleep one by one.

As long as she was ignored, Lakshmi had no reason to set Charlie after them, but occasionally one or two kuravas would emerge from the maidan and taunt her. Then she would release her hold on Charlie. He would run after them, his low growl like distant menacing thunder, and chase them back into their settlement, dodging the stones, bottles and other missiles that they threw at him. His innate animal instincts told him exactly how far he could go without exposing himself to danger, and he knew the maidan itself was enemy territory. As soon as he crossed the road and came to the edge of the maidan, he would stop, bark furiously and return to Lakshmi. But when he retreated, the kuravas who gathered at a safe distance to watch the spectacle would laugh heartily and slap each other on the back.

One evening, a young kurati girl who challenged Charlie to a duel was not quick enough to run to safety in time. Just as she was leaping over the imaginary boundary that surrounded the maidan, Charlie's sharp teeth that had never penetrated anything harder than an unripe mango's skin before sank into the girl's calf through her enormous skirt as easily as a knife slicing through freshly made butter. The girl screamed in pain and fell to the ground. A few elders who had witnessed the chase came rushing to help her to her feet. Charlie decided it was time to retreat, and he ran back to where Lakshmi stood in the narrow space between two kiosks that sold newspapers, magazines, cigarettes and bidis, bananas, cheap sodas and sweets.

After inspecting the girl's calf for a few moments, some of the elders came out of the maidan brandishing sticks. Having the good sense to recognize danger, Lakshmi dragged Charlie by the collar and disappeared through the maze of narrow, crowded streets that led her back to her house.

Later that evening, under the mango tree behind my house, Lakshmi shivered with excitement as though she had played truant for the first time.

'They're not after you,' I assured her.

'Shh!' she hissed back, her eyes darting to and fro like a lizard's. 'I finally showed them, those pigs!' she exclaimed gleefully. 'You should have seen Charlie's mouth—he had this much of the girl's flesh between his teeth! That ought to keep the kuravas away from us for a while.'

She chattered away excitedly, narrating the whole episode once more in case she had left out some of the finer details the first time around. By the time she finished, her eyes were steadier, she was talking more calmly and slowly, the conspiratorial whisper had given way to her normal voice.

She then settled herself comfortably at the base of the tree, nibbling at a sour, unripe mango. 'Do you know why they wander?'

I shook my head.

'I know,' she replied. 'Listen . . .'

To my amazement, that evening she told me what she'd overheard them telling each other. She told me that the kuravas had been in search of their lost tribesmen ever since they could remember. For centuries they had been passing through the City in groups big and small in search of an island to the south for which their ancestors had first set out, leaving their ancient homeland far to the north and west. Long ago—so long ago that nobody remembers any more—a man from their tribe had brought back stories of this island, which he had serendipitously discovered during his travels. It was so fabulously rich and overflowing with pearls that he thought he had stumbled upon paradise. He opened a bagful of pearls in front of his astonished tribesmen to prove his story. Since pearls were the most prized possessions of their tribe, the stories they heard from the man were enough to galvanize some of them to go back in search of the island with him.

When this first batch of kuravas left their homes, promising to come back with pearls, the rest of the people believed they would be rich soon and waited patiently for the prospectors to return. But months turned into years, and the lone traveller's tale took the form of a legend: exaggerated, embellished and reinvented with the passage of time, so much so that people started believing that in search of this fabled island the prospectors had lost their way and were wandering aimlessly in the jungles and deserts in between. When enough people started believing this theory, they sent out a search party to find the original prospectors. But the search party did not return either. Still more people went in search of the missing tribesmen, never to return.

Over time, wave upon wave of them left their homes, a few at a time, with only legends that described the places on the way as their guide and hopes of reuniting with their families as their motivation. They crossed unknown territories of blistering deserts, mountains, wild jungles, flat, red plateaux and finally the sea, beyond which they hoped their promised island lay. For generations they wandered in those alien lands, eating what they could find—fresh meat and fruit when they were fortunate, rotting carrion when times were hard. From generation to generation they faithfully handed down their collective wisdom, the elders urging the younger generations to carry on, while they themselves fell by the wayside, too old and infirm to take one more step, swallowed by the alien earth even as prayers for the reunification of their descendants escaped their lips.

That was how their clan had been wandering for centuries, lost in the unending stretches of land between their home and the fabled island. Nobody remembered any more where they came from; their ancient homeland was now as much a legend as was the island they were in search of, the mythical place of peace and contentment their elders spoke of ruefully right before they died, as though their visions of death and their ancestors induced remorse; yet it was too late to rectify the ancient folly, for their inherited memory had failed them, their old eyes unable to penetrate the amnesiac fog that swirled around them, the path they had taken from their homes now obliterated by encroaching jungles and shifting sand.

'That is why for centuries they have been passing through the city,' she concluded. 'They don't know where they're going. But they think one day they'll reach their island of pearls.'

By the time Lakshmi paused, her voice was softer and more tender, her face had lost its mysteriousness. I had been listening to her spellbound, so engrossed in what she was saying that I did notice how late it was. 'It's a sad story,' I said eventually.

She stood up, brushed her pavadai and threw away the unfinished mango. 'Do you believe them?'

I was surprised by the question. 'Why, don't you?'

She shrugged. 'They're kuravas,' she said. 'I don't believe a word of what they say.'

A few days later, Charlie the Dog disappeared. When she returned from school Lakshmi did not find him at the water pipe she normally tethered him to, and her grandmother did not know where he was. For a few moments Lakshmi was quiet, digesting the news, registering his absence. Then she screamed and ran out of the house. 'It's those kuravas! It's those dirty, thieving pigs! They've got him!'

'Perhaps they've already made a chutney of his bones,' a neighbour remarked rather thoughtlessly.

Lakshmi let out another yell and ran towards the maidan. I ran after her, afraid that she might do something foolish. When we arrived at the settlement I watched, astonished, as she shouted at the kuravas in a mishmash of languages. A crowd gathered around us, all the faces smiling, marvelling at this non-kurati girl who not only spoke a little of their language but could even abuse them in it. I guessed that Lakshmi, without even a preamble, had accused them of having stolen Charlie and cooking him over a low fire for dinner, for slowly the smiles on their faces were replaced by angry looks and they kept shaking their heads.

While Lakshmi kept insisting that they had Charlie, a few men sneaked out of the group and returned with stout sticks. I held Lakshmi's hand, sure that they would strike us. They brandished the sticks as they approached us. With one forceful tug at her hand I pulled her and broke through the circle of kuravas around us. The kuravas followed us. They hurled rocks at us once they realized we were way ahead of them. One of the missiles hit Lakshmi on the back of her head and she cried in pain. 'You dogs!' they shouted at us as another rock caught her on her ankle. I pulled her to safety in the narrow passage between two buildings where, fortunately, the pursuing crowd did not follow us, because just as Charlie knew where his limits were, I suppose, the kuravas knew it would be foolish to chase after Lakshmi into her own territory.

Lakshmi limped home, her head and ankle bleeding profusely. Upon seeing her, her grandmother became alarmed. 'My baby!' she fussed, 'how did this happen?'

Despite wincing with pain, Lakshmi looked at her and, without batting an eyelid, said, 'Some urchins were throwing stones at each other and one of them accidentally hit me. Ask him,' she said, turning and looking at me full of innocence, 'he saw it happen.'

Taken aback by her cool, calculated lie it took me a few moments to realize why she had made up that story. So confident was she in her ability to tell a convincing lie that she had not thought it necessary to first take me into confidence.

'You've got a scheming mind,' I was to tell her later, and she only giggled in response as though I had praised her.

While her grandmother continued to fuss over her, a doctor was summoned and Lakshmi sat grimly, still breathing hard from all the anger and excitement. The wound on her ankle had to be stitched. As the doctor worked on it, Lakshmi alternately stifled her tears and inaudibly cursed the kuravas. After her wounds were dressed, the doctor patted her on the back and said to her grandmother, 'Other children would have brought out the whole city with their screaming by now.'

All evening she stayed in her room simmering with anger, ignoring her grandmother's calls to come down. Mistaking her sullen silence for agony, her grandmother massaged her head and feet, brought her food and water, fanned her with a wooden hand-fan, and even sang to her in an embarrassed, half-humming, half-mumbling way. Through all this Lakshmi remained unmoved, oblivious to her surroundings, brooding darkly.

Early the next morning, after bathing and praying, her hair still wet with bath water, when Lakshmi's grandmother opened the front door to draw kolams on the steps as she ritually did every day she was horrified to find a large mound of animal guts right before her. There were pieces of freshly hacked flesh entangled with intestines from which blood and other bodily fluids oozed and ran down the steps in several little rivulets. The way they were strewn on the steps made it clear that the guts had been flung down violently, for drops of blood and bile were splattered on the door and on the road. Usually there were stray dogs at the end of the street, rummaging through the garbage bin, but that morning there were none. At the other end a boy was driving a herd of buffaloes to be milked. The neighbours had not yet woken up and there was nobody else in the street.

Lakshmi's grandmother turned her face away. The sight of animal flesh and its odour overpowered her. She leant on the door and retched. She hawked and spat with such violence that a few neighbours came out of their houses. Upon seeing the flesh, they too recoiled in horror. A few moments later, when she had stopped retching and steadied herself to close the doors she noticed that an 'X' was marked in chilli paste on each of the doors. She suddenly realized what this meant. She swiftly bolted the doors from inside. After washing her mouth she ran up the stairs to Lakshmi's room. Lakshmi was still asleep, curled like a baby, her fist clenched and stuck under her chin. Her grandmother shook her hard, making her wake up with a start.

'Lakshmi!' she whispered hoarsely, 'What did you do to the kuravas? Tell me what really happened yesterday.'

Recognizing the seriousness in her grandmother's voice, Lakshmi sat up in bed and remained still.

'What did you do?'

Lakshmi was silent. She had resolved not to talk about the previous evening. It would remain inside her and fester like a septic wound. And if it was up to her it would remain that way forever, her secret savage encounter with the kuravas, her first humiliation at their hands, her exposed weakness without her ally, Charlie the Dog. The thought made her even more desperate for Charlie's company, even angrier with him for having disappeared.

'Are you going to answer me or not?' her grandmother asked again, fiercely.

Lakshmi pursed her lips tight, as though afraid that her thoughts might involuntarily spill forth.

Her grandmother raised her hand, and in a quick motion slapped her hard on her cheek.

'Do you want to get killed by them?' her grandmother demanded. 'Do you want me to die? This house to be burnt?'

Fighting back her tears Lakshmi turned her face away from her grandmother, and despite being shaken vigorously she did not turn back.

'Where did you get this insolence?' her grandmother shouted. She slapped Lakshmi again; this time so hard that her palm stung. This made her angrier. 'Answer me, you ungrateful wretch!'

Lakshmi, who would later learn that ingratitude was the most unforgivable of offences in her grandmother's book, turned to her grandmother and, despite her eyes being full of tears, looked at her with such defiance that her grandmother suddenly felt scared. Scared of the little girl, scared that her granddaughter's insolence was not unlike her own indomitable determination. For a moment or two she looked around in confusion. Then she stared at Lakshmi, searching for even the tiniest chink in her defiance. But Lakshmi continued to stare back unblinkingly. Finally, as she left the room she said, 'You're going to get nothing to eat till you decide to open your mouth and tell me what happened.'

Lakshmi turned away from her grandmother and went back to bed in the curled-up foetal position. It was only after her grandmother was out of earshot that she allowed one sob to escape.

Later in the morning a man was summoned to clear the steps. As he swept the animal entrails into a plastic bag he pronounced, even though he hadn't been asked, shaking his head sympathetically, 'Looks like a dog, amma. It must be those kuravas there. Only they eat dogs.'

Lakshmi's grandmother, who was in the courtyard by the tulsi plant, got up without a word and sat by the tap and retched. This time the food she had eaten all alone, without Lakshmi by her side, came up.

In the evening, after school, when I went to Lakshmi's house her grandmother welcomed me with a grim nod. Wilting under her gaze, without her having to prod me, I blurted out the truth.

'She went there looking for Charlie,' I said.

Her face softened a little bit. 'But how do you know they have him?' she asked, turning to Lakshmi. I was surprised that despite her prejudice against the kuravas she had taken the reasonable line of thought.

Lakshmi too was apparently taken aback by this, for she stuttered in confusion, forgetting that she had made up her mind not to talk about what had happened. For the first time since the previous evening she looked miserable, 'But, amma, what else can happen to him? You know they hate him—and me!'

Her grandmother pursed her lips into a thin line and a severe expression clouded her face. I could see one of her periodic outbursts of anger coming on. 'Look, Lakshmi, I've told you so many times that you are not to go there to that filthy place. And every time you've disobeyed me. I've warned you it doesn't take much to provoke those savages. Now look what's happened. If it hadn't been for Vasu you would not have escaped. They would have captured you and sold you off, or cut off your limbs or even killed you. Or, do you want to run away with them like your mother did?'

The viciousness of her grandmother's tone affected Lakshmi deeply. She turned away and whimpered.

Unrelenting, her grandmother forcibly turned Lakshmi's face towards her, her fingers squeezing her cheeks so tightly that her lips parted, shaped like a sparrow's beak. Her grandmother looked directly into her eyes. The old forbidding expression began to reappear on her face as she pronounced her final threat, 'They've already killed Charlie. You could be next. If I ever catch you going there, I'll brand your legs with a hot iron rod!' To back up her threat she pointed to the iron rod with a pointed tip that stood in the courtyard below.

Uncharacteristically, there were tears in Lakshmi's eyes. I don't know what hurt her more: the wounds on her body or the sudden lack of her grandmother's support.

Without a word she wiped her tears and went upstairs to her room. She had shed her last tear over the incident. Later, when her grandmother left a plate of food in her room—her first meal of the day—she refused it, continuing to lie in bed in the foetal position. Only that was familiar, comforting.

I returned home confused. I didn't understand her grandmother's threat, nor did I understand her ruthlessness. How could she, who treated Lakshmi like a long-lost treasure, suddenly turn so violently against her? And what did she mean by that remark about her mother? Wasn't *she* Lakshmi's mother? It didn't make sense.

It was my father who told me that she was Lakshmi's grandmother, not her mother.

'So did her mother really run away with kuravas?' I asked.

'No,' my father said, sighing, 'her grandmother says that just to frighten her.'

But it still didn't make sense to me, as it wouldn't for many years. Some years later, leaning against the mango tree behind our house, Lakshmi would speak for the first time about what she knew of her mother. 'When she was still a girl my mother ran away with a group of kuravas who were passing by. They cast a spell on her. Why else would she have run away with them? She went wherever they went, roaming from place to place, doing what they told her to do, living like they did, in filth and without any morals. After many years, when I was born, my grandmother rescued me from my mother. Otherwise I too would have grown up among those filthy people.'

'Do you really believe those stories your grandmother told you when you were little?'

Lakshmi became angry. 'Of course that's exactly what happened. Are you saying I'm lying or my amma's lying?'

She had the same earnest look in her eyes as when she had lied to her grandmother about how she had got injured. It was a look of unquestioning belief in her version of the story.

Many, many years later I realized why her grandmother had told her such a story, and why Lakshmi had continued to believe it, even when she was old enough to have understood the truth. It was a story that explained away her past without her having to confront difficult truths. Like all myths, it was comforting, for nobody is ever expected to justify or provide a rationale for myths.

A few days later, after dusk, Charlie returned just as mysteriously as he had disappeared. He seemed very pleased with himself. His tongue hung out and he woofed contentedly as he crossed the threshold as if to announce his return. His flint-coloured paws were now caked with mud. He did not look like a dog that had spent the last few days in captivity amongst the kuravas. Lakshmi—who was sitting in the courtyard, leaning against a pillar, still sullen and refusing to talk to anyone—was at first startled and happy to see him. But her happiness vanished instantly, leaving within her a vague feeling of something having gone wrong, of having been wronged and betrayed. She looked at him accusingly, aware of a sense of inexplicable disappointment at a time when she should have been happy to see him. Charlie waddled up to her and when he reached out to lick her face she struck him in the chest with her elbow. He let out a surprised yelp and retreated.

Her grandmother did not say anything. She took Charlie away from Lakshmi and dragged him to the sink in the courtyard where she gave him a bath. As she doused him with soapsuds she slapped him gently time and again, admonishing him. 'Do you know how much trouble you've caused?'

Charlie yelped in confusion, trying to break away and run towards Lakshmi, to find out why she was angry with him. And Lakshmi, who noticed how gently her grandmother dealt with the real troublemaker, became even more resentful and refused to look back at him.

After the bath, Charlie broke away from Lakshmi's grandmother even before she had had a chance to dry him with his towel and bounded up to Lakshmi, his ears perked up, furiously wagging his tail, barking and whining and snivelling. Lakshmi clearly understood what he said, but she did not look at him. When he ran around to face her she turned away, making him run to the other side again.

Moments later, irritated with this game, Lakshmi got up and ran to her room with Charlie at her heels. Just as he was about to cross over the threshold into her room, she slammed the door on his face. Even as she did that she felt a tinge of regret, for she understood everything Charlie said and she knew he was sorry for what he had done.

She picked up a tattered doll, the only one she'd ever had, a doll she had not touched since she'd brought Charlie the Dog home for the first time. It was one of those English dolls with frizzy silver hair, a dainty dress and little pointed feet. She did not know how she had acquired it, but she'd had it ever since she could remember. After months of neglect the doll's hair had become unruly, its dress had sloppily slid off the shoulders and was covered with dust, and the buttons on it had lost their shine. She set about grooming the doll just as she used to groom Charlie.

At first Lakshmi could hear Charlie snivelling and found it distracting. But with the passing minutes, as she became more and more engrossed in the doll, she found it easier to ignore him as well as the feeling of regret within her.

It was December now. The retreating winds brought rain and lashed the City with unprecedented fury. Low-lying areas were flooded, trees and electricity poles toppled like matchsticks, overflowing sewers opened their mouths wide and sucked in a few unwary pedestrians. On the streets, even in relatively safe areas like ours, there were shin-deep rivers of mud and garbage. Rain water seeped in through the concrete into homes, leaving stains and festering, peeling paint on the walls.

Lakshmi spent her days locked up inside, looking down on the street from the window in her room all day. She had not stepped out of the house since that incident. She knew her grandmother too well. But she used the only weapon she had: she still refused to talk to anybody.

During those long, bleak days she sat on her bed and looked out of the window at the monotonous sight of clouds and rain. Ochre rivulets ran down the street in which, under ordinary circumstances, she would have dropped paper boats and watched them float away, bobbing up and down in the streams of water that wove in and out of each other like the strands of her own pigtail. Wet buffaloes walked by every afternoon for the second milking of the day, driven by boys under plastic sheets, wielding their bamboo sticks like batons and clicking their tongues to keep the herd together. Black umbrellas floated by below her as if by their own will, without anybody under them. Occasionally urchins ran past, dripping wet, excitedly crying out to each other and splashing muddy water on passers-by.

During those days of incarceration, when, like a prisoner, she watched the world outside her window, Lakshmi's resentment slowly turned into rage. The silent, indefinable rage of an abandoned child. The loneliness of a child who unabashedly sought attention wherever she went. Years ago her mother had spent silent days in this room too, but that was the silence of their times, not of punishment. She had accepted the silence and loneliness with the resignation of a meek child. But Lakshmi was different. Unused to silence, unused to lack of attention, voraciously in need of the approval of people around her, her rage festered inside her. But with the perversity of someone inflicting punishment on oneself, she sought the very loneliness she hated. When her grandmother came to her room and asked to her to come down and eat, she would turn the other way and go down only after she was sure her grandmother had finished eating and had left the kitchen. When I tried to talk to her she would turn to the window and pretend she could not hear me. And every time she heard Charlie the Dog snivelling outside her room, she picked up her doll. She groomed it, made it sit in prim poses on her pillow, and spoke to it as she used to speak to Charlie.

At first Lakshmi's grandmother merely tolerated her silence as that of a sulking child. She felt that in not trying to cajole Lakshmi too much she was teaching her an important lesson: that defiance and disobedience would get her nowhere.

The more Lakshmi sulked the more her grandmother was determined not to give in. She could punish her in return with silence of her own, to make her learn the consequences of not being obedient and grateful. And the more her grandmother refused to give in, to forgive her, the more Lakshmi felt resentful. But slowly, with every passing day, this determination to teach her a lesson crumbled. Lakshmi's silence was a defiance of her punishment, of denying her the moral authority. Sometimes she felt that in continuing to let Lakshmi be she was spoiling her, allowing her to gain the upper hand by martyring herself. But sometimes she was simply too overwhelmed by the silence. She, who had spent years in stoic silence interrupted only by whispers, now found it oppressive. She wanted to talk to Lakshmi, for she realized that the silence of the past had served no purpose other than to break up the family, sending each member in a different direction in search of succour.

So, one day, she marched into Lakshmi's room, sat down on her bed and turned Lakshmi's face towards her. 'How much longer are you going to refuse to talk to me?' she asked.

Lakshmi turned her face towards the window and said nothing.

'Is this some kind of drama that I don't know about? Or is it a cinema?' Lakshmi's grandmother said with great contempt, because ever since her daughter had left home for Nasser the moplah her dislike for the cinema had turned to loathing.

Lakshmi, who had inherited this loathing from her grandmother, turned around. She looked angry and it seemed as though she was finally going to break her silence to deny this hotly. But, yet again, she chose to keep quiet.

Lakshmi's grandmother flew into a rage. 'Stubborn mule! Such defiance, such contempt!' Then, noticing that Lakshmi's pavadai had inched up almost to her knees, she pulled it down roughly and pinched her. 'No modesty either! You're turning out to be the tulukan's daughter I didn't want you to be. Any more of this drama and I'll brand your tongue with a hot rod. Then let's see you scream and beg for mercy! That's the only way to straighten you out.' So saying she left in a huff, her threat ringing in Lakshmi's ears.

For a long time after that Lakshmi wondered what her grandmother had meant by calling her a tulukan's daughter. At first she was puzzled and doubted what she had heard. The significance of those words did not occur to her until later, and then she was overcome by distress. She remembered the spite with which her grandmother had called her a tulukan's daughter. What was a tulukan's daughter supposed to be like?

For the first time Lakshmi wondered who she was. She had

always known, in an amorphous, unarticulated way that unlike most other children she had no father, but she had never questioned her grandmother about it. Now, for the first time, she became achingly aware of what she'd always known. It suddenly scared her, hurt her. She became aware of the silence in the house, her own lack of words, how the void, which she was getting accustomed to, was the void of an incomplete family that was now fractured even further.

She started talking increasingly to herself and to her doll. Charlie the Dog came by frequently and sat by the door, never going in (he knew Lakshmi too well). When Lakshmi talked to her doll in the language she had earlier reserved for Charlie, he would howl in protest until Lakshmi got up and slammed the door on his face.

One evening I accompanied my parents to her house. 'Maami, maybe you should be a little more lenient with her,' my mother said, noticing Lakshmi's serene face staring at us through the open doors of her room upstairs. 'She's a child after all.'

Her grandmother, clearly irked at my mother's advice, replied airily, 'She's just sulking. She'll be all right soon.' Then, looking at me, she said, 'You should come more often and cheer her up.'

'But it has already been so many days, maami. I'm worried.'

'You mean I'm not worried? She's all right,' her grandmother insisted. 'Just too stubborn for her age, that's all.'

My parents, unwilling to push her further, turned to idle chitchat and drank coffee. All through our visit Lakshmi kept staring at my father through her fog of silence. If he stood up and walked around the courtyard her eyes followed him. When he sat down in the easy chair that had once been the sole preserve of Lakshmi's grandfather she leant forward slightly, for one of the pillars in the courtyard obstructed her vision. When he finally got up to leave she craned her neck till he disappeared into the passage leading to the front door and watched him from her window till she could see him no more.

'There's something about the girl,' my mother said on the

way home. 'In nine days she's lost nine years of childhood.'

My father, pensive and reflective so far, shook his head and pronounced, 'She never had a childhood. She's only now beginning to mourn what she never had.'

One day, when she could bear her own silence no more, Lakshmi screamed so loudly that it woke my mother up from the nap she was taking a few streets away. Frightened crows, sparrows and pigeons fled from their roosts, squawking, furiously flapping their wings and disappearing into the sky. When Lakshmi paused momentarily to catch her breath a stunned silence descended upon the agraharam.

My mother and I rushed to her house, but by the time we arrived the entire neighbourhood was already there. Lakshmi was in her room, screaming her lungs out. As I fought my way through the crowd I caught a glimpse of her and became scared. Her hair, which seemed to have not been combed for days, was untied and fell all over her face. Her eyes were large, red, and demonic, her face wet with tears and perspiration. Her nails were long, dirty, claw-like, some broken jaggedly at the tips. All around her were signs of ravage: the plaster on the walls had been dug out in places, leaving gaping craters; the bedsheets lay on the floor in the middle of the room; the pillow had been ripped open, its cotton stuffing, stained, rancid from years of absorbing hair oil, was strewn all over the room. In a corner was a pair of scissors with which she had cut her pavadai in numerous places.

A few neighbours went in and threw buckets of water on her, but she continued screaming. They tried to subdue her, but she fought back like a wild cat and scratched their arms with her nails till they bled.

Her grandmother panicked. 'Someone bring incense, lime, garlic and chilli powder,' she called. 'She's possessed!'

While two women ran to fetch these items from the kitchen and prepared to exorcise Lakshmi, someone else went to call the doctor. I stood at the doorway and watched the women light the incense, tie the garlic and lime together with twine and wave it in front of Lakshmi. But she continued to scream and throw things at them.

'Throw the chilli powder into her eyes!' her grandmother shouted frantically. But as she dipped her hand into the cup of chilli powder, the other women held her arms and pulled her back.

'Maami, please leave this to us!' my mother said firmly and led her to the kitchen where she sat on the floor with her head in her hands.

It was only after the doctor arrived and gave her an injection that Lakshmi stopped screaming. Then, as the tranquillizer began to take effect on her, she became subdued and her eyes started drooping. Moments later she was asleep, but even in her sleep she continued to whimper.

After the crowd had left, I stayed back. Lakshmi's grandmother was still in the kitchen, looking dazed. My mother was by her side, calming her down.

'My baby,' her grandmother lamented. 'My beautiful baby granddaughter! I punished her for her own good. How was I to know this would happen?'

'That's okay, maami,' my mother said, 'she'll be all right.'

But Lakshmi's grandmother looked sad and resigned because she was sure she had now lost her granddaughter just as she had lost her daughter. She turned to my mother and sobbed, 'Do you think she'll ever forgive me?'

That evening when Devaki arrived, looking worried, Lakshmi's grandmother spoke to her almost as distantly as she always had. When Devaki wanted to go upstairs and take a look at her sleeping daughter, Lakshmi's grandmother pulled her back weakly more out of instinct than out of any strong conviction. If she wanted, Devaki could have shaken off her mother and gone upstairs. But she obeyed, reluctant to kick a stumbling woman.

Devaki and her mother sat talking about Lakshmi and her future. 'Amma,' Devaki said, 'I know you still don't want me to raise her. I have no right to come and claim her now. But, after this—'

'I know,' her mother responded and stared quietly at the dark, greasy wooden rafters in the kitchen.

'Perhaps you'll allow her to be sent to a boarding school?' Devaki continued gingerly, searching her mother's face for a reaction. To her surprise her mother looked at her with none of the disapproval she had expected. Devaki was enormously encouraged by this; after all this was the first time in so many years that something she had said had not displeased her mother. So she decided not to tell her that it was Nasser Sharif who had suggested this arrangement; she did not want to wreck the plan.

Before leaving, Devaki paused at the doorstep for a moment. She felt the urge to rush up the stairs and embrace her daughter. But when she noticed how sad and defeated her own mother looked, she remembered how badly her mother wanted to prove herself.

She went home without having set eyes on Lakshmi, but she was happy anyway because she could finally make plans for her child.

That rainy season, at the age of nine, after having lived all her young life exactly the way she wanted, Lakshmi left her grandmother's house early one morning in a rickshaw. She was helped into it by my father, who looked into her eyes only for an instant before hastily turning away from her. He said Lakshmi looked so awfully crushed that it was like looking into the face of an old and defeated woman. Her grandmother stood out of the way as neighbours loaded the two steel trunks that contained Lakshmi's clothes and books on to the rickshaw, her sari wrapped tightly around her shoulder, her mouth covered by the free end, watching with deep, forlorn eyes as her granddaughter avoided all eye contact with her. No doubt she suffered that day to see Lakshmi leave her, but she knew there was little she could do to prevent it.

After Lakshmi's luggage was loaded onto the rickshaw, my father, looking out of place in his dun-coloured suit and thin silk tie, boarded the rickshaw himself and sat on the wooden bench next to Lakshmi with his arm protectively around her. As the rickshaw groaned and creaked and lurched forward in the semi-darkness on its way to the railway station, the noise it made rang in my ears. The rickshaw puller's straining calf muscles rippled visibly through his dark skin that gleamed in the light of a street lamp. It was going to be a long journey, and my father was going to accompany her to her destination. He would enrol her in the boarding school run by Irish nuns to which she had already gained admission, thanks to her father's connections. My father would stay back in the small town in the mountains for a few days so that he could see her every evening during visiting hours, and to ensure that she was well settled in the dormitory. And cloistered in the dormitory like the nuns who ran the school, Lakshmi was to live for the rest of her school years, returning to her grandmother for a few days every summer and winter.

Suddenly, the enormity of the journey Lakshmi had just embarked upon hit me like a thunderbolt, and I forced my eyes open from my half-sleep and chased the rickshaw down to the street corner, shouting, 'Lakshmi, please don't forget me!'

After I had given up the chase and retraced my steps slowly, I suddenly realized that Charlie the Dog was nowhere to be seen. He had not come out of the house that morning; it was very unlikely that he was still asleep. I went in and found him at the threshold of her empty room. Even in her absence he had not entered the room. When I peered at him through the darkness he turned away from me and put his face in the gap between the open door and the threshold, but not before I noticed that there were tears in his eyes.

Cloistered

For many weeks after Lakshmi's departure I spent my time walking around the neighbourhood, listlessly throwing pebbles at stray dogs and cows, refusing to play with my friends, answering grown-ups in monosyllables and even shooing away Charlie who invariably barked excitedly and bounded up to me whenever I went anywhere near Lakshmi's house.

In the hours that I spent alone, I slowly became more aware of myself and my feelings. When Lakshmi was around, her presence demanded that I pay more attention to her than to myself. I had to be aware of every subtle change in her mood, anticipate her every need, listen attentively when she spoke. Even when she was quiet everyone around her was aware of her. Now, in her absence, I was startled by the realization of the extent to which her feelings had dominated mine. Whatever I felt had been a mere reflection of what she had expressed. For instance, I now discovered that I really did not care much for Charlie or any other dog. When he came to lick me and drool all over me I found myself being annoyed at him, and often, to his dismay, I pushed him aside.

Even though in Lakshmi's absence I had no reason to go to her house, I went there in the afternoons and was surprised by the affection with which her grandmother greeted me. As soon as she saw me cross the threshold she would get up from her customary place on a palaka placed in a shaded corner of the quadrangle, where she usually sat fanning herself and reading magazines or simply leaning against the pillar and dozing all afternoon. She would pat me on the head, lead me to the kitchen, and heap snacks on a plate for me. And while I ate greedily, my mouth usually full to the point of choking, she sat facing me, happy to watch me eat. Sometimes she recalled Lakshmi's idiosyncrasies, trying to hide the heaviness in her sigh by forcing a smile. After eating and listening to her for a long time, I would leave, feeling a little lighter from having relived Lakshmi's presence.

One evening as I stood outside the maidan, a group of kuravas appeared from nowhere and stood in front of me. I looked up at them nervously, half expecting them to give me a sound thrashing for no reason at all. A woman with a scarf tied around her head and a wrinkled and weather-beaten face stepped up and said, 'We know that nasty girl has been sent away.'

I looked at her in astonishment. *How in the world did they know?*

'We know everything,' she said and nodded for added effect. 'She tried to kick us out, but, look, she herself got kicked out before us.' She looked at her companions and laughed. Then she became serious and brought her face close to mine and whispered a warning. 'I hope you don't try to do what that little devil did. Otherwise, this time we'll take you away first.' She carelessly flung around her large skirt, and cackled with laughter as she straightened up.

I ran to Lakshmi's grandmother's house and breathlessly shouted from the doorway, 'Did you send Lakshmi away because you were afraid the kuravas would take her away?'

Lakshmi's grandmother looked up from the quadrangle in surprise. She considered my question for several moments. 'It had nothing to do with the kuravas, Vasu,' she finally said, sighing. 'It had everything to do with me.'

Her answer puzzled me deeply.

'You're too young to understand, Vasu. Come in and eat something.'

As I sat eating upma, her grandmother emerged from her reverie, and asked, 'Did Lakshmi ever tell you that she hated me?'

I've always imagined cloisters as establishments from another age: archaic, forbidding, austere, where the laity and temporal matters have no place, where the only human emotions are those that are filtered and sublimated through the stern spiritual sieve of religious strictures, making their inhabitants either appreciative of mundane human sentiments or wholly contemptuous of them.

If the purpose of a cloister is to isolate its inhabitants from the outside so that they may focus on the spiritual, it is hard to see what the architect who designed the cloister in Lakshmi's school had in mind. Architecturally it was a cloister, but it was a large, imposing building—too large for its purpose, really—with a grand courtyard flanked by colonnaded porticoes inspired by those in Bologna. There were numerous spacious rooms that were occupied by the nuns who ran the school and those of their order who came there from other parts of the country to recuperate and contemplate. One of the large corner rooms on the ground floor was a chapel, its windows made of stained glass, its walls covered with arabesques. The inner walls of the building overlooking the courtyard had gargoyles grinning from every corner. In the courtyard, in geometric patterns between the fountains, the nuns grew such brightly coloured flowers that it made the place look more like a small Andalusian castle than a nunnery. From there one could see the mountains, fold after fold of rising crests covered with eucalyptus trees, blue and dark. The clear light that filled the building made it cheerful. Even when the fog descended from the mountains, instead of bringing on gloom it gave the place a dreamy, joyous appearance.

It was into this cloister hidden deep among eucalyptus trees that Sister Cecilia brought Lakshmi the day she arrived. Sister Cecilia would recall later that she could not bear to see the sadness and mute terror in Lakshmi's eyes when my father left her. It reminded her of the terror of her own childhood. She gently guided Lakshmi around the building, showing her the rooms, the fountains, the flowers, the ivy, and the mountains, giving her time to absorb the surroundings, to marvel at the geometric precision of the columns and the arcades.

But the silence and serenity of the building frightened Lakshmi, and she clung to Sister Cecilia, who put her arms around her and spoke to her gently in her strange accent, in nonjudgemental, undemanding tones. Lakshmi listened quietly without looking up. They sat beside a pillar and gazed for a long time at the courtyard, listening to the tinkling of the breeze among the eucalyptus trees, watching bees flit from flower to flower.

After a long time Lakshmi looked up at Sister Cecilia, who wore black plastic-framed spectacles that were too large for her small face. Her wimple not only covered her ears and held her spectacles tightly in place, but also encroached upon her cheeks, making her look like a fish seen through a magnifying glass.

Slowly Lakshmi realized that the silence they sat in was the silence of contemplation, not of anger or disapproval.

That night Lakshmi slept next to Sister Cecilia in her bed, clutching her ragged doll like a security blanket. Sister Cecilia wrapped her arms tightly around her. At first Lakshmi was uncomfortable, but soon she was soothed by the rhythmic sound of the woman's breathing. When she was younger she used to wrap her arms around her grandmother's waist and bury her face in her sari, feeling the starch-stiffened fabric against her cheek. Her grandmother smelt of fresh turmeric and sandalwood paste and as her stomach rose and fell with her breath Lakshmi felt so content that she could fall asleep in that manner. That night she felt the same contentment in Sister Cecilia's arms and slept more restfully than she had in a long time.

In the morning Sister Cecilia opened the cupboard and showed Lakshmi her collection of dolls and puppets. They were neatly arranged on several shelves. Rag dolls with woollen curls, plastic dolls with blonde hair that looked like peach fuzz, wooden soldiers that bent at the hip, smiling egg-shaped figures that wobbled happily when touched, simple stuffed dolls that did not regain their shapes once pressed, and terracotta figures of female dancers whose heads wobbled when displaced. Then there were the puppets. She took them out carefully and showed Lakshmi how to make them come alive. She handled them deftly, with minimum movement, effortlessly controlling them as though she had a dozen hands, tugging a string here, nudging a rod there, and they danced to her command. They were of many kinds: marionettes, guignols, water puppets with rods and levers, simple farm animals made from sticks, flat shadow puppets, even a few kathputli puppets.

'Do you like my collection?' she asked proudly.

Lakshmi, fascinated by what she saw, spoke for the first time since she had arrived, mumbling, 'Yes.'

Encouraged, Sister Cecilia picked up two of the three guignols and, in two different falsetto voices and in two different accents, talked as she made the puppets move.

'Welcome, pretty face!' cried one of them. 'What lovely eyes you have!'

'Flatterer!' retorted the other, smacking the first one with the back of its hand.

'You're just jealous that I could think of something nice to say,' responded the first evenly.

'Eh? Jealous of what? Your oversized nose, your piggy eyes, your chicken legs?'

Lakshmi smiled tentatively. Sister Cecilia smiled back encouragingly.

The first puppet turned to Lakshmi again and said, 'Don't mind my foolish friend. He's usually cranky in the morning until he has had his breakfast.'

'Stop it! Can't you see she's not interested in what you think of me? "Who are these strange foreigners?" she asks. "And why do they have such funny accents?"'

'That's because I'm Italian and you're French, you donkey,' said the first.

'Who did you call a donkey?'

'You, who else?'

'Watch your big dirty mouth! Or she'll have to clean it with soap.' He pointed to Sister Cecilia. 'And when she does that you'll cry like a baby. Waa, waa, waa!'

'Stop squabbling!' the first one said, exasperatedly. 'Is this the way to behave in front of a new student?'

The second puppet, suddenly becoming conscious of Lakshmi's presence, bowed shamefacedly and said, 'Our apologies, lovely young lady. We only wanted to welcome you.'

'Yes, welcome, pretty lady. Don't think badly of us. We aren't usually this silly.'

'That's right,' interjected the other one. 'We aren't usually this bad. We're usually worse!' The puppet chortled uproariously.

Lakshmi giggled and clapped. It was as though the sun had broken through the clouds after a long bout of gloomy weather. Her tense expression slowly gave way to smooth, relaxed lines, bringing back some of the childish innocence she had recently lost.

Sister Cecilia put away the puppets and beamed at her. She put her arm around Lakshmi and pulled her close to her. It was a chilly morning and Lakshmi felt warm against her. As they walked down to the refectory for breakfast she was startled by the clearness of the light. There was no wintry fog. The contours of the mountains behind the building were crisp, and the comforting smell of eucalyptus wafted in with the breeze. The colours of the flowers in the courtyard were bright, multihued, sharply contrasted.

Still holding Lakshmi close to her, Sister Cecilia said, 'See, there's nothing to be afraid of here. It's safer than home.'

What characterized Sister Cecilia for Lakshmi in those early days at school was her predictability and punctuality. Most of Sister Cecilia's activities were dictated by her duties towards the school and her order. Everything she did was according to a schedule that rarely wavered. Hers was a strict regimen of prayer, contemplation, study, teaching and domestic work. Like an industrious squirrel, she was always busy. But she always managed to find some time for Lakshmi. For many months she came to the dormitory at 9 p.m., slipping out of the convent after the night prayers to tuck Lakshmi into bed. Lakshmi could hear the distinct sound of her heels clicking along the granite floor from a long way down the hallway and would know what the time was. When Sister Cecilia arrived, all noise on the floor would cease and the girls would regard her with deference. Sister Cecilia would sit at the edge of Lakshmi's bed and indulge in small talk till the warden, who clearly resented Sister Cecilia's presence in her territory, came around, eyeing the two of them balefully before ringing the warning bell and turning off the lights. Between the warning bell and lights-out, the warden, Sister Cecilia and all the Christian girls in the large dorm would hurriedly kneel on the floor beside their beds and pray. Sister Cecilia knelt beside Lakshmi's bed and prayed for forgiveness for her sins, although Lakshmi could never imagine what sins the nun could have committed.

Perhaps it was all the rules Sister Cecilia broke. There were rules for everything the nuns did: the amount of starch they used to stiffen their fluted veils, what kind of snacks they could eat between meals, how they made their beds, what they could write to their families . . . Lakshmi had noticed this even during her first few days. The night she went down to the refectory with Sister Cecilia for the first time, the nuns stopped talking when the small bell at the Mother Superior's table tinkled softly. With minimal movement, they went about their chores in silence, gliding to and fro like pucks on ice. Lakshmi found it strange that so many women should suddenly stop talking to each other and get busy doing what they had to. But just as the novelty of the situation was giving way to anxiety—for it reminded Lakshmi of her own recent silence at home—Sister Cecilia pulled her aside and whispered, 'It's all right. I can talk to you.'

Sister Cecilia always seemed to get away with bending, or worse, disobeying rules when it came to Lakshmi, not just in the matter of speaking during enforced silences or being able to visit her in the dormitory, but, more significantly, in the most fundamental gesture that defined their relationship: giving Lakshmi the privilege of coming to the cloister almost at will. Lakshmi could never figure out what Sister Cecilia said to convince Mother Superior to ignore her infractions. But, much later, she understood the significance of her gestures, especially considering that even minor flouting of rules by other nuns resulted in harsh reprimands. Lakshmi could sense that the other nuns sometimes resented Sister Cecilia for the privilege of bonding so closely with a student. What was more striking was the envy from which their resentment sprang.

Over time the other girls in school came to envy Lakshmi too. But Lakshmi barely noticed it. She did not talk to the other girls very much. They mostly came from rich—even aristocratic—families. They were self-assured, proprietary in their attitude towards the school. Some were openly haughty. For Lakshmi, knowing Sister Cecilia was enough. She liked the fact that this was not home. Things were so much simpler. At home there were all the ambiguities and maddening suggestions of non-existent relationships: a grandmother who was a mother, the ephemeral mother with translucent skin, who was not quite a mother, a father whom she'd never seen and whose name was never uttered at home, a dog who was more human than animal and was just as capable of betrayal. Here she only had to deal with Sister Cecilia. Lakshmi felt safe in her presence. She felt comforted by her smile, her slow speech, as if sprinkled with semicolons, her soothing, monotone voice, her strange accent, her arcane dress. She treasured the anonymity, for there were fewer demands on her that way. This was a new beginning.

Over several weeks Sister Cecilia coaxed Lakshmi little by little out of the protective shell she had withdrawn into, scraping the edges gently, probing and clearing out the debris, curious, but never prying. These conversations reminded Lakshmi of the small talk she and her grandmother exchanged in the kitchen after school.

Sister Cecilia gave her a blank notebook one day. 'Write down your thoughts in it at night,' she said.

Thoughts? Lakshmi wondered. *How can one capture one's thoughts and write them down?* But she accepted the notebook and that night sat over it for a long time before writing in it in exasperation: *I don't know what to write!*

Sister Cecilia also coaxed her into writing to her grandmother, to tell her that she was doing fine and to not worry about her. As Lakshmi wrote unsteadily—for she had never written a letter before, and because this too required her to capture her thoughts—Sister Cecilia watched over her, prompting her when she hesitated, reassuring her with a smile when she looked doubtful. When she was done, Sister Cecilia showed her how to fold the inland letter sheet into a compact rectangle and lick the narrow flap to seal the letter.

Her grandmother's response arrived a few days later on a postcard with every possible space crammed with words. There were the usual questions about her health and her school. She wrote about Charlie (but made no reference to his listlessness) and their neighbours. What Lakshmi did not see then was the undertone of relief her grandmother had desperately tried to hide, to sound normal by being excessively chatty.

Lakshmi reread the letter immediately, more slowly this time. When she was done she looked up and smiled at Sister Cecilia. The process of having exchanged words with her grandmother brought relief to her. The disquieting burden that had lodged itself in her mind lifted somewhat.

Sister Cecilia responded with a wide, toothy, fish-like smile of her own. 'You're ready to see your grandmother again, aren't you?'

Lakshmi stopped smiling. Anxiety gripped her. She clung to Sister Cecilia's arm.

'Not yet, I guess. You'll understand one day how much your grandmother loves you.'

'I want to stay here forever.'

Sister Cecilia laughed. 'And wear this boring habit like me when you grow up?'

Lakshmi nodded.

'You're being silly. Why would you want to live here?'

'I don't know. But I do!'

Sister Cecilia turned solemn. 'You're still a child,' she said. 'You don't know what you're saying.'

On Sundays at half past one, when the other nuns retired to their rooms for contemplation, Sister Cecilia came to pick up Lakshmi for an afternoon walk. They walked up the cobbled path under the vines and creepers that formed a canopy over it, past the cloister to the small iron gate in the back. Nobody ever seemed to come to this part of the school, evidently not even the gardener, for an untrimmed trellis partially obscured the gate. Beyond it the hill rose steeply, covered with eucalyptus trees, their bark peeling like scabs to reveal lighter, tender skin underneath. They climbed the hill till they came to a clearing on a promontory that overlooked the valley below. Here they paused to take in the breathtaking scenery. The vast tea estates to their left and right swathed the small towns all over the hills like blankets. Numerous settlements dotted the hillside, some perched on cliffs like bird-droppings. In the valley floor a river snaked its way to the plains.

Directly below them were the ornate buildings belonging to their school and the boys' school nearby, interspersed with lush lawns and trees. They were built on the estates of an eccentric French mercenary who had made a fortune in the employ of several rajas and nawabs. Many of the buildings were from his time. His large mansion with its statues, fountains and grand archways was now the main building of the boys' school. The garden leading up to it was a small-scale copy of the gardens at the Tuileries. From the promontory they could see parts of the building that were not obscured by greenery: its solid stone walls, its mansard roof, the large weather vane revolving lethargically in the wind.

On one occasion, chaperoned by an older nun, Sister Cecilia took Lakshmi to the highest peak in the mountains, jostling in a crowded bus through a series of hairpin turns. Lakshmi was particularly excited, for it was a clear day, and Sister Cecilia had told her that on clear days one could see the pearl-drop island far away. At the peak, from the small observatory shaped like a lighthouse, they could see the speck of an island through the grainy lens of the telescope. Sister Cecilia's veil flapped about in the strong breeze as she pointed it out. Lakshmi was outwardly calm, even nonchalant, but her heart was beating fast. The vivid descriptions she had overheard from the kuravas came flooding to her. She strained her eyes for topographical details: the emerald hills, the silver sands, the necklace of ruby rocks between the island and the mainland, the kuravan pearl divers who leapt out of the water to gasp for breath before leaping back in like delirious fish. But all she could see was the blurred outline of land that was often indistinguishable from the surrounding sea. Everything looked muddy brown, even the sky on the horizon. She was disappointed. Why had the kuravas made such a big deal of this island that looked nothing out of the ordinary? Where were the riches they'd talked of? Why had they taken such a long time to reach an island that was so easily within grasp even from this far?

She stared hard for a long time, her face hardening. She felt cheated.

'Isn't the view lovely?' Sister Cecilia asked, still excited as a schoolgirl.

'There's nothing to see here,' Lakshmi answered angrily, turning away from the telescope and looking down at the valleys below. 'The kuravas are fools. They are blathering nincompoops who believe their own silly stories.'

Horrified by her belligerence, Sister Cecilia fell silent.

That night, kneeling at Lakshmi's bedside Sister Cecilia prayed audibly, 'O Lord, deliver us of our anger and teach us to forgive those who cause us pain. For we know that there can be no happiness without forgiveness.' She opened one eye to look at Lakshmi, who sat crushing a mosquito till the blood and sticky fluids from its belly coloured her fingertips crimson. And when she raised her newly hennaed fingers triumphantly, Sister Cecilia closed her eye and whispered urgently, 'Lord, forgive us so that we may have the grace to forgive others.'

Sister Cecilia turned into a different person when she held puppets in her hands. She laughed a lot and took on the characters of her puppets, which seemed to be mostly crazy and irrepressibly silly, made even more so by the falsetto voices she spoke in. Now and then she would bring out some of her puppets and put up impromptu shows to amuse those around her, and Lakshmi would giggle at Sister Cecilia as much as she did at the puppets' antics.

All of Sister Cecilia's puppets had names and special characteristics. Lakshmi's favourites were the querulous puppets Sister Cecilia had welcomed her with. Sister Cecilia called them Frédéric le Fou and Patrizio il Pazzo. Patrizio il Pazzo, the crazier of the two, was a rotund puppet with a Groucho Marx-like moustache, rosy cheeks that lent him an air of mischief, a perpetual gleam in the eye, a silly grin and an absurd laugh. The voice that Sister Cecilia used for him was shrill; it at once matched his quarrelsome nature and made him appear ridiculously effeminate. He quarrelled with everyone, including his puppeteer. Frédéric le Fou could be just as querulous, but he could also wipe the foolish grin from his face and in an instant turn into a suave, trim gentleman, whose excessive courteousness and self-conscious air of superiority was just as hard to take seriously.

Then there was Scaramouche, the cowardly braggart. Sister Cecilia always placed him next to the hunchbacked Pulcinella with the oversized, hooked nose, the exaggerated, pointed chin, the crooked mouth and large ears, who looked comic and pathetic at the same time. Despite the funny, rowdy roles he played, this character always confused Lakshmi, for she could never be sure if she should laugh at him or feel sorry for him. This was the only puppet she felt uncomfortable looking at. Sister Cecilia usually took him out along with a pretty little girl puppet to act out Punch and Judy scenes, and when Pulcinella wobbled too close to her, his silly cap flopping over his large eyes, he seemed to Lakshmi to be almost hideous.

Once, as Lakshmi recovered from a bout of typhoid, she sat up in bed one day and held a marionette for the first time. She tugged at one of the strings and the puppet danced wildly, exaggeratedly jerking its legs in impossible directions. Both she and Sister Cecilia burst out laughing. Even after Lakshmi steadied her fingers the marionette jerked around for a few moments as though it had springs for joints. Even the slightest twitch of her fingers produced a cascade of movements that was impossible to control. But when Sister Cecilia took it in her hand, it behaved itself perfectly. It did exactly what she asked it to do. If she asked it to lift a hand just so much, it did exactly that. If she asked it to bow, it didn't plop over, but bowed majestically. Lakshmi was enthralled.

When Lakshmi was well enough to walk about, Sister Cecilia took her to the music room adjacent to the chapel downstairs. 'We need some music for the puppets,' she said. She handed over an assortment of marionettes to Lakshmi and played a lively tune on the electric organ. In Lakshmi's unsure hands the marionettes danced madly. The wilder they danced, the wilder Sister Cecilia's music became; soon, she and Sister Cecilia could control themselves no more and they howled with laughter.

'Shhh!' Sister Cecilia said, controlling her laughter and looking anxiously at the door. God forbid if Mother Superior should be in the chapel next door. 'You like the music?'

Lakshmi nodded.

'Listen to this, now.' Sister Cecilia played a few notes that sounded very familiar to her. 'You know this, yes?' She then played the notes a little differently, and Lakshmi, to her horror, instantly recognized it as a film song that had recently become very popular. The girls from the north often hummed the tune in the dorm when the matron wasn't within earshot. The older girls even sang it, often pirouetting on their heels, their smiles concealing a secret: *Aajaa sanam, madhur chandni mein hum/ tum miley to viraane mein bhi aa jaayegi bahaar.* What was

Sister Cecilia doing playing this song next door to the chapel? The kind of song her grandmother wouldn't allow even at home. It sounded so out of place, so hedonistic, so naughty. But Sister Cecilia seemed to be enjoying herself. 'It's a popular film song, is it not? It was inspired by an Italian tarantella from the south. Here, listen to the original.' She giggled, her eyes dancing mischievously. Sister Cecilia tapped her heels lightly on the parquet floor to the lively rhythm of the tune. 'Come on, make the marionettes dance.' Then she got up and danced a few steps, swirling around in place with her hands clacking an imaginary pair of castanets. Lakshmi was surprised to see this side of Sister Cecilia. Did nuns dance? But somehow her dancing did not seem obscene; in fact, there was a certain innocence to it, as if she were dancing for the sheer joy of it. There was grace in her movements despite the slight wiggling of her hips visible through her ballooning habit. She then stopped and looked at the door to make sure nobody had witnessed her little performance. Lakshmi giggled again, fascinated, even though she was still quite surprised. Sister Cecilia laughed. 'Don't look so nervous. Music doesn't always have to be serious. There is joy in this music and dance. People dance like this with tambourines, mandolins and guitars at weddings. Something this joyful can't be bad, can it?'

To Lakshmi, brought up on her grandmother's rigid and austere notions of what constituted good entertainment, it was a new and revealing way of looking at music and dance. Slowly she began to enjoy them just as she began to enjoy being around Sister Cecilia's puppets. They had a magical effect on her. From being passive and silent she opened up to become cheerful, even talkative at times. Her imagination was galvanized. Puppets were better than dolls because they were animated, lifelike. Over time they became uncomplaining, undemanding friends, witnesses to her every mood and her secret thoughts. But, more importantly, more than all the moments of loneliness they filled in her life and the mirth they provided her, she could persuade them to do anything she wanted. Controlling the puppets gave her a sense of power, of being in charge of their destiny, which in turn made her feel like she could control her own destiny. And the wounds within her slowly began to heal.

Soon Sister Cecilia began writing her own scripts for puppet shows with Lakshmi's help, usually based on their lives at school, with generous caricatures of students, teachers and nuns.

The students loved the shows. The falsettos, the strange accents and voices, and the lively music played on the record player added to the allure. Sister Cecilia had the ability to bring all these elements into each show. Lakshmi stayed with her behind the curtains, handing over the puppets in the right sequence, controlling the music, sometimes even lending her own voice to the act.

Lakshmi and Sister Cecilia secretly named several of the people around them after puppets. 'If you painted a moustache and a beard on Mother Superior she'd look like Orlando Furioso,' Sister Cecilia remarked once, and the two of them burst out laughing. 'And if you put spectacles on this one, it's you,' Lakshmi said, pointing to a colourless, prissy marionette with pursed lips. Sister Cecilia pretended to be shocked by the unflattering comparison, but laughed good-naturedly afterwards.

But the most puppet-like person in the school was a servant boy who did odd jobs. He helped the cook, moved flower pots and dug the earth for the gardener, swept the Principal's office and carried her books for her, and cleaned the windows every Sunday. When they first saw him both Sister Cecilia and Lakshmi were taken aback. 'He looks like Pulcinella!' Sister Cecilia exclaimed in Lakshmi's ear.

The boy had exaggerated, grotesque features, as though someone had played a cruel joke on him. He was slightly hunched, had a protruding chin, a curved, beak-like nose, and large, magnified eyes. He was so dark that the whites of his eyes gleamed. His hair was springy and unruly, and his crooked mouth gave him a permanent sneer. He wore shorts that were a few sizes too big, his long, bony, hairy legs appearing like stilts under them.

But there was something about him that made Lakshmi want to look at him. She watched him go about his tasks from afar. For all his ugliness—or perhaps because of it—he had a presence, almost an omniscience that she would come to recognize only much later. Everything about him was pronounced: his features, his loping walk, the effort he seemed to put into even the simple act of speaking. It was impossible to ignore him. And yet to her he had a child-like innocence. He didn't seem to be aware of himself. Nor of the world around him.

'He doesn't seem to mind it,' Lakshmi said. 'He doesn't know he's ugly.'

Sister Cecilia nodded. 'Yes. I suppose if you don't know you're ugly you really aren't.'

Lakshmi felt sorry for him, nevertheless. 'I don't think we should bring out Pulcinella again. He might recognize his ugliness in the puppet. And then what would happen?'

But she needn't have worried. The boy was not as oblivious as she'd imagined; in fact, he was painfully aware of everything he did, everything about himself. His face, for instance. He could hardly bear to look at himself in the mirror. He had already learnt to hate who he was.

'Faith,' Sister Theresa, the Indian nun who taught moral science, intoned devoutly, 'is believing that the Lord, our Saviour, will guide you over every puddle, that He is the invisible force that makes you remember the answers to examination questions, that He is the one who magically wipes away your tears and takes care of you when you fall ill.'

Lakshmi was even more confused. Sister Theresa had introduced the concept of faith in class earlier that day, and Lakshmi, confounded by the abstract terms in which she had spoken about it, had sought her afterwards, not because she had wanted to appear studious, but because she dreaded confusion. 'But I still don't understand.'

'You're very close to Sister Cecilia, aren't you? So you probably know how much she has suffered.'

Lakshmi shook her head.

'Okay, I'll tell you, listen. When she was a girl Sister Cecilia lived in France with her parents. They were a very happy family. But during the war her parents disappeared one day. They were taken away by the police. Do you know why? Because they were Jews. Sister Cecilia escaped only because their neighbours hid her for many months and secretly took her to Italy so that she could live safely with distant relatives. She had to change her name and live with strangers. Do you know how she was able to get through those horrible years? It was because of her faith in Christ the Lord. Because she, a non-Christian like you, allowed Jesus into her heart and accepted him as her saviour. She trusted Him and He held her hand and guided her to safety. That is faith. Do you understand now?'

Lakshmi did not. This was going nowhere. Sister Theresa made as much sense as Shakespeare did in *The Merchant of Venice*, a text that the English teacher sonorously read aloud in class. But Sister Theresa beamed with hope and Lakshmi didn't want to disappoint her, nor did she want to listen to the nun's unconvincing explanations any more. So she shrugged ambivalently.

Misinterpreting this as interest, Sister Theresa pressed ahead. 'Do you want to give faith a chance, child?'

Bored, Lakshmi shrugged again.

'Glory be to the Lord!' Sister Theresa exclaimed ecstatically. 'Join us for High Mass on Sunday. I'll tell Sister Cecilia to come and get you from the dorm.'

The next Sunday Lakshmi dressed as Sister Theresa had instructed: in her best dress, with a matching hairband, her black school shoes polished till she could see her face in them, and her face daubed with Pond's talcum powder, which she borrowed from another girl.

Sister Cecilia looked pleased. 'You've dressed appropriately for Mass,' she said and escorted her to the church.

By the time they arrived at the church in the school's premises, the Christian girls had already begun taking their places at the pews. They were well dressed and quiet. Sister Cecilia did not make Lakshmi sit with the rest of the girls. Instead, she took her to the front and seated her in the first row with the nuns. As the nuns occupied their places they nodded at Lakshmi approvingly. Sister Theresa squeezed her hand.

The choir, comprising students of all ages, gathered behind the pulpit. Sister Cecilia gave Lakshmi a book and opened it to the right page for her. When the nun playing the organ gave the cue everyone started singing earnestly, even the little girls in ribbons in the rows behind her. Sister Cecilia looked down and smiled at her, pointing to the appropriate line in the book. Lakshmi noticed that the hymn looked much shorter and simpler on paper than it seemed when sung. Sister Cecilia then sang louder, opening her mouth wide to articulate the words better, as though speaking to a deaf person. She softly tapped her leg to bring out the rhythm and ran her fingers across the words as they sang. Lakshmi followed her finger but did not sing along.

Between hymns, during the momentary silence in which some people slapped their hymn books shut and others cleared their throats softly or adjusted their dresses, Sister Cecilia bent and whispered into Lakshmi's ear, 'Don't be so shy. You can sing with us.'

But Lakshmi's attention wandered from the hymn book. She looked at the large wooden cross behind the choir illuminated by numerous little bulbs, and thought Jesus Christ looked pained. She noticed how the pillars around the apse had figures of angels and saints carved on them, how the pillars curved upwards and met close to the ceiling. She looked up at the high ceiling and imagined the spires outside rising above it, the tallest of them all the bell tower whose bell she heard every Sunday morning to signal the beginning of Mass. She looked at the tall windows that wouldn't open, their translucent glass not allowing much light into the church. The church looked very old, grey and gloomy. She suddenly realized when she turned around and looked at everybody singing from the hymn books, how strange it all was, how alien, how out of place she looked here.

When Mass was over and everyone streamed out of the church in an orderly fashion, a few nuns—including Sister Theresa who beamed, feeling personally responsible for Lakshmi's presence—stopped her on the way and said how happy they were that she had joined them. 'Hope to see you every Sunday, child,' they said and Lakshmi nodded obediently.

Only Sister Cecilia was silent and distracted all the way back to the dormitory.

The next Sunday as Lakshmi and Sister Cecilia emerged from the church Sister Theresa walked up to her and asked, 'Child, why don't you sing the praises of the Lord like the rest of us?'

Lakshmi considered the question for a moment and replied, 'I don't understand the songs.'

Sister Theresa looked incredulous. 'But it's simple English, my dear. You speak languages I've never even heard of. What is it in those hymns that you don't understand?'

Lakshmi shrugged. Even the *Vishnu sahasranamam* her grandmother had made her learn by heart and chant regularly held some meaning for her, if only because of repetition and ritual.

Sister Theresa clucked impatiently. For a moment Sister Cecilia looked like she would, too, but then she said, 'She's just shy. She'll get over it soon.' Sister Theresa went away looking unhappy, and Lakshmi was grateful to Sister Cecilia for having made her go away.

But every Sunday she and Sister Cecilia walked back to the dormitory in silence. For a very long time Lakshmi did not understand Sister Cecilia's temporary post-Mass silences. Was it piety? Sadness for Mary? Was she lost in thought? She was sometimes afraid that Sister Cecilia might have forgotten how to smile during Mass.

It was Sister Theresa, forthright as always, who took her aside once more and asked, 'Child, are you happy to be here?' There was more annoyance in her tone than concern.

Lakshmi shrugged in response.

Sister Theresa took a deep breath and said, 'You know, all sorts of amazing things happen to those who sincerely believe in the word of God. Do you know the other day the miraculous statue of Mother Mary in a church over the mountains shed tears? Just like that tears started flowing down her cheeks. She was crying for us. Can you imagine that? Haven't you heard that lepers who go to that church and pray come out cured? Haven't you heard of the hot springs near Sister Cecilia's hometown in France that has miraculous powers? One dip in the bubbling whirlpools is all you need to wash you of your diseases and your sins.'

Lakshmi yawned. Sister Theresa looked disappointed. 'You know,' she said, sighing and getting up. 'Sister Cecilia does so much for you. At least you can sing for her.'

Lakshmi could hear the insinuation in her criticism. Was that why Sister Cecilia refused to talk to her after Mass? Was Sister Theresa implying that she was not grateful? Did that mean Sister Cecilia would stop caring for her now?

Suddenly anger mingled with panic welled up inside her. 'I just don't understand all this,' she shouted and rushed away from the church, running all the way to the dorm, to her bed where she buried her face in her pillow and lay still, refusing to cry.

Sister Cecilia came to see her later that day. She ran her fingers gently through Lakshmi's hair and asked her to get up. As soon as Lakshmi heard Sister Cecilia's calm voice she jumped up. There was no complaint or accusation in it. Sister Cecilia looked as though she was unaware of what Sister Theresa had said. Yet she must have known, otherwise she would not have come at that time.

'Are you not well?' Sister Cecilia asked.

Lakshmi nodded vaguely, neither in affirmation nor in denial.

'Let's go for a walk. It'll make you feel better.'

Relieved, Lakshmi got up and accompanied the nun to the hills.

That day neither alluded to Sister Theresa. But later, when

Lakshmi was old enough to be curious about these things, she asked Sister Cecilia, 'Sister Theresa says you suffered a lot as a child.'

Sister Cecilia shrugged. 'I suppose so. You can't help it when your parents disappear one day, and the only hint you have of what might have happened is when your neighbours ask you to pretend to be someone you're not.'

'Did you ever find out what happened to your parents?'

'No. But I'm sure they died in a concentration camp.'

'And yet why did you become a Christian?'

'A few terrible men do not make a religion bad,' she said abstractedly. 'Besides, I didn't have the choice. I was always afraid. I had to pretend to be a Catholic. Even after I was smuggled into Italy to live with a distant cousin in Turin. That's how it was for a lot of us then. My cousin even married a Catholic. But with time pretence wears off, and it becomes your reality.'

Lakshmi wondered how it was possible for her to obliterate her true identity, replacing it with her doppelganger, with what had once been make-believe when she finally entered a convent. 'Still, don't you bear any grudge against the oppressors of the Jews?'

Sister Cecilia looked pensive. She screwed up her eyes and looked towards the far hills where they were chopping down trees and bulldozing the hillside to plant tea bushes. She sighed. 'The loss of your home and your identity can make you sensitive to other people's troubles. Or it can turn you into a misanthrope.'

Sadness clouded Sister Cecilia's face, and all the talk of faith and miracles sounded trivial. Lakshmi admired Sister Cecilia. For her wisdom in being able to separate a system of belief from those who abused it. For her ability to forgive. By then old enough to recognize her own losses, Lakshmi wondered what *she* would become. Would she be caring like Sister Cecilia, or rapacious in her demands on others and unforgiving if they failed her? 'I hope I grow up to be like you,' she whispered into the breeze even as she knew deep down that it would not be the case.

★

Lakshmi returned to her grandmother's house for every break between terms. Every time she arrived or left Devaki came to the station and stood in the recesses of the platform, behind the crowd, far enough not to be seen, yet close enough to get a glimpse of her daughter. Lakshmi remained unaware of her mother's shadow on her, oblivious of her mother's joy and pain.

To her grandmother's dismay she came home in pinafores and skirts, in two-ribboned pigtails, with no pottu on her forehead. The first thing her grandmother did as soon as she arrived was to silently hold out a pavadai, and, as she grew older, a davani, into which she changed after an oil bath that became akin to a purification ritual. She emerged from the bathroom with a small pottu on her forehead, her eyes lined with kohl, her hair doused with coconut oil, braided into a single thick plait pulled back so tightly that one could see the tension at the roots of her hair. Her grandmother would then instruct her to go to the prayer room, put a cotton wick into a lamp after soaking it in oil, and light it in front of the gods who stared down from sundry photo frames in small altars. While she did this, her grandmother stood behind her muttering shlokas.

Lakshmi went through this ritual uncomplainingly, as though she saw no dichotomy between her life at home and the one at school, sliding naturally into the different rhythms, the different sets of rules, rituals and superstitions.

The chasm that had opened between her and her grandmother remained. On her first visit, as she sat eyeing the feast of karudams, vadai, ven-pongal, avial, payasam and therati paal that her grandmother had prepared for her, the tension was palpable. After a long silence her grandmother attempted conversation. 'Are they feeding you well there?'

Lakshmi nodded.

'Do they give you rice, sambar and curry? Or is it that Christian food of bread, butter and jam?'

'They give us proper food,' Lakshmi responded tersely.

Her grandmother sniffed, unconvinced. 'Are they taking good care of you?'

Lakshmi nodded again.

'Do they wash your clothes properly? Are there doctors to take care of you when you fall ill? Is there anybody to help you with your homework? Are there a lot of children in the school? Do you have friends there? Are the girls nice to you?'

She nodded in response to every question. Her grandmother made it easier for her by asking her questions that could be answered non-verbally.

After a while the conversation flagged. Her grandmother sat back on her palaka and they finished the meal in virtual silence.

Subsequent trips were no better. But over time the chasm became less awkward. It was no longer threatening; it was just there. It grew into the crevasses and tiny pits between them like a live, amorphous creature till it found a comfortable posture, an optimum size, and settled between them, soft, cushioned, spongy, resilient. Her grandmother sought comfort in the renewed activities around the house, and Lakshmi was happy with the familiarity of home, its flaws and its strengths.

Lakshmi and I spent most of our time under the mango tree behind our house, which in the hot season overflowed with flowers and fruits and insects and sap, while at other times it was inert except for diligent ants that scurried up and down its trunk.

I don't quite remember when adolescence crept up on us, but I suddenly became aware of Lakshmi's grandmother murmuring to her, telling her that she was not a child any more. Lakshmi would brush aside her grandmother's advice and continue to spend the afternoons under the mango tree with me. One day when her grandmother caught the two of us sitting on one of the branches of the tree, she ordered Lakshmi to get down and said in a distressed tone, 'You're growing up to be a tomboy. At least for my sake have some modesty.'

Lakshmi went home with her then, but was back at our house a few minutes later. 'I thought your mother wanted you to stay away,' I said.

'My grandmother!' she corrected me peevishly. 'There's nothing wrong with my coming here. Even your mother thinks so.'

I was startled. 'Do you know she's not your mother?'

'Of course,' she responded with contempt. 'I always knew she was my grandmother.'

'But how?'

'A motherless child knows,' she said.

'So do you know who your mother is?'

She nodded. 'But I've never felt the urge to meet her. I don't want to see her, in fact.'

'Why?'

She shrugged. 'What do I want with a mother who abandoned me?' Her eyes lost their brightness. She turned away from me and moodily sat at the base of the mango tree ripping a leaf apart vein by vein.

'But, still, not even once?'

'No,' she said firmly and walked away.

One summer I overheard my mother telling my father, 'How beautiful she's turning out to be. Just think of the day she'll come into this house as a bride!'

I heard my father grunt in response before I moved away in confusion.

I had already noticed subtle changes in the way Lakshmi behaved with me. She wasn't coquettish, but there was something in her gestures that made me uncomfortable, something about the way she'd suddenly break out into a secret smile for apparently no reason or throw darting, oblique glances at me. She and my mother held several whispered conversations that sometimes culminated in giggles, and when they became aware of my presence they would stop abruptly, making me feel awkward.

One day, during the break before our final year in school,

Lakshmi stood close to me under the mango tree, smiling secretively for a long time. Then, all of a sudden, she asked me, 'Have you ever kissed anyone?'

I shook my head, startled at the turn in the conversation. I suddenly became aware of her proximity and moved away a little.

'I have,' she said in a revelatory tone and giggled.

I was shocked. 'You're bluffing!'

She shook her head emphatically, a little hurt that I did not believe her. Without much prodding she told me about Pulcinella.

Ever since Pulcinella had started working at the school he'd been staring at Lakshmi quite openly, unabashedly. One day, while she was walking back from the convent to her dormitory, he attracted her attention from behind a hibiscus bush. Lakshmi stopped in her tracks, scared. Then he whispered, 'Have you ever been to the forests outside the school?'

His voice was gruff, gravelly. Lakshmi nodded.

'Come here after dark in the evening,' he said, nonetheless. 'I want to show you something.'

After dark when she went back to the hibiscus bush, nervous, afraid, but overcome by curiosity and excitement, he was already there. He instructed her to follow him past trees and bushes, past the pergola near the convent, to the gate at the back. He had a key to it and opened it. Lakshmi followed him out, aware that she was breaking the rules. It was dark and she couldn't see where they were going. But he apparently knew, for he strode confidently, sure-footed, clicking his tongue impatiently when she fell behind or stumbled on a stone or a fallen branch. She heard wolves baying in the night, owls hooting, the smell of eucalyptus overpowering her. Shivering, beginning to regret her decision to go out of the school, she nevertheless continued to follow him because it was too late for her to turn back. After several minutes of climbing they came to a halt at a clearing. He paused and went down on his hands and knees, searching for something. Then he took out a box of matches from his pocket and lit a match. She could see the ghostly outlines of what looked like a molehill. He gingerly took the match into the hole, and in the dancing yellow flame, she saw several tiny, glassy eyes sparkling at them. She suppressed a cry and held on to his bony shoulder. He slid one hand into the hole and a moment later brought out a small struggling rodent. It was dirty, possibly even flea-infested.

'We eat them,' he said, enjoying her shock.

The match had burnt out now, and Lakshmi was grateful for the darkness. But he lit another one and brought the flame so close to the rodent's eyes that she could see it reflected in them. The terrified animal began to squeal. She shut her eyes tight.

'I know you rich people find it unthinkable, but we're so poor, this is all we have to eat,' he said, forcing her to open her eyes. He released the rodent and let it scurry back into the hole. Lakshmi wasn't sure what he was trying to say, but she knew then that he wasn't as much of a simpleton as he appeared to be. She saw intelligence in his wild eyes, sophistication in his speech, pointed rebuke in his voice. But there was also something vulnerable about him. He seemed painfully aware and ashamed of his appearance, of his stature and position in society.

'Ei,' he said, grinning. 'Come here.'

She shook her head.

'What are you afraid of?'

He scuttled towards her, still on his haunches, crab-like. She moved away. But he lunged at her and put his arm around her. She shivered. The second match had also gone out. This time he did not light a third. In the darkness she felt his chapped lips seeking hers. 'Like the dorais,' he whispered. She tasted his briny saliva in her mouth, his slobbering lizard tongue clumsily lapping hers. She stopped breathing, afraid that she might smell him and throw up. When he released her lips she gasped for breath. She pushed his arms away and got up. 'I want to go back,' she said in a small voice, wiping her mouth on her sleeve.

He escorted her back in silence. He waited by the hibiscus bush till she had stealthily entered the dormitory.

'In the light of the matchstick he looked like a brute,' Lakshmi said to me now, enjoying the memory. 'He dislikes everybody who's not poor. Tell me, is it my fault that I'm not poor like him?'

As I listened my ears burned. But with what I could not tell. She had combed her hair carelessly that day, for curls and wisps stuck out of the sides of her head, giving her a waif-like appearance. She looked artless, completely natural, and, for the first time in my life I noticed how incredibly lovely she was.

Then she gave me another one of her secretive smiles. 'Look, this is how he kissed me,' she said, and before I knew what she was doing, she pulled me behind the tree so that nobody from inside the house could see us, and planted her lips on mine, prying them open by wedging her lower lip between them. I felt suffocated as she slid her tongue into my mouth and smothered me. Her saliva was soon all over my lips, oozing into my mouth. Its taste repelled me. I summoned all my energy and pushed her away, sputtering and spitting and coughing and gesticulating as though I had swallowed poison.

'Lakshmi!' I cried. 'Don't you have any shame?'

After spitting out one last gob of spit I rushed to a tap nearby and rinsed my mouth a few times. In doing all this I had hardly looked at her, but when I emerged from under the tap and looked up, to my surprise, I saw that her eyes were full, her face red and stricken. Before I could open my mouth she hung her head and rushed past the side of the house and disappeared from sight.

I sat down on the steps leading to the back door of the house with my head in my hands. Charlie the Dog, who was the only witness to the episode, sat beside me with a puzzled expression. I felt ashamed, disgusted, sorry. But, above all, I was confused.

Later that day I went to her house. Her grandmother was

at the door, worried. The first thing she asked me was, 'Do you know what happened to her?'

I shook my head, pretending ignorance for Lakshmi's sake. She had locked herself up in her room and refused to come out.

'It's important,' I whispered so that her grandmother couldn't hear. 'I need to talk to you.'

But there was no answer from within.

'I'm sorry.' I tried again. I waited for several minutes: for a response, a grunt, a sniff, the rustling of her pavadai, the flip of a page, anything. But there was none. Charlie the Dog barked anxiously. I ran out of the house and looked up at her window from the street. She was sitting on her bed by the window, her head bent, holding her rag doll, incongruous, a woman looking like an abandoned child, finding comfort in a doll with cheap woollen hair. When she saw me she flashed her eyes and slammed the window shut with such vehemence that I was afraid the wood would splinter and come crashing down. It was that rage again, that inexplicable ferocity, a point from which there appeared be no return. But this time it was suffused with humiliation as well.

I knew she would not open the window, no matter what the cost. Yet I stood in the street, leaning against the building across the street, staring at the closed window all afternoon. When I staggered home, feeling light-headed and dehydrated from the heat, I realized that for the second time in her life Lakshmi had lost her innocence.

When she left for school at the end of the break one stifling morning, my father sitting beside her in the rickshaw with an assortment of steel trunks and his valise under his feet, it was an all-too-familiar scene. She did not raise her eyes to look at me. I felt a crushing sense of responsibility, the burden of guilt, the enormity of my foolishness. The loss was irreparable.

★

The day she got back to school Lakshmi walked up to Pulcinella, interrupted him while he was digging a new flower bed, and said to him, 'I want to see those rats again. Take me there.'

Pulcinella dropped his shovel as he stood up. When the look of surprise faded, a smile appeared on his face, contorting it.

That night they met behind the hibiscus bush and sneaked out of the school. At the top of the hill he lit a match and they saw the marble eyes staring back at them. Lakshmi did not avert her face; instead she leant forward and studied them, remarking how they shone like fireflies. He put his hand into the hole and pulled out a rodent.

'Let me hold it,' she said, taking the squirming creature in her hand. A wave of disgust engulfed her, but she steeled herself and held the rodent firmly till it gave up all hope of escape. 'One day I'd like to eat it too,' she said. She spoke a different dialect, a rustic one—crude, her grandmother would have said—like him. It gave her the sense of speaking a less civilized language, one she had never spoken before, but it came to her quite naturally as though she'd spoken it all her life.

Pulcinella laughed, both at what she said and how she said it. 'No, maydum,' he said mockingly, taking the rodent from her. 'A Brahmin like you better stay away from our food. What will we have left then?'

The moon was bright enough for them to see each other even after the matchstick had burnt out. She noticed how his skin shone in the diffused light, how the dark edges of the mountains and the ghostly shadows thrown by the tall trees behind him that usually formed an unearthly, forbidding backdrop at night now looked less menacing. She noticed that he was more relaxed, less threatening than he had been when they had come here the first time. Perhaps it was because she was speaking *his* language, the way he did, with all its earthly intonations, sounding disarming, without any pretences.

The fresh scent of pine and eucalyptus mingled with the odour of the rodent in his hand. When she leant forward she could smell his body too: the dank smell of an oil cellar, of recently cooked animal flesh. How did animal flesh taste? Was it soft and chewable, or hard and leathery? She had seen the girls in the non-vegetarian section of the mess eat meat, but their food had never interested her. It was too well-cooked, full of the aromas of familiar spices to arouse any curiosity. And what about his tongue? His briny saliva? A wilful sense of self-destruction made its presence felt. A sense that would appear again and again in her life. She wanted to taste his tongue again, feel the forbidden touch of his rough hands.

He reached for her and swung her into his arms with surprising ease. She stiffened and tried pushing him away. But he was surprisingly strong.

'Let me go,' she said, but her voice drowned in confusion.

They rolled on the ground, crushing fallen eucalyptus leaves under their bodies, the freshly squeezed juices releasing a heady odour into the night air. They could see a few pairs of incandescent eyes looking at them through the trees, but they let them be because wolves do not speak, nor do they recognize illicit passion.

During the day she would make up her mind to never see him again, but as night approached, she found herself helplessly propelled, moth-like, towards Pulcinella, who waited behind the hibiscus bush even though they never agreed to meet there. He seemed to know that she would come, and she would follow him obediently, like a sleepwalker, into the darkness.

When she crept back into the dorm the warden sometimes saw her and would mutter resentfully, 'Sister Lakshmi! She has a special pass to the convent.'

Lakshmi never asked Pulcinella what his real name was. Everybody in school called him Yesudasan; he had been baptized by a priest at a nearby church without his realizing it a few years ago. He never asked her why she called him Pulcinella. He never questioned her; he just wasn't curious to know more about her. When she offered any information about herself or the school he would listen with disinterest and shrug as though he knew everything she said. On the other hand he became animated when he spoke. He told her about life in the mountains, the remote settlements his family had left behind, wandering from place to place, scrounging through the forests for fruit, birds and animals. And live rodents. They—he, his parents and his younger siblings—lived in a shack up in the mountains. When she asked if she could visit his house he pointed vaguely in the direction of the highest peak and said it was so deep inside the forest that the only time he saw anybody else was when he came to work at the school. But when she insisted he became irritable and said, 'Maydum, what does a Brahmin like you want to do in our shack?'

One day he told her he was learning to read and write. He showed her a slate on which he had written *a, aah, e, ee* and *oo, ooo.* The letters were written in an unsteady hand; they were large to make up for their lack of confidence and occupied both sides of the slate. The liberal embellishments on them made them look like bad calligraphy. Lakshmi's first impulse was to laugh, but the dead seriousness of his expression doused her mirth.

'What do you think of it, maydum?' he asked, challenging her.

She shrugged. 'It's okay.'

'Only okay?' He suddenly grew angry. 'I spent all night learning this from a book meant for little children. I burnt five candles. Look at my eyes, they are sleepless. And it's only okay?' He shook his head in disbelief.

His reaction surprised her. 'It's good,' she said at length in a placatory tone. 'It's good.'

'Then why did you look as though you were going to laugh?'

'I remembered the first time I wrote the alphabet on a slate and showed it to my grandmother,' she lied. 'She said it looked like the knots that formed in her sewing thread if she left it unwound for a while.'

He calmed down. 'I want to learn to read and write like you people,' he said, placing emphasis on 'you people'. There was a touch of contempt in his voice. 'You have the money to live in a big school, wear those short skirts and talk like the dorais as though you are one of them. But I have to get out of the hovel we live in. I don't want to be somebody's servant all my life.' He brought his face close to hers. There was passion in his eyes. 'Eating rats may be a novelty to you. But I don't want to hunt them for my food.'

Lakshmi turned her face away. She let him be. She let him mock her. She let him insist on focusing on the differences in their social standing. She let him vent his anger. She listened calmly when he railed at the rest of the world for shunning his people as savages even though they were the original inhabitants—the adivasis—of these mountains. She didn't tell him that all that bile made his saliva sour.

But, one day, she wrote in her diary: *P is bizarre. He has surely come from another planet. He is so intense that one day he is going to burst into pieces. SC says he's a revolutionary. But I don't believe her. He has no followers. In fact, nobody pays attention to him.*

She asked him obliquely, 'What is it about the mountains that makes you so angry?'

'It's not the mountains.' His look made her aware of the preposterousness of her question. 'How can mountains make you angry? It's the world. To everybody we're invisible, even when we're standing in front of them. We're savages. We don't belong in society. But, I tell you, we were here before any of you.'

He identified with the tribals in the mountains. He was one of them, but that was not the full story. There were things about himself that he never told her. He never told her that a group of kuravas, while migrating south, had made the wrong turn at Mannarkudi and had made their way up the mountains. That, there, lost in the dark blue mountains, a kurati girl, fascinated by his father's abilities to catch scurrying rodents in the forest, had run away with him. That she had settled amongst his father's people with the malleability and adaptability of a kurati. That a year later he, Pulcinella, had been born to her. He did not tell her that his nose, his chin and his eyes were exaggerated representatives of his mother's people in him. A tiny piece of information left untold, unaware that it would have had enormous significance had he mentioned it.

The day Lakshmi threw up her lunch she was whisked away to the convent under a cloud of whispers by the grim-faced nuns. Sister Cecilia appeared before Lakshmi as she lay in bed in one of the rooms in the cloister. She was calm, but Lakshmi could see anger simmering beneath the surface.

'You have committed a grave sin,' Sister Cecilia said grimly.

Lakshmi turned her face away.

'There's no need to be insolent,' Sister Cecilia said with surprising belligerence.

Lakshmi turned to look at her, but said nothing. Sister Cecilia was still seemingly calm.

'Normally students are thrown out of school for far less serious offences. Do you want us to send you back home?'

Lakshmi was stung by the tone of her voice. She didn't think Sister Cecilia was capable of issuing threats.

Sister Theresa, who was also in the room, interjected, 'All this wouldn't have happened if you had accepted the Lord as your saviour.'

Sister Cecilia put a finger on her lips and escorted Sister Theresa out of the room politely, but firmly. Then, shutting the door, she said, 'You have betrayed my trust in you. What should I tell the Mother Superior now? And why should she listen to anything I have to say on your behalf any more after what you've done? Why don't you answer me?'

It wasn't often that Lakshmi shed tears, but now her eyes clouded over. She avoided Sister Cecilia's insistent stare and willed her eyes to clear by opening them wide and taking a deep breath.

'Why don't you answer me?'

'What can I say?' Lakshmi said weakly.

'You could at least have the humility to ask for forgiveness. To acknowledge that you have sinned. Sinned so badly that repentance will have to be severe.'

Lakshmi was shocked by the harshness in her voice; it reminded her of her grandmother. She had never imagined Sister Cecilia employing that tone with anybody, leave alone with her. Were even the softest of people capable of becoming hard?

Sister Cecilia sat silently for a while, waiting for a response, and when there was none, she got up and left.

Outside the room Lakshmi could hear the faint voices of Sister Cecilia and some other nuns down the hallway. 'She's an intelligent girl,' she heard Sister Cecilia say. 'She knows what she has done. The torment of her realization is punishment enough. She'll repent one day.'

'What do you think we should do with her in the meantime?' the Mother Superior asked.

'Can't we let her stay here? If we send her home her grandmother is sure to throw her out. And she's too proud to go to her mother's house.'

'But that's not *our* problem.'

Sister Cecilia seemed to consider this for a few moments. 'It is,' she said with a sigh. 'We—*I*—gave her too much freedom.'

The next day the school's gardener escorted Pulcinella out of the school, holding him by the scruff of his neck. 'Amma says you shouldn't come anywhere near this school again,' he said balefully, referring to the Mother Superior.

Pulcinella wriggled to free himself from the gardener's grip. 'Why?' he demanded.

The gardener shrugged. 'I don't know. You must have done something.' He relieved Pulcinella of the key to the back gate and released him.

'But you can't throw me out without an explanation!'

The gardener guffawed. 'I see you've learned to talk like the big people.' He slammed the school gate shut.

Pulcinella fumed. 'Just see if I don't come back and demand justice! I'll complain to the police about you.'

'Dai, go away,' the gardener said, wearily. 'I don't know anything about this. It's between you and amma.' He turned and walked away muttering to himself, 'Justice he says! The boy doesn't even know to write his own name, and he talks like the big people about justice!'

From the other side Pulcinella now screamed. 'They can't do this to me! My family depends on the money I earn here!'

The gardener was now out of earshot. It was evening; there was nobody else around except for the watchman who sat lazily at the gate with his lathi all day long and monitored the traffic through the front gate. And even he was slumped on his stool, ignoring the raving boy.

Lakshmi's belongings were moved to the room she now occupied in the cloister. She'd slept in the room on a few occasions in the past when recovering from illness. But now it looked different, having been refurbished recently. For the first time she noticed a cross nailed to the wall in such a way that it was directly in front of her when she lay in bed. A small, red night lamp lay on the table directly under it, its light directed up at the cross. There was a black plaque on the wall below the cross. The silver cursive letters on the plaque read: *Domine, non sum dignus*—Lord, I am not worthy. On the table was a copy of the New Testament.

Lakshmi could hardly keep any food down. She attended classes sporadically. The rest of the time she spent lying in bed staring at the cross and studying the exaggerated shadows thrown by the light under it. Her final school-leaving examinations were fast approaching, and even though she did not know if she was going to take them, she made half-hearted attempts to study for them.

Sister Cecilia came to her room every day, grim-faced, speaking to her in matter-of-fact tones, and supervised her food and studies. When, for a period of time, Lakshmi was particularly indisposed and weak due to morning sickness, it was Sister Cecilia who stayed by her side, feeding her liquids and taking care of her needs. Their conversations were now more deliberate, more ponderous and often to the point. Lakshmi recognized in Sister Cecilia the kind of resentment her grandmother had exhibited, a silent accusation of ingratitude. It hung between them, this accusation, like the folds of a curtain. Lakshmi responded by retreating into bouts of silence and melancholy, watching helplessly and, in moments of defiance, wishing more and more folds to appear between them so that she could hide behind them. Sister Cecilia simply left her alone at such times, and Lakshmi cherished these moments as victories.

Not once during those long hours in bed, when watching the cross and identifying its changing shades at different times of the day had become a hobby of sorts, did Lakshmi pine for Pulcinella. He had served his purpose. The fleeting moments she had shared with him were now long gone. She had already forgotten the smell of his breath, the taste of his tongue, the glint in his eyes. She could not remember the cause of his constant anger. Sometimes it seemed as though he had never existed, as though she had dreamt everything. But once Sister Cecilia brought in a crumpled piece of paper to remind her of his existence. He had tied it to a stone and had shot it into the convent with a sling, breaking a window in the process.

'Here,' Sister Cecilia said, thrusting the piece of paper into her face, 'he has the nerve to send this to you.'

Lakshmi examined it. Scrawled on it was a message she could not decipher. In his unlettered way he had strung together letters that did not make sense. She tried reading them backwards and forwards, at all angles and upside down. But they still didn't make sense. She gave up. She figured he'd sent this either to tell her he loved her or to warn her and 'her people' of some dire consequences that she would not understand anyway. She tore up the paper and threw the pieces into the waste-paper basket.

Sister Cecilia visibly cheered up after that.

The term drew to a close. Christmas, too, was fast approaching. After the examinations most of the students would go home. The only ones who would remain in both Lakshmi's school and the boys' school were the ones whose parents lived abroad and those who had nowhere else to go. This time Lakshmi would be counted amongst the latter.

Christmas was usually celebrated in a grand way in the big community church between the schools. Choirs made up of the students who stayed back and people who lived on tea plantations and in towns in the neighbouring hills had begun practising every week after Mass. Lakshmi was careful to avoid them after service, running back to the convent feigning sickness even when she felt fine.

Sister Cecilia's changed attitude, her newly acquired harshness, rattled Lakshmi. Everything the nun did seemed like a deliberate reminder of what Lakshmi had done, of how she had let everybody down. Sister Cecilia seemed to do everything more slowly to maximize the effect, whether it was to walk her down to the refectory or to pray audibly by her bedside umpteen times every day. And those moments when she struggled with her nausea, when Sister Cecilia was by her side, helping her to the toilet or urging her calmly to drink ginger water to calm her unruly stomach were particularly weighed with torment. She wished Sister Cecilia wouldn't do all this, wouldn't make her live in perpetual guilt.

'Why are you doing all this for me?' Lakshmi asked Sister Cecilia one day after she had wiped the vomit that had accidentally stained her dress.

Sister Cecilia appeared unprepared for the question. She looked about in confusion, then said brusquely, 'Who else will take care of you?'

'That's not reason enough.'

'Well, that's the only reason I know.' Sister Cecilia looked particularly uneasy at having to explain her actions. She looked around the room. Her eyes fell on the Bible that had remained undisturbed since the day it had been placed on the table. 'I hope you remember that you still haven't asked for forgiveness. You still haven't repented.'

Sister Cecilia stood looking at her as if expecting a reply. But when none was forthcoming she turned and walked away, leaving Lakshmi to contemplate the light on the cross, nursing her growing determination to not do what was expected of her.

Like the mists rolling down the mountains Sister Cecilia's punishing gestures enveloped her in gloom. She remembered the days before she was sent away from her grandmother's house, the similar feeling of being adrift and alone, of the harshness that tried to break her spirit, of how people were unwilling to forgive her for her mistakes. Just as she had spent days in her room as a child watching the world go by under the window, she now began spending all her time staring at the cross on the wall till the psychedelic light of the bulb under it spun webs in front of her eyes, rippling through the room till it was suffused with a mesmerizing glow.

She feared it hypnotized her, addled her brain, enfeebled her. For in her worst moments of nausea when she wished whatever was in her guts would just come out and deliver her, she began wondering if there wasn't more happiness in obedience. Perhaps in submitting to others there was relief, for the burden of making decisions was on someone else. Perhaps that was why the nuns in the convent were usually happy; their path was clearly marked, all they had to do was follow blithely. It was such an easy option. And repentance would give her that option.

One night she heard Sister Cecilia singing in the chapel. Her voice appeared all of a sudden, through the silence of the night, needle-thin, delicate, spasmodic, as if from a faraway gramophone. It stirred her. She found the energy to get up and tiptoe downstairs. Sister Cecilia was alone at the organ, singing *Ave Maria*. It was a version Lakshmi had not heard before— Caccini's, as she would find out later. There were no words other than the two to Hail Mary, repeated over and over again. But it was the music, the fluidity of the melody, overlaid by the rich harmonics of the organ that caught her by surprise. She hadn't heard anything this lovely in a long time. She stood outside the chapel, leaning against a pillar in the shadow thrown by the moon. Sister Cecilia's voice was devoid of the grating harshness that had set in of late. There was distilled purity in it. It was as soft as it was on Lakshmi's first day at school when Sister Cecilia had calmed her. As the voice soared, it enveloped Lakshmi and lifted her with it, till she felt as though she were floating above the cloister and then rising even higher as the pitch and the volume of the music rose. This is what they must mean when they talk about heavenly music, this bodily flight from one's shackles, this sense of omnipotence and glory.

By the time Sister Cecilia had finished singing, Lakshmi was aware of a deep ache within her. How she longed for the Sister Cecilia she *used* to know, the giggling, fish-faced nun.

Lakshmi hummed the melody to herself softly, absent-mindedly, breaking off occasionally when her throat swelled with the hurtful feeling of having lost something forever.

The next day was Gaudete Sunday. The large church in the valley between the hills was dark and gothic, an anachronistic imitation of European churches with spires and gargoyles and stained-glass windows. But inside it was simple, almost bare, its cruciform nave flanked by tiny unadorned chapels. But the altar had marble floors, mahogany choir stalls, a red carpet leading up to it, a pipe organ fused into the wall on one side, and oversized candelabra with cherubs carved on their stems. The purple candles on a large wreath from the previous Advent Sundays had been replaced with pink ones.

The priest, in a richly glittering chasuble, reminded them of the Christmas spirit in his sermon. There were the usual homilies and stern warnings against Satan's seductive charms, but there was also joy in his voice. Even the choir sang joyously, unlike their soulless rendition on most days. Everybody smiled; they clutched each others' hands and exchanged greetings and good wishes. Nobody else seemed to have any doubts in their minds; nobody seemed to wage battles within. They all appeared genuinely pleased at being part of the congregation, in being obedient, in following the others. How easy it was for them to be happy!

After Mass, Sister Cecilia stayed back to take part in the

rehearsals for the forthcoming Christmas celebrations. The choir regrouped for practice. From a bare sacristy the deep intonations of a Gregorian chant oozed through the walls: *Agnus Dei, qui tollis peccata mundi: miserere nobis* (Lamb of God, who takes away the sin of the world: have mercy on us). Sister Cecilia sat at the organ after the chant had ended and played the opening chords of the aria she'd sung the previous night. Hearing them again did not diminish the power of the notes. Lakshmi felt herself being propelled from the pews. She approached Sister Cecilia and stood by her side, her head bent. Just as Sister Cecilia started singing, Lakshmi joined her. Startled, Sister Cecilia stopped. Then she broke into a big smile, her first to Lakshmi in many weeks, her wide money-purse mouth becoming even wider. She resumed from the beginning. This time Lakshmi sang all by herself the melody she had heard only the previous night. She remembered it perfectly as though she had known it all her life. *Aaaavvvayy Marriiiiiiaaaa,* she sang over and over again, repeating the words, contracting and lengthening the syllables. A few people who had lingered on after the service stopped to listen. Sister Cecilia beamed. Sister Theresa rushed up and held Lakshmi's hand as she sang without looking up at anybody.

By the time she'd finished singing she wanted to burst into tears. It was the applause of those who'd gathered around her that stopped her. Sister Cecilia stepped down from the organ and held Lakshmi in her arms. Lakshmi's eyes welled up. She buried her face in Sister Cecilia's shoulder and cried. She felt Sister Cecilia gently push her down. Obediently she fell to her knees, sobbing.

'Repent, my dear,' Sister Cecilia said. 'Repent, and you will be forgiven.'

When they left the church later that day, walking side by side towards the convent, Lakshmi felt an enormous sense of relief. There was a glimmer of hope; she could be accepted, pardoned for what she had done.

It was the same sense of hope that engulfed her when she sang the aria again at Mass on Christmas Eve, and afterwards the Mother Superior clasped Lakshmi's hands in hers and said excitedly, 'What a wonderful Christmas it is, my child! God bless you and your baby!' When Sister Cecilia stood by her side smiling proudly as strangers surrounded her outside, remarking not only how wonderfully she sang, but also how beautiful she looked. She noticed some boys from the neighbouring school hanging around, stealing sly glances at her, trying to nudge their way past the eagle-eyed nuns. She didn't want to leave. She wished all these people would stay, mill around her, talk to her, smile, hold her hand. She wished this moment would last forever.

A certain calm descended on her by the time she and Sister Cecilia went back to the convent, a feeling that she was at peace, her seething mind finally quietened. Even the stern warning, 'Quod non est aeternum, non est—What is not eternal, is not', that Sister Cecilia had written quite pointedly on a piece of paper and had left on her desk several days ago, did not ruffle her. Eternal or not, she had to savour this moment.

But the next morning she was in for a shock. Before breakfast, Sister Cecilia took Lakshmi down to the chapel Mother Superior was already there, a thin pendant with a cross in her hand. Sister Cecilia knelt down on the prie-dieu and gestured to Lakshmi to follow. Then she whispered a prayer, pausing after every sentence for Lakshmi to repeat: 'Lord, forgive me, for I have sinned. I am not worthy of your mercy and grace. I let the devil instead of you into my heart. He led me to destitution. But, now, I beg for your mercy, to show me the way. Lord, protect this unborn child conceived in grave sin. I entrust it to you. Lord, I am not worthy, I am not worthy, I am not worthy.'

The happiness she had experienced the previous day evaporated instantly against the onslaught of these harsh words. She was baffled by the sudden turn of events. What was the significance of this act? What was she really admitting to in uttering these words? When had she consented to this? Was this the price to pay for acceptance? She repeated Sister

Cecilia's words feeling weak, disoriented, her lips moving involuntarily to emit unfamiliar sounds. She had the dreamy sense of observing herself from outside her body, while she did someone else's bidding like a marionette. When she had finished uttering the prayer she bowed her head even further till her chin rested snugly in the trough of her collar bone.

Then the Mother Superior, who had been monitoring the proceedings, got up with a sigh of relief and pressed the cross into Lakshmi's hand, saying, 'Child, wear this. Hold the cross every time a sinful thought crosses your mind. It will give you strength in your time of need.'

Again, like a marionette, she felt an invisible force controlling her actions as she accepted the pendant, uttered words of gratitude, and wore it.

Back in her room, she lay in bed in a daze. She was unworthy. The words on the plaque on the wall flashed before her eyes even when she closed them, for the psychedelic red light on the table that refused to be put off like some mysterious self-sustaining fire could penetrate not only her eyelids but also, it seemed, walls and great distances, following her wherever she went. *Domine, non sum dignus*. A part of her wanted to get up and cut the plaque into shreds, but the invisible force kept her down, making her utter those words over and over again till she feared she would start believing them.

Lakshmi did take her final school-leaving examinations but she did not return home immediately after that. My father, who had gone as usual to pick her up, returned alone. 'They thought it was best for her to stay back and prepare for college,' he lied to her grandmother.

'But why?' her grandmother asked.

'She did poorly in one or two subjects. So they're going to give her extra help in those subjects before she goes to college.'

'But why does a girl have to go to college? In a year or two I want to have her married off.'

My father looked at her uneasily. 'But, maami,' he said

gently, 'girls do go to college nowadays.'

Her grandmother was unconvinced. 'How much longer will she be there?'

My father hesitated. 'The college term starts only in July. So she'll be there for a few more months.'

Lakshmi's grandmother was unhappy. 'A grown girl shouldn't be away from home like this. What will people think?'

'It's all right, maami,' he said, looking guilty. 'It's only a girls' school. What can happen to her there?'

Lakshmi's belly had now begun to show. One day the Mother Superior took her hand in hers and said, 'Child, have you decided what you're going to do with the baby?'

Lakshmi shook her head. She had spent her time thinking of nothing but the future. It looked bleak to her. Where would she go with the baby? Who would take her in? Should she go in search of Pulcinella? She did not know where her life was headed; she had no control. But there was nothing she could do. She was condemned. By an unborn baby, no less. There were moments when she felt deep revulsion towards the baby when it made its presence felt by moving inside her. And she would place her hand on her belly and press down on it till the baby stopped moving and the revulsion would ebb. It was easier to *not* think of the child, to pretend there was none.

'Your grandmother won't take you in, will she?'

Lakshmi shook her head again.

'What about your mother?'

Lakshmi shook her head even more vehemently.

The Mother Superior nodded solemnly. 'Unfortunately, there's not much in the world for someone like you. Life will be very difficult outside. You have to decide what you want to do with your life and your baby.'

'I don't know, Mother.' Against her will, Lakshmi looked at the Mother Superior pleadingly. 'I just don't know what to do. Believe me, I've thought of every possibility.'

The Mother Superior took her hand. 'I know, my dear. It is hard enough for an old woman like me to think clearly about this. I can only imagine how much harder it is for a child like you.'

Lakshmi sat up. There was genuine sympathy in the Mother Superior's eyes. At that moment a sudden hope took hold of her. But also the urge to give in finally. To admit to her sins. To repent and to submit herself. 'Mother, please tell me what I should do.'

'There are no easy answers, child.' The Mother Superior took a deep breath. 'The only solution I can think of is for you to join our Order. Dedicate your life to the service of the Lord. That's the only way to repent for your past sins.'

Lakshmi looked up, stunned. When she got her voice back she asked fearfully, 'And the baby?'

'Our Order runs an orphanage in the City. They'll take good care of your baby.'

The Mother Superior spoke as if she had already thought this through and had made the decision for her. Lakshmi did not know what to say.

'Tell me, what other choice do you have? But take your time to think about it.'

'Yes, Mother,' she replied obediently, realizing helplessly that it wasn't she who had responded, but the marionette in the Mother Superior's hands.

'God bless you, my child,' the Mother Superior whispered, and left her alone.

Lakshmi spent the rest of her confinement battling the red lamp in her room. No matter what she did to obstruct its light, no matter how strongly she squeezed her eyes shut, she could see red ripples of light spreading out before her.

'Your behaviour should reflect humility, obedience and gratitude,' the Mother Superior had once remarked. And this light strove to enforce that.

She had plenty of time on her hands. She observed the novices who came to stay in the convent for their spiritual training. Most looked happy, albeit solemn, but some looked burdened and scared as they carried their missals back and forth from the chapel, bowing as they passed the nuns in the ambulatory. Were the oppressed-looking ones there against their wishes? Did they feel homesick as she had been during her early days at school? What went through their minds when they meditated all afternoon before vespers, sometimes with theological books open in front of them, sometimes with eyes open? Were they praying for release when they knelt silently like statues, their faces hidden by their palms? Did they sacrilegiously think of lost love during Benediction, in the midst of those ancient chants of adoration? She wanted to reach out to them, but they would glance at her large stomach and hurriedly walk away.

She would join their ranks one day. Would she join the happy lot or the miserable ones? Or would she continue to be impassive, letting the flow of life take her where it pleased?

When her baby was born the nuns in the convent sighed with relief. The baby girl had all of Lakshmi's features, fortunately, and Pulcinella's colour. She was dark and beautiful.

On Sister Cecilia's recommendation the Mother Superior named the baby Ruth as atonement for her mother's actions. She would be baptized in a few weeks. Lakshmi's baptism as well and her initiation into the Order would take place after a few months, when the baby was old enough to be taken away. She waited for the inevitable.

But the afternoon before the baby was to be sent away to the orphanage, Lakshmi stood in the quadrangle in the cloister and remarked how clear the light was that day, as if she were seeing it for the first time. Everything around her was sharp, bright and vivid. For once the omniscient red haze of the lamp in her room didn't cloud her vision like cataracts. For once she did not feel the tug of the invisible strings that the Mother Superior held. And those words, those hideous words on the wall, she could not recall them.

She ached to see her grandmother again, to fall into her arms and to share a conversation with her, as a mother now. She remembered her softness, her strict regimen, her ritual recitation of the *Vishnu sahasranamam* in her off-key voice every Sunday morning. She thought of her discipline and routine, her constant activity around the house, how dutiful she was, how everything she did was somehow related to Lakshmi, how she hardly had any time to think of herself. She thought how even her harshness was familiar and comforting, how her slaps stung at first, only to give way to a warm rush of blood that soothed her. She remembered how even in her silence the bond of kinship was evident. She could vividly see the wounded expression on her grandmother's face as she left home the first time. It occurred to her then that a mother cannot be acquired outside the home.

Lakshmi rushed in and peered at her sleeping baby. It looked vulnerable, uncomplaining. She was born with resignation, with the wisdom to know that it was sometimes good to not have a will. Lakshmi picked her up and held her close. The baby's little fingers curled around her index finger, grasping, even in her sleep, at whatever was available. Lakshmi could smell her breath, her baby skin. The smell of a newborn, which she had not recognized until that moment. The smell that would remain in her memory forever. The smell that awakened something instinctive, primordial, within her.

That night Lakshmi took out a bag and hastily stuffed into it a few of her things: a few clothes, the comb her grandmother had given her, her rag doll, the money my father had given her when he last saw her. Nothing else she possessed mattered. In another small bag she stuffed a few of the baby's things. Slinging a bag on each shoulder, holding the baby tightly to her, she hesitated for a moment. Then she yanked the red light from its socket, lifted one of the desk's legs and crushed the bulb under it. The crunching noise it made gave her great satisfaction. She looked at the plaque on the wall. She decided against pulling it down as well. She was already feeling lighter. She tiptoed out of her room in the dark, opened the cloister door and ran towards the gate as fast as she could. Having trodden that path numerous times with Pulcinella, she knew how to negotiate her way over the hills in the dark towards the town nearby where there would be buses to take her to the plains.

On her way to the bus stop Lakshmi paused several times to look at her baby in the moonlight, to smother her in her arms. That night, as she kissed her daughter, she realized that she had never kissed her before.

But when Lakshmi's grandmother saw the baby she staggered. 'Which parayan's daughter have you brought here?' she asked hoarsely.

'She's *my* daughter, amma,' Lakshmi blurted out, floundering in confusion. 'I didn't know where to go. They wanted to give the baby away to an orphanage. They wanted me to become a nun. They wanted to take my baby away from me, amma. They said I could not keep the baby there. They told me I had to forget that she's my daughter.' Lakshmi stopped, realizing that she was beginning to sound hysterical.

When her grandmother spoke, it was with a wrath Lakshmi had never seen before. 'Take that thing and get out of my house!' she shouted. 'I won't touch that vile thing. God alone knows which wretched man's daughter she is!'

Lakshmi shivered. 'Amma, she's *my* daughter! Your granddaughter.'

'It's your mother's granddaughter, not mine. Take it to her. I've done my part by raising you. Take it away immediately!'

Lakshmi hesitated. Again, instinct impelled her to act. She could not take the baby wherever she went. She inhaled deeply her baby's smells one last time before placing her on the floor. Suppressing her tears, she picked up her bag and swiftly turned and ran out of the house. Her grandmother ran after her, shouting, but Lakshmi disappeared. The baby began to cry. Lakshmi's grandmother stared at her in revulsion for a long time. Finally she left her where she was and went into the prayer room where she chanted loudly to drown the baby's cries. All afternoon the baby cried from hunger and insecurity. Lakshmi's grandmother did not come out of the prayer room even once.

My first reaction upon seeing the baby was guilt, an overwhelming feeling that I would battle all my life. Lakshmi, who was supposed to be *my* Lakshmi, was hitting back at me, avenging herself through this baby. A baby brought into this world only to remind me of my folly.

And I could see that my mother, who'd brought the baby home, was stricken too. 'What made her do this? Why did she have to destroy her life like this? Who knows what kind of man the father is.' She winced at the baby, allowing herself to be repulsed by its uncertain paternity.

'Amma!' I admonished my mother.

'I know, I know. But she was supposed to come to this house as a bride!'

I picked up the baby gingerly. I'd never held a baby before and was afraid it might disintegrate in my clumsy hands. But I needn't have worried. I seemed to know how to hold her, as if I were her father. As she lay in the crook of my arm, she opened her eyes and smiled, and I felt a tenderness I'd never experienced before. Wasn't I too young to feel this way? It was absurd, as absurd as the idea of Lakshmi being a mother.

Lakshmi's grandmother, who'd done nothing but talk about Lakshmi during her absence, about how harsh she'd been with the motherless girl, now refused to allow even her name to be mentioned. And yet, at the same time she looked pale, terribly old and weak, a woman who was counting her days on her prayer beads. Her anger mingled with a sense of fatalism. 'Andavané!' she whispered. 'Why are you tormenting me like this?'

That evening Lakshmi's mother came and picked up her granddaughter. Without any fuss she left, cradling the baby, joyfully cooing to her, offering her an index finger to hold on to.

'I've got my daughter back,' she whispered joyfully at the door. 'My daughter has returned to me!'

Arangetram

Nasser Sharif cradled the baby in his arms, and when he beamed Devaki remembered why she had been so attracted to him. He was old, but he still had the chiselled features of a god. He stood ramrod straight by the window cooing to the baby. He hadn't been this joyful even when Lakshmi had been born.

They stared out of the window. The front gate was firmly shut, as it usually was. Over the years there had been fewer and fewer visitors, ever since Nasser Sharif's career had taken a nosedive after Independence, when the demand for a rugged, patriotic hero was replaced with an insatiable appetite for the soft romantic type who could break into a brooding song for no reason at all. People could not envision Nasser Sharif running around trees and he found the new heroes too effete to even try and compete with. And over time his admirers drifted away, finding increasingly facile excuses to forget appointments with him.

'But why did Mahtab not come to us?' he turned suddenly and asked Devaki rhetorically. He still called her by the name he had given her, a name everybody else had forgotten.

Devaki sighed. 'Don't talk about things you cannot change,' she said gently. They had had innumerable conversations of this sort over the years. 'Why would she come to us after what we did to her? At least if we were dead her life would have made sense to her. But how it must feel to have parents and yet not really have them!'

'We should never have given her up.'

Devaki never responded when he expressed regret over their decision. How could she tell him that she had never wanted to give Lakshmi up either? How could she tell him that she did so only to protect his reputation and that she could have faced the world had it not been for him? How could she tell him that it was because of the moral responsibility *he* felt towards his admirers, *his* sensitivity to how he was perceived in the world (even if it was another matter that in hindsight these were irrelevant, considering how quickly everybody forgot him)? How could she tell him that she did this out of gratitude to him?

'We should not have let her go to the boarding school,' Nasser Sharif continued. 'You should have brought her home that day.'

'And killed my mother's spirit?'

'But we've ended up killing *Mahtab's* spirit. Look what she has had to do.' He turned to the baby. 'And even after that so many times I told you we should bring her home. But you never listened. It was always about what your mother would think. Did you ever think how it would affect our daughter? I should have gone to her school without you and taken her away from there myself. God knows what she's going to do now. Go, bring her home.' Devaki placed her hand on his shoulder to calm him. 'She won't come even if she has to die in a gutter,' she said gently.

'So what are you saying we should do? Nothing, as usual?'

'What choice do we have?'

'You may not. But I do. If I can't find her a job and provide her with a roof over her head, how can I call myself her father? There are still a few people who respect me and will do what they can to help.'

So saying, he handed over the baby and walked out of the house. And till he returned that evening, Devaki anxiously hoped he would not be foolish enough to try to find Lakshmi. He was more fragile than her. He would not be able to deal with Lakshmi's anger. She knew her mother well, and in the same way she also knew her daughter.

Movies were in Lakshmi's blood. Even though she detested movies passionately, like her grandfather, her father and her mother she inevitably wandered into the make-believe streets and cheap opulence of the film city, impelled towards the studios involuntarily by her legs that had become compliant to her destiny in this moment of desperation. Half consciously—or perhaps half unconsciously—she found herself walking through a great arched gate made of simulated ivory, into the portals of the most famous of all the studios in the city. There, a young and upcoming director's lackey welcomed her and, to her great surprise, guided her to the green room where she was told to dress up. The man was of course only following the orders he had received from the director, who, after making a great show of bestowing a favour, had promised Nasser Sharif to give her a try. 'But first only in a supporting role till she proves herself,' he had grudgingly offered.

Now decked up in clothes that gaudily shone of imitation silver and gold thread, her hair smothered with plastic flowers, and her face painted twice over, Lakshmi felt like a tart and considered tearing it all away and fleeing. But the woman who made her up exclaimed, 'An apsara to put all the other apsaras in the world to shame! Go, my daughter, you'll be a great star one day.'

Lakshmi was then presented to the director, who examined her from head to toe and muttered impatiently, 'Now go to the dance director there. He'll show you your steps for the audition. We'll decide after that.' With a wave he dismissed her and proceeded to discuss something with his assistant.

The chain-smoking, pot-bellied dance director who wore rings of precious stones on all his eleven fingers (his left hand had two thumbs), put a cigarette between his lips, raised one hand over his head, put the other on his waist and wiggled his hips with the ease of a belly dancer. He took a couple of steps in either direction, pirouetted a few times, jumped in the air like a fleeing gazelle and landed gracefully on his tiptoes. He removed his cigarette from his mouth and then said, 'Now do that.'

Lakshmi quivered. She had never danced before; she had not even secretly tried a sideways movement of the head or the coy glances like many of the girls in school did in front of a mirror. What would her grandmother say if she saw this? But she wavered only momentarily, and soon her usual steely resolve came back and she stood on the stage, waited for the music to be turned on and followed the motions she had seen the dance director demonstrate.

Barely had she started dancing than the director, who was watching her, came forward and interrupted her, 'Stop! What's this? You call this dancing? You're prancing like a monkey on the roof! Go learn dancing and come back later.'

Lakshmi was stunned. She could not believe her ears. She, the one who broke hearts in every street and alley, was being dismissed because she could not imitate a few silly dance steps that even an obese man could perform? She looked at the director with anger and humiliation flashing in her eyes. She ripped off the plastic flowers in her hair and threw them in his direction. Then she ran out of the studio without even bothering to change into her regular clothes, without looking back to see if the crew was laughing at her.

Watching the proceedings from his cushioned chair near a rotating table fan was the film's hero. He sat smoking meditatively, but his eyes followed Lakshmi as she stomped off the stage. After she was gone, he rose and approached the director.

'No good,' the director said, shaking his head. 'I called her on Nasser Sharif's recommendation.'

The hero smiled at him. 'Balu,' he said in an avuncular tone, 'didn't you see she had promise?'

The director looked up, startled.

'Sit,' the hero said, sitting in a chair and patting the seat of the one beside his. 'Film-making has more to do with the intuition, which no university in America can teach you.' He was referring to the director's American degree in film. 'Just by looking at that girl I can tell you that she has promise. You know why? Because she's wounded. Acting is for the wounded, for those who've suffered.' He paused and leant toward the director. He pointed in the direction of the heroine's dressing room and continued, 'She, for instance, is not an actress. What she is is a pretty face, someone who can imitate a few of the basic expressions, the mudras of our classical texts: happiness, coquetry, anger, sorrow. And prance around a bit. And even that she does badly. Tell me, what else can she do?' He stopped and frowned. The director knew that the only reason Mutthu had agreed to do a film with the heroine was because she was popular enough to draw crowds, but not enough to overshadow him. Mutthu stuck his thumb in the direction of the door. 'But she—she has felt more emotions than our heroine can name.'

Then he fell deep into thought and scowled as he usually did when he was contemplating something. He had often spoken to the young director, who was the son of an old friend, about his struggle to enter the world of films. He talked about the indignities he had had to suffer as an awkward, asthmatic young man who had come to the city with a dream and little else. It was a dream he'd dreamt ever since he'd been a little boy, when his friends began calling him Hero. Over the years he had started believing in that dream. He was sure his friends were prophetic, sure that he was destined to become a film star. But one day, when he caught his friends snickering behind his back after calling him Hero, he realized it was all a cruel joke. The irony of the nickname finally dawned on him, for he was a timid, stuttering boy. 'Hero, watch out, here come the girls for you,' they'd call out when he was a little older, and they'd laugh uproariously when he darted to safety from non-existent pursuers. But the more his friends teased him the more he sought refuge in his dreams and the more he believed in his destiny.

'I was a pathetic boy when I ran away from home and came here,' he said, lighting another cigarette. 'Pathetic!' He emphasized the word with a touch of bitterness. 'And naïve.

I thought I'd walk into a studio and they'd welcome me. What did I know about acting or about the world?'

The young director listened solemnly. He was accustomed to Mutthu's periodic bouts of self-deprecation. Usually when he lapsed into such moods, people would gather around him, clicking their tongues in sympathy and obligingly refute his self-deprecating statements. 'But at that age everyone is like that,' the director said soothingly.

'No,' Mutthu insisted, brushing his words off. 'I knew nothing. I came here thinking I would live in one of those mansions they showed in movies. But where do you think I lived for many years?'

'On the footpath,' the director obliged, having heard this story before.

'Yes, on the footpath alongside beggars and drunkards. I earned some money by hanging about the film crews like a leech, and they would take pity on me and give me two annas and a cup of cold leftover coffee for appearing in a crowd. But that was nothing compared to what I went through when that girl Devaki appeared. I suffered, Balu, I suffered.' He snorted dramatically, sounding like a croaking frog. 'I contemplated suicide when she went to live with that old lecher, Nasser Sharif. He was old enough to be her father!

'So what I'm trying to say is: it is the suffering of those days that made a man out of me. It also made me an actor. A good actor! Without the suffering I'd have been like the others: a dog that only knows how to wag its tail. Give the girl a chance, I say. I can see that she has what it takes to be a star.'

Lakshmi was staying with a distant uncle, a half-forgotten nephew of her grandmother, the only relative she could think of going to for shelter after having left her baby with her grandmother. She went to his house because she remembered him as a quiet, non-interfering man who smiled at everything, the only relative who would take her in without asking any difficult questions. When she arrived at his house not only was he smiling as usual, but he was also waiting for her at the door. He didn't ask her anything; he just seemed to know.

To her astonishment, a few days after her visit to the studio, a messenger from the director knocked on the door.

'You can be a star,' he said, and smiled toothily. 'A superstar.'

She stared at him stonily.

He looked away uncomfortably. 'But you have to know how to dance. That's how it is in this industry.'

'Tell the director he can go to hell,' she replied angrily.

'But he wants you in his films,' the man responded. 'All he wants is for you to learn to dance and come back when you're ready. He has even convinced Mahadevan Iyer to take you as his student. You surely know who Mahadevan Iyer is.'

'I'm not interested in films.'

The man was flabbergasted. 'What are you saying, madam? It's a break very, very few people get. A second chance like this is unheard of. You know what all unknown actresses have to go through to get even a small part? Please think it over.'

But Lakshmi was not interested. She showed him to the door and slammed it behind him.

Her uncle, silent witness to all this, spoke up. 'Why, dear, why all this anger?'

'Should I accept all kinds of humiliation silently?'

Her uncle looked distressed. 'He's only asking you to learn to dance.'

'And what should I do with that?'

He did not respond. He did not know the answer.

She went to the veranda. She liked to spend her time there in the evenings. She watched the neighbours return from the temple, their hair adorned with jasmine flowers, their foreheads smeared with vermilion and vibhuti, their hands clasping coconuts and betel leaves, talking loudly about silk saris and jewellery. Their dark skins had patches of a yellow hue from the turmeric paste they had applied while bathing. They sounded content in their chatter. She liked these moments outside the house alone when she felt free, when the contented sounds of the evening soothed her into contemplation. She liked the moist, briny sea breeze, the first sounds of the crickets, the crackling murmurs of radio news bulletins, the hiss of petromax lamps on the carts of flower sellers heading for the temple nearby, the cycle rickshaws trilling softly, the sputter of frying onions and the whistling of the pressure cooker somewhere, muffled and distant.

But that evening her mind went completely blank, a searing void. It was only a long time afterwards, when it grew dark, that she became conscious of her surroundings and of the dull ache somewhere within her. She heard the cries of children returning home for dinner. Through the trees she could see a sliver of a moon appearing tentatively in the darkening sky. She recalled a conversation she had had with my father a couple of years ago. They had gone to the beach and were not far from the very spot where delirious crowds had felicitated her father on Independence Day. They could see the faint outline of a full moon appearing in the wake of the retreating sun. My father had stood at that spot and had turned a full circle as though he was looking for something, somebody. He had told her then that her father had named her Mahtab after the full moon night on which she was born. She had felt hurt upon hearing this. Why would she be named after the moon? It was pockmarked, full of the ugly textures of a once pimple-ravaged face. It was also fickle, unreliable.

But, now, looking at the crescent hiding behind the tree, shy, persecuted, tentative like a hunted deer, she felt differently. She realized that it wasn't fickle but vulnerable. In its delicacy and smooth milky whiteness it looked beautiful. *Mahtab,* she thought. *What a lovely name! Mahtab!* Then she became angry. She was the daughter of a moplah everybody in the world knew. Except her, that is. She had never seen him. She had never felt his touch. He had never held out his finger for her to grasp. She had never even heard him utter her name, her beautiful, brittle name.

'Whatever you decide, I'll support you,' her uncle said.

She picked up the piece of paper on which the messenger had left the well-known Bharatanatyam teacher's address. It was in a town an overnight train journey away. She looked at it for a long time. She did not know who was going to pay for her expenses. Surely the producer wouldn't, nor would her teacher. And, yet, how perfectly everything had fallen into place. Again there were forces nudging her. Unseen, but not unknown. Yet she was afraid of the answer, afraid that she might have to admit to herself that her mother who had run away and her moplah father deserved to be acknowledged, that the people she had so assiduously excised from her life still existed and had at least a peripheral influence on her. They were the other puppeteers in her life. And they were tugging at her again. She wanted to resist, but she didn't have the strength for another battle. At least not yet. Besides, how long could she burden her uncle? She would just have to learn to let go.

★

It wasn't as much an academy as it was an old sprawling house past the town's noisy market, the kind well-to-do men built for their extended families in the nineteenth century: a large dung coloured veranda, with pillars of great girth flanking the stairs leading up to it from the street; an inner courtyard where one could not only do all the washing and cleaning, but also raise a cow or two; large rooms with thick stone walls, wooden windows and high ceilings. On the double doors leading to the house were two vermilion 'Om's with a swastika above them. On the floor was a freshly made kolam, the paste made of rice powder still wet, the circular pattern emanating from a central 'Om' like ripples in a pond. If this was the academy, its reputation seemed exaggerated, for it hardly looked like the kind of place where famous dancers learnt and honed their skills.

As soon as she entered the house she felt as though she had stepped into a world of midgets. The house was as large as the people in it were small. In one of the front rooms she saw a group of small children, most of them girls with kohl-blackened eyes and hennaed hands, and a middle-aged man in only a veshti and bands of vibhuti on his torso and arms instructing them. He occasionally struck the tiny brass cymbals in his hands to reinforce the rhythm. Even he looked small in that large room; one could stack up four men his size on one another's shoulders and still not reach the ceiling.

And, she, self-consciously large (although in reality no larger than the guru himself), was beginning to wonder if it was the rattling overnight train that had skewed her vision when the teacher turned around, as did the distracted students, and glanced at her only for a moment. He then looked away, as any respectable man would from a woman who was not related to him, and remarked, 'I was expecting a little girl.'

Before Lakshmi could decide whether it was an accusation or an expression of disappointment, he went back to his students, leaving her to swallow the words that she had begun formulating in response.

The students resumed their exercises. With every passing moment it became increasingly clear to her that the guru had no intention of talking to her. She wished she could shrink down to the size of the girls. Perhaps then he would not ignore her as he now did. As she watched the students form tiny equilateral triangles with their limbs and torsos, which, as her eyes swept through the entire class, appeared like the self-replicating geometric designs in a kaleidoscope, she wished she could simply vanish instead of gaping foolishly, waiting to be acknowledged.

After half an hour, when the session came to an end, the teacher breezed past her, as if she did not exist at all. The youngest of the students, a girl no more than seven, with two pigtails looped up and tied at the base with red ribbons, gazed at her with large, curious eyes. Lakshmi tried to imagine herself at that age, and she realized that she didn't remember. She was seven not that long ago, but it already seemed like it was in a past life. In this life she was large as a giant from Brobdingnag, and invisible.

Just as the humiliation within her began to assert itself, the guru's wife appeared. She had clearly been doing housework, for her hair was tied up in a knot and the thalapu of her sari was tucked in. She smiled warmly, the first person in the household to do so, and gestured to Lakshmi. Instantly, Lakshmi forgot her anger. She followed the teacher's wife through a series of corridors to a small room.

Lakshmi sat on a bamboo mat on the floor and listened to the various sounds of her new world. She could hear Mahadevan Iyer issuing laconic instructions punctuated by the metallic ping of the cymbals. The students stomped on the stone floor in time to his words, softly when he spoke softly, loudly when he raised his voice. In between the claps of their feet and the teacher's hands, she heard the muffled sounds of traffic outside in the street: rickshaws trilling, buffaloes being driven from the river, a scooter or two sputtering by. Somewhere far away she could hear the sounds of a kitchen brimming with activity.

As she listened to these sounds dread welled up within her because she was so big, because everyone around her was so small, because she fit so badly into this new world of hers. Like Alice in a tiny world into which she had accidentally stumbled.

The teacher's wife sat down next to her. 'Don't mind him,' she said. 'Like all geniuses he has rigid ideas. As one grows older one's body becomes less flexible and it becomes harder to learn. Besides, all his students come here when they're young. They grow up under his care and guidance. We don't have any children of our own.' She paused and sighed. 'With you all he can do is teach you to dance. And even that without the liberties he can take with a child. But don't worry, he'll come around sooner or later.'

Lakshmi did not know what sooner or later meant. A few hours, a few days, a few weeks? Perhaps even his wife did not know.

Lakshmi followed her back to the kitchen and stopped at the threshold. Even for such a large house the kitchen was larger than she had expected. It was smoky. There were several people in it: extended family members and older students. An elderly lady, only a little younger than Lakshmi's grandmother, was stirring something in a large vat with a long-handled ladle. She was a widow: the thalapu of her plain ochre sari covered her shaven head and she wore no blouse. Lakshmi couldn't help staring at her as she flitted energetically from stove to stove stirring and tossing, instructing the younger women, making sure everything went smoothly. The enthusiasm with which she worked reminded Lakshmi of her own grandmother.

When the widow paused to wipe the sweat from her face with her sari she caught sight of Lakshmi and smiled at her, buck-toothed, a gap between her front two teeth. 'Welcome, dear,' she said. 'No, no, don't come in. This is only your first day. Go and rest. Why do you want to stand in this smoke and heat?'

But Lakshmi stayed at the threshold and watched. The kitchen was familiar, its air thick and overpowering with the selective memories of the days in her grandmother's kitchen, of the murukku and modakams, the snacks and sweets she made, not of the chilli powder and her enraged screams. Her grandmother, breaking with tradition, had never let her help her in the kitchen. 'Once you get married, this is where you'll spend most of your time,' she, for whom cooking for the family was an act of love, would say. And, yet, Lakshmi used to stay back, just as she did now, watching her grandmother, but learning nothing of what she did. She realized now that despite the time she had spent in her grandmother's kitchen she could not, even if she wanted to, help these women.

So when dinner was ready, she jumped up, happy to be of assistance, to carry the food to a large room where all the students had already gathered. To her relief there were older students besides the young ones. The guru, with fresh vibhuti and sandalwood paste on his body after a bath, sat on a palaka at the head of two rows of plantain leaves placed on the floor. He muttered a shloka—which the others repeated after him—and picked up the brass jug beside him, filled his cupped palm with water and poured it all around the plantain leaf that was now filled with food. Not until he'd taken the first bite did the others start eating. The students were noisy, but the teacher ate silently looking neither here nor there, as if the act of eating was a continuation of the prayer.

After the meal, Lakshmi stayed behind to help wipe the floor and serve the women who had earlier laid out the food.

The old widow smiled. 'Your very first day and you're working here as part of the household. Your parents have brought you up well.'

Lakshmi, taken aback, bent her head, pretending that she had not heard her.

As the women ate, the teacher's wife again said to her, 'It will be all right. Give him some time.'

Lakshmi nodded. She was willing to give him all the time he needed. It wasn't as if she had somewhere else to go. Besides, in those first tentative moments in that house, despite the teacher's aloofness, she'd sensed a certain warmth that existed in large families. She had felt the faint stirrings of the contradictory sense of unfamiliarity and belonging, as if she was visiting distant relatives she had never met before. True to its appearance, it was a home rather than a school. The guru was Maama, everyone's uncle. His wife, Maami, and the grandmotherly widow, Paati, were surely women she'd known before. There were a myriad other maamis and maamas, older students, relatives and assistants, prefixed by their names to distinguish them from the teacher and his wife. They were like the cousins and aunts and uncles who'd flitted in and out of her childhood. The younger students were like the children of extended families.

It was a feeling she'd never had in school, this feeling of comfort among people she'd never seen before. Even during times of contentment at school, she had not thought of Sister Cecilia as family, for she was too white, her wimple and her spectacles made her look too fish-like, too alien. Whether what she felt here was a real sense of belonging and comfort or simply an illusion created by her mind in a moment of desperation, fabricating kinship where none existed, she could not tell. But even before the day was over she wanted to plunge headlong into the cauldron of this extended family, for, however preposterous it sounded at that time, there was the very real possibility that this might, one day, become a surrogate home, if not a real one.

For several days Lakshmi went to the dance room where Maama taught his disciples in batches depending on their age and the level of their skills. These sessions were scheduled around the scholastic activities of those who went to nearby schools or to one of the three colleges in town. After lunch and a brief rest, he sat bare-chested and cross-legged on a bamboo mat in the centre of the dance room and discussed the theoretical and aesthetic bases of dance, drama and music with his older students. He spoke with scholarly ease, throwing in wide-ranging references to the Natya Shastra, the Puranas, the bhakti poetry of Purandara Dasa and Jayadeva, classical dramas like *Meghadutam*, and the different talas of classical music and how they related to the rhythms of the dance. During the course of these lectures he would spontaneously break into song to demonstrate his point, emphasizing the rhythm with his right hand, and then explain the many layers of meanings contained in the words. He sang with natural self-confidence, his baritone voice emerging from his navel, which, according to Lakshmi's grandmother, was invariably the mark of a gifted singer. His enunciation was precise and brahminically fastidious, as was everything else he did. He always looked grave and abstracted, yet alert and ready to rectify the minutest errors of his wards. Lakshmi observed that the disciples were either awed by him or regarded him with great deference. He had an undeniable presence.

During the dance and music lessons Lakshmi stood in a corner, prepared to come forward and join the others at the slightest gesture from Maama. But there was never any indication that he was even aware of her presence. 'Tei yum dat ta tei yum ta ha,' he exhorted his students, instead, in the cryptic language of dance. And the students followed the instructions, hitting the floor with the balls of their heels to the beat of the imagined rhythm, their toes up, sometimes with one leg extended to the side or the front. The more skilled among them executed corresponding hand gestures and facial expressions, which, without music and words, appeared as arcane and mysterious as a mime's code.

Eventually she gave up, her will wilting, not so much under the assault of Maama's determination to ignore her as by her own volition to retreat, out of ennui, for she was still not sure if she cared for dancing. She did not really understand it. Besides, the older women inside were far more welcoming, and she went in to help manage the household. She spent a lot of time squatting next to Paati in the kitchen, bent over stoves, learning to cook. Paati, in a strange echo of her own grandmother, periodically tried to make her leave. 'Why do you want to spend your time at the stove at such a young age?'

'That's all right, Paati,' she'd respond. 'I like being here. In any case I'm not all that young.'

One day, she made rasam all by herself. As he ate his dinner, Maama commented, addressing nobody in particular, 'This is very good.' Coming from him, the praise was significant. When Paati mentioned that it was Lakshmi who had made it that day, he didn't seem particularly surprised. It was his lack of surprise more than his praise that flattered her. And, yet, for unfathomable reasons, she remained invisible to him when it came to dance. It must be some sort of test, Lakshmi would say to herself, sensing her growing humiliation, comforting herself with the thought that Maama was an eccentric sage testing her will power before revealing the secrets of the world to her. And when he did, she was sure, the world would be hers and the director who had compared her to a monkey would find out how wrong he was. So she waited, biding her time, gaining strength from the possibility of delicious revenge.

About two months after Lakshmi's arrival Maami lost patience with her husband. She called Lakshmi out of the kitchen and took her to a small room adjoining the larger one where the students practised. She tied her hair up into a loose bun with a couple of twists, fastened the loose end of her thalapu at the waist, and performed the namaskaram. 'You don't start dancing without paying your respects,' she said. She repeated the gestures for Lakshmi's benefit, touching the floor for Mother Earth, holding her hands above her head for the gods, bringing them to her forehead for the guru and finishing by touching her heart to signify the soul. Lakshmi repeated these gestures, and immediately realized how awkward her movements were, and how much practise she would require to master even such a simple act.

But Maami didn't seem to notice. She stood straight. There was something very striking, very distinguished in that simple act of standing straight. It was as though one of the gracefully sculpted figures in the gopurams of the ancient and famous temple nearby had come alive. 'The first thing you must learn is to stand properly,' she said. 'Posture is everything. Without it, dance is merely moving your hands and legs, which everyone can do.'

Lakshmi stood erect, with her feet together, facing forward. Maami looked at her with a critical eye. 'Your arms are supple,' she commented. 'That's good. But don't let them droop like that. Keep them firm but flexible.' She sounded like Maama.

Lakshmi tensed her arms a little. 'That's better,' Maami said. 'It's the most basic position in our form of dance. It is from this balanced or samabhanga position that all other positions and gestures emerge. For instance, turn your feet sideways like this and bend your knees outwards. Another very simple posture, but this one, too, forms the basic building block of any dance sequence.'

Lakshmi remembered seeing sculptures in the ardhamandali position. She also remembered a preponderance of this posture among the beginners, often with their hands on their hips, a series of triangles, symmetric around the imaginary central vertical axis.

Lakshmi stood in that position. She was aware of how stiff her body was, and she stood frozen that way. Moments went by, but Maami did not ask her to get up. It had seemed easy enough when Maami did it, but now Lakshmi's thighs and the small of her back ached and she wobbled unsteadily on her legs. Finally she let go.

'Nothing is easy at first. But once you've mastered the basics you can dance even in your sleep. Watch . . .'

As Maami danced, she was filled with a sudden glow of energy, her eyes and her expression animated, entranced. She performed a series of patterns, and Lakshmi saw for the first time how discrete, seemingly static positions could be strung together, causing them to fuse and yield a kind of fluidity she had never seen. Lakshmi watched in astonishment. She had only seen Maami hurrying about the house taking care of everybody's needs, dressed clumsily in old saris that were sometimes dirty. But now, even though the sari was old and the blouse did not match and the kohl in her eyes had begun to run down the edges and her vermilion pottu was smudged, she looked elegant, confident, dignified, a different person. Lakshmi watched her in wonder, listening to the clap of her feet against the floor, and even in the absence of words and music she understood the story Maami was conveying through her dance.

By the time Maami had finished dancing, Lakshmi had goosebumps all over her body, for this was a moment of epiphany, the secret code of the dance suddenly shattered to reveal the beauty and grace within. She was jolted alive from the torpor into which her life had slid. What rich possibilities of expression it offered! The subtlest movements were pregnant with meaning and references; they were a reflection of one's inner self, a perfect vehicle for self-expression. Everything she'd heard Maama say to the disciples suddenly made sense, his vision of perfection, to which he goaded all his disciples, had come alive before her eyes, like the unfolding of the petals of a fast-blooming lotus.

Paati, who had come to watch, smiled and patted Maami

on her head when she stopped. 'She has always been the better dancer,' she said, turning to Lakshmi. 'He is the better critic and teacher.'

'But why don't you dance more often?' Lakshmi asked.

Maami smiled. Paati shook her head and said, 'After marriage your priorities change.'

'So you haven't danced at all since then?'

'No, I have,' Maami replied. 'Sometimes.'

'But never in public,' Paati added, making it clear that she didn't disagree with the notion that women from decent families did not dance in public.

'Never?'

'Never.'

So saying the two women walked through the courtyard towards the kitchen.

Lakshmi went to her room pensively. She forgot about her own lessons. She thought about Maami's dancing, her talent. How could she not want to dance? Was she not aware of the metamorphosis dancing brought about in her, like a butterfly breaking out of its cocoon? Did she not realize how happy and carefree she appeared to be while dancing? How could she bottle up so much talent and skill under the pretext of running a household? How did she feel watching so many of her husband's disciples—all of them from ostensibly decent families—perform their arangetrams at the end of long hard years of training, knowing that she would never be, nor could dream of being, on a stage like them? Did she not want to be one of them?

She got up and ran to the kitchen. 'But you must dance!' she cried out. 'You *must*!'

There was so much vehemence in her command that both Maami and Paati turned around and smiled in bemusement.

'I want to dance like you,' she continued. 'Please teach me. I don't care how long it takes.'

So it was Maami who taught Lakshmi the basics of dance. She demonstrated the basic adavus slowly and patiently, one adavu at a time. She ensured that the angles at which Lakshmi's body bent were perfect, that she stamped the floor with the full face of her feet, that her arms and legs moved smoothly during the transitions from one position to another. It was she who taught Lakshmi to listen to the music even when there was none, to hear the stories in the silence of the gestures.

A few days later Maama walked in on one of their sessions and Lakshmi stopped abruptly, mid-sequence, her hands in the air, her right leg stretched sideways, guiltily, as if caught doing something forbidden. For several moments he didn't say anything.

'Continue,' he said at last.

Lakshmi hesitated. Then, on Maami's cue she continued from where she had left off. Maami followed up with a more complicated series of steps, stringing a few adavus together. Lakshmi repeated after her, self-consciously, nervously. When she was done, Maama nodded. 'I've been hasty. I can see that you're a determined woman.'

'That means he'll teach you,' Maami said excitedly after he left as abruptly as he had appeared.

But a sudden anxiety gripped Lakshmi. Did that mean Maami wouldn't teach her any more? And that she wouldn't dance either? 'No, I want you to continue teaching me,' she said, insistently.

Startled, Maami asked, 'Why would you want me to teach you when you can learn from the master?'

But Lakshmi nodded slowly, insistently. Maami then smiled, flattered, but looking doubtful. 'With all the work to do around the house, I don't know . . .'

'You can make time for dance.'

'Don't be silly. He's a much better teacher.'

'I want only you to teach me, and I want to perform my arangetram with you.'

The significance and the irony of her offer were not lost on Maami. 'But arangetrams are solo performances,' she said weakly.

'That will be my gurudakshina. I want to share my stage with you. I want you also to dance. If you don't, I'm going to hang up my ankle bells, too.'

Maami turned around and smiled, not without some excitement.

Not long after she started to learn to dance, Lakshmi's grandmother died. Upon hearing the news she got up and bathed, as was expected of her. She never understood why one was supposed to take a bath when someone died. It was no ordinary bath. It even had a Sanskrit name: snanam, with oils and shikakai, signifying purification. Perhaps it was a substitute for bathing in the Ganges. Her wet and oily hair glistening, the earthy smell of shikakai in her nostrils, she spent the rest of the day in the kitchen with Paati, cooking for the household with the kind of energy she had rarely felt. She made dishes she had never made before, but she knew exactly how to make them, for the recipes appeared before her eyes with the clarity of her grandmother's dreams in the kitchen. She shred coconut meat, pounded the chillies and spices into paste, chopped an assortment of vegetables, and watched them simmer and meld into one another. When she was done she was surprised to find herself surrounded by food in vessels of all kinds and sizes, like a wedding feast, surprised that she had prepared all of that almost single-handedly. As she watched everyone devour the food she looked on with satisfaction, and for the first time she understood why her grandmother had always equated food with love. But in that moment of sudden realization she got up, looked away from the two rows of disciples eating happily, and wished her grandmother had not sometimes confused the two and substituted the former for the latter.

For the next few days she constantly thought about her daughter for the first time since she had given her up. The baby daughter who had never cried, who had had the wisdom to resign herself to her fate, which was murky, nebulous, like the mountain fog in which she was born. What she knew of the baby then and what she remembered now was the creamy smell of the baby's skin, musk emanating from the crinkles of her navel, her milky breath. It was headier as a memory. It was an animalistic way of remembering her, the way, perhaps, Charlie had recognized her.

For days the smell overpowered Lakshmi, driving her crazy with its power and intangibility, a mother wolf reminded of her lost cub. For days it curled around her nostrils, inducing her to sniff periodically, driving her to obsession. It became a searing pain soon, a canker that consumed her days and kept her awake at night. She must have appeared a somnambulist during the day, for Paati patted her gently one day and said, 'What's the use of thinking constantly about the dead, dear?' And Lakshmi started with fear for a moment till she realized that Paati was referring to her grandmother and not her daughter. But Lakshmi did not correct her. How could she? What words could she use to describe why her mourning her grandmother had segued into yearning for her daughter? How could she tell Paati that she could not possibly raise her daughter, that perhaps she was unworthy of being a mother, that perhaps she would not see her daughter again the way her mother did not see her? That, one day, her daughter would want nothing of her, the way she wanted nothing of her mother?

But there was wisdom in what Paati said. What's the use of hanging on to the memory of something that one cannot have? It was then that she decided to bring out the scalpel and hack away those parts of her memory that troubled her: the olfactory centres of her mind. Slowly, painfully, layer by cellular layer she made incisions. With every layer that she was able to cut through, the pain reduced—or, perhaps, she grew increasingly numb—until the excision created a hole in her memory that was completely excavated, leaving behind only a dull, accommodating, comforting pain that she could live with.

The surgery was so successful that she could not smell her baby any more, no matter how much she sniffed. She could not smell any other baby either. When past students brought their babies on visits, she watched them from a distance, unmoved, while everybody else in the household fussed, remarking how beautiful they were even when they were not, even when the black mark on their cheeks to ward off the evil eye—a blot to deliberately introduce imperfection—appeared unnecessary. These babies held her attention, but she could not bring herself to hold and cuddle them, for she could not smell them. She envied everyone for being able to simply celebrate these babies for what they were. She especially envied Paati. Paati, who had never been a mother, glowed with joy, unencumbered by her own misfortune, every time a baby came by. She was so comfortable with them that one would have thought she had raised a dozen children of her own. 'Hold the baby,' she would say, handing over a baby to Lakshmi. And when Lakshmi hesitated, sniffing in vain, she would smile toothlessly. 'Go on, there's nothing to it. Holding babies comes naturally to women.'

'You wouldn't know, Paati,' Lakshmi would want to say. 'You've never had a baby of your own that you've given up.'

★

For ten years Lakshmi learnt to dance under Maami's tutelage, melding indistinguishably with the other women who helped run the household, becoming a 'maami' herself in the process.

She was a quick learner and mastered the techniques in a short time. The fact that almost everything in the house had some connection to dance and music helped her. They influenced life to such an extent that sometimes the women sang ashtapadis—the love songs of Jayadeva—even while cooking, or hummed refrains from a raga that came to mind.

Sometimes when she practised with Maami in the smaller room, Maama and a few other students would come and watch. Maama would not say a word unless Maami prodded him gently, and then he would point out to Lakshmi with astonishing accuracy even the tiniest misstep or the subtlest misinterpretation of the bhava—the essence—of the piece.

As she learnt the intricacies of dance she found herself experiencing new emotions and re-experiencing those she had forgotten while lying numb in the cloister with her baby. It was not just the nine rasas of the classical texts that she experienced now, but also the numerous subtle emotions in between. She found herself becoming fuller as a person, wiser from having understood their meaning and their rationale.

And every year, amid a flurry of activity during the second half of the year when some of Maama's disciples prepared for their arangetrams, Lakshmi grew more confident. She shared their excitement and their nervousness. She'd known right from the beginning that, unlike several of the students who came there and dropped out after a while because they could not deal with the rigours or because they lost interest, she would go all the way. So her promise to share the stage with Maami at a time when she did not know if she even had talent for dance or if her body was supple enough to conquer its demands, came from innate self-belief—or rather the complete absence of doubt—and not from arrogance. And every time another of her fellow students prepared to venture out, this self-belief became stronger. Watching them ascend the stage and face hundreds of people that included critics and connoisseurs she'd feel overcome by a certain confidence, for that stage would be hers too one day. It was only a matter of time before her turn would come, when Maami would pronounce that she was ready.

She heard those words quite unexpectedly in her ninth year at the academy. But it was Maama who uttered them, not Maami. One evening, several members of the household gathered in the dance room to relax as they often did after a day of hard work. One of the girls picked up the veena and idly played a few notes of raga Hamsadhwani. This caught everyone's attention. The violinist picked up his violin and continued from where the girl had left off. As if on cue the mridangam player whipped off the cover of the mridangam and accompanied the violinist. Then Maama started to sing and Maami emerged from the kitchen where she had been helping prepare dinner. Raga Hamsadhwani was a favourite of Lakshmi's, which Maami knew. She augmented Maama's singing with a jathi. She then looked at Lakshmi, pointing her chin towards the open centre of the room. Lakshmi stood up, tucking the thalapu of her saree into her waist. Then Maama, the violinist and the veena player stopped to allow Maami to utter the dance syllables unencumbered by the raga. Lakshmi attempted a string of particularly difficult adavus. Maami smiled and challenged her by increasing the tempo of the jathi. After several minutes of steadily increasing tempo, when, at the climax, the syllables Maami uttered, the beat of the mridangam and the stamping of Lakshmi's feet on the floor merged like three streams into a single reverberation, they stopped. In that moment of silence, the unison of rhythm, voice and movement became starkly clear. And immediately afterwards the music resumed from where it had left off, as if there had been no interlude. Lakshmi, too, resumed dancing, and then held out her hand and invited Maami to join. Maami did, and they danced, Maami as Krishna and Lakshmi as Andal, the adoring devotee.

At the end of the impromptu concert, as Lakshmi wiped her brow, Maama spoke, 'You should start preparing,' he said.

Lakshmi looked at Maami in astonishment.

'We!' Lakshmi squealed, holding Maami's hands.

Maami looked surprised at being reminded of Lakshmi's promise. 'How can an arangetram have two dancers?' she protested, resurrecting her old argument.

But Lakshmi would not listen to her objection, because she knew that despite her weak attempts at refusal, Maami really wanted to dance in front of an audience. Lakshmi could see it in her sparkling eyes.

Lakshmi went to bed that night with fevered thoughts racing through her mind. In a few months she would be on stage herself for all the world to see. In a few months she would have metamorphosed into a dancer. Newspapers would review her performance, perhaps even carry a photograph of her; critics would praise her; the audience would adore her. She, who pranced like a monkey on a roof, would wear glittering silks and jewels and give the most intricate and complex of recitals.

But as she drifted into sleep she was confounded by mixed emotions because the excitement of her arangetram was balanced by the imminence of her departure from the cocoon in which she lived, isolated from the real world and immune to its realities. Larva-like, she had retreated from the world after having faced and fought it. Now the thought of emerging from the cocoon into the harsh light outside left her riddled with anxiety. She felt like an animal being released into the wild for the first time after having been lulled into unlearning its naturally predatory abilities.

In the morning she said to Maami what she never imagined she would say, 'I don't think I'm ready this year.'

'Don't be silly. Even *he* thinks you're ready. You're just nervous.'

'You don't understand. I don't want to leave.'

'Who's asking you to leave? You can stay with us till you get married.'

But that was the problem. Who would marry her? She couldn't possibly stay there forever.

'I don't understand you,' Maami continued. 'After all these years of hard work, how can you refuse this?'

What could Lakshmi say? Maami wouldn't understand, anyway. She smiled and nodded, but braced herself to tackle the oncoming dread that would surely engulf her.

In the early days Maami had described dance as a prayer, but Lakshmi had not understood her. Now, sitting by the tulsi plant in the courtyard, after an oil bath, as she placed a new wick in the earthen lamp, carefully smearing it with oil and twisting it, she could see how the ten years had been a penance, a disciplining of the mind and body, and their union with the soul. At first she had lit the lamp by the tulsi plant and by the Nataraja statue in the dance room merely to please Maami and Paati. But the ritual of lighting them every morning after bathing slowly became a sacred act, the point of focus for her meditation, the sadhana she'd begun undertaking of late. She wasn't expected to believe in its significance, nor did she. The mere act was becalming and cleansing. And that was enough.

It was with the same sense of sanctity that she placed the new clothes and jewellery for the arangetram in the prayer room and lit lamps as Maami placed vermilion marks on them. She had spent the entire day with Maami, Paati and a few of her fellow disciples, scouring the town for them, looking for a sari that was exactly the shade of mauve she wanted, for the red stones in the jewels that would match the sari, for the precise width of brocade in the fan of her costume, and for a melaku—the upper portion of the costume—that would contrast perfectly with the colour of the pyjama. She did not ask Maami where the money came from, but just as she quietly accepted a small bundle of notes every month after the postman had delivered the money order, she accepted the much thicker bundle that day without fuss. She placed all the pieces of jewellery in front of the gods, all of them in their individual red and purple boxes: the chandrasuriyan and the rakudi to adorn her head and forehead; the jimiki, thodu and mattal for the ears; the mukkutthi and bulaku for the nose; the heavy gold odiyanam, the waistband; the chavari and kunjalam for her hair; and finally the salangai, the ankle bells.

For four months she meditated and practised every day. She took music lessons every day even though her sense of music wasn't too good. But she sang with a tambura for an hour every day as part of her sadhana. She spent a lot of time trying to gain control over her senses, for her hands, feet, eyes, ears and her own inaudible singing while dancing had to be in perfect harmony.

On the day of the arangetram Lakshmi placed her ankle bells and cymbals before the statue of Nataraja. She formally invited Maami into the prayer room and offered her a silver tray containing a silk sari, a garland of marigolds, betel leaves and fruit. Then she knelt and touched Maami's feet. When she got up there were tears in Maami's eyes.

'I should be the one shedding tears, Maami,' Lakshmi said.

Maami wiped her eyes. 'I didn't think I would ever teach someone to dance.'

Maami picked up her ankle bells and gave them to Lakshmi,

who then touched them devoutly to her eyes before wearing them. She shivered with excitement at their tinkling. This was the moment of her maturity as a dancer, of her independent existence, the culmination of years of slow, often imperceptible progress.

Maami struck the cymbals together and Lakshmi rehearsed the pushpanjali with which she would open the recital.

When she turned around she noticed Maama at the threshold. She hesitated for a few moments. He was grave as usual, but his manner was approving, even proud. She went to him and touched his feet.

'For what?' he asked. 'For being foolish enough to try and kill your aspirations?'

'You're my guru, too.'

He turned away. Lakshmi could sense shame in his voice. At that moment the enigma of his refusal to teach her became irrelevant; the questions she'd asked herself all these years about his behaviour were no longer important. She felt sorry for him. Despite his aloofness she'd learnt a lot from him. Despite his initial rejection he'd been generous with his knowledge and exacting in his criticism. 'God bless you, ma,' he said as he walked away. 'You have a bright future ahead of you.'

The large auditorium was full. A lot of people, including influential critics and cultural figures, usually showed up at the arangetrams of Maama's disciples, especially those that took place in the city during the annual festival of music and dance. But that day it appeared as though all of the city's cultural elite had come to see the performance. When Maama introduced Lakshmi and Maami he was particularly grave. 'One of them I failed to discourage despite my best efforts,' he told the audience. 'The other I never encouraged even though she deserved all my support. It's a happy day for me because they've both succeeded despite me. It's a happy day for me because one of the dancers is my wife, and the other is her disciple, one of the best students I've ever seen.' When he walked away from the microphone Maama looked burdened with guilt and sadness because this day almost didn't happen.

Lakshmi peeked at the crowd from behind a red velvet curtain on the stage. She had imagined this moment numerous times in bed just before falling asleep. She thought she knew exactly how she would feel, how she would walk onto the stage, how the musicians would sound to her, how she would take the first steps that would form the prelude to her recital. But what she now felt was something she had never imagined before. The enormous significance of the moment dawned on her. But with it came fear. She looked across the stage at the musicians sitting cross-legged on a carpet at the other end: the singer, the flautist, the violinist, the mridangam player, and Maama as the nattuvanar with his cymbals. It occurred to Lakshmi that the stage wasn't wide enough. She had choreographed her movements for a large stage. But this stage appeared so small that she was afraid she would fall off. She looked back at Maami in panic. But Maami smiled self-assuredly. 'Go on,' she urged her. 'They're waiting.'

Lakshmi pictured the image of a monkey on a roof. It still hurt to think that she was that monkey. She steeled herself with a deep breath and walked into the spotlight before any other thoughts crossed her mind. Fortunately, with all the bright lights on her she could barely see the audience. That eased her mind considerably; she could now dance for herself.

Up until the varnams Lakshmi was barely conscious of her surroundings and danced as if in a daze. She only heard the music, her feet and her heart beating wildly. It was only when she ended a varnam with a particularly complicated series of movements that she became aware of the audience when she heard the applause. It seemed far away, shrouded in fog. She looked, but could see nothing; she put her hand out, but there was nothing to grasp. She came back to the green room and sat still, for her ears were buzzing with a cacophony of sounds, until Maami gently prodded her to get up and change into a sari for the second half of the recital.

With Maami on the stage with her for the three padams

and the tillana that formed the second half, Lakshmi felt better. The padams would require her to be fully awake and aware of her surroundings, for she would be by turns Swadheenapathika, the proud one, Khanditha, the spurned one, and Radha as an abhisarika, the infidel. Lakshmi was conscious of the feelings she was attempting to express, and all those years of imbibing the many-layered essence of the lyrics, of being able to interpret them in many different ways helped her. This was what abhinaya was all about: forgetting one's self and one's worldly fears and entering another consciousness, of donning the nayika's garb and wresting her very soul.

When the recital ended, the audience erupted with applause. Maami smiled proudly. Lakshmi could tell that she was relieved. Instinctively she fell at her feet and touched the ground with her forehead. The audience cheered even more at the spontaneous gesture. Maami picked her up by her shoulders, smiling in embarrassment. For a moment Lakshmi thought Maami would embrace her, but since they were still on stage they stood still. The two women who'd only moments earlier expressed the deepest emotions vividly through dance now stood staring at each other, uneasy at their inability to express themselves in words, like tongue-tied orators.

When they got off the stage, they were blinded by a couple of cameramen and their large circular flashes. Mothers pushed their daughters—and some sons—forward, hissing, 'Do namaskaram!' Someone garlanded all three of them. A well-known dancer of yesteryear was there, too. She lifted Lakshmi's chin with her forefinger in a maternal manner and said, 'You looked like a rati on stage.'

Lakshmi had thirsted for such attention for a long time, and it was every bit as enjoyable as she had imagined it. Through the haze of giddiness she noticed that the crowd gravitated towards Maami, praising her lavishly. 'You danced like a sixteen-year-old!' the well-known dancer exclaimed. 'You inspire me to don my ankle bells again.' But Lakshmi didn't pay much attention to it then, or the next morning when she snatched the newspapers from the mridangam player and furiously flipped through them to read their reviews.

'. . . like urvashis they adorned the stage,' Lakshmi read.

'Look at what this says about you,' Maami read from her newspaper. '"Lakshmi definitely appears to be the most talented dancer to emerge in a long time. Her sense of time and space is impeccable, as is her understanding of the emotions expressed in the music. Her performance was an embodiment of geometric precision. Her abhinaya can serve as a manual of the nava rasas."'

Lakshmi giggled. She turned to the most widely circulated English-language newspaper. It carried a half-page article with a large photograph. 'A photo!' she exclaimed. But she stopped short when she saw past the make-up and the jewels that often made dancers look alike; she had almost failed to notice that it was Maami who was in the photograph, not her. The photograph was particularly flattering, with Maami in profile at her expressive best. She remembered the man photographing both of them, yet the one they published was Maami's. She skimmed through the review. It was also extremely positive. But it devoted a lot more space to Maami's performance than to hers. Lakshmi went back to the other reviews. As she reread them, she realized that every one of them had heaped more praise on Maami. The theme was common: a middle-aged woman who matched the abilities of a much younger woman. One article even went into the realm of hyperbole when it talked about how Maami had battled against all odds to fulfil a lifetime's dream at an age when normally she would have been preparing for her daughter's arangetram. Then there was the other angle to the story: of the teacher and disciple coming out at the same time. The reviewers found this interesting, even ironic.

Lakshmi went back and forth between the articles, reading and rereading, hoping against hope that her eyes were deceiving her. But in every one of them Maami had overshadowed her. Maami, her age, her abilities, her being the best-known teacher's wife. And Lakshmi was just a side-note, an accompanying interest story, the praise for her beginning to take on the texture of wise old connoisseurs patronizing a newcomer.

Suddenly all the attention and praise she'd received the previous evening began to ring false. Maami was still giggling over the rave reviews. Gloating over her, it seemed. How could she do this to her, especially after it was she who had forced Maami to dance? How could Maami have hogged all the attention when she, Lakshmi, had selflessly shared her stage? Lakshmi felt used, betrayed. She became aware of a small burning sensation in the pit of her stomach—the beginnings of humiliation. She flung the newspaper away and got up. She felt like crying. But she shut her eyes and stopped her tears. 'It was supposed to be *my* arangetram!' she shouted when she reopened her eyes, pointing an accusing finger at Maami. She stomped out of the room while everyone watched, aghast. 'You stole my arangetram from me!'

As she fled the room a familiar irrational rage overpowered her and she willed the destruction of the delicate chalaza that bound her to Maami and the rest of her household. A sense of morbid satisfaction coursed through her as she mentally destroyed everything in sight. But there was also that familiar sense of loss, of helplessness—of wanting to be helpless, of wanting to be the victim lest she turn out to be the perpetrator— as she barrelled out of the house, for she knew then that she would never see Maami again. But like all destructions in her life this had to be surgical too, complete in every way, for she knew that remnants of a relationship were always problematic and caused far too much misery.

Mutthu

I was at the arangetram, as were Devaki, Nasser Sharif and Ragini, Lakshmi's daughter. Nasser Sharif carried a walking stick even though he wasn't weak enough to need it. Ragini, in two pigtails, so quiet that it was easy to overlook her, constantly held on to Devaki's arm as though she were afraid of losing her. The four of us sat in the back so that Lakshmi would not see us. Devaki and Nasser Sharif sat silently throughout the recital, beaming proudly, and at the end when the audience gave a rousing applause Devaki leant towards me and said, her voice choking with emotion, 'My baby!' Ragini patiently looked on as her grandmother wiped her eyes and walked out of the auditorium sobbing.

I was—and still am—a journalist with an English-language newspaper in the city. Although I wasn't there as a representative of my newspaper, my natural inquisitiveness propelled me close to the crowd that had gathered around the dancers and Mahadevan Iyer. Lakshmi was not only as beautiful as ever, but looked particularly divine that evening, bejewelled and made up, smiling and acknowledging the felicitations she received. The Vedas describe the dawn, Usha, in the most beautiful of terms, personifying her as a woman; that woman must surely have been Lakshmi. Caught up in the moment, I recklessly waved and called out to her. She turned to look in my direction. I was also sure she saw me, for there was a spark of recognition in her eyes. But just as suddenly her eyes turned hard and narrow, as if she were looking at something far away. I turned around to see if she was staring at someone else, but there was nobody behind me. I staggered away, ashamed and wounded, seeking refuge behind the crowd, understanding for the first time why Devaki always stood in the shadows, why it was easier for her to suppress a mother's love than to be seen by Lakshmi.

In the crowd around Lakshmi that evening was Mutthu, threading his way towards her. When they noticed him, people stepped aside and gawked at him. 'I will not attempt to praise you,' he addressed Lakshmi in his characteristically self-mocking manner, 'because others would have said everything there is to say. But I'll tell you this much: I finally understand why dance is considered divine.' A man accompanying Mutthu handed him a bouquet at that point, which Mutthu, in turn, presented to Lakshmi. 'A small token of appreciation for a great dancer.'

Lakshmi accepted the bouquet and thanked him. She dimly remembered having seen his face on numerous movie posters: smooth, cherubic, heavily made-up, with disconcertingly red lips. In real life he looked very ordinary, very unremarkable. He was darker, gaunt, his skin beginning to sag, his lips blackened by cigarettes. Only his hair was as black as it was in the posters, a little too black, and artificially so. She'd never seen any of his movies—she hadn't seen a movie in a very long time—but somehow he had a much smaller presence in person than she imagined he had on screen.

He whipped out a card. 'Call me when you're ready to act. I'll get you the finest roles.'

How presumptuous of him, she thought, to assume she'd want to act in movies.

'But I must go now,' he continued, unconcerned that she had not responded. 'My fans are waiting for me.' He gave a small smile, as though having fans was an occupational hazard and not a privilege. He turned around and walked away with sprightly steps, tossing his head nonchalantly like a hero.

Lakshmi did not remember the encounter for several days until another bouquet, also wrapped in a shiny plastic cover, arrived at her uncle's house. And then she remembered his walk, the walk of an adolescent imitating his favourite film star. The walk of a man imitating himself. Everything about him—including his pomposity—had that veneer of being an imitation, and it made him look ridiculous. All he needed was a floppy three-cornered hat and he'd look like a harlequin or one of the many Shakespearean clowns. She laughed at the thought.

The next day another bouquet arrived for her. This time there was a short note attached to it: *To the most beautiful dancer on earth.*

For a week she received a bouquet every morning with flattering notes enclosed. Surprisingly, they succeeded. Usually they were corny, vapid: *The stage you graced is a shrine in my heart.* But, once, surprisingly, the note quoted from classical literature: *Your sinuous walk so shamed the swan that he hid among the lotuses of the pond,* prompting her to wonder if someone else wrote the notes for Mutthu. Instead of discarding the notes contemptuously, as she would have normally done, she read and reread them, alternately feeling amused and thrilled.

On the seventh day, the man who delivered the bouquet also delivered the note separately and waited for her to read it. Mutthu was going to celebrate the release of his hundredth film, if one counted the films in which he had played bit roles. Not only did he invite her to the celebrations, but he also wanted her to dance. And she could name her price.

Lakshmi's first instinct was to refuse. What would she want to do with people in the film industry? Dancing to an audience of philistines wasn't a good start to her career. Don't the shastras say that the ideal audience is one with no preconceptions, so that it can recognize the union of dance, music and drama with the divine? But she hesitated. It would be madness to refuse her very first commission. Accepting his invitation would mean wider exposure and, more importantly, it could even present an opportunity for delicious revenge.

'I'll give my answer later,' she told the delivery man and sent him away.

After that she received two bouquets every day—one in the morning and one in the evening. Very soon there was an embarrassing profusion of flowers and noisy, gaudy plastic wrappers around her. The flowers began assaulting her already damaged sense of smell till she could stand it no more and accepted his invitation.

He sent a car to pick her up. A '60s Morris Minor with tan leather seats, walnut wood-grain panels driven by a liveried chauffeur. Mutthu himself arrived in a new Mercedes. She was impressed.

The celebrations were an ostentatious day-long affair, kicked off by the release of the film in the morning at an auspicious hour amidst prayer and chanting, a team of priests ready at hand to bless Mutthu and his new film. All afternoon along the roads leading to the studio, festooned with streamers and banners and loudspeakers on poles, members of his fan club held celebrations of their own, playing music from his films, holding competitions to impersonate him, beating drums and in general milling about in anticipation.

Mutthu made an unscheduled stop at one intersection where a group of young men was dancing to one of his film songs on a gaudily decorated dais. Without being prompted, Mutthu joined them. As the dancers became aware of his presence they stopped one by one, awed, till, finally, he was the only dancer left on the dais. The cheering crowd egged him on and he danced energetically like a man in his twenties, and without inhibitions. When the song ended, a large crowd gathered around him. He fell headlong into the crowd and allowed it to mob him. While his assistant held a large box of sweets he pressed a laddoo into every hand, regardless of how dirty or gnarled it was. His fans fought with each other to shake his hand and to fall at his feet.

Lakshmi witnessed the scene from a distance. It was oddly touching. The crowd reacted spontaneously and with admiration, clamouring, and like children his fans could not be bothered with niceties. Their acts of deference were simple: they untied their turbans, shook off their slippers as if outside a temple, and unfurled their casually tied lungis. Some prostrated with alacrity.

Mutthu, too, had suddenly changed. Lakshmi was struck by the total lack of self-consciousness, by the genuine pleasure with which he interacted with these men, not bothered by the odour of their bodies, their dirty clothes, their prickly, unshaven faces, their insistence on invading his personal space, the few ravenous hands that appeared repeatedly for more laddoos.

He walked towards the studio, continuing to distribute box after box of sweets. More and more people came running, some just to see him, others to talk to him, still others for the sweets. An old rickshaw puller who was passing by stopped his rickshaw by the side of the road despite his passenger's protests, and ran bent-kneed towards Mutthu, wobbling from side to side. Lakshmi couldn't help laughing. He could be a good Bharatanatyam dancer, she thought, what with his already bent knees.

Upon noticing the rickshaw puller, Mutthu stopped. The man bent down to touch his feet, but couldn't go far enough. The veins on his calf were ready to pop open, his fingers so crooked that they appeared knotted.

'Why are you walking like this?' Mutthu shouted over the noise, giving the man a laddoo.

'What to do, aiyah?' the man shouted back and grinned. 'My joints have given way. Years of pulling that rickshaw.'

'You look terrible. Don't you feel any pain?' Mutthu frowned with concern.

'Of course I do, aiyah. But what can I do?'

'Come to the studio tomorrow to see me,' Mutthu called out to him before the crowd pushed him farther down the road. And then to his assistant, he said, 'Give him money to fit his rickshaw with a motor.'

In the late afternoon, after the crowds had dispersed film personalities, musicians and other people gathered for the main celebrations. Lakshmi's recital kicked off the evening's programme after the long-winded speeches and felicitations. Mutthu himself went to the microphone to introduce her to the audience. She kept her recital short, and at the end of it the audience was on its feet. Mutthu, with his wife beside him, sat imperiously in the front row, one leg resting on the other, still wearing the heavy garlands he had been felicitated with, smiling with satisfaction.

Later, at the dinner table, Mutthu was back to being a hero. The glint of a star looking arrogantly into the camera was back in his eyes. He introduced Lakshmi to everybody who mattered. But he did not bother to introduce her to his wife, who sat beside him at the dinner table glowering at her suspiciously, her face darkening every time Mutthu so much as looked at Lakshmi. It was a while before Lakshmi noticed her, she was small and looked much older than Mutthu, with unhealthy grey streaks in her hair. She was dressed in a loud toffee-pink silk sari, her hair thick with flowers that sat clumsily on her head. She seemed harassed and ill at ease. Nobody seemed to pay any attention to her, and next to Mutthu she hardly had a presence. Lakshmi thought there was something cruel in the way Mutthu ignored her, even more so when just that afternoon he had delighted in the company of strangers on the street. She noticed how his wife seemed to recede farther into the background in reaction to his ignoring her. Lakshmi felt indignant on her behalf. She tried to engage her in conversation, but the woman remained uncommunicative, recoiling farther back into her chair, scowling suspiciously at everyone.

It was not until several days later that Lakshmi saw Mutthu again. After the celebrations, he had taken to sending her flowers every day and inviting her to the shooting of his latest film. She did go eventually, partly out of boredom, but also because she was curious. There was obviously more to Mutthu than met the eye.

After shooting was over he took her to a restaurant nearby where they sat in a secluded cabin under dim lights and sipped soft drinks: she a Fanta, he a Thums Up. The waiters greeted him with great deference, especially the one who took their order, a boy not much older than seventeen.

'Are you happy with your new job?' Mutthu asked him.

'Aiyah, what's there to complain? This is so much better than what I did before.'

When the waiter had gone with their order Lakshmi turned to Mutthu. 'You don't behave like a film star with these people.'

He looked surprised. A what-kind-of-a-question-is-that look clouded his face. 'How do I behave?'

'Like one of them.'

'Why shouldn't I? I was one of them at some point. I wasn't born in a palace. Besides, I know him.'

'How?'

'He grew up in an orphanage I visit sometimes. That's where I met him when he was a boy.'

She blinked in confusion and embarrassment. 'It was very kind of you to buy a motor for that rickshaw puller,' she said, instead.

He waved her praise away. 'It cost me nothing. But it means everything to that man.'

He sounded sincere, nonchalant, as though there was nothing special about his gesture. There was no artificial humility in his voice. Lakshmi realized it was a mistake to have pictured him in a clown's hat, in tight leggings, prancing about, foolishly mistaking himself for a wise man. He was no buffoon.

So a few days later she allowed him to bring her back to the same restaurant. This time she asked him about his wife. He shrugged in response, as though he'd rather talk about something else. After several moments of silence, he leant forward, lowering his voice, readying for a confession. 'We were married before I became famous,' he said and paused as if that were explanation enough. 'Then the world opened up to me and I stepped out of our anonymous existence into the spotlight. But she has always lived behind closed doors. She has refused to open up and to adapt to our changing circumstances. She's still the woman of our past. She doesn't know how to talk to people, she has no interest in the arts and knows very little about what's happening around her. All she can do is wear the most expensive saris and jewels. She just doesn't know how to be a famous man's wife!'

Lakshmi wasn't sure if he expected her sympathy, and she offered none.

'Look at women nowadays,' he continued. 'Consider all their accomplishments. Look at yourself: you're beautiful, educated and talented. High-class.' He sighed and blew his nose into his large checked handkerchief. 'You should not waste your talent. You'll make a great heroine with all your refinement and beauty.'

She felt flattered. Once he was past his self-conciousness, his on-screen persona, and dropped the artifice of a hero, he appeared sincere and willing to reveal his vulnerabilities. Unlike the previous occasions when he had complimented her, he wasn't putting on an act now. The artificial brightness in his eyes, the exaggerated sprightliness in his gestures was gone, revealing an ordinary, even plain man with a bead or two of sweat gleaming on his forehead. She was willing to believe him, not only his compliments, but also what he said about his wife. Perhaps she did hold him back.

Then he suddenly placed his hand over hers. She yanked her hand away and lowered her eyes in confusion. 'My world will grow dark without you,' he said, undeterred.

She almost burst out laughing. But then she realized it was he, not the hero—his alter ego with whom he often confusingly changed roles—who had spoken. She looked at her fingers in embarrassment. 'I think we should go,' she said in a small voice, getting up.

Mutthu looked pained as he escorted her out. 'Forgive me if I've offended you,' he said when they went to his car. The driver looked back and smiled meaningfully. Lakshmi was even more embarrassed. Thankfully Mutthu did not attempt any further conversation.

'Don't you know he has a reputation?' one of Maama's past students asked her.

'What reputation?'

'Don't you read the gossip columns? He's considered a

ladies' man. Every few months he's linked to a different woman, usually an actress. See for yourself.' She pulled out a few film magazines and pointed out the innuendoes, gossip and suggestive photographs. 'His affair with this actress has been going on for months now. Don't get involved with these film people. They'll only drag you into the dung heap with them.'

But Lakshmi had seen no dung heap around him. She saw no other women. The actresses did giggle and flirt with him in the studios. But once they left the sets they went their own ways. Perhaps his reputation was all made up to keep him in the news.

Still, for several weeks after that Lakshmi did not respond to his repeated requests to meet him. He began sending her flowers again. They irritated her. *Please stop this*, she scribbled curtly on the wrapping of a bouquet and returned it unopened one day.

She did not hear from him after that for several days. But on her birthday, he showed up at her doorstep with a box containing a pearl necklace. As she stood at the threshold wondering what to say or do, a crowd began gathering.

'Let me in,' he whispered, 'before the whole world comes here.'

'It's not my house,' she said. 'I can't let you in.'

'Then come with me tomorrow. The film unit is going to the hills for a few days of shooting. There'll be nobody there. I'll send the car in the morning. Please be ready.' There was urgency in his voice, a plea.

Even after he was gone, his car honking madly, the crowd hung around and gawked at her. She shut the door and looked at the necklace. They were real pearls. Natural, each with a different blemish. She wore the necklace and stared into the mirror. It was beautiful. What people said about him must be true. If he could woo her, then the stories about all the other women must be true too. She took off the necklace and put it back in its box, resolving to return it through the driver when he came to pick her up the next day. What would she want with a man old enough to be her father? A married man. A man with a reputation.

She stopped herself there. How easy it was to cast aspersions on someone else's reputation, even when one's own wasn't particularly clean. She did not sleep that night. She sat on the floor, picking apart the threads from a rag. When she was done there were threads all around her legs. She swept the floor with her hand and picked them all up in a fluffy ball. She was struck by how soft they were as a mass of individual threads even though the cloth woven out of them had been quite coarse. To her surprise she caught herself searching for the threads, trying to break him down into individual characteristics that she could latch on to.

The next morning when the car arrived she was waiting for it. They picked up Mutthu from the studio. He sat beside her with a broad smile and took her hand. She pulled away instinctively. 'You're like a delicate flower that hasn't blossomed fully yet,' he said. The driver looked in the rear-view mirror and grinned lasciviously. Lakshmi began to dislike him. He must have seen numerous women in the back seat with Mutthu and heard some of the soupiest lines the latter remembered from his films. This must all be a big game to him. She began to resent Mutthu for making her simply one in a long list of his women. Was she too a mere plaything? Someone even his driver could leer at? She looked out of the window wondering if she should order the driver to stop and turn back. In the event, the passing scenery started blurring, and the debate in her mind became incoherent as sleep overtook her.

The hills were familiar. She remembered the light and its startling clarity. It hadn't changed in all these years. The smell of eucalyptus was everywhere, wafting down from the higher slopes.

The evening they arrived they went to the large garden where the shooting was to begin the next day. Mutthu was deliberately dressed dowdily in very old clothes, ordinary slippers, sunglasses even though it wasn't sunny in order to achieve a measure of privacy. They went boating in the natural lake bordered by weeping willows and oaks transplanted from Europe over a century ago. They walked through the rose garden and sat on an embankment that had a large clock whose dial was a flower bed. He and the heroine would dance around this clock and romp through the rose garden for a song sequence. The heroine would run, for no reason at all, into the fountain in the middle of the rose garden and get wet. Lakshmi turned to Mutthu and asked, 'Don't you find it all mindless?'

Mutthu blinked in bewilderment. He didn't seem to understand what could be mindless about a film. 'Everybody loves it,' Mutthu responded. 'This is what romance is all about.'

She laughed. She, who had experienced inexplicable passion, could not understand the romance in running through fountains with fatuous smiles or holding hands with swooning expressions. 'You really think so?'

Mutthu looked surprised. 'Why, don't you?'

She shrugged nonchalantly to blunt the criticism implicit in her laughter.

'It's all in the style. Everybody wants to see us do things in movies they usually don't have an opportunity to do. They want to experience emotions through us. They want to live their fantasies through us. And sometimes, they try to capture some of that fantasy themselves. Why do you think so many men imitate my style, my walk, my hairstyle?'

She had to control herself from laughing at such a self-deluding response. It was not arrogance but an innocent belief that what he did served a terribly serious purpose, a belief that left no room for doubt, a wide-eyed wonderment that made her healthy scepticism sound perverse. 'Even you imitate yourself,' she said to herself.

'Look at them,' he said, pointing to a honeymooning couple. The man lay on the grass with his hands behind his head, the woman sat beside him, bent over him in rapt attention. 'See, he's posing like me. He thinks he's a hero too. What's the harm in a little make-believe?'

She could see that he was trying hard to prove his point, a challenge he had probably never faced because everybody around him seemed willing to accept his word unquestioningly. It was clear that her unimpressed look ruffled him. He looked petulant, his lips pouting and arching downwards like those of an admonished child. 'I'm a superstar,' he said rather vehemently. 'Have you seen even one of my films? A more famous actor is still to be born. The people of this state and around the world adore me. They will build temples for me one day.'

Lakshmi was rattled by the tone of his voice. She'd never heard him speak so harshly. It wasn't her intention to anger him. She didn't want him to turn against her for such a trifling disagreement. 'What do I know about films?' she said by way of placating him, and distracted him by admiring a squirrel that had appeared in front of them, flicking its bushy tail and standing on its hind legs. And like a child Mutthu could be easily distracted. He lost his pout and stretched his hand out towards the squirrel.

'I don't have to see one of your films to see why you're a superstar,' she lied to him later, allowing him to hold her hand, speaking in gentle tones the way she used to with Pulcinella when he was angry.

Back in the cottage she allowed him to pull her close to him. He held her tightly, but she did not move. 'You're the love of my life,' he whispered to her. She did not believe him. It sounded like a line from one of his films. But she felt strangely reassured and let herself be engulfed by his embrace.

As she tried to sleep that night, lying next to a satiated Mutthu, who slept hugging his plump pillow, smiling in his sleep, she wondered why she had been meek, why she had lied to please him, why she had, uncharacteristically, quashed her own pride and her opinions to make amends for having vexed him. She could not understand what had prompted her to handle his fragile and bruised ego so delicately, even to the point of deception. She wondered what price she would have to pay for this in the future.

When he rolled over in his sleep and put his arm around her, she did not move. She felt herself stiffen but she resisted the urge to move his hand away.

★

Rumours about Lakshmi's involvement with Mutthu shocked me. I did not believe them at first. But nobody entirely disbelieves rumours no matter how strenuously they claim to.

What was Lakshmi doing with a man like Mutthu? I imagined him to be a sleazy, lecherous character in real life, an uncouth, greasy-haired Lothario in his waning years preying on women like Lakshmi to prop up his own ego. But what about her? What was *she* thinking? What was she to him? What impelled her to debase herself in such a fashion?

Nothing about her actions made sense to me. Especially this. The illogic of the situation and the thought that Lakshmi was just as capable of falling, angered me. I turned this anger on others: on my mother, for instance, who foolishly suggested once that it was just as well that Lakshmi didn't come into our family as a bride. 'Shut up, amma!' I snarled at her. 'What do you know about her life?'

But the gossip made me furious. Some of it was vile and personal. But there was nothing I could do to stop it. How many wagging tongues could I rein in? And, besides, how could I refute anything? And yet, when I overheard one man at the journalists' club referring to Lakshmi as Mutthu's mistress I couldn't help interjecting. 'What do you know about their relationship? Did they come and give you an account of all their activities?'

'Relax,' the man responded, taken aback. 'I'm just saying what everybody knows. Why are you getting offended?'

What could I have said to that? That the truth was unpleasant? That it hurt? That it should have been me and not Mutthu? 'It's none of our business. That's all.'

'What's she to you? Why are you defending a small-time dancer who's sleeping with a film star just to get a break in films?' There was suspicion in his voice.

I was bound to her in so many ways that I could not even attempt to say which of my relationships with her I would betray if I responded. I became angry with Lakshmi for making her position so utterly indefensible.

'She's a fool!' I said to her mother accusingly, for foolishness is often inherited. 'A nincompoop.'

Devaki and Nasser Sharif were dismayed and embarrassed. 'She should know better than to get involved with these film people,' Devaki said fretfully, sounding like her mother.

I looked at her in bemusement.

'Don't look at me like that. My father and her father are different. They belonged to a different generation. They had a different set of values.'

Despite the ironies—indeed the hypocrisies—in her argument, I nodded.

'He was an extra in those days. Look where he is now. What fortune!'

'But no amount of fortune can make up for his lack of education and culture,' Nasser Sharif said, snorting. 'He's there now only because everybody wants such crassness. In my day we were not just actors, but artistes. We had a stage presence. We held the audience's attention with our talents, not with the antics like these fellows perform. In any case, don't worry, ma, I'll do my best to keep her away from that extra.'

'What can you do? You think she's going to listen to you?'

'I'll talk to him.'

'On what basis?'

'Because I'm her father.'

'You're going to tell him that?'

'Yes. We've kept quiet for too long. Why should we be ashamed? Let the world know that she is our daughter.'

Devaki smiled. 'At least now.'

Nasser Sharif telephoned Mutthu. 'I'm Nasser Sharif, Lakshmi's father,' he said.

There was a long silence at the other end. Finally, with humility that surprised Lakshmi's father, Mutthu said, 'Saar, vanakkam. How are you?'

'I'm hearing stories about you and my daughter. So naturally you'll understand if I worry about her. Every father wants the best for his children.' He paused.

'Yes, of course.'

'Don't mind my saying this, but this is not the best option for her.'

'Saar, with all due respect you should be having this conversation with your daughter, not with me.'

'Look, all I'm trying to say is this: you're a mature man and I'm requesting you to do the right thing and stay away from my daughter.'

'You are a man of the world, too. So you can understand that it is not so easy to turn my feelings on and off.'

'I'm not discussing feelings,' Nasser Sharif responded irascibly. 'I don't want her to ruin her life. By getting involved with her you're taking on a big responsibility, and I hope you'll fulfil it.'

'I'll do the best that I can.' Mutthu's tone was cold.

Nasser Sharif was despondent after the call. 'He has no respect for elders. He has no class. Devaki, go bring Mahtab home.' But he said it without conviction this time. 'I should never have got her involved with the film crowd. What did I think I was doing? Now she's his plaything. My little girl in the arms of a lecher. Allah, what kind of test is it?'

★

The only woman from his past that Mutthu ever spoke to Lakshmi about was his deceased mother. She attempted to wheedle out information about the women he was supposed to have been involved with. She tried interrogation, petulance, cajoling, threats of blackmail, sweet-talking. But his standard response was always: 'What women? Do you believe everything you read?'

His mother he introduced to her (with the help of a photograph) a few months after they'd first met. It was an old photograph—brown, with frayed edges—and the name of the studio etched in gold in a corner, the kind that, like the memory one has of the deceased, glossed over human imperfections and idealized its subjects. His mother sat stiffly, probably wearing her best sari, self-consciously staring at the camera, unwilling to smile at the strange contraption that would capture her forever. Frozen in time, she was a younger version of his wife.

At first Lakshmi resented his silence about the women in his life. Why couldn't he tell her about them? At least to confirm or deny everything she had heard. Didn't he trust her enough? Their first real fights were over the ghosts of these other women. When her curiosity boiled over and she shouted at him in frustration, he would hold her by the shoulder, laugh his hero-laugh and say, 'How you glow when you're angry, my dear!'

And she'd get angrier, not only because he was so patronizing, but also because he couldn't even be bothered to come up with something more original than a line from a film.

In the end it took only one serious response, not even an answer, for her to make her peace with his secrecy. 'You may fear that I'm lecherous,' he said one day when he was in a contemplative mood, 'but even I have some values.'

That was when it occurred to her that there were lots of things about her life that she wasn't willing to reveal to him. If he tried to pry into her past she'd clam up. So she had to allow him his privacy, his secrets, just as she wanted to maintain hers.

And she would never find out in all her life that his silence was not out of secrecy but respect for her, because of all the women who really mattered to him, the first was her mother, the one who broke his heart by ignoring him and clinging to a man old enough to be her father.

One day, in a magazine, Lakshmi saw a photograph of her

and Mutthu at the glitzy social do that they had been to the week before. She had worn an expensive Kancheepuram sari that he had given her. He looked natty in a suit and had his arm around her shoulder.

She threw the magazine down. Even the modicum of ambiguity surrounding their relationship now lay shattered, her privacy pried open by a nosy cameraman. This was what she had been afraid of. What did his wife feel seeing her husband with another woman? How would he explain the photograph to her? How did he explain his long absences from home?

Lakshmi never saw his wife after that first meeting. She remained hidden in the closed world of her home, probably seething with jealousy, probably waking up every morning to spit on her photograph and cast evil spells on her. When Lakshmi had started appearing in public with him she had been constantly filled with the dread of running into his wife. She imagined his wife coming after her with the rage of a spurned woman, her eyes brimming with fire, her hair loose and wild, her tongue as sharp as a scythe. But Mutthu behaved as though it was perfectly understandable and natural for him to share his public life with Lakshmi and not his wife. He seemed untroubled by guilt; perhaps because he felt none. Sometimes she wondered if he even knew whether his wife was alive or dead. He never explained her absence to anybody, nor did he ever try to prevaricate or offer excuses when asked.

Overwhelmed by guilt, Lakshmi asked him that day, 'Isn't it unfair to your wife for you to be seen with me and not her?'

He clucked his tongue impatiently. 'But what can I do if she doesn't want to go out anywhere?'

Perhaps she feels humiliated, Lakshmi wanted to tell him. But she had too many doubts and questions about her own relationship with him to fight on someone else's behalf. Did people talk behind her back? Did they mock her?

'Don't you care what people think of us?'

He shrugged. 'Let them think whatever they want. Why do you care so much about what people think of us?'

But how could he not? How could he ignore the sharp glances of ridicule, the meaningful smiles? Or be unconcerned about her having the dubious honour of being the other woman, the home-wrecker?

'Go back to your wife,' she wanted to tell him, but her tongue became leaden and she could not utter those words, neither then nor the numerous times later when she felt she should.

For the next several days she refused to see him. But that only increased his ardour. 'Like a peacock I thirst for your love,' he proclaimed over the phone.

'I'm not a stupid heroine in your film,' she retorted angrily.

He showed up at her doorstep half an hour later having cancelled shooting for the rest of the day. His make-up was wearing off, giving his skin a pasty texture. His eyelids drooped under the weight of mascara. Did all actors wear mascara like women? The combination of stale make-up and fatigue made him look crazy. 'My love,' he sighed. 'You're my whole world. You're my heartbeat. You're the rhythm of my music.'

The resentment she'd begun to harbour at being the other woman now welled up against the emptiness of his nonsensical words. She pushed him aside.

'What's happened, my love?'

She turned away and did not respond.

'Did I do something wrong?'

How could he not know what was bothering her? She wanted to shout at him for being so insensitive.

He held her chin in his fingers and looked at her. 'How can I see you unhappy? I'll do anything to see a smile on your face. You only have to tell me.'

'Then give me what every woman wants,' she snapped, guilt easily giving way to anger, sympathy to self-centredness. 'Give me the respectability I deserve.'

Weeks later, at the end of a trip to a small town for the shooting of his latest film, instead of returning to the City, to Lakshmi's surprise he took her to a small nondescript temple in the middle of nowhere, the kind of temple with a plain gopuram and garishly painted compound walls that one usually ignored. But according to local legend couples who sought blessings there led long and happy lives together. Mutthu purchased two garlands from the flower seller outside the temple. There was nobody inside. The priest recognized Mutthu and welcomed him obsequiously. To Lakshmi's utter shock, Mutthu asked the priest to conduct their marriage.

Relishing Lakshmi's disbelief, Mutthu broke into a wide smile. 'My love, I said I'd do anything for you. You didn't believe me, did you?'

As if to prove that this wasn't a practical joke, he pulled out a thali from his trouser pocket with the flourish of a conjurer pulling out a rabbit by its ears. The thick yellow thread and the gold pendant looked authentic. Disoriented, unable to decide whether she should be happy or nervous, Lakshmi looked on as the priest started chanting hymns, allowing words to bleed into one another, skipping the ones that were hard to pronounce. By the time they had exchanged the garlands, the scene around her had ripened into something familiarly surreal—the sanctum became a tableau on a stage, and she, Mutthu and the nonsense-uttering priest were the marionettes that played out a scene for the amusement of school children. When Mutthu tied the thali around her neck the priest raised his voice a few decibels over the high-pitched clinking of the little brass bell in his hand, and she accepted it with bemusement, barely realizing the significance of this act or the staccato incantations of ancient hymns of bliss and well-being. Before she knew it, the ceremony was over, and Mutthu led his new bride towards the waiting car, proclaiming the obvious: 'Darling, you're now my wife!' Lakshmi, his bride, smiled at him—she didn't know what else to do—feeling the coarse thread of the thali against the back of her neck, remarking to herself how the symbol of marriage chafed so.

They had their first bitter fight the moment they emerged from the temple. She didn't shout or raise her voice. In fact, she did not utter even a word. She just sat beside him in the back of the car, leaned against the window and shut her eyes. 'But, my dear . . .' Mutthu tried to get her to open her eyes. But she pursed her lips as tightly as she squeezed her eyes shut.

He took her to Singapore and Australia on their honeymoon. As he plied her with exotic food, expensive gifts and took her to see the sights, she was neither happy nor unhappy. She sat by his side, placid as a frozen lake. Only the occasional tension in her gestures and the sting in her voice betrayed her anger. At first Mutthu appeared befuddled. 'But, my dear . . .' he'd start to say. Lakshmi would look at him askance, and his voice would trail away, and he'd laugh hollowly and try to joke as he always did when she was angry with him.

Immediately upon their return he took her to one of the houses he owned in the city. It had been the first house he'd bought years ago, and he had lived there with his first wife for many years until he had moved to his present larger, much posher house. It was a small two-storey independent house. The upper floor had a large balcony shaded by a mango tree that looked on to the small garden below with a patch of grass bordered by roses, hibiscus, jasmine and bougainvillea creepers. In the back was a tamarind tree, one that Mutthu himself had planted the day he moved into the house.

'This will be our private retreat,' he said, stretching his arms wide as he stood at the gate.

He led her in. As soon as she stepped in she became aware of his mother's presence. There was a large garlanded portrait of his mother in the front room hanging from the wall at an angle, gazing down at them. This was the first time he had ever brought her to one of his homes. He prostrated himself in front of the portrait, making room for Lakshmi to follow suit beside him. But she remained standing, arms folded, surveying the scene with some detachment.

Yes, they were married, but what did it really mean? Illegal, unwitnessed, barely celebrated, how legitimate was it? Surely he would not leave his first wife for her? Who would he go to in times of crisis, his first wife who represented his hearth, or her, his recent acquisition? With whom would he celebrate festivals and perform pujas?

When he stood up Mutthu looked hurt. But he sighed and held her in his arms. 'Isn't it insulting enough to her that I married you while she's still alive? Why should we insult her further by making a show of it?'

'Don't make excuses. Nobody knows we're married.'

'What do you care what others know? I married you in god's presence in a temple.'

'If god were the only one who mattered why do people make such a spectacle of marriage?' The edginess in her voice returned.

'The spectacle is for the world. What really matters to me is what I do in the presence of god and my mother.'

Even in her uncharitable mood she knew what he said wasn't hyperbole. He had always spoken of his mother reverentially, as if she were the family deity. He had even consecrated her in the large mansion he had bought for her in their small town of Kuppam. He called the house Annai Illam— Mother's Abode. He performed pujas and charitable work in her name. And now, he had brought Lakshmi to his mother as his bride. Surely it was symbolic of something.

Lakshmi softened and sat down next to him. They were silent for a while, he looking up at his mother's portrait longingly, and she watching him.

Finally he broke the silence. 'Everything I am now is because of her. She was the only one who always believed I'd become a star. Unfortunately she did not live long enough to see her son as a hero. You know, in those days I still did supporting roles. She would see every film of mine in the theatre in Kuppam, no matter how small my role. The screening of my film was a big event. She'd take a platoon of neighbours and relatives, and fight with the one-anna crowds for her place in the front benches. If it weren't for her blessings I'd never have become successful.' Mutthu paused. 'She had a hard life. She used to knit plastic baskets to feed me and send me to school. "Eat well, my son," she'd say. "How else will you become a hero?"'

'What about your father? How come you never talk about him?'

Mutthu's face darkened. 'I don't have a father.'

'You mean he died before you were born?'

'No, no, the man who married my mother lived a long life. Or so they say. But I hardly saw him. He spent all his time with his mistress.'

Lakshmi was startled as much by what he said as by the way he said it. He was matter-of-fact, speaking without any sense of irony. It was clear to Lakshmi that he disliked his father virulently. She understood then why he traced back everything positive in his life to his mother. In his need to dislike his father he had not only chosen to deify his mother, but had also been—and would always be—blind to the irony of his life: that he did exactly what he hated his father for and that, in some ways, his life was a mirror image of his father's. Just as Lakshmi had committed the same mistake she so hated her mother for.

Unaware of the profound paradox exposed by Lakshmi's questioning, unaware of the sudden clamminess of her hands, the tremor of her lips, Mutthu continued loquaciously that day, an over eager new husband, telling her about his mother and his childhood in Kuppam, about their future together. By the time it became dark, he had suggested that Lakshmi live in this house, with servants to take care of her needs, a car and a driver to take her wherever she wanted to go. He had suggested that his manager, a young, eager man who worked silently and efficiently, should also manage her professional commitments.

She could see that he was trying hard to defeat the irony of his life by ignoring it, by waving magic wands of normality in the face of the demons from his father's life. She realized that in his victory lay her own salvation, that if indeed he succeeded there was hope for her too, for she could wrest some of that normalcy and make it her own. She needed him for her battles as much as he needed her for his. This, then, was the best compromise: a marriage that took care of moral dilemmas without invoking any legal ones.

She got up and prostrated herself before the portrait of his mother. A new bride paying respects to her mother-in-law. Mutthu, surprised and pleased, got up with alacrity and fell to the ground by her side, and a newly-wed couple sought a mother's blessings.

The Role of His Life

It was *her* home. People would sometimes refer to it as 'chinna veedu', the little house, a term that was both a euphemism for her ambiguous status as his second wife and recognition of its lesser importance than the one his first wife lived in. She would start hating the house later, for what it stood for, for the insinuations it attracted. But for now she didn't think it would have a name. It was a place she could call her own, even if it was Mutthu who had given it to her. And she moved into it with a kind of joy she had never known.

Unobtrusive, shaded and obscured by trees all around it, it did not draw attention to itself. And it suited her fine. It was cool and comfortable, and she could mould it to her personality. She set about furnishing it to her tastes, allowing Mutthu only the indulgence of hanging a large black-and-white photograph of himself standing with the Maharaja of Mysore next to the Maharaja's prize-winning '26 Bugatti.

She spent several hours a day in her dance room downstairs. It was large enough to give her the sense of a stage. She kept it bare, except for a record player—a gift from Mutthu—on which she played the music for her practice when her musicians weren't present, and a large bronze statue of Nataraja with a lamp next to it in an alcove. At the foot of the statue were the words of the first shloka she had learnt from Maami. It was a shloka she recited every time she danced. *Angikam bhuvanam yasya/ Vachikam sarva vangmayam/ Aharyam chandra-taradi/ Tam vande sattvikam shivam* (We bow to him, the benevolent Shiva/ Whose limbs are the world/ Whose word is the essence of language/ Whose costume the moon and the stars.)

She read extensively about historical and mythological characters in search of new material. She sought out those who were well versed in antiquity. The new themes she added, as she later realized, were usually centred around women: Andal and her devotion to her lord; Kannaki's righteous wrath; Radha, instead of the traditional narratives about Krishna; Mirabai, the Mewari princess who ignored her husband in favour of Krishna.

She loved explaining the legends and stories that were part· of her repertoire, their significance, their historical and mythological allusions. At every recital she demonstrated how each element was added to another to create fluid, graceful movements, and how in conjunction with music and poetry these movements produced a fluent narrative. She could explain the art in simple terms, with the deftness of a storyteller, in a language that was accessible to everybody.

Mutthu's manager, who had also begun managing Lakshmi's career, worked unstintingly to ensure that she remained in the public eye. He chose—and sometimes even sought—invitations that would give her the most exposure. Her reputation as a dancer began to grow. She received invitations to perform at every important event, some of them in other cities. She found the applause during and after her performances exhilarating. They always gave her the sense of being transported to another world where her hitherto insatiable appetite for attention was finally sated. But when the temporary euphoria of praise subsided, it left within her an emptiness, a desire to feel it again even more strongly. She knew she was becoming increasingly dependent on praise as if it were a narcotic, and like an addict she sought increasingly larger doses of it to satisfy herself.

Once after a lecture-demonstration at the university as part of a week-long cultural festival, students and faculty members mobbed her. They all had the look of people who'd experienced an epiphany. Several students pressed notes into her hands. She read them to Mutthu later and laughed. 'Look, this one is so presumptuous: "Will you be my Parvati? Signed, Shiva." And this one's so touching: "I didn't know such ethereal beauty existed till I saw you dance. How I wish I had not come to watch you. You have now shattered my small world, for I have now begun to yearn for the unattainable."'

Mutthu was neither amused nor impressed. He said nothing. Lakshmi noticed his lips arch downwards. She cast a sideways glance at Mutthu's pouting face and let out a peal of laughter. 'You're as jealous as an adolescent! Who would have thought a star as big as you would be jealous of mere mortals!'

'Of course I'm not jealous,' he protested.

But she did not believe him. 'Here, I hope this makes you feel better.' She ripped the notes and threw them into the garbage bin. She put her arms around him and stopped smiling. Something akin to tenderness—an emotion she rarely let herself experience—stirred within her. 'You have nothing to fear,' she said gently, as if addressing a child, the tone she wished he would use with her. 'Our age difference doesn't matter to me.'

He snorted in a peremptory sort of way and changed the subject. What she took for jealousy then turned out in reality to be something more.

Some years later Lakshmi was invited to perform at the Independence Day celebrations at the Red Fort in Delhi. Mutthu looked pleased. 'You'll find that the President is a cultured man,' he said with an air of familiarity, no doubt recalling his encounter with the President a couple of years ago when he had won a national award for a role in a particular film. 'But I've heard that he's not as good as he appears to be. Beware of his groping hands when he greets you.'

Lakshmi smiled. 'I can't believe it. You're still jealous.'

Mutthu looked startled. 'Jealous? Why should I be jealous? That man has hardly any teeth left.'

Nevertheless, Mutthu accompanied her to the capital and sat in the front row with the other celebrities. At the reception after the evening's programme when the President approached to greet her, Mutthu rushed to her side and put his arms on her shoulder in a proprietary manner.

'I've seen you somewhere . . .' the President, not known for being particularly sensitive, said to Mutthu and paused for a moment. 'Ah, now I remember—you're the film star from the south! I don't watch films myself, but I'm told you're good.'

'You're being silly,' she said to him later as he sat pouting at her. 'I'm sure he didn't imply anything about you.'

Again, later that year, during the annual music and dance festival in the City when Lakshmi was specially feted with the title of Kalaimamani, Mutthu sat through the entire evening looking downcast. He was silent all the way home.

This time, however, she was irritated by his childish behaviour. For some time now she'd taken care not to dwell too much on her successes in his presence.

Upon reaching home he picked up a framed photograph of Lakshmi with the President and said, 'You can reach for the stars.'

'You've been there for years! What are you upset about?'

Mutthu turned around and looked at her inquiringly with a half-smile. 'I'm very happy for you.'

'Then what's the problem?'

Mutthu didn't respond right away. He went to the balcony. 'Don't you see? I'm hurtling downwards.'

Leaning on the railing he lit a cigarette and looked upwards as though he could see himself literally falling from the sky. It was then that Lakshmi realized that more than being envious of her success he was mourning the decline of his own career. The renewed surge of popularity after he had won the national film award had been deceptive. In real terms it had marked a turning point in his career. Such achievement awards usually went to old people, those who had retired from the film industry, sometimes to the dead, as an act of contrition rather than appreciation. It was as though once he received the award the industry had belatedly taken notice of the fact that he wasn't young any more. They began acknowledging his true age and came to him, with the usual deference, and with new kinds of roles. They did not see him as the impetuous, romantic, action-oriented character any more, but as a more mellow, dignified man, one who was expected to speak in a deep, authoritative voice, one who fondly watched other younger characters romp through gardens. In his earlier films he had blackened his hair to hide the strands of grey; now they asked him to touch up his artificially black hair and moustache with a silver brush. Earlier he had applied layer upon layer of make-up to hide the lines on his face; now they asked him to wear a fake paunch under his shirt. He was still the star of these films, but the other characters were getting increasingly prominent roles. The roles of the avuncular lawyer, the family patriarch, the police commissioner who would embarrass even Raja Harishchandra with his honesty were euphemistic ways in which the industry hinted that his eventual retirement was looming on the horizon.

Lakshmi understood that her rise only accentuated the sense of his decline. And Mutthu, who took his on-screen persona all too seriously and played it out even in real life, sure of himself and his place in the world, was panicking at the downward spiral of his career. She touched his arm and pressed her face against his shoulder.

'What am I doing!' Mutthu exclaimed, shaking himself up and opening his arms wide as if remembering that he was still a hero. 'I should be reliving my successes through yours instead of drooping and shrivelling.'

He smiled, but not convincingly. For all his brave words he would not be able to get over his distress. It remained with him for months, a passive malaise, rearing its head only occasionally, but when it did it manifested itself in petty complaints that Lakshmi quickly got used to. His distress turned, inevitably, into gloom; the gloom of a spent man, the gloom of a fallen king. But the showman that he was, how could he stay low forever? The gloom would eventually lift, but he would have to reinvent himself and play the role of his life for that to happen.

Slowly, he began to change. He became increasingly

avuncular in real life as on screen. He became less cavalier, less conscious of his status as a hero. He did not attempt to hide the grey in his hair any more.

'You're growing up,' she commented to him with a smile and he laughed good-humouredly.

But rather than fading from the public eye he remained as popular as ever. The smaller his on-screen roles became, the more time he spent getting involved in everybody else's troubles. To some extent he had always been involved with other people. Journalists who came to interview him left after being interviewed by him. When strangers sought him out, he rarely turned them down. He knew everybody in all his film units by name, from the peons who brought the crew frothy, piping-hot coffee in stainless steel tumblers to the directors' assistants and members of the producers' extended families. He treated them like his own extended family, encouraging, scolding, advising them even without being asked. The laughter and the banter he shared with them was infectious ('Hey, Soda Bottle, I hear you have all your four eyes on some woman. Is she pretty or is she like our heroine?'). He was a natural crowd-puller, a magnet that made people lose their sense of bearing and gravitate towards him.

When he forgot himself in the honeycomb of admirers, he also forgot his handkerchief. Even though he carried several of them—his respiratory ailments forced him to use them prodigiously—in his most candid moments he never made an attempt to reach for them when he wanted to blow his nose, which he did between his thumb and forefinger, and wiped his hands on the nearest rag he could lay his hands on. This was one indulgence everybody allowed him, and those with more delicate tastes suppressed their winces and sent for servants discreetly to clean up after him.

Although Lakshmi hated this habit of his, and over the years she would shout at him on innumerable occasions for his lack of hygiene and concern for others, it was at such handkerchiefless moments that she paradoxically admired him the most. This was the real Mutthu: slightly uncouth (or, perhaps, more accurately, lacking sophistication), but very human, the kind of man even a stranger on the street would not only recognize, but could also approach and ask for help. They often did, and he never refused. They came to him seeking all kinds of assistance: from job recommendations to exerting his influence to get their ration cards approved. A wispy bumpkin stopped his car outside the studio one day and requested a role in a film, and instead of telling the driver to brush him off, Mutthu rolled down his darkened window to admonish the stranger: 'Simpleton! Have you seen your face in the mirror?' and asked his producer to hire the boy as a peon instead. 'You never know, he might become a star one day,' he said to the producer. 'Just like me.' In a way, there was very little difference between the Mutthu on screen and the Mutthu in real life. He wanted to be and succeeded in becoming a hero even in real life.

It was no wonder then that he had more admirers than his stature as a superstar justified. So many people were willing to do his bidding. Like the rickshaw puller whose rickshaw he had fitted with a small motor, who often came by the studios just to touch his feet and willingly ran errands for him as though he were an old family retainer. Or the newly hired peon who would follow him around for the rest of his life. Or the America-returned director who had turned Lakshmi out all those years ago, to whose career he had lent his name when it needed a fillip.

This was the source of his charisma: his lack of pretence, his ability to connect with everybody, his paternalistic concern for them. Lakshmi realized later, much to her dismay, that she, too, had succumbed to his charisma, that despite her repeated insistence that she had got involved with him of her own volition, it was possible that he had held sway over her in much the same way as he did over his admirers.

As time went by people had taken to forming queues outside his various homes. They came to him for advice and help not only on personal matters, but also, increasingly, on political and social issues: workers who wanted to unionize against management, industrialists who wanted him to have a word with the unruly leader of their workers, people with social welfare schemes in mind. Farmers sought him before agitating, autorickshaw and taxi drivers wanted his support in their protests against the hike in petrol prices, opposing clans wanted him to mediate in their quarrels, college students wanted his approval before going on strike. Sometimes he spent several days at a time writing recommendations and calling up his contacts on their behalf, sometimes personally participating in their activities, from demonstrating for better working conditions for tanners, to demanding a pay raise for government school teachers.

One day he got into an argument with a councillor over the demolition of illegal tenements on a plot of land owned by the city. In front of the bulldozers that had come to tear the structures down and surrounded by the residents of the slum the two men had almost come to blows. Like the characters he played, Mutthu was never averse to using force to make his point. He'd advanced towards the councillor, fist clenched, fully intending to sock him in the jaw, but someone with presence of mind pulled the councillor back just in time.

'Why do you get involved in everything?' Lakshmi asked him once after he returned, grimy-faced, his sweat-soaked shirt sticking to his back. 'You look like you've been out in the sun all day.'

'What to do? How can I refuse if people want me to intervene in their troubles?'

'I hope you don't get into trouble yourself for taking sides.'

He laughed. 'Don't worry. Who will dare raise a finger against me? Besides, I always take the side of the truth.'

She shook her head in incomprehension. 'Whose truth? I don't understand why you can't mind your own business.'

'Is it that I don't spend enough time with you?'

'No,' she lied, after a moment's hesitation. 'It doesn't bother me. But why strain yourself? Why this unnecessary tension?'

'You don't understand, my dear,' he replied and sighed. 'There's no tension. I love it. It keeps me in touch with people.

I can't understand how you can be content being by yourself.'

'That's not true. I want people around me, too. But within limits.'

He was silent for a while. Then he replied, contemplatively, 'I'm afraid of limits. I'm afraid of being left behind.'

His response startled her.

He was unusually quiet for the rest of the day. Later he came up to her and said, 'I suppose I'm doing this more for myself than for the people who approach me. Does that make me selfish?'

Lakshmi gazed at him. For once he appeared to doubt himself. She could see a streak of fear in his expression. The fear of being forgotten, of being unloved. The fear of going off narcotics. The fear she knew so well. 'No, it doesn't,' she said gently. 'Do what you believe you should.'

It was in Kuppam that he finally made up his mind. It was only natural that he should go home to make such a life-changing decision. He always went to Kuppam to cogitate or to recuperate, and this time Lakshmi went with him. As always, the morning after his arrival in Kuppam a group of twelve lepers showed up at the gates of Annai Illam. They always knew when he arrived in town. Word got around fast in Kuppam, travelling with the breeze from door to door. The lepers had begged for a living ever since he'd known them. But he never gave them money without making them earn it. That morning, too, the caretaker of the house opened a side gate for them, allowed them to fetch the brooms and pans and disinfecting liquids from the small outhouse near the compound wall. After the lepers had cleaned the ditches all around the house and poured disinfectant till the reek of ammonia and chlorine suffocated them, Mutthu strode up to the gate, surveyed their work, nodded approvingly and dropped coins and notes into their mutilated hands. As he watched the lepers leave, excitedly counting the money, he pulled his silk bathrobe over his striped European-style pyjamas, one hand in a pocket, the other holding a pipe, and announced, 'I've decided to enter politics.'

Lakshmi burst out laughing. He lit his pipe with a flourish and frowned. She dimly remembered that he'd bought the maroon robe and slate-grey pyjamas in Mauritius where he had recently been to shoot a film. He had also taken to smoking a pipe around that time, like the benevolent, pipe-smoking industrialist character he had played in it.

'People need me,' he explained, pacing the veranda, puffing smoke in short, rapid bursts. 'Yes, they need me, now that this thalaivar is too weak to take care of the Party.'

He was referring to the leader of the regional political party he had been a card-carrying member of for over two decades now. He had campaigned on behalf of the party in past elections, but had done little else. In the past it had stood for regional pride. It drew its support by promising the restoration of the state's ancient pre-eminence. But in the last few years, with the leader's failing health, it had had no vision to offer. Its ideology had degenerated to a farce. Infighting amongst the leaders ensured that its supporters fled to other parties. Not long ago some office-bearers of the Party had come to meet him. 'Saar,' they had said, 'only you can turn around our fortunes. We need your help.' And he had sent them away that day pleased at being sought out, but not making any promises.

'So what are you going to do?' Lakshmi asked.

'So many things! I have to get involved in managing the Party. We need to shake it up, to rejuvenate it by infusing new blood and new ideas into it.'

'It will take up a lot of your time and energy.'

'But I'm already spending a lot of time solving everybody's problems. How's this going to be different? Besides, I have to do it for my people.'

'But what do you know about politics?'

Mutthu looked flabbergasted. 'What's there to know? You make dramatic speeches, act like you're the centre of a grand epic, and get people to vote for you. The more people you convince the more power you have. In this I already have a big advantage over everybody else.'

Mutthu was serious. He visited the president of the Party at his home and spent several hours in private consultations with him. Rumours started floating around that he was going to take over the reins. But, strangely, he spoke very little about his political involvement in public. The press renewed its interest in him. When asked by a reporter what his long-term plans were, he replied, 'Films, films and more films!'

'But, saar,' the reporter persisted, 'what about the rumours?'

'I'm only helping the thalaivar, who's a dear friend of mine, in some Party-related work.'

But the rumours persisted. One day the office-bearers voiced for the first time what the rumours had been hinting at. 'With the thalaivar bedridden you've been taking all the responsibilities. It is time you took over the leadership as well, saar.'

Mutthu looked horrified. 'Cheh-cheh-cheh! How can you talk like that when he's still alive? Don't insult him like that.'

The men went away shaking their heads, apologizing. But Lakshmi knew he had not meant it. He had been actively propagating some of the rumours by dropping hints to various people, and the relish with which he read about those rumours later in newspapers and magazines horrified her.

'Why don't you tell everybody exactly what you're doing instead of continuing this sham act?' Lakshmi asked him.

Mutthu laughed. 'If I am going to join politics, I should do so to my greatest advantage. Don't you see I'm creating suspense? People like drama. They want to be able to participate in it. By not telling them everything, I'm giving them an opportunity to contribute to the story. How boring it would be if I simply stood up in front of everybody one day and announced, "I have decided to take a plunge into politics. Please give me your support." Once the story is reported, there would be very little else to write about. But now everybody is speculating, everybody is talking, everybody is predicting the future. They're all playing the part of scriptwriters and directors.'

Before long Mutthu was back in the limelight, heightening

everyone's interest by coyly refusing to confirm or deny whatever was being said and written about him. The more he denied he had any aspirations to lead the Party, the more his fans and the press speculated that his elevation was only a matter of time. This assumption became so widespread that in the end it became a self-fulfilling prophecy. When some months later the Party president died, thanks to Mutthu more people followed him in death than they ever had in life. Mutthu's election as the Party president became a mere formality, for there was none to oppose him.

Lakshmi was present when he formally took charge of the Party. Hands folded, beaming under the weight of heavy garlands, Mutthu looked a different man. He wore a white shirt, a white veshti and a silk angavastram over his shoulder. Over the last few months his transition from film hero to politician had been so smooth that she hadn't even noticed it. He was completely at ease in his new avtar, as if he had been preparing for this, the greatest role of his career, all his life. She began to understand how his humility concealed shrewdness and how effectively he charmed everybody with it. It was the same charm she herself had fallen for several years ago, a charm not so overt as to be obvious, yet not too subtle to be ineffective.

As he stood in front of the Party workers acknowledging their support, Lakshmi couldn't help admiring the deftness with which he had stage-managed the whole show. If he hadn't joined politics he would have faded from the public eye without even a whimper. Watching him energized and full of verve Lakshmi understood that his need to be in the centre of things essentially sprung from the same reason as hers: once the stage lights were turned off, the world became frighteningly dark.

Initiation

Ragini and Nasser Sharif were inseparable. Burdened by guilt like Devaki, he was both father and grandfather to the girl; it was thus a doubly pleasurable experience watching her grow. Forgotten by his erstwhile admirers, he lived anonymously and had all the time for her. He delighted in her joys. He watched her with the fascination of a new father, following her wandering, curious eyes, seeing the world the way she saw it, from her height. And she clung to him like a vine. Tenaciously, desperately, literally clambering up his legs when she was little. As if making up for the loss of her mother.

He was the only one who thought she was a good dancer. 'Like your mother,' he'd say, burdening her with her mother's reputation even before she had begun dancing. After Lakshmi's arangetram, when Ragini also wanted to dance like her, he sent her to the best dance teacher in the city. For all the love and affection she showered on Ragini, Devaki was not blind to her awkwardness. Her body was just not supple enough. There was too much of her father's ungainly bone structure in her.

Even Ragini knew she was not a good dancer. But she continued taking lessons only to please her grandfather.

One day after a field trip to an orphanage as part of her school's social service club's activities, she came home subdued. As usual Nasser Sharif called her out to practise.

'Not today, thatha,' she said. 'I don't feel well.'

'No, no, you must. Success does not come without hard work.'

'I visited an orphanage this afternoon, thatha.'

'Orphanage? What orphanage? Where's the need to go there?' His voice rose. 'This is why I tell you to come home straight from school. It's affecting your dance practice. How will you be a great dancer if you don't practise? There are plenty of people in the world to care for orphans. Only you can take care of your dancing. No more social service for you, understand?'

Ragini looked on in despair. Devaki came and gently led Nasser Sharif away. 'Leave the poor girl alone today.'

'If she doesn't become a well-known dancer it'll be because of you. Allowing her to be undisciplined.' Nasser Sharif wagged a finger angrily at Devaki before hobbling away.

Later Ragini asked her grandmother when they were alone, 'Paati, is it because I almost grew up in an orphanage myself?'

Startled by her perceptiveness, Devaki looked up. 'Yes, dear. You know he treasures you. Don't give him another reason to feel guilty.'

Nasser Sharif watched her practise every day. 'I want you to perform your arangetram before I go,' he'd say, aware of his advancing age, and Ragini would give him a small smile to conceal her fear. After practice, when he read the newspaper, she'd sneak up behind him, sit on the threshold of the room, and stare at his thick greying hair visible over the back of the chair. She'd sit absolutely still, barely breathing, trying to block all thoughts from her mind—for they stemmed from fear, a fear all too familiar to her mother—till her grandfather stirred and called out to her for his evening coffee. Rousing herself from her meditations and allowing the world around her to come flooding back into her mind, she'd get up with a sigh and go into the kitchen to get coffee.

One day, she could bear it no more and told her grandmother, 'I just wish he'd stop talking about dying as though it's a trip to the vegetable market.'

Her grandmother smiled. 'He's at that age. You mustn't take him too seriously.'

'It's not a joke. If he doesn't stop talking like that I'm going to stop dancing.'

It was only natural that when he did pass away it should be Ragini who would first find out. That day he had been watching her practise, as he usually did, sitting in his chair, smiling proudly at her. It was only when that smile on his face had remained fixated for too long, when it had turned eerie and cold, when the chair's curved canvas, lumpy, knobbly under his weight had become still that she knew something was wrong. When she poked him with her forefinger, she found that his flesh had acquired the plasticity of clay, and she instantly knew that he had not been joking.

Later, weeping over him, she looked up at her grandmother and asked, 'Shouldn't we tell amma?'

Devaki, resolute in her sorrow, hesitated only for a moment and replied, 'That's not necessary.'

Ragini understood why. She was precocious, way beyond her years. I'd seen her from close quarters, visiting her quite frequently. I was her Vasu-maama, the one who brought her news about her mother, news that I heard from my journalist colleagues. Devaki and Nasser Sharif would always say how eagerly she looked forward to my visits. But she would welcome me like she would any other family friend, with a smile and reserved courtesy. Sitting between her grandparents on the sofa she would listen with curiosity, but also with detachment, for she understood a lot, especially what to crave and what to let go.

But the moment she saw me that day she looked childlike. She came running to me and leaned against my chest with her fists under her chin. She wanted me to clasp her in my arms. I did so. Even when I let her go she did not move. She had never overtly sought comfort in my presence, not even as a child when I sat her on my knee. And now she wouldn't move away from me. I half expected her to cling to me the way she had clung to her grandfather. It was only then that I understood her earlier reserve, her transferring of that attachment to me now. I began to have an inkling of the enormous responsibility she was now entrusting me with. She was just as needy as her mother.

Mutthu took his job very seriously, as if it were divinely sanctioned. He met the members of the Party and listened to their complaints and advice. He spent hours behind closed doors in meetings, chalking out strategy with senior office-bearers. He travelled all over the state to meet functionaries and to assess the situation for himself. Wherever he went he helped recruit new members, often paying the fee of one rupee on behalf of the poor who were herded into regional offices with no money on them.

After several weeks he drew up a blueprint for the Party's reorganization. It called for the creation of new centres where the Party lacked presence, consolidation of existing ones where there were too many, replacing incompetent or disloyal local leaders with those who exhibited the right amount of talent and enthusiasm. He appealed to his fans to volunteer their time and talents for the cause of the Party. He gave them access to the Party's infrastructure in return for their services.

Lakshmi did not share his enthusiasm for all the running around, for the sweat-stained back, yellowing armpits, grimy hands, and greasy hair. She was content with her dance. Recognition came easily for her. She got used to the spotlight, and the silks and precious stones she wore. She continued to be delighted with the admiration she received, the little girls who wanted to be dancers themselves gathering around her and staring at her in awe. Her increasing popularity gave her a sense of confidence. She observed how other exponents of dance were transforming the art by bringing in new ideas, by borrowing themes and structures from other forms of dance, sometimes even creating a fusion of styles. She, too, began experimenting with form, particularly the dance-drama, which gave her a lot of scope for creativity. There were other dancers and musicians who were willing to collaborate with her, and soon they formed an informal dance troupe.

She began by choreographing the epics: parts of the Ramayana and the Mahabharata. Then she created dramas based on well-known works of literature like *Meghadutam*, *Geetagovinda* and *Silappadikkaram*.

Her reinterpretation of *Silappadikkaram* was controversial. Deviating somewhat from the original story, she had Kannaki initially refuse to pardon Kovalan, her wayward husband. Indeed she had Kannaki wrathfully turn out the repentant Kovalan and relent only when he fell at her feet and promised to banish the courtesan Madhavi from his mind. Even then Kannaki never completely pardoned him. When she later turned her wrath on the Pandya king her lament was not so much at Kovalan's wrongful death as it was at her loss.

Purists criticized Lakshmi for her feminist reinterpretations. One of them wrote in a review: 'It is not simply a misrepresentation of an ancient work that has stood the test of time; it is an assault on the concept of womanhood in our culture and, hence, an assault on our culture itself.'

The review stung Lakshmi. This was the first time she had been criticized in public. The mud that he had flung stuck to her. She had been taken by surprise, helpless in the face of the assault. And she couldn't even fling it back at the reviewer. She could not confront him; he was simply a name, perhaps even a fictitious one.

But in the long run the negative publicity the controversy generated was good for the troupe and for her. People flocked to see the dance-drama. The troupe was invited all over the country to perform. Weeks later, basking in her increased popularity, secure in the knowledge that her supporters outnumbered her critics, she sent a note to the man who had started it all: 'Thank you for everything. In one stroke you have done more for my cause than all my admirers and I have in all these years. I'll be sure to send you a complimentary ticket to the premiere of my next dance-drama.'

When elections were announced in the state Mutthu began working like a man possessed, with the kind of energy he claimed he had never had. The number of people who wanted to meet him was astonishing. And it kept increasing with every passing day. People trailed him wherever he went. They even followed him to Lakshmi's house, converting the front room to an auxiliary office. Mutthu and Lakshmi had very little time together. It seemed that whenever she saw him he was surrounded by a mob of people, sometimes so thick that she would have a hard time finding him at all. The constant buzzing around him irritated her. She specially disliked the Party workers who hovered around him for no reason whatsoever, whose obsequious ways she despised.

'If you go to the toilet they'll even follow you there,' she remarked to him once, during a rare moment of privacy.

'They do,' Mutthu replied in good humour. 'Even if they don't have to go, they'll stand there pretending as long as I'm there.'

'Doesn't it annoy you?'

Mutthu laughed. 'What you see as annoyance I see as admiration.'

'What an uncouth way of showing admiration.'

'You've led a very privileged life. You're too cultured. And that convent school you went to didn't do you any good either. You don't understand the common man.'

He seemed to enjoy irking her with his comments on her upbringing. He did so on purpose.

But soon after, during that early stage of election fever, even before parties had announced their candidates, there was trouble in one of the rural districts. Members of a rival party beat up some of Mutthu's men in an argument over a perceived insult while they were drinking at a toddy shop. But instead of retaliating, the district leaders inexplicably split into two camps and beat each other up in public.

A few days later two of the senior members of the Party from that district arrived at Lakshmi's house looking for Mutthu. They hobbled in, scowling and refusing to look at each other. They were covered with cuts and bruises and plasters.

'So, tell me what happened,' Mutthu asked impatiently.

'Saar,' began one of the men, smiling toothily. 'Those

rascals started the whole thing. Our men were sitting quietly as cats drinking when the goons . . .'

'Not them. What happened between you two?'

The man straightened himself and looked balefully at the other. 'You should ask him, saar. He was the one who stormed into my house with his men and started abusing me for no reason at all.'

The other man, who had drifted into a trance after seeing Mutthu, woke up at this point. 'Saar, saar,' he sputtered, overcome with indignation. 'I've known him for twenty-five years. When his daughter was born I was the one by his side to celebrate her arrival as though she were my own daughter. And, now, he doesn't even tell me that he has fixed his daughter's wedding. I have to hear about it from strangers. This is how he rewards our friendship. Twenty-five years, saar.'

'You're a loudmouth,' the first man countered. 'Everything you poke your nose into turns sour.'

'Is this poking my nose? Expecting a friend of twenty-five years to have the courtesy to inform me of such a major event in his life?'

'Even over the last two weeks all you've been doing is complaining about me all day to everybody at the district office. It's common knowledge that you and your circle of good-for-nothing fellows in the Party do nothing but sit around and spread gossip.' Then he sealed his argument by switching to English to pronounce his opinion: 'Bleddy fools!'

'Oho, is this how you feel about your fellow partymen?'

'Yes. I didn't want to take any chances with my daughter's wedding.'

'How dare you put your personal needs over the Party's? Saar, you should punish him for his anti-Party activities.'

Lakshmi watched the proceedings with increasing amusement while Mutthu's expression hardened. She chuckled softly when Mutthu interrupted the squabbling men with the imperious wave of an irritated school matron. He often scolded those around him, even strangers, but now he was really angry. The two men fell silent.

'Is this how you two clowns run our affairs?' Mutthu thundered. 'Instead of thrashing those ruffians at the toddy shop soundly you spend your time hatching plots against one another and indulging in fist fights. And you two wanted to be nominated for that seat? What kind of leaders are you? Idiots! I'm going to throw both of you out of the Party. Now, get out of here!'

The two men fell at Mutthu's feet and pleaded with him to reconsider. 'We're good lifelong friends, saar. It was only a small misunderstanding. You mustn't take it too seriously.' They smiled sheepishly.

But Mutthu turned away and left. The two men hesitated and blinked at Lakshmi who was trying hard to conceal her smile. The first man then walked over to her. 'Amma, I'd be honoured if you and saar attend my daughter's wedding. It's on the fourth of next month. Saar's secretary has all the details. Saar is really angry. But please convince him. It will mean a lot to my family.'

'I'll see what I can do,' she said, and the two men retreated, smiling through the patches of bandage on their faces.

Lakshmi went in looking for Mutthu. 'What charming gentlemen,' she remarked.

Mutthu was not amused. 'Half the time I have to deal with idiotic issues like this.'

'I thought you liked all this. Helps you strengthen your bond with the masses.'

'Stop it, Lakshmi!'

'I think you should attend that man's daughter's wedding. He might start a riot if you didn't.' She let out a peal of laughter in response to his flashing eyes.

'You could help me out,' Mutthu said to her after a long, particularly tiresome and contentious day of drawing up a preliminary list of all possible candidates for the elections. 'A woman's touch will make things go smoother. Your popularity will only enhance our reputation.'

Lakshmi was quiet for a while, thinking not about the

question, but contemplating his face. His pencil-thin moustache quivered. It was shining black. He must have recently dyed it. It looked out of place on his face, for his skin was beginning to wrinkle like a prune. She wished he wouldn't dye his hair. The streaks of grey looked good. They made him look avuncular. Avuncular—perhaps that was exactly what he didn't want to appear. He was the hero, the man who jumped from building to building, chasing crooks, the man who took on fifteen bad guys at a time, the man who set all the evils of society right, the man whose very appearance set hearts a-flutter. Both his moustache and hair were trimmed carefully, nourished with the best oils and gels. She remembered that she was supposed to answer. He was waiting for it, so there was no way to ignore his question.

'But I don't know anything about politics.'

'Nobody knows anything when they enter politics,' he declared. 'All you have to do is make a few speeches and smile even at your enemies. The rest you'll learn along the way.'

'I'm not going to make any speeches or smile when I don't feel like it.'

'No, no, you don't have to. That was just a way of speaking. You don't have to do anything you don't like.'

'But I don't like these petty quarrels and the constant ego clashes. I don't know how you can stand those people day and night. Leave me to my dancing.' Mutthu looked disappointed. Then, more gently, she said, 'Where will I have time for all this?'

'Come and help whenever you can. No expectations. Just come with me every now and then. Just having someone I can trust next to me is enough.'

She did not respond. But a few days later she went with him reluctantly. Sitting cross-legged on cushions covered by freshly laundered white cloth, bolstered by plump pillows, the office-bearers around the room stared at her wordlessly, like stuffed frogs.

Mutthu explained her presence airily. 'I've asked her to help us out.'

They smiled, but Lakshmi noticed their discomfort. She looked around the room. There was Sundarapandian, a portly man about Mutthu's age, who dyed his hair, too. She had met him before. He had been the previous leader's right-hand man. He resented Mutthu's pre-eminence, but had wisely refrained from contesting internal elections to take over the reins. 'I have to handle him carefully,' Mutthu had told her earlier. 'He has a loyal following in the Party. So I have to watch my back.'

Mutthu had also told her about S. Sushila, the sole woman in the group, one of the legislators from the City, a veteran of many elections, who had been in the Party for years. It was rumoured that Sundarapandian had a thing going with her.

There was the economist, who faded in and out of the meeting, bored with all the talk of fund-raising, which was not his forte. There were representatives from every part of the state. All of them spoke warily and self-consciously, glancing at her periodically as if to ascertain if they could trust her with their words. Many exuded the earthy loyalty of those who'd risen from the ranks after years of hard work. Perhaps that was why they were cool to her, resentful of her facile entry into the decision-making body of the Party.

The discussions that day focussed mainly on the issue of finances. It cost money to bring in truckloads of people to election rallies, to plaster the entire state with posters, to erect loudspeakers at every intersection, to distribute food and clothes to the poor, to pay off journalists to write positive articles about them.

As the meeting progressed and Lakshmi continued maintaining her silence, she noticed a perceptible difference in their demeanour. By the end of the meeting the office-bearers were better disposed towards her. She had been right in keeping quiet. They greeted her one by one, said a word or two on their way out. When his turn came, Sundarapandian bowed to her slightly with folded hands and declared in English, 'Welcome, madam! It is a pleasure to have a well-educated, accomplished lady in the Party.'

Lakshmi acknowledged his flattery. But she didn't like his smile. It was leering, insincere.

Later, as Mutthu walked with her to his waiting car, he said, 'Why were you so quiet? You should have said something.'

'What was there for me to say?'

'Plenty!' He gestured in mock exasperation. 'Do you think the others are any better qualified? You just have to talk. You have to make it sound as though you know what you're talking about even if you don't.'

'You're such a cynic!'

Mutthu laughed. 'I'm just worldly-wise.'

'Leave your worldly wisdom outside when you come home. And leave politics there, too. I'm already tired of your involvement with these people.'

Mutthu could coax her. He could make her walk barefoot on a bed of burning charcoal if he wished. Later, when she felt his absence most strongly, she would often wonder how he had managed to do it. He held some sort of power over others, the way, as she would discover, she did. Power that made people want to follow him, power that had mesmerized her without her knowing.

Despite Sundarapandian's presence, she accompanied Mutthu sometimes to the Party's general council meetings. She hated Sundarapandian even though she could not say why. When the opportunity arose he was unduly courteous, never failing to bow slightly, to show humility. She detested those yellow teeth he showed every time he smiled, those gem-studded rings on his fingers, his hairy arms, the ostentatious silk shirts he wore, the bands of vibhuti he smeared on his forehead, those fleshy, ever-hungry lips.

One day, when they were discussing the election manifesto, after a particularly intense debate over whether it would be economically feasible to promise to hand out rice to everyone below the poverty line or not, he turned to her and said in English, 'Madam, you have been so quiet throughout our discussion. What is your esteemed opinion on this topic?'

Lakshmi was caught unawares. She had been listening to the discussion with some interest. The cost the economist had estimated for this scheme was staggering. She instinctively agreed with him that it would be a financial burden the state could not handle. But she could not think of anything intelligent to say. She blinked. 'I don't know . . .' her voice trailed off, and she wished the discussion would move on without her.

'What, madam? You're an educated person. How can you not have ideas when even country bumpkins like us do? Please speak freely: we're like a big family here.'

She shot an angry glance at him. Everybody looked at her and waited for her response. She had to rise to the challenge and say something. She thought furiously. Rice was too expensive because they would have to give a lot of it to make it a meaningful venture. Could they promise something else? Something cheaper? She thought of Mutthu's fondness for tamarind, the acres of tamarind trees he had planted in his estates in Kuppam. Normally it would have elicited a smile, but now it did not seem so absurd to her. Why not tamarind? It plays an especially important part in the poor man's diet. 'One kilo of tamarind,' she announced. 'One kilo per family per month is enough.'

The others were flabbergasted. Sundarapandian laughed. 'With all due respect, madam—' he said, unable to conceal his glee.

But Mutthu, who had been smiling slowly, did not let him finish his sentence. 'What a brilliant idea!' he exclaimed, his eyes widening with delight. 'Tell me: who doesn't use tamarind? It is almost as important as rice, and a lot cheaper to distribute. It is more drought resistant, and best of all, who doesn't like the taste of tamarind?'

Lakshmi, encouraged, looked at the economist who had objected to rice, for approval. He nodded slowly. 'It is certainly more sensible economically than promising rice,' he said in measured tones. 'It also poses fewer logistical problems because we consume far less tamarind than rice. But don't you think one kilo is too much?'

'One kilo is fine,' Mutthu said. 'People don't know its medicinal value. It purifies the blood. It stimulates the pancreas. In the West scientists have found that it even helps fight cancer.'

The others in the room began to nod in approval as well. She looked at Sundarapandian in triumph. He was sullen.

'We're so glad to have you with us, madam,' he told her as the meeting broke up and walked away without waiting for her to respond.

Moments later, walking down the corridor of the Party headquarters, she overheard him talking to some other members in a room. 'Tamarind, she says! Who has heard of anything more absurd than that? People will laugh at us if we tell them we'll give them free tamarind. Does she think we're buffoons? Just because she can speak English like a dorai does she think every idiotic idea of hers will be accepted? But what to do? She has Mutthu in her fist. He'll jump into the ocean if she asks him to. I don't know why he gives so much importance to his mistress, that whore!'

Lakshmi stopped and swivelled on her heels. A whore! That was what he really thought of her. She wasn't all that surprised to hear that; his leers had been indication enough. She had, over the years, grown accustomed to leers and smirks. But nobody had ever said a derogatory word, not even an oblique comment, in her presence. Whether it was out of respect for Mutthu or for her she could not tell. But it galled her to actually hear someone insult her in this way.

She pushed the door open and stormed in. She stood inches away from Sundarapandian, close enough to smell his nicotine breath, and glared. He edged backwards and attempted a smile. He opened his mouth to say something, but she did not give him a chance. She took off a slipper and lashed his face with it. Once, twice, thrice . . . She did not stop. Every time the hard leather sole of her slipper smacked his face it sounded like two bamboo sticks clapping together. She could hear no other sound. Every clap only infuriated her more, and she delivered each successive lash with even greater force. And with each lash he moved a step backwards till he was up against a wall. She did not know how many times she hit him, her arms just flayed about indiscriminately. It was only when Mutthu arrived and pulled her away that she stopped.

As he led her away she became aware that she had been overpowered by a familiar rage. The rage of a nine-year-old girl in her room upstairs staring at the world outside through the prison-like window grilles even as her world within lay sundered. She allowed Mutthu to lead her to the car. Once they were inside he brought his hand close to her eyes. She instinctively evaded it and snarled at him. Only later did she realize that he didn't have chilli powder in his hand; he had simply wanted to close her eyes.

They drove to Kuppam in silence. He had called for his favourite car: a '60 Jaguar, elephant grey with satin window curtains. It had cost him a fortune. The first time he'd tried to impress her with his knowledge of cars he'd explained its features to her. 'It's a Mark IX Saloon, six-cylinder, 3781 cc, 220 bhp engine, wire wheels, power steering, Dunlop disc brakes and Vaumol leather. Only 5984 of these cars with right-hand drive were produced. It's already a classic.'

'What's Vaumol leather?' she'd asked, bored.

'Who knows!' he'd responded, shrugging, for he knew practically nothing about the facts he'd rattled off. He couldn't tell the difference between a four-cylinder and a six-cylinder engine. 'Whatever it is, I'm sure it's something posh and expensive.'

And they'd laughed.

He rarely took this car out and cared for it as one would care for a prized racehorse, but the occasion demanded privacy and comfort. She was still exhausted and had not recovered from her recent fury. He was preoccupied, reticent in his concern. The grand gestures were now replaced with an economy of actions, the inward-looking brooding expression giving way to nervous distraction as he periodically parted the curtain and watched the rural scenery pass by.

He had cancelled all his work for the next few days to be with her. She was dully aware of the whispered confabulations he had held with his aides before coming to her room to tell her that a change of air would do her good. She wasn't sure if she had acquiesced or not. But now, after the muggy, depressing air of the city, the lightness of the countryside gave her back her sense of balance that she had lost upon hearing Sundarapandian's words. She began to like the idea of going away for some time. A change of air to him always meant going to Kuppam and she'd accompanied him there on numerous occasions over the years. She had never been to his home—his real home—in the city. She had never asked to go there out of respect for his wife. So going to his home in his village was the closest she could come to entering his bastion.

As soon as they arrived she set out to wander through the house. The numerous corridors still confused her, there were still many rooms whose purpose she had not understood, but they were familiar and she felt like she belonged in the house. Despite being vacant most of the time the house felt lived in and with every visit she discovered something new. Once it was a well camouflaged cupboard in the wall that she almost didn't notice, inside which was a safe the previous occupants had used to store their jewellery and money. Then there were occasions when she discovered a mahogany writing desk, a tulsi plant in the courtyard, an ornate brass doorknob, a Raja Ravi Varma painting carelessly relegated to a locked, dust-covered room. It was like going to one's grandfather's home for summer vacations and discovering new facets to its personality every year. Except that for Lakshmi her grandfather's home was too painfully familiar, too much like a jail to hold any wonders or nostalgia.

Mutthu had told her a grand story about the origins of the house. It had belonged to the local raja's family and had been built by the last raja's great-uncle. The chettiar had built it in the late nineteenth century for his favourite chettichi in the middle of nowhere because the chronically ill chettichi could not stand the noise and the crowds in the town. He had furnished the house with care, and he had good taste: mahogany and teak furniture from Burma and Thailand, drapes made of the finest muslin, artwork and statuettes from around the world. But the chettichi tore down all the drapes saying it made her house look like a tulukachi's. In all her life she did not use any of the furniture either, for only the dorais ate at dining tables and slept on four-poster beds. For years most of the furniture and paintings remained locked up in the back rooms to be devoured by termites and moisture. She spared the statuettes, that too grudgingly, only because many of them were of gods and goddesses. 'The last raja had no idea what the house contained,' Mutthu told her. 'I rescued as many items as I could. But I still threw away a truckload of rotting furniture and art.'

After a tour of the house Lakshmi went out to the grounds. Acres and acres of land were filled with tamarind trees, most of them planted after Mutthu had purchased the house. At regular intervals were nameplates of the house as if to remind visitors and residents where they were: on the outer walls, at the main gate and side entrances, on the walls of outhouses, even on tamarind trees. All of them shining brass plates, engraved with the same rounded letters, announcing grandly: Annai Illam.

As she wandered through the grounds under the quiet, cool shade of the tamarind trees, she found Mutthu leaning against one of them, chewing a tamarind pod pensively. A servant stood beside him, poised in anticipation of his next command. 'What have you discovered this time?' he asked.

Lakshmi shrugged. She had discovered a cool, dark corner in an empty room where the wall curved just enough so that she could sit down on the floor and lean against it cosily. The room had no windows and was at the end of a long, dark corridor. It had perhaps contained some of the chettiar's paintings, for there was still dampness in the air, a smell of mildewed artwork. She could sit there and contemplate undisturbed if she wished. But it would be her secret refuge and she wasn't going to share it with Mutthu.

Mutthu led her by the arm back to the house. They sat down on the swing in the veranda and he gently pushed it back. As it oscillated to and fro the hinges in the ceiling squeaked. He smiled. 'I'm impressed,' Mutthu said leaning towards her, snorting like a pig. She could see a gold chain around his neck. She had never liked it. Only women were supposed to wear chains. She pulled his collar so that she could not see it. 'I've never seen you cry. Even yesterday, not a teardrop.'

'Did you expect me to be a Draupadi while he pulled off my sari?'

'You're a fiery woman,' he replied and laughed. 'A furnace.' He touched her hand gingerly with his forefinger. 'Oooh! I've burnt myself!' He sucked it.

His levity exasperated her. It usually meant that he was beating about the bush. 'So what is it that you want to tell me?'

His smile disappeared and he sighed. He put his arm around her. 'I met him afterwards and lashed out at him myself. I told him how by insulting you he had insulted me too. It was really pitiful the way he begged for my forgiveness.' Mutthu paused. 'Please allow him to apologize.'

Lakshmi did not respond. The chain was visible once more. Again she pulled his collar over it. He took off the chain and put it in his pocket. 'He said he'll come here,' Mutthu said. 'Give him a chance. He's really ashamed of himself. He won't misbehave again. Just allow him to come and apologize.'

'As long as you don't expect me to ever talk to him again or pardon him.'

'Of course, of course.' Mutthu looked relieved. He took the chain out of his pocket and put it around her neck. 'Looks so much better on you.' He smiled as if urging her to smile back. She did not. She disliked being appeased with trinkets; she felt bribed.

But she let him hold her in his arms and be soothed by the gentle swaying of the swing and the call of a mynah somewhere in the tamarind trees. She wasn't sure if she could do without these baubles: his dependence on her, his ingratiating smiles, his awkward attempts to appease her. Where would she be without them? Who else could she lean on?

Back in the city, Lakshmi woke up in the middle of the night for no reason that she could fathom. Her mind was clear, her thoughts lucid from the very moment she opened her eyes, as though sleep had wiped out all the random noise and distractions that muddle one's brain. Like the moments immediately following her bouts of rage, when there was such stark clarity in her mind that she could observe herself and her thoughts as if reflected in a pool of spring water. She remembered how red the world always appeared around her at such moments, how images of knives dripping with blood, dogs exposing their fangs with bits of human flesh stuck on them, lightning streaking across darkened skies and piercing the earth like daggers were conjured in her mind. In those moments of lucidity there were never the kinds of doubts that usually plagued her, never a reason, a need, to forgive. On the contrary, there was pleasure, a savage, cannibalistic joy in raging, in inflicting pain on herself and others. She had felt that perverse joy while she had hit Sundarapandian.

She shuddered at the recollection. She went to the balcony and looked at everything around her: the shadow of the mango tree, the nightwatchman below, asleep on his stool by the gate, the neighbouring houses illuminated off and on by the flickering street light, the Mercedes that was now virtually hers covered with canvas, a still ghost. It was silent. She would have normally appreciated the peace, but now she found it maddening, for the stillness reminded her of the terrible moments of lucidity. She wanted to hear the noise of the traffic, the insects buzzing around the mango tree, the distant blare of film music on loudspeakers, neighbours shouting at their children, the crowds of sweating, panting Party workers at her door looking for Mutthu. She wanted to fill her head with all their noises, to crowd out her recollections, to muddle her thoughts. She sought comfort in chaos, for her moments of lucidity were scary, and she always emerged from them with the feeling of having lost something, a bit of innocence, perhaps, or a bit of humanity.

For several nights she continued waking up and walking to

the balcony, uncharacteristically seeking noise and comfort in noise. But in vain.

Then one morning she decided she had to do something. She left with Mutthu on a tour of the state. She had to counter her dehumanizing experiences and she could do that only by connecting with others. She was determined to enjoy contact with people the way Mutthu did, for although she made fun of his claims of being a man of the masses, she envied him the ease with which he did so. She had always been squeamish about touching the poor and the dirty. It was a Brahminical, deeply ingrained trait she had inherited from her grandmother. But now she was determined to quash it and reach out without flinching.

'I want to feel what you feel when you're with a crowd,' she said to Mutthu. 'Can you teach me to be one with them?'

Mutthu smiled. 'There's nothing to teach or learn. Just forget yourself and look at others. That's all there is to it.'

She could do that. How many times had she been a nayika, forgetting herself and submitting herself to dance?

From district to district they went, meeting with local politicians, social activists and the crowds that followed them. They stopped at nameless villages on the way. At every stop they were mobbed; crowds would gather around the car even before it had come to a halt, sometimes with someone jumping on to the bonnet and rapping at the windshield urgently till the driver stopped. At first only men gathered around them. But as word of her presence spread, women started appearing, tentatively at first, collecting around her, requesting her to visit their homes. She walked into the villages, past open sewers in which pigs lolled pleasurably, past squawking hens and smelly goats to their mud houses, whose outer walls were studded with round patties of cow dung like ornaments, and she had to remind herself to not flinch. Inside, while her eyes adjusted to the darkness, the women unfurled their best mats and hurriedly made coffee and sweets for her, using up all the sugar and milk they had, proud to have her in their homes. And before she left they'd request her to talk to Mutthu on their behalf for more handpumps or jobs for their sons or the prosecution of a local gang lord.

The days were long, filled with visits and meetings, requests, complaints and random talk. It took her time to get used to the multitudes around her, their chatter, the familiarity with which they spoke to her, their insistent hospitality, their utter confusion and hurt if sometimes, overwhelmed by the occasion, she was curt with them.

But in the evenings, when she and Mutthu shut themselves in a guest house or hotel or a local landlord's home, the day's cacophony acquired meaning, filling her with a warm and soothing feeling.

At one stop a fight broke out among the women who had crowded around her. 'Come to my house, amma,' a woman urged, shoving the others away, grasping her hand and guiding her through the crowd.

'How dare you take her to your place?' shouted another woman. 'Do you even have a mat to offer her?'

'Shut up, Valar!' retorted the first. 'And get out of my way.'

But the second woman was not about to give up so easily. 'Who are you to tell me to shut up?' she screamed and pushed the first woman away. As a fight erupted between the two women, another woman with sunken eyes and uncombed hair startled Lakshmi by touching her hand so lightly that it felt surreptitious. Silently she motioned Lakshmi to follow her. Leaving the women and their respective supporters to argue raucously, Lakshmi followed the quiet one out of curiosity. The woman led her to a hut made of palm fronds with a tarpaulin roof. Inside its dark interior she pointed to a man lying sprawled on the floor, reeking of alcohol. The man opened his eyes momentarily, revealing large eyeballs floating in pools of blood. He grunted peevishly and turned his head before passing out again.

Lakshmi regarded the drunken man. It was obscenely early to be drunk. The woman did not speak. Perhaps she was mute. Perhaps she had communicated all that there was to communicate. Lakshmi didn't know what to say. She hesitated for some moments. 'I'll do what I can,' she stuttered.

The woman touched her arms reverentially and brought her palms together. As Lakshmi prepared to leave, the woman put her hand out, attempting to stop her. 'Stay,' the woman's eyes seemed to say. 'I'm afraid.'

Lakshmi hastily left the hut and rushed towards the car, ignoring invitations and messages from the other women.

'You mustn't take everything to heart,' Mutthu said to her later. 'You can't solve everybody's problems, and you'll only find yourself crushed by their weight.'

'But the woman thought I could do something for her.'

'They all think that. We're supposed to be superhuman. We're supposed to be able to solve everybody's problems. They set themselves up with these expectations.'

'But isn't that because *we* make them believe we can help them?'

'That may be so. But leadership is not about making everybody's lives happy. It's about doing what we can. There are lots of people we're not going to be able to do anything for. For instance, there's no law to prevent that woman's husband from being drunk at ten in the morning.'

But his words made no difference. Something about the woman made her problem so stark, so real. It put her own problems in perspective. It humbled her. There was more to life than what Sundarapandian or someone else thought of her. Surely she could—she *had to*—do something for the woman?

Perversely, the more time she spent thinking about the woman, the lighter she felt, for her mind was getting cluttered again and there was no room for her own thoughts. It was comfort clutter.

A few days later at a press conference attended by journalists not only from all over the state but also from all parts of the country, Mutthu announced that Lakshmi had officially joined the Party and would be a special advisor to him and the rest of the leadership on all matters pertaining to the campaign. Along with him on the dais, behind a confusing array of microphones, sat Sundarapandian, still sullen.

One journalist from an English-language periodical from Bombay, to the delight of everybody in the room, asked cheekily, 'So, Mr Sundarapandian, how does it feel to have the woman who beat you with her chappal share campaign responsibilities with you?'

After the laughs had died down, Sundarapandian, without a change in his expression, said, 'You journalists have the habit of exaggerating everything. There were no slippers involved, no beating. She is an honourable woman, and I am a respected senior member of the Party. There was a small misunderstanding between us, but we have already sorted it out. In fact, I welcome her to the decision-making body of the Party and will give her my whole-hearted support.'

The man had been punished enough. Lakshmi interjected, 'Mr Sundarapandian is correct. We are on good terms and anything you're told otherwise is false.'

Sundarapandian, surprised by her spontaneous statement, was visibly relieved. He bent towards her and held her hand. A smile broke out on his face. Cameras began to click furiously at this juncture.

She looked around uncomfortably. What had she got herself into? Why had she allowed Mutthu to coax her again into accepting campaign responsibilities? 'You're a natural campaigner,' he'd said to her at the end of the tour. 'How happy you look, my dear.'

The journalists then wanted to know if she would contest a seat herself.

'No,' she declared hastily. 'I'm not a politician. I'm simply helping the Party in its election campaign.'

Lakshmi noticed Sundarapandian's smile widen. The journalists nodded solemnly, approvingly, it seemed to her. Their attitudes now changed; they were more respectful. A non-politician working for a political party. Somehow it sounded more respectable even to her. It had the connotations of trustworthiness, uprightness, dignity and principle. One could help formulate a party's policies without having to make unpleasant compromises to ensure continuation of one's popular appeal. One did not have to indulge in back-room negotiations and skullduggery. One was above all the crassness that characterized the typical politician like Sundarapandian.

The next day the newspapers gave significant coverage to the press conference. They hailed Lakshmi's induction into the inner circles of the Party. They all saw her entry as a step towards taking deviousness out of politics. Moreover, she had guts, for, despite the public denial, it was apparent that they believed in the rumours regarding her treatment of Sundarapandian. 'A breath of fresh air to blow away the noxious miasma of politics,' claimed one newspaper editorial.

Her misgivings were somewhat allayed as she read the front-page articles. They were just as gratifying as the praises she received from dance critics.

That evening, feeling flush, she lay in Mutthu's arms when he said, 'I thought you handled yourself quite well at the press conference. That was very gracious and diplomatic of you.'

'I hope Sundarapandian doesn't think I've forgiven him.'

'He's a veteran. He's too shrewd.' Mutthu paused for a few moments. 'Now that you have had your victory, I need to give him something to pacify him. I think I'll give him the parliament ticket he so desperately wants.'

Lakshmi shrugged. She didn't care. 'Give him two if he wants. The longer he's away the better.'

The Curtain Rises

Curtains. There were curtains everywhere she looked, draped one over the other, covering windows, doors, shelves and even in the little doll's house in the glass cabinet. Their variety astonished her more than their numbers: thick opaque ones, translucent ones, sheer ones, patterned, plain, frilly, pleated, embroidered, laced, in cotton, silk, chintz and muslin. Lakshmi half expected someone to peel the curtains away one by one as in the dance of the seven veils.

She could see them only because Surya had parted the thick window curtains a little to allow sunlight in. And even that skein of light vanished when Gloria entered the room and pulled the curtains together. It was only then as they sat in the darkness that it became apparent how equally dark the rest of the house was. From the outside it had looked like any other posh house: high compound walls topped with shards of glass; the black iron gate manned by a watchman, with a 'Beware of Dogs' sign on it; a decorative red-tiled Iberian roof; two lupine Alsatians tethered to their doghouses along the long concrete driveway. But inside the house looked drab; it had an air of secrecy. Lakshmi suspected that the curtains were meant to keep out prying eyes.

It was surprising that even in such a dark house Surya could continue smiling and looking bright, as if he carried a vial of magical sunlight—as his name implied—everywhere he went, which made people take notice of him. He was short and stocky, and had sharp, precise features on a round face. His mannerisms were languorous, and he moved about with a permanent smile and the self-assurance of the wealthy. He sat with one leg over another, his foot dangling in mid-air, his hands spread along the back of the sofa, looking expansive and comfortable. He laughed at all of Mutthu's jokes and even his complaints sounded good-humoured.

'What, saar,' he said, 'we live right on the coast and yet there's no water in our taps. Water, water everywhere, but not a drop to drink, as they say. Year after year they promise to build a desalination plant, and year after year they ration water like a precious commodity. Useless fellows! Who takes interest in these matters? Who cares if we have water or not?'

The air-conditioner hummed loudly in the background. Even if it hadn't, Lakshmi wouldn't have heard Gloria come in and stand beside her, for she came in soundlessly like an apparition. And when she said hello, inches away, in her voice that sounded muffled like an echo, Lakshmi jumped out of her skin.

Surya chuckled. 'She has that effect on everybody,' he explained, but stopped short to make room for her beside him.

Looking at the two of them beside each other, Lakshmi couldn't help noticing how dissimilar they were. Gloria was not at all like anything she had imagined. Her complexion was pasty, pallid, like weathered marble. She was thin and tall, and had she not been wearing a sari she would have appeared angular as well. On her broad forehead was a tiny pottu, visible only because of its contrast with her skin. Her black hair was so tightly held together in the back with a pin that the roots on her forehead pulled at the skin. Her expression was severe, humourless.

They had met in Milan when Surya had gone there on business. She was working for a company Surya wanted to do business with. She was asked to show him around town because she spoke good English. And Surya duly fell in love with her when she had let him lean over and kiss her awkwardly while they sat at the foot of Vittorio Emmanuele's statue in front of the Duomo. It must have been an odd sight, for the pigeons in the square fluttered away excitedly, the crowd turned and looked at them curiously, a couple of straw-haired gypsy women who were approaching them for money changed their minds and walked away.

They married soon afterwards, twice: once in an ancient church in her native Turin, the second time in an equally old temple whose eight hundred pillars resounded with the echoes of their wedding chants.

Surya was a self-made businessman. He came from a traditionally wealthy family that owned a lot of land. In addition, his grandfather had made a fortune in shipping, with vessels making calls on ports on five continents. But his father inherited very little of that wealth. Surya's older uncles had swindled his father of his share of the shipping business, leaving him only with a lot of uncultivable land in the dry district of Pudupettai. But, unlike his father, Surya was shrewd and ambitious. He dropped out of college and began making money in a variety of business ventures. By the time he met Gloria he had made a modest amount of money. But after marriage his wealth grew phenomenally, mainly due to his association with Mauro Tedeschi, his Italian business partner who was a childhood friend of Gloria's.

Mauro Tedeschi arrived late that evening. He had visited the tanneries on the banks of the Shakadai that afternoon. It was their latest venture, and he had wanted to see the tanning process for himself. It was an oddity: a man in designer clothes who reeked of sewage. Nobody who went within a mile of the tanneries came back without carrying their abominable stench. And Mauro Tedeschi had worn gumboots and gambolled in knee-high muck like a naked child, delightedly watching the tanners at work. And yet, despite the stench (that would not leave even after repeated baths and application of unguents and cologne), he looked regal. He exuded confidence, and if it weren't for his refinement, which was immediately apparent, he would have perhaps appeared a tad arrogant. His luxurious hair was black and sleek. He had an aquiline nose, and animated, intelligent eyes. He was handsome. *Too* handsome. Lakshmi would much later be fond of telling him:

'If you weren't so handsome I'd have fallen in love with you.' And he would laugh uncertainly, not understanding Lakshmi's private joke.

'What fantastic leather you have in your country,' he said, his eyes lighting up with enthusiasm. 'So cheap, so durable. And what fine workmanship!'

Surya interjected at this point. 'But, saar, these tanners are so unreliable. The way they do business it seems like they don't want to make money. If their wives sneeze they take the day off, if some distant relative gets married they take a whole week off. In the meantime European distributors pester Mauro for their shipments. Half our time is spent on just finding out when we'll get the stuff. Lazy fellows from top to bottom!'

Mutthu nodded sympathetically and Surya continued, encouraged, 'And then the red tape to get an export permit. Let's not even talk about that. I've been trying to start a factory to manufacture leather garments and handbags, but my application has been pending for years. I even said I don't want any government-sanctioned land, but who cares? At this rate how can we do business with foreign countries?' Surya looked unhappy for once.

Mutthu listened gravely, knowing that he had to say something. 'If I get elected, my top priority would be to promote business,' he said finally in a campaign tone. 'People like you will be taken care of.'

Surya and Mauro Tedeschi were delighted. They raised their wine glasses to toast Mutthu's victory.

'To a new era in the history of this state!' proclaimed Surya.

'To prosperity worldwide!' Mauro Tedeschi added, not wanting to be left behind in expressing grandiose sentiments.

Gloria, silent all through this conversation, remained in the background, intently gazing at everybody. Something told Lakshmi that Gloria's mind was furiously at work, that she, not Surya, was behind this meeting. As if to confirm this, when, after dinner and a couple of liqueurs and cigars, they rose to leave, Mauro Tedeschi kissed Gloria on her cheeks and thanked her. 'Where would we be without your ideas!'

'What ideas was he referring to?' Lakshmi asked Mutthu on their way home.

Mutthu shrugged. 'Maybe the dinner meeting?'

'Speaking of which, what was that all about?'

'Just a social visit, what else? Surya is a young and ambitious businessman. He's a supporter of the Party.'

'Are you sure they don't have a hidden agenda?'

Mutthu shrugged again. 'Maybe they do. But don't we *all* have hidden agendas?'

Days later, at a party, Mauro Tedeschi, garrulous as ever, deftly and rapidly jumping from one topic to another, his mind apparently teeming with all sorts of thoughts, leaned over and said, 'Dim the lights and she'll be gone.' He guffawed. It took Lakshmi a moment to understand the joke. 'When we were young we used to call her La Sindone, The Shroud.' She laughed. For there was something mysterious, even spooky, about Gloria. Her features, sallow, shadowy, unclear, undersculpted, except for the eyes, did have the effaced quality of the real Shroud. And when she wore dark glasses and covered her hair with a scarf, her face degenerated to a blur, a colourless oval. The Shroud of Turin! 'But she's such a dear person! One has to look past her appearance to get to know her. She's the reason behind Surya's success. She's the brains behind his ideas. When we were kids I wouldn't have imagined her doing this. She was so devout and unworldly that we used to think she'd become a nun. But look at her now,' he said, pointing to her rich Kancheepuram sari. He then called her with mock deference: 'Suora! Suor' Gloria!'

Gloria and Surya walked over to them. 'You've been telling her about my nickname, haven't you?' Gloria asked Mauro Tedeschi in an admonishing tone.

'Ah, Gloria! How could I not tell her about the fun we used to have when we were young?'

Gloria looked unperturbed. It was interesting the way Mauro Tedeschi and Gloria behaved with each other. There was that comfortable familiarity that can exist only between childhood friends, a familiarity that comes from knowing and understanding each other's foolishness, indiscretions and dreams. There was that certain level of taking each other for granted. But when they spoke it was apparent that they were genuinely fond of each other. This, despite, or perhaps because of, the fact that Mauro Tedeschi often made fun of her in ways adults normally don't tease each other, sometimes with what might appear to be cruelty to the outsider.

As the conversation veered off towards cars, Lakshmi fell silent, listening to the men only intermittently, avoiding eye contact with Gloria in order to discourage her from starting a conversation. Mutthu was boasting about having driven the maharaja of Mysore's Bugatti once. And Mauro Tedeschi hooted. 'Signor!' he exclaimed. 'How fortunate! What a classic car! But I prefer our modern cars myself. Ferrari is coming out with a new model next year. Testarossa—Redhead—they're going to call it. I've seen its design. Che bella!'

'Ah, Ferrari,' Mutthu responded wistfully. 'I've always wanted to own an Italian sports car.'

'You should come to visit us in Italy. I'll get you behind the wheel of as many Ferraris and Maseratis as you want.'

'Can you get me entry into a racetrack?' Mutthu's voice rose with excitement.

'Of course. I'll take you to the tracks.'

'We don't have a single racetrack here. Not one. And on our highways, if we reach a hundred we think we're flying a plane.'

Lakshmi moved away.

All the way home Mutthu remained excited like a child. He talked on and on about race cars and jet-powered engines and Alfa Romeos and Aston Martins. Lakshmi interrupted him, 'Can you stop your car madness for a minute? I don't think you should associate yourself with them. I don't trust them. Especially her.'

Mutthu laughed. 'They're harmless business people. And she doesn't even speak.'

'But that's the problem. She says so little.'

'What's wrong with that?'

'Nothing, usually. But she's the brains behind those two. I don't have a good feeling about her.'

Mutthu clicked his tongue irritably. 'Stop imagining things. She's a perfectly nice and quiet person. And even if she is the brains behind them, what's wrong?' He closed his eyes, signalling that he didn't want to carry on this conversation any more.

Lakshmi's suspicions deepened further when a few days later one of Surya's employees brought a bag full of money to the Party headquarters. It was an ordinary cloth bag, the kind that people took to the vegetable market, yellow, with the name of a provision store printed on it in bright red. Surya had already made a contribution to the Party. So Lakshmi was astonished not only to see another large contribution from Surya, but also the casual manner in which it was delivered. Perhaps that was precisely the idea: to not draw attention.

'I just don't understand,' she said to Mutthu. 'Why is he giving the Party so much money? It's not merely a campaign contribution. Even I can tell that.'

'This is an investment for him,' Mutthu responded. 'He's a businessman. Besides, it could be from that Italian fellow.'

'What does *he* stand to gain?'

Mutthu regarded her for a moment as though he wanted to make sure he had heard the question correctly. Then he chose to keep quiet.

'Isn't it wrong?'

'What's wrong? Where's the law against making contributions to political parties?' Mutthu looked irritated as though she was being childish and purposely difficult. It wasn't as though she did not understand all this. But she wanted a validation of her understanding from him. She wanted him to spell out everything, to leave nothing to inference. But Mutthu was in no mood to explain. He turned his attention elsewhere. It was just like him to not be bothered by moral ambiguities.

For her things had to be either right or wrong, and anything else was just confounding. Perhaps, she reflected, worldly wisdom lay in allowing some matters to remain ambiguous, unquestioned and unanswered

On several occasions when Lakshmi ran into Gloria at chance encounters or at the Party's functions she would go the other way. Gloria's presence unnerved her. The unwavering gaze, those dark, shadowy eyes hidden deep inside their sockets that pierced everything and unravelled every secret, those black eyebrows, that lipless mouth opening ever so slightly when she spoke. But once Gloria managed to corner her and she had no choice but to indulge in small talk.

'I admire your dancing,' Gloria said. 'Ever since I watched you dance I've wanted to learn to dance, too. But Surya only laughs every time I bring up the topic. You tell me, is it too late for me to take lessons?'

Lakshmi shook her head out of politeness. She could not see Gloria dancing. She was too monotonic in her expression.

'There's grace in your dance. I see the same grace in the way you interact with people.' Lakshmi was surprised to hear that. 'It must be hard to always be that way especially when you meet so many people.'

'I'm learning from Mutthu.' Lakshmi couldn't help being pleased that her efforts had been noticed.

'Do you plan on going everywhere with him on campaign?'

'I don't know yet. I'm not even thinking about it.'

'It can't be easy, eating no two meals at the same place, spending every night in a different room, meeting all kinds of people, and still looking fresh, energetic and leader-like.'

'Yes, I hope I can find a reason to stay back.'

'Don't say that. I think it's wonderful what you've done so far. Your presence will make a big difference.'

'That's what Mutthu also says. But, you know, I'd rather—'

'I also think it's wonderful that the Party has begun providing meals for the poor.'

Lakshmi herself hadn't been particularly enthusiastic about it. 'It's an election gimmick,' she'd told Mutthu. 'Of course,' he had responded candidly. 'You have to during elections. Otherwise people will vote for our opponents. Look at it this way: because of this gimmick at least a lot of hungry people are getting to eat something.' She hadn't disputed that. But she had remained unconvinced. And so Gloria's praise surprised her. 'But it's only for a short while,' she said.

'Yes,' Gloria responded. 'I was thinking that as well. How long can you provide meals? Besides, a meal is useful for about four hours. And then what? Have you considered something more long-lasting? Like clothes, shelter, training?'

Lakshmi liked this line of thinking. 'We can't start training programmes or build houses that easily. But clothes . . .'

'Yes, a sari would remind a woman of her benefactor for as long as she wears it.'

Lakshmi mulled over the idea. The more she thought about it, the more she liked it. She walked over to Mutthu.

'What a wonderful idea!' Mutthu hooted when she told him. 'She's a shrewd woman. We could use more of her ideas.'

Lakshmi felt a tinge of regret at having told Mutthu about it. She looked for Gloria in the crowd. But Gloria had receded into the background. Silent, almost undetectable. As though she wasn't even there. As though she hadn't spoken those words at all. Simply minding her business.

The saris arrived within a week. They were from a textile mill owner Surya knew. This first batch was the mill owner's contribution to the Party. Surprised at the speed with which it was delivered, Lakshmi asked Surya about it.

'That fellow already had these in stock,' he replied.

'So many?'

'Mass production. They were sitting in his godowns for a long time.'

'How long?'

'Oh, I don't know,' Surya said vaguely.

Lakshmi picked up one of the saris from the pile. She felt the fabric. It was coarse cotton, the kind used in cheap lungis. It felt coarser than the sample the mill owner had presented to her a few days ago. She handed it over to the delivery man and had him unfurl it in front of her. The sari was stiff with starch. It was clear to her that the weaving was shoddy: in some places the threads were sparse and crooked, in others they were thick and knotted. The mango patterns on the sari were also uneven: if one had a thicker eye, another had a sharper curve, and the third had fewer whorls on top.

'It smells like it's been in a godown for months,' Lakshmi commented.

The delivery man coughed. 'It's possible that he had trouble selling this batch to the wholesalers.'

'So it's rejected material.' She looked at Surya questioningly.

Surya looked at the delivery man balefully. He shifted his weight from one foot to another. 'I won't pretend that this is very good quality. But the women who're going to get this will be happy.'

There was not much she could do. They had come for free and she couldn't possibly reject a gift, especially one they had solicited. She would have to make the best use of them.

So with great pomp a few days later Lakshmi and Mutthu inaugurated the free sari scheme in Kuppam. A pandal was erected on the premises of Annai Illam, festooned with marigolds and streamers. There were hordes of Party officials and workers, local bureaucrats and policemen walking about here and there in the compound with an air of importance. Journalists and photographers had turned up in large numbers. All the poor women from Kuppam and the surrounding areas had been rounded up by the Party workers and were made to stand in a queue outside the gates of Annai Illam, which were not opened yet. A large crowd had gathered on the road and in the open patch of land across it.

As the air became heavier with expectation, someone in the crowd outside shouted over the other voices, 'Mutthu vazhgai! Lakshmi vazhgai!'

Taking the cue from him, the crowd began chanting as well. Then the women in the line joined them. Even the Party officials inside the compound lent their voices. Soon the chants rose to a crescendo. 'Vazhgai, vazhgai, Mutthu vazhgai!'

Mutthu, Lakshmi, Sundarapandian and a dozen local dignitaries got on to the low dais under the pandal. The Party's local chief grabbed the microphone and ordered the crowd to be quiet. Unidirectional speakers had been installed on the wooden poles of the pandal and outside the compound in clover-shaped bunches of four. With a sense of great self-importance and solemnity, the local chief then intoned, clutching the microphone with one hand and raising the other in the air. 'It gives me great honour to welcome our supreme leaders Mutthu and Lakshmi to Annai Illam!'

'Yo!' someone in the crowd outside shouted. 'Who are you to welcome them to their own house?'

The crowd twittered and the speaker was taken aback. Clearly he had still to get used to heckling. With the absurdity of his words dawning on him, he laughed sheepishly. Then, bravely, he garlanded the three dignitaries on the dais. Being the consummate speaker that he was, he quickly recovered from the embarrassment and gave a speech. He hailed Mutthu, he hailed Lakshmi, he hailed Sundarapandian. With such leaders they had nothing to worry about, he assured everyone. Victory would be theirs.

Half an hour later he handed the microphone to Mutthu, who was greeted by lusty cheers. An adolescent in a flaming red shirt unbuttoned down to his stomach in the manner of film heroes stood on the compound wall, straddling the barbed wires on it. He took the opportunity to sing one of Mutthu's hit songs. He flicked his long hair nonchalantly from his forehead, mimicking Mutthu's style. 'Oh, my beloved,' he crooned, his hands spread out, 'the birds are singing, the bees are frolicking, but where are you?'

The crowd cheered and egged him on to sing the entire song. And he readily obliged.

'This young man reminds me of myself as a young man,' Mutthu shouted into the microphone when the man was done. 'I used to roam the streets of Kuppam too, dreaming of becoming an actor. Like him I was—and still am—one of you, a man of the streets who has risen to this position through hard work, because of the love of my people and my mother's blessings.' The young man jumped down with an ecstatic smile. He had had his day.

As Mutthu continued speaking, people craned their necks to see him. Many had climbed over the wall or were perched on trees outside the compound like an army of monkeys. They listened to him in rapt attention. Oration came to him easily. As an actor he was known for his delivery, and special monologues were written for him to accentuate his rhetorical skills. His experience with long monologues came handy now. His intonations were just right, the modulations in his voice apt. There was emotion in his words, drama in his gestures. 'I am now your humble servant, and I will do all I can to provide young people like him with all the opportunities they deserve. What will the other parties do for you?' he asked the crowd. 'Nothing! Nothing!' the crowd roared back. 'As for the fools who go around with the rising sun as their symbol, do they even know in which direction the sun rises? In America there's a party that has a donkey as its symbol. These rising sun fellows shouldn't even field donkeys as their candidates, because a braying donkey makes more sense than they do.' The crowd broke into laughter. 'Ask one of them what his party stands for and he'll answer—henh-uhhh-henh-uhhh-henh-uhhh!' the crowd brayed and laughed uproariously.

When he finished speaking, the crowd clambered over the wall and rushed towards him. They wanted to touch his hand, to hold it for a moment so that they might imbue at least a little of his greatness. Mutthu climbed down from the dais and held his hand out to the crowd. They fell over each other to reach him. In his inimitable style he touched everyone he could reach.

Then the policemen rounded up the intruders and escorted them out of the compound. Through a smaller gate, the women, who had been waiting patiently, were allowed in, between the ropes that marked the path from the gate to the dais. Several female Party workers, clad in their best saris and jewellery, their hair dripping with jasmine, their faces and necks heavily powdered, came up to help Lakshmi distribute the saris. Surya and Gloria sat on steel chairs under a tamarind tree, monitoring the scene. The owner of the mill ordered his men to arrange the saris in piles next to the dais. One by one the poor women came to receive their saris. There were old women hobbling with sticks, girls who were too young to wear a sari, mothers with little children sitting on their hips, pregnant women heaving under the weight of their babies. They were all clad in shabby saris and rags. Every one of them received a starch-stiff sari made of lungi cloth with mango patterns on it in pink and red and maroon. 'Go, ma,' the policemen shouted, pushing the women away, 'you can examine the sari once you're outside.' Some women touched Lakshmi's hand as they accepted their saris and wiped their eyes with the rags they were wearing. One of them fell at Lakshmi's feet and said, 'Amma, now I have something to wear to my daughter's wedding.'

Lakshmi paused to look at her retreating figure. 'Where is your daughter?'

'At home, amma, blushing,' the woman replied with a smile. 'Her wedding is tomorrow.'

'Here,' Lakshmi said, handing another sari to her. 'Take one for her as well.'

The woman fell at Lakshmi's feet again.

The owner of the textile mill grinned, his head bobbing from side to side, for this event was clearly a success, and said eagerly, 'Yes, yes, take that for her. She'll look pretty in that sari. Pretty as a bride.' And he laughed with glee.

Lakshmi walked down the general ward of the government hospital. Rows of steel cots with peeling paint and wafer-thin mattresses. Bags of IV fluids hanging like bats from hooks, tubes snaking their way into outstretched arms. Some family members were wailing, others dazed, were staring at those lying on the cots. Lakshmi hated the smell of hospitals. But she had to come today because Mutthu was out of town campaigning. The supervising doctor walked beside her, a crowd of Party workers and journalists following them.

'Twenty have already died, madam,' he said. 'There are forty more here.'

'What was in the arrack?'

'Rat poison.'

'Why would anybody add rat poison to brew alcohol?'

The doctor shrugged. 'Could have simply been a mistake. Or perhaps the brewer thought a little poison would add kick to the drink and miscalculated the amount.'

'Rat poison!' She still couldn't believe it.

'This time it's rat poison, the next time it will be something else. Happens regularly somewhere or the other. Madam, you won't believe the amount of destruction arrack is causing our people. Only a few are lucky enough to die.'

One of the victims retched violently, flailing his arms, pulling at the tubes. He had to be restrained. In the neighbouring cot another man slept with his eyes open, his eyeballs ready to pop out of his sallow, unshaven, wrinkled face.

Lakshmi remembered the silent woman who had taken her to see her husband. She remembered the woman's wordless plea, her own confused reaction, her helplessness. What could she have done to help the woman then? What could she do now? What could anyone do for the forty men and women lying unconscious in the hospital fighting the effects of spurious liquor?

She remembered reading a feature in a magazine about a group of women who were fighting to keep arrack out of their village. Because the men spent most of their earnings on arrack, it was ruining their families, reducing them to abject poverty and making their men slaves to alcohol. Fed up of their men, these women had taken matters into their own hands and had forced the owner of the liquor store to shut his shop and leave the village. She wasn't sure this success could be replicated elsewhere. Perhaps the women who had banded together were unusually strong willed. Perhaps the owner of the arrack store was essentially a good man and had left because he sympathized with their point of view. Or perhaps he was weak and chose not to stand up to them even though he hadn't done anything illegal. Besides, their victory could turn out to be temporary until someone else decided to set up shop. The solution to this problem should not have to rely on vigilante intervention—she had to do something.

She brought this issue up at the Party's next general council meeting. They were to finalize the ten-point programme that would form their election manifesto. She proposed that the Party promise to ban country liquor if elected to power. She looked around and was surprised to sense disapproval. Sundarapandian objected to it, of course, and was quiet for some time.

'Why arrack?' he burst out finally. 'Why arrack, I say? What's wrong if people who toil all day drink half a glass of arrack to ease their hurting bodies? Are we communists or something? It is arrack today, it will be cigarettes tomorrow and milk the day after.'

The economist looked doubtful, too. He said, 'Banning country liquor will cut the state's revenues drastically. As it is the budget is in deficit. Besides, prohibition only encourages corruption.'

'Exactly!' exclaimed Sundarapandian triumphantly. 'That's what I'm saying! Only people who work hard with their hands know what it is to come home with every bone in your body threatening to fall off.'

Mutthu looked surprised at the ferocity with which Sundarapandian objected. 'Sundarapandian-saar,' he said, trying to placate him. 'It will appeal to all women. It's only a manifesto. You know better than everybody here that not everything in it will be implemented.'

Sundarapandian calmed down a bit. The others, too, appeared less agitated. Mutthu had that effect on people. A few words here, a few words there was all he needed to say to allay their fears.

Now Lakshmi had to say something to drive home

the advantage. 'Remember,' she said, avoiding Sundarapandian's gaze. 'Half the voters are women. Even those who normally don't vote will do so if we include this. I can feel it every time I meet women across the state. How many of the women who come for free saris do so because their husbands have spent all their money on arrack?' She looked at Sushila, who was hesitant at first. After a moment Sushila nodded, almost imperceptibly, as if she wished nobody would see her. Lakshmi warmed to her for being brave enough to express her opinion; Sushila's nod was encouragement enough. 'You need to be a woman to understand another woman's pain. All you men think about is money and votes. It is women who think about food and clothing and medicines for the family. They're the ones who are most affected when their husbands squander their money, to see their children drink thin kanji before going to sleep at night. We'll pay a heavy price if we ignore their feelings.'

Sushila looked up now. 'Yes,' she said. 'What she says is correct.'

Sundarapandian looked indignant. 'If everybody has made up their minds, what is there for me to say?' he said.

'No, no, saar,' Mutthu interjected. 'We haven't decided yet. That's why we're even talking about it. We want your opinion.'

'I'll agree to this only if you promise not to implement it after the elections,' he said with renewed vigour.

Mutthu nodded. 'Don't worry. There are enough things as it is to keep us busy for two terms.'

Lakshmi wanted to protest, but she realized what Mutthu was doing. Only a few days earlier he had told her, 'When fighting battles, advance one step at a time. If your opponent loses all his ground in one shot he's likely to be a lot more displeased than if he lost an inch at a time.'

The ten-point programme looked impressive:

1. Strive for social equality.
2. Eradicate poverty.
3. Increase irrigation to drought-prone areas.

4. Prohibit the production and sale of illicit country liquor, i.e., arrack.
5. Food subsidies for families under the poverty line.
6. Subsidies to export-oriented industries like leather and textiles.
7. Fight corruption.
8. Build more rural schools.
9. Improve health care for women and children.
10. Stabilize prices on essentials.

Later, on the way home, Mutthu sighed contentedly. 'You argued your case very effectively today,' he said, taking Lakshmi's hand. 'Explaining it in terms of votes and constituencies is exactly what you need to do with these lifelong politicians. That's all they understand. For a woman who calls herself a non-politician you've begun thinking like one. You're as shrewd as Gloria.'

Lakshmi protested. She took her hand away and admonished him for making everything look crass.

Mutthu leant over, tapped her on the nose and smiled indulgently. 'Don't fool yourself for too long.'

She slapped his hand away. 'You don't know anything,' she said sharply and ended the conversation. But she knew he was right. She had not realized that she had been thinking of these issues in terms of their popularity and votes. Was she turning into a politician herself? Perhaps people were innately political in their thinking. Wasn't the will to succeed, to achieve one's goal, inherently selfish and, hence, political? Perhaps the very instinct for survival was a political act.

The next morning she began her previously scheduled press conference with a vehement declaration: 'I'm here simply as the spokeswoman of the Party. Please note that I'm not even a registered member.'

She repeated this wherever she went, and to her increasing annoyance Mutthu laughed at her whenever she brought it up. 'Wipe that smile off your face,' she hissed at him once. 'It makes you look silly.'

But Mutthu continued to smile . . .

★

The run-up to the elections was an exciting time because it gave us a new pastime. Devaki, Ragini and I improvised a little game Nasser Sharif had devised to teach Ragini how to read when she was little. He'd open up his bureau and take out newspaper cuttings from the old days, a few at a time, and spread them on the floor. Then he and Ragini would bend over them and count the number of instances they saw his or her great-grandfather's name in them. 'Five,' he'd say, and she'd squeal, 'Six! I saw one more than you.' And he'd counter, 'That's because I haven't read this column yet. That's eight. Now, how about you?' And she'd look crestfallen till she saw a few more instances and then would jump with joy. 'Ten! Thatha, I win!'

We'd taken to counting the number of times we saw Lakshmi either in person (from afar) on the campaign trail, or in a photograph. We each had different reasons for wanting to see her. Like avid birdwatchers we took our binoculars wherever we went just in case an opportunity presented itself. Framed within the incomplete, overlapping circles of the viewing area, we watched her feed the hungry and distribute saris and sometimes lungis to the poor, happy just to get a glimpse of her.

The entire state was plastered with posters of the Party's candidates. Large cut-outs of Mutthu and the local candidates, abnormally cherubic, larger than life, always smiling benevolently, appeared at strategic locations. Often Lakshmi was featured with Mutthu in these cut-outs. Ragini took to counting the number of posters and cut-outs she saw of her mother.

I made it a point to attend all the rallies in the City, and sometimes took Devaki and Ragini along. I never entered the press enclosure because it was always near the podium. Instead, I sat with the crowd in the dust or on pavements. Sometimes people around me chanted slogans of support, sometimes they were bored and fidgety. Sometimes these rallies were occasion for celebration for the workers of the party and they'd arrive well ahead of time with bottles of liquor and drink till they were in the mood to make merry. And then they'd sing raucously and dance, bottles in hand, handkerchiefs tied around their necks and heads like bandanas, while vendors selling Mutthu's posters, groundnut, sundal, and sticky, fly-infested sweets hovered around them, running a brisk business. Lakshmi only attended a few of these rallies and never addressed the crowds. Instead, she sat on the dais with the other leaders and folded her hands to greet the people. Through my binoculars I could see her close at hand, and sometimes I would forget that she was far away and reach out for her, only to brush against the back of the man sitting in front of me who would swat my hand away thinking it was an insect.

Lakshmi and Mutthu complemented each other. He attracted the masses with his popularity and earthy histrionics, she the press and the educated with her articulate, urbane, intelligent ways. She met the press almost daily. She made all the formal announcements, fielded questions, articulated the Party's policies and stand on various issues (not that there were many). The media liked her photogenic face, her polished sentences, her stance as a non-politician amongst career politicians. So my colleagues forgave her more easily than they did the others, even when she made mistakes or could not answer unexpected questions raised by the opponents.

Periodically Devaki, Ragini and I met to compare notes. I'd share photographs and paper clippings and audio cassettes of press conferences and anecdotes. Devaki would always smile proudly. 'She's so beautiful,' Ragini once said while we watched her on the evening news on the television, unaware that she herself was just as beautiful. ('Even more beautiful than her mother,' Nasser Sharif had insisted once. 'Dark and beautiful.')

At the end of the day I'd always be the one with the most number of sightings to talk about, and the other two would look at me with envy. Ragini even pretended to resent the advantage I had over them. I never derived any pleasure from winning this sorry little game of ours. But I continued to play it to humour Ragini and Devaki till I realized that they were doing the same thing, till we realized that we were equally pathetic in our efforts to make up for Lakshmi's absence.

★

Mutthu took to arriving at campaign stops in a rented helicopter, which suited his hectic schedule as well as his love of histrionics, as he descended from the sky in the belly of a giant bird. Crowds of peasants watched in awe and cheered when he walked out of the craft, keeping time with the staccato rhythm of the rotors.

'It's all part of image-building,' he said.

'Any more image-building and people will think you're a god,' Lakshmi countered. He laughed and did not deny it.

Lakshmi, always looking fresh and beautiful in her carefully chosen saris, accompanied Mutthu to most of these campaign stops. Ever since she had announced the family-friendly points of the Party's manifesto, women clutching their children began arriving in large numbers to her campaign stops. Her popularity grew steadily, so much so that at one campaign stop she was mobbed more than Mutthu. As the women shoved their babies towards her so that she could touch them, Mutthu stood aside in amusement. 'At this rate you'll become more popular than me,' he told her and laughed.

But there were times when Mutthu went alone either to meet delegations or to campaign in remote villages. One of the delegations he met once was of government employees trying to settle their disputes with the government. For months the employees of the state's electricity board had been murmuring darkly about their salaries and the union representing them had demanded an increase in salary. The minister whom they had approached kept vacillating between agreeing to their demands and taking a tough line with them.

For months the union had threatened to strike, but the government had managed to avert it every time with appeasing talk. Ever since the date for the elections had been announced, the union leader's demands had become more insistent, his threats vociferous. When the government failed to meet his demands, the employees went on strike. For days electricity was erratic. Transformers that had burst were not repaired, downed electric poles were not put back in place, wiring of new areas was suspended. Factories closed down, electric trains were cancelled and offices came to a grinding halt. Under the immense pressure of public ire and the impending elections, the government agreed to renegotiate with the union. At the same time the union's leader publicly appealed to Mutthu to help resolve the impasse. Mutthu obliged, and after the meeting the union leaders announced that they were lifting their strike and reluctantly agreed to the government's offer only because Mutthu had appealed to them. Pictures of their handshake appeared in all publications for the next few days. This event alone, more than anything else he'd done before, catapulted him out of the reach of his opponents.

Lakshmi was the only one who remained unimpressed. 'Why did you have to stage this drama? That man was once the president of your fan club.'

Mutthu laughed in good humour. 'You're so difficult to understand, my love! One day you talk like a child, the next day you have the wisdom of—what's that historical character's name?'

'Chanakya?'

'Yes, Chanakya.'

She brushed it aside. 'Despite doing nothing you come across as the saviour.'

'Nothing of that sort, my dear,' he responded airily. 'If I hadn't talked to him he would not have withdrawn the strike. That's what people get from me. I have the ability to get things done.'

'He would have done anything for you.'

'Do any of the fools in the government have the kind of

leverage I have? Besides, if you are going to do something good for the people you might as well do it front of the camera. What's the point in doing good deeds behind a curtain when it's your popularity that determines whether you get another chance to do good or not?'

'You always have a justification for everything.'

'I'm not going to pretend to be a saint; I'm *not* one. I'm running an election campaign. Besides, saints can't feed the poor, but an elected leader can.'

The victory celebrations were held by the seashore in the city one night, at the very spot where Lakshmi's father, the moplah, and her mother, the star-dazzled girl, had celebrated the country's Independence almost four decades ago. Coloured lights scoured the dark sky in anticipation of Mutthu's arrival by helicopter. Mutthu had decided that he would drop from the sky like a superhero. It was a perfect opportunity to lend a mythical dimension to his popularity. Like the god Vishnu he wanted to ride on the back of Garuda, with Lakshmi beside him as his celestial consort. But procuring a bird-shaped aircraft proved to be hard and he settled for a helicopter.

The podium on the beach from where he would deliver his victory speech was covered with a sheer muslin curtain. It was Gloria's idea. As his helicopter appeared over the podium, the beach burst into cheers above the sound of the live orchestra playing hits from his movies. The helicopter hovered above the podium for several minutes. Then a rope ladder, not long enough to reach the ground, was unfurled from it, and Mutthu appeared at the door, waving to the crowd. With the orchestra playing an action score, the crowd watched in astonishment as he climbed down the ladder, swaying dangerously in the strong wind that blew in from the sea. When he reached the last step of the ladder he remained suspended in mid-air for several suspenseful moments, still a good thirty feet above ground. As the music score approached its crescendo, strobe lights danced all around him and the podium was engulfed by a smokescreen behind. To everyone's horror, coinciding with the musical crescendo, Mutthu let go of the ladder and plunged downwards, feet down, hands stretched up, cutting through the wind and smoke, landing behind the curtain on the podium with a loud thump. The orchestra fell silent abruptly and the helicopter took off towards the sea and vanished. There was stunned silence. Seconds passed and there was no movement around the podium. Just when everyone had begun to fear the worst, the orchestra suddenly came alive with violins and drums and trumpets and cymbals playing at the same time, and the curtain rose to reveal a coughing, spluttering Mutthu working his way out of the smoke. The crowd erupted with relief and Mutthu responded by pumping his fist in the air.

It was like an action scene in a film, with the difference that the audience was part of it, its reaction genuine, unlike the make-believe descent by Mutthu's stunt double while Mutthu himself stood concealed behind the curtain and the fake smoke. The stunt proved enormously successful and believable, for the cheering went on and on. And for a long time afterwards people would tell stories about how Mutthu flew down to earth from the heavens. If only he had had a Garuda-shaped vehicle with Lakshmi beside him, the myth would have been complete.

Finally, as the smoke cleared, the others on the podium came into view. Sundarapandian and Lakshmi flanked him. Behind them was Mutthu's first wife, making one of her rare public appearances, looking far from happy, for Lakshmi was standing next to her husband, a place that rightfully belonged to her.

Lakshmi turned around. Mutthu's wife hid behind everybody else, fidgeting with her sari. For an instant she looked up and their eyes met and clashed. Lakshmi half expected her to pull her back and hiss: 'You tart! Have you no shame? I'm the faithful one, the dutiful one like Kannaki. And, you . . . you're a common dancer, the courtesan without morals, the—'

Lakshmi averted her gaze. Mutthu's wife went back into the background. She said nothing at all. The bright lights shining on the stage cast shadows on the people at the back.

Lakshmi's shadow fell on her. She was almost invisible, her head bent with humiliation. Lakshmi felt a twinge of pity and guilt. She nudged Mutthu and pointed in his wife's direction.

Later, as the celebrations wore on, Mutthu, with characteristic diplomacy, restored his wife's dignity somewhat by inviting her to stand beside him on the other side. He was truly the superhero that day.

The Peacock-Eyed One

Lakshmi sat cross-legged on the floor next to Mutthu, crouched over the plantain leaf and eating in silence while the excited orphans—'Mutthu's orphans', as they were called—chattered around them, raising their eyes every now and then to look shyly at the two guests of honour and giggle behind their clenched fists.

The election campaign had depleted Mutthu of all his energies. For two days after the victory celebrations he had slept like Kumbhakarnan, snoring appropriate ragas at different times of the day. He had emerged from his ursine sleep, heavy-lidded, dishevelled and wan. He had come over to Lakshmi's house in that state and said that he wanted to celebrate his election victory with them, his orphans, many of whom he had known since they were abandoned babies. Lakshmi had been reluctant to come, but she hadn't been able to say why. Mutthu had insisted, and so she had come. There were dozens of children, snot-nosed, sandy-haired from lack of care, many of them weaklings, with stilts for legs and knots for knees. And this after the administrators of the orphanage had spruced up the kids for the visitors. The children had swarmed all over Mutthu as soon as they had entered, tugging him towards the little playground, shooting at him with toy guns, throwing a ball to him, clambering over him with a rubber stethoscope and pretending to examine him, and pouring him make-believe coffee in a plastic cup. They had performed a skit for him in one of the rooms, an older boy overdoing an imitation of Mutthu, and Mutthu had laughed delightedly at all the jokes in the play. He had hugged them, tickled them, taken them on his knee, given them new toys. 'Hero!' he had called out to the boy in the play. 'Comb your hair like this. There. Now you look like a real hero!' And the waiter from the restaurant near the film studio had returned to his old home, insisting that he serve Mutthu and Lakshmi their dinner, grinning toothily as he ferried buckets of sambar and buttermilk, trays of vegetable curry and rice and appallams.

After the meal she waited for all the children to get up before getting up herself so that she didn't have to stand with them at the tap to wash her hands. On the way out she did not look into their eyes, not even when a little girl gave her a bouquet, and she smiled, not at the girl, but at some abstracted, smiling face, unclear and effaced like a memory from a long time ago.

Outside, Mutthu shed his excited demeanour and said, his tone unusually sharp, 'At least you could have made an attempt to enjoy their company. You know I've had a long association with the orphanage. At least for my sake you could have smiled at them.'

Lakshmi turned her face away and sighed. She could not answer. What could she say? Like an unused well the hole in her memory had partially filled in over the years, and she had begun to remember baby scents she had earlier willed herself to forget. She didn't realize then that her silence was not callousness, but a cry for sweet forgetfulness that would soothe her back to normalcy.

★

A man with magnified eyes sat down with a few kuravas, leaning against an ancient Impala that the kuravas had driven into a clearing in the forest, and drank arrack from a stainless steel tumbler. The other men leaned against an even more ancient Fiat parked alongside. They were already drunk.

'Where did you excavate these relics from?' the man asked.

'Oh, these cars?' they said when they understood his

question. 'We've owned them for years. Handed to us by our fathers who got them from their fathers and so on.'

'I didn't even know these cars still run. Where do you get spare parts?'

'We make them, we smuggle them, we steal them,' they said. 'Just like we get our guns and bombs.' They walked up to the cars and took out various guns from the dickey and brandished them in the air.

The fish-eyed man was surprised by their frankness. Perhaps the arrack had made their tongues loose. Arrack did that to him too. Made him talk about things he'd never known, made him see visions, made him write poetry that everybody said was beautiful. It was the smell of arrack that had brought him to the clearing. When he needed it he could smell it from miles away and sniff his way to the source. Like all strangers, these kuravas were generous with their arrack.

They drank in silence for some minutes, contemplating their drink, the still air, the setting sun, the stream that flowed by. Then one of the kuravas woke up and asked, 'What's your name?'

'Mayilkannan,' the large-eyed man responded.

The kuravas burst out laughing. They had obviously not heard of him or his poetry yet.

'Have you seen a peacock's eyes?' they asked as they fell over each other in mirth. 'Peacock eyes, he says!' They paused to catch their breath. 'You have cruel parents!'

Mayilkannan was used to this reaction. 'I gave myself this name,' he said calmly, gulping down the rest of the drink in his tumbler. Indeed he had, in a moment of profound irony, when he was staring at his reflection in a mirror to consider a pseudonym to write poetry under. He had considered other names, but they were neither ironic enough nor cruel. He remembered being called Pulcinella years ago when he worked at a girls' boarding school. He considered the name seriously because, even though he did not know what it meant, he knew it was a joke on him. But he ultimately rejected it because it was an alien word that nobody would be able to pronounce or understand.

The kuravas now laughed even more loudly. Mayilkannan watched them impassively and poured himself some more arrack from the tin can. Finally, when it seemed as though the name had lost its effect and the men fell into drowsy silence, Mayilkannan said to them, 'My mother is a nomad, too.'

The words woke them up instantly. They looked at him for a moment in disbelief as though he were joking. They got up, ready to assault him, for even in their drunken state they knew that being a kuravan was no joking matter. But the expression on his face was serious and he was not drunk. They jumped with joy and embraced and kissed him.

'We thought we were the only kuravas for miles and miles,' they cried, overjoyed.

They pressed more arrack to his lips. One of them collected some twigs, paper and other rubbish from the clearing and lit a bonfire in celebration. Then they danced around it, forcing Mayilkannan to join them. They stumbled over each other, but they laughed and sang and took swills of their drink. Mayilkannan broke away from the group and took the tin can away from them. 'My brothers,' he said, 'you shouldn't drink any more.'

But they continued dancing and stopped only when they grew tired. They slumped against their cars again and fell asleep instantly.

Mayilkannan watched the fire crackle and leap towards the sky. The arrack began to have its effect on him. He could imagine these men deep in the forests, in the hills, where only wild animals and poachers roamed, training hard for battle, crawling up the hill on bleeding elbows, being indoctrinated in the virtues of killing, in the sanctity of martyrdom. They came as boys and would leave as men, to go back home, to their island to fight to reclaim the pearls their ancestors had dreamt of, which they believed was rightfully theirs. He said aloud, addressing the sleeping men,

Drink the scented water
From these unwashed mugs
Fling your paper money
Let them fly like wingless birds
Ease your broken back onto the grass
Caress your calloused hand
Let the fire in you rage on
For they try to kill you, maim you
For they make you an outsider
In your own home
Brother, I know why you dream
With your eyes open wide.

In their sleep the men raised their hands and mumbled in appreciation. When the fire went out Mayilkannan too eased his back on to the grass and fell asleep.

After being thrown out of Lakshmi's school Mayilkannan had not returned home. He had wandered around for a year, sleeping in the open when he found no shelter, hunting for his food when he had no money. Hard rocks, brambles and leaves, sweet-smelling hay, urine-sprayed footpaths: he was used to them all by now. He used his wits and his hunting skills to survive. And the fire within him. The fire that impelled him to teach himself to read and write. The fire that burst forth periodically in the form of poetry that he recited along the way to whoever was willing to listen. He wrote them down on loose sheaves of paper that he stuffed, crumpled and oil-stained, in the frayed jute bag he carried everywhere with him. They were his treasure. But he was unaware of their value till people started asking for them, and he would distribute them carelessly, often not remembering whom he gave them to. 'Of what use is treasure to a kurava?' he would ask. But people convinced him to be more careful, to be more possessive. He learnt the rudiments of acquisitiveness as a result of his poetry.

His reputation as a wandering bard grew. People gathered around him and listened to him recite poetry and recount how he had taught himself to read and write. Strangers would shudder at his ugliness, but they would be drawn to him because of the gravity and passion in his voice. There was always a lesson to be learnt from whatever he said, whether he meant to edify or not; he was both a poet and a teacher. At the end of his recitations, children came to him to have him explain difficult passages or verses in their books and to help them with sums that they could not do. Adults who could not read asked for help filling out forms, or for him to read out letters relatives wrote to them. 'You must learn to read and write,' he would tell them. 'How much longer will you ask for help?' And he would click his tongue impatiently, admonish them, and demonstrate to them how easy it was to read when one split words into individual syllables and characters. He would write them clearly to demonstrate his point. The alphabet, suddenly made easy, its arcane code cracked, was not forbidding any more. To press home the advantage, he would tell them why it was so important to be literate, how only literacy could vanquish ignorance. He would teach them the alphabet till they began to recognize the shapes and sounds. Then he would move on to another place in his constant wanderings, to teach another group of illiterates.

Soon his random poetry recitations gave way to a daily routine of public readings. At night, in the light of an oil lamp or a hurricane lamp or a street light (if he was lucky) he would sit cross-legged, smacking himself when mosquitoes bit, and read to his audience. He read anything and everything: newspaper articles, informational flyers, booklets left behind by missionaries, literacy primers, school textbooks, his own poetry, any random scrap of printed material. *What* he read was secondary. It was the habit of reading that was important, a habit he wanted his audience to develop.

Then, one day, he came across a group of volunteers from a literacy movement—they called it Ezhutharivu—herding people into the village headman's courtyard to teach them the alphabet. He stayed in that village for a few days and observed the volunteers as they went about their tasks. They carried a portable blackboard and charts with pictures and words. They handed out thin books, primers and slates. They sang songs and told stories. They followed a curriculum, a strict regimen of lessons of increasing difficulty. They took their mission seriously. He liked the energy these volunteers had, their patience with stubborn students, their good humour. They seemed to enjoy themselves.

He realized that in contrast he taught people not for the pleasure of it, but because he felt burdened by their ignorance. The work of the volunteers made him realize how incomplete and unstructured his own methods were. The volunteers didn't leave as soon as their students learnt to recognize the alphabet; they persisted till their students gained a certain level of proficiency. He realized that he had never paused to consider what became of the people he taught after he left them. Did they build upon the skills they had learnt from him till they became proficient? Or did they forget everything as soon as he turned his back on them?

At the end of a fortnight he went over to the volunteers and asked, 'Do you need a wandering teacher?'

Mayilkannan had visited Pudupettai before. It was an overgrown village that was elevated to the status of a town because it was the district headquarters. There were no other towns in the tiny district, and Pudupettai had an apologetic air to it. It wasn't clear where the town ended and the surrounding countryside took over; there were swathes of small farms interspersed with urban streets right in the middle of the town.

Mayilkannan had been particularly keen on going to Pudupettai this time. He had heard of the new district collector, a woman, who supposedly had radical ideas and had procured government funds to support the group's literacy drive in the district.

Mohana Devi, the district collector, surprisingly turned out to be a plain woman who lacked the airs of an educated, accomplished bureaucrat. She wore a simple sari; her hands were unadorned, as was her neck, save for the yellow twine of her thali. She could have been mistaken for a local housewife. But when she spoke she was a different woman, so articulate and confident that Mayilkannan was immediately impressed.

'Arrack,' he told her when he got a chance to speak. 'Look around us. Half the men in this district are lying drunk on the wayside. How can there be sustained development when so much of what the poor earn is wasted? Illiteracy, arrack and lack of development are all facets of the same social problem.'

She nodded. 'The new government is talking about banning country liquor.'

Mayilkannan had heard about it. He had recognized Lakshmi's face on election posters. The girl who had been the reason for his dismissal from the school, the girl who had patronized him, the girl who had, for some strange reason, borne his anger patiently. He felt nothing upon recognizing her face; only the general, impersonal suspicion and disdain he felt for the rich.

'The new government means business,' Mohana Devi continued. 'It's exactly the kind of law we need. You'll see what a difference it can make.'

'Like all our other laws it will change nothing,' he responded. 'These are just to keep our educated people busy.'

Mohana Devi appeared surprised by his cynicism. 'No, this is different. That new woman especially. She's not like the other politicians. I've met her before and I know she's sincere. She'll influence real change. Mark my words: she will.'

Her enthusiasm was infectious. He felt the stubborn cynicism within him dislodge ever so slightly, giving way to hope, and a new emotion akin to pride to hear the collector praise Lakshmi. 'Yes,' he replied. 'I suppose we should give them a chance.'

Later, when he left the district collector's office his mind teemed with ideas to bring out the correlation between arrack and illiteracy in a street play. A play that would address two significant issues at once. 'Arrack,' he muttered, sniffing it in the air. 'We must get rid of it.'

Involuntarily, like a Pavlovian dog, he followed the whiff of alcohol and turned his cycle towards the woods outside town, to the clearing where he was sure to find the kuravas who would gladly share a drink with him. He wrote the play that night after his acquaintances had fallen asleep and after he'd drunk a jugful of the remaining arrack.

Half an hour before the scheduled opening of the new street play he had written, Mayilkannan discovered the joy of beating the drum. On a whim he had borrowed a thavil from a local musician to help him publicize the play. He walked through the alleys of the poorest part of town beating the drum to attract everyone's attention. He rather liked the sound it made and beat it with gusto even though he had no sense of rhythm or music. *Ticki-tacka-thadam-thap-tick*, he beat, enjoying the sound. He had never had a toy, even an improvised one, as a child, and this loud toy delighted him like nothing had in a long time. It made him uncharacteristically light-hearted, frivolous.

Residents peeped out of the doorways and windows of their ramshackle tenements on either side. 'Yo!' shouted someone irritably. 'Why are you making such a racket? Have you lost a screw?'

Mayilkannan, unfazed by the criticism, shouted over the noise, 'If you want me to stop go to the street corner and watch the play.' Then he stopped beating the drum and looked around at all the curious but passive faces. They would need something more than noise to get out of their homes. 'A super-hit drama!' he announced, imitating a well-known radio announcer in a deep voice. 'A story of greed, ignorance and misfortune. If the world has ever been unjust to you—and you all look like you've been victims before—you must see it. World-class acting, cinema-style scenes, right here, at the street corner in a few minutes. And it's free!'

The excitement that followed his announcement gratified him. Children started running towards the intersection. He caught a few passing by him and turned them around. 'Children cannot watch the drama alone. Go and bring your parents along.'

'But I live with my uncle,' protested one girl.

'Mother, father, uncle, aunt, neighbour: bring anyone. Bring a grown-up along.' *Ticki-tick-tacka-tack*. 'Jatha, drama,' he now cried like a vegetable seller. 'Hey, where do you think you're going alone? A grown-up. Bring a grown-up along, boy.' *Tacka-tacka-tick-tick*. 'If you don't like my beating the drum wait till you hear me sing.' *Tacka-tick-thum*. 'Go, amma, the drama is at the street corner, not here.'

In a very short time he had managed to drive everyone out of their homes with their hands on their ears. A large crowd gathered at the intersection in front of the makeshift stage. The district collector arrived in her official car with several bureaucrats.

The play itself was very simply produced. A few benches had been put together to form a stage, behind which hung a plain white cloth on two poles. The actors were volunteers of Ezhutharivu. They were dressed in ordinary clothes, wore no make-up and did not adopt any stage persona. They simply played themselves: lungis hitched up, saris tucked in as if ready for household work, hair uncombed, dirty pieces of cloth covering the heads of those who appeared to be involved in manual labour. The play was titled *Karuppaiah's Misfortune*. It was about a quarry labourer, who, at the end of a hard day's labour, drinks more than he earns. The arrack shop owner, despite being aware of Karuppaiah's financial condition, goads him to drink more. He even offers Karuppaiah a loan to meet his expenses and draws up a document explaining the terms of the loan. Karuppaiah cannot read and does not know what the terms are. But he puts his thumbprint on it and gratefully accepts the money. Meanwhile his wife works in fields owned by rich landlords, earning a pittance and bringing the money home for household expenses. Before he realizes it, Karuppaiah is neck-deep in debt, and the shopkeeper harasses him to pay up. Unable to repay, he drinks even more and comes home to take out his frustrations on his wife by beating her every night. Then, one day, the shopkeeper's men arrive at his doorstep and demand immediate repayment of the debt.

Karuppaiah has nothing to give them. But the men are in no mood to sympathize. They take whatever they can find: utensils, a steel trunk, even his children's clothes. Then they confiscate the house, a meagre structure of mud and dung and hay, which Karuppaiah had built on land that did not even belong to him. Karuppaiah and his family are now destitute.

The audience nodded in appreciation, in recognition of familiar themes throughout the play. Nothing in the play was new to them. Karuppaiah's story could be seen repeated in countless homes. Yet the tragedy of his family compressed into a play of forty minutes had shock value. The women, in particular, identified with Karuppaiah's wife. They mobbed the woman who played the part of Karuppaiah's wife and expressed their sympathies for her without realizing that she had only been acting.

After the play Mayilkannan spoke briefly to the audience about the moral it contained. He then invited Mohana Devi to also speak.

'Selling arrack will soon be against the law,' she told the crowd. 'Once the law is enacted I will send the police to close down all the shops that continue to operate. But every one of us also has the responsibility to root out this evil. You who drink, I urge you to stop. Those who don't, especially you women, if you see anybody selling liquor, I urge you to come together and force them to shut their doors. Soon you will have the right to shut them down. The law will protect you.'

Afterwards Mayilkannan waited for the crowd to disperse and gave Mohana Devi a crooked smile. Her eyes were twinkling with enthusiasm. There was every reason to hope that she would help him bring about real change. He began to respect her. 'I'm happy our paths have crossed,' he said before hopping on his bicycle and riding away.

When he went to return the thavil to its owner, the percussionist was horrified at its condition. 'What did you do to it? Did you beat it with rocks?'

Mayilkannan laughed sheepishly.

The man tapped it at several places, cocking his ear. Then he tugged at the straps. 'The pitch is off,' he said waving his hands about in distress. 'There is no reverberation. It's beyond repair.'

Mayilkannan was only too happy to keep it as his own.

A few days later in a village outside Pudupettai local volunteers brought together a group of women for their first lesson in reading. They gathered outside the temple, under a banyan tree. An electric bulb, its wire stretched taut all the way from the temple, lay suspended from one of the branches. In front of the class, a blackboard had been placed against the tree. The volunteers began by distributing slates and chalks to the students. The teacher was a young girl of fifteen who lived in the village. She was nervous even though she knew all the women because she was teaching for the first time. Mayilkannan sat down on the steps of the temple with his newly acquired drum beside him. He had beaten it to help herd the women to the temple, but now he silently observed the proceedings. The teacher wrote out the first few letters of the alphabet.

'This is *uh*,' she said. 'It is the first letter in the alphabet, like the *uh* in amma.'

'*Uh*,' they repeated after her like school children. 'Amma.' Then they giggled, for they had never held a slate and chalk before; they didn't know that the alphabet had sounds. But they were also proud that one of their own, this girl looking nervous and anxious in her half-sari, was now teaching them. They were also aware of the stranger who claimed to have peacock eyes sitting in the shadows, and felt self-conscious. They covered their mouths with their saris and giggled. Two other volunteers moved among them and helped them write out the character, the first character with its pot belly like that of the temple priest, the stem hanging off it like his kudimi. The second letter *aa* was the priest with a dog's tail curled between his legs. The volunteers giggled along with the students.

Mayilkannan smiled in the shadows. He had never thought of the letters of the alphabet in those terms. When he had learnt the alphabet it had been a sacred task, a painful, excruciating effort, a self-inflicted punishment that precluded any humour, any naughty analogies.

All the women seemed to be enjoying the exercise. But there was one woman sitting behind everybody else in a rumpled mass, almost lost in the shadows of the aerial roots of the tree. She was painfully thin, sickly. She was the only who did not giggle. She looked preoccupied.

For the rest of the evening Mayilkannan watched this woman. She seemed to be aware of his stare and turned away slightly so that he could not see her glazed, swollen eyes any more.

After class he asked one of the volunteers about her. 'Oh, Thenmozhi,' the volunteer said. 'We had to force her to come even though we know she's not going to learn to read and write. But we wanted her to get away from her father at least for an hour or two.'

'She's a vazhavetti, aiyah,' another woman said. When Mayilkannan stared at her without responding, she continued, as if to explain, 'Her husband threw her out last week and now she's back at her father's house. What's she going to do learning all this? Her life is over.'

'I know what it means. But why did he throw her out?'

'Who knows? She says he's married to arrack, and he says she's a witch. And her father, after beating her mother to death now beats *her* every time he's drunk. Says she's a shame. Poor woman.'

'But why is her life over?' he asked. A rhetorical question, it was wisely left unanswered.

He left the women and rushed after Thenmozhi. He found his way in the moonlight. He stumbled over rocks and sleeping buffaloes, but finally caught up with her. 'You must learn to read and write,' he told her, his voice betraying his anxiety. 'It will change you. It will give you self-respect. Your life is not over yet.'

The woman smiled sardonically. On her cheek was a scab, a cut that must have been quite deep, for the flesh around it was still tender, turbid, in danger of being infected.

'What happened?' he asked.

'I fell down.' The answer lacked conviction, and he did not believe her.

'Where do you live?'

She did not reply.

'What about your husband? I want to talk to him.'

She looked scared. Before he could ask her any more questions she ran away into the surrounding woods and into the darkness.

The following evening, after class, Mayilkannan stopped her before she disappeared again. Her eyes were swollen with recent tears. The wound on her cheek looked even more dangerously close to infection.

'Your father's drunk again, isn't he?'

'They all are,' she replied with sudden anger. 'Not just my father.'

'But they all don't beat their daughters. He's a beast.' It was his turn to get angry.

She did not respond.

'I'll have the shops shut down,' he swore, 'so that no one comes home drunk.'

'But you also drink,' she said. 'Who are you to criticize others?'

The response startled Mayilkannan.

'I've seen you drink by the stream,' she continued. 'With those kuravas.'

He did not know what to say. Nobody had pointed out the obvious hypocrisy in his stand before: not the volunteers, not the masses among whom he moved. He suddenly felt exposed, naked, the moral high ground shifting and crumbling under him.

'But I don't have a family,' he said feebly. 'I don't beat up or starve anybody. I only write poetry.'

Thenmozhi looked back at him unblinkingly, the look of a hundred words.

'You're right,' he said at last. 'I don't have the right to criticize others.'

Thenmozhi turned away, knowing she had won a trifling, meaningless victory.

Mayilkannan made no attempt to stop her.

The jatha troupe stayed in Pudupettai for an unusually long time. They rarely stayed in one place for more than a day or two, after which they would move on to the next town or village or hamlet. But Mayilkannan kept delaying their departure because he wanted to meet Mohana Devi again. He wanted to talk to her about expanding the role of the local group and to push more aggressively throughout the district. He wanted to talk to the local members about their everyday problems and help them plan their activities. He wanted to ensure that the fledgling literacy class in the village nearby did not wither away in a few days. But, most importantly, he wanted to know what would happen to Thenmozhi. He desperately wanted to talk to her husband, but nobody could or would tell him where he lived. Not even the girl who taught the women. Their answers were always vague. One woman pointed towards the woods and said he lived in a village beyond it. Another said he lived in the neighbouring district and there was no easy access to it. Finally he told the rest of the troupe to leave without him.

A few nights later, after a class in which the women learnt to recognize the differences between *ka* and *sa*, he overheard one woman telling another, 'She's going to her husband's house tonight. To see if he'll take her back.'

Mayilkannan immediately looked around for Thenmozhi.

He caught sight of her just as she disappeared into the darkness in the direction of the waterlogged rice paddies, away from her father's house. Without a moment's hesitation he followed her, keeping a safe distance so as not to be detected. He took off his slippers, for the hard leather soles and the nails that held them in place grated against the pebbles underneath, sounding like glass being crushed. He followed Thenmozhi all the way to her husband's house, past the paddies, beyond the bore well that did not work, into a clump of trees beyond which lay a hamlet where farm labourers lived. He stayed hidden behind the trees as she walked into one of the huts. Immediately the silence of the night was broken, and a wrathful man dragged her out. Behind him appeared another woman, hastily wrapping her sari around herself, shouting as though she had been robbed.

'Witch!' the man shouted. 'She's back, the witch!'

Despite his unsteady hands and legs, the man summoned enough strength to shove her towards Mayilkannan hiding behind the trees. Thenmozhi stumbled and fell down. Mayilkannan wanted to emerge and help her to her feet. But he knew that the humiliation of being seen thrown out of her own house would be far more unbearable than the scraped skin she had suffered.

With a whimper she picked herself up and retreated. She did not look back to see the neighbours come out and watch the spectacle. Mayilkannan followed her silently all the way back to her father's house and left only after he was sure that her father had taken her in. Perhaps he was too drunk to notice that his daughter had returned.

The next morning, before Thenmozhi's husband left for the fields, Mayilkannan arrived at his doorstep. 'Dai!' he called out. 'Come out of there, you dog!'

The husband, steadier, but perplexed, appeared at the door.

'Don't you have any shame?' Mayilkannan continued. 'Throwing your wife out in front of the other woman!'

Riled, Thenmozhi's husband retorted, 'Dai, poruki! What's she to you? What do you care if I throw my wife out?'

Mayilkannan advanced with an outstretched hand, incensed at the insinuation and the insult. But someone pulled him away. A couple of other men coaxed Thenmozhi's husband inside. A woman he suddenly recognized from the literacy class stood at the doorway of a neighbouring shack. He took a couple of steps towards her, angry with her for not having told him about Thenmozhi's husband's whereabouts when he had asked her. Her lack of cooperation was evidence of complicity. The woman fled inside. Constrained again by bystanders, his attention reverted once more to Thenmozhi's husband. 'If you don't take your wife back I'll set the police on you!' he shouted, quickly realizing how empty, how impotent, how ludicrous his threat was.

'Leave him alone, vaadhyare,' another man said, gently pushing him away.

Despite the words of respect, or perhaps because of them, Mayilkannan felt the man was being patronizing. He was angry with himself for his ineffectual outburst, for looking like a fool. The man pointed to the mud path that led back to the village. Mayilkannan let himself be led away. 'Tell her never to show her face here again,' Thenmozhi's husband called out after him.

That night neither Thenmozhi nor her husband's neighbour came to class.

'What did you expect?' a student rebuked him gently. 'You've scared that woman away. Thenmozhi too.'

'You don't bring about change by setting everything alight,' the fifteen-year-old teacher said patiently, as if talking to a child.

Mayilkannan felt humbled. He, who had seen a village for the first time when he was seven, should have known better than anybody else how change was to be brought about. He, born on the fringes of society, in a world that was older than civilization itself, where nothing had changed in thousands of years, should have known that ancient peoples have little regard for time, that they are not easily threatened by it, for they are secure in the knowledge that they have survived and will continue to do so. He was becoming impatient, a characteristic—and perhaps the exclusive right—of the privileged. But what he was getting impatient with he could not say.

He left the group of women and went to Thenmozhi's father's house. He knocked on the door softly. Thenmozhi appeared, and upon seeing him became scared. She was about to shut the door on him when he stopped her. Seeing the futility of forcing the door shut, she stepped out and shut the door behind her.

'Is your father in?' he whispered.

She shook her head. 'What do you want?' she asked instead in a small voice. Without waiting for his response she walked away from the house, towards the coconut trees that formed the border between the row of houses and the fields. He followed her.

'You don't have to be scared,' he said. 'Nobody can do anything to you. Don't stop attending class because of what I did.'

She did not reply. Hidden from the houses they stood in silence. She did not make any attempt to leave. The wound on her face had still not healed and now there was a fresh one next to it. She had fallen on her face the previous night. He reached out and touched it. Startled, she jumped back. He could not say if it was out of pain or fear.

'I'll try to give up drinking,' he said to her at last.

Thenmozhi turned and ran home.

Mayilkannan went back to the temple and unlocked his bicycle. He did not ride it; he simply pushed it and walked alongside slowly. He did not go back to town. Instead he went to the clearing by the river where the kuravas sat slouched against their cars, drinking. Upon seeing him they got up and welcomed him and offered him a glass. But he pushed it away. 'Not today, brothers,' he said.

The kuravas, surprised, slurred, 'Why? Is it an inauspicious night to drink?' they guffawed. Mayilkannan did not even smile. 'Come, brother, drink,' they insisted. 'We can see that your heart is heavy. Here, take this. This is the universal medicine.' They pressed a glass against his protesting lips. He gave in.

Later, he wrote:

Why do you run away from me,
frightened like a deer?
Why do you flinch when I soothe
your wounds with peacock feathers?

Is your body so scarred
that you fear
a caress might hurt more than a slap?

That night he knew he would be in Pudupettai for a long time.

The Law . . .

Lakshmi was struck by Mohana Devi's self-assurance, her enthusiasm to implement the new anti-arrack law. She was the first official in the state to try and enforce the law.

'You won't believe how much confidence it is beginning to give the women here,' Mohana Devi said to Lakshmi, bubbling with energy. 'Why, only the other day a group of women from a neighbouring village came to my office and asked me to have the local distiller arrested. A few years, even a few months ago, this would have been unthinkable. Women travelling by themselves to town to take on their men and the rich distillers?'

Lakshmi was gratified to hear that. It had been surprisingly easy to pass the anti-arrack legislation. She had been afraid that Mutthu would treat it simply as a campaign promise to be forgotten. But he hadn't forgotten it. It was he who had asked, 'Are you ready to see your idea legislated?' Sundarapandian had not objected. Perhaps he was preoccupied with national politics in Delhi. Perhaps he had buckled under pressure from various anti-liquor groups. Perhaps Mutthu had offered him something in return for his silence during the debate.

'You must meet the Ezhutharivu people,' Mohana Devi said, leading her to another room in the district headquarters. 'They're doing a phenomenal job not only by spreading literacy but also by bringing about real social change.'

But Lakshmi wasn't listening. She stood frozen at the threshold. Pulcinella! The rat-catcher! Her heart missed a few beats and then it rattled in her chest. She took deep breaths. At first she thought she'd mistaken someone else for him. But those crooked lines on his face could not possibly be reproduced on another human being. She remembered his breath, how it mingled with the smell of crushed eucalyptus leaves, how heady and repulsive it was. And the ferocity of those eyes, how scary and fascinating she used to find them. What was he doing here? Would he recognize her? Should she show signs of recognition? Did he know anything about her confinement and her departure from the cloister? Did he know about her baby—their baby? Had he gloated to his people that he, an outcast, had conquered and polluted the high-caste through her?

And what about him? She didn't know what to make of his reaction. Was that a smile of recognition? A mocking gesture? The smile of a murderer before he goes for the final kill?

She quickly took control of herself and acknowledged his greeting stiffly. Then she pretended nonchalance and moved on to greet the others, spending more time with them than necessary, just to avoid looking at him. She noticed that the smile on his crooked lips had disappeared and he had looked disappointed, perhaps even a bit foolish. He then settled into a chair and remained silent for the rest of the meeting.

'How many distillers have you put out of business?' Lakshmi asked, studiously avoiding his gaze.

'Several,' Mohana Devi responded. 'We've already collected over one lakh in fines. But many of them simply move to a new location or defiantly reopen after a few days. There's one particularly bold fellow nearby who's paid his fines six times already and still continues to operate.'

'Why don't you have him arrested?' asked Lakshmi.

'He just posts the bail and returns to his shop.'

'Take me to him.' Lakshmi got up, relieved at the opportunity. She had been carefully steering the conversation so that it did not force her to address Pulcinella directly, but it was becoming increasingly difficult to do so with Mohana Devi eager to involve him. Besides, his brooding silence had begun to unnerve her.

Selvamani, the local legislator who had accompanied her on this visit, was outside ordering his men around. He immediately stepped up his activity several gears as soon as he was told that they would go to an arrack shop. 'Collect all the workers!' he ordered his aides. 'We're going to witness something important.' He turned back and smiled sycophantically at Lakshmi. He pulled up one of his assistants and whispered, 'Dai, do something quickly. Knowing her, she'll want to shut the shop down. The whole thing will be a flop if nobody is around to witness it.'

Instantly the men sprung into action. Selvamani himself ran up and down the corridor, holding up the hem of his veshti, shouting commands. Others scurried in and out of the compound; mopeds and cars and bicycles made a mad dash into town; small arguments ensued amongst Selvamani's minions over the most efficient way of spreading the word. A few minutes later a sizeable crowd gathered outside the compound. A megaphone was procured. Party flags and placards appeared out of nowhere. A few photographers were busily taking pictures.

Lakshmi was impressed. How easily Selvamani had gathered a crowd. She liked him. He was a very simple and humble man, most unlike the politicians she knew.

She smiled at him, which made him almost faint with pleasure. But when someone told him which arrack shop they were headed to, his smile vanished immediately and he became pale. 'No, no, madam,' he said, looking stricken. 'Not that shop, madam. Any other would be fine, but not that one.'

'Why not?'

'It's owned by Sundarapandian-saar's nephew.'

Lakshmi was shocked. For confirmation she turned to Mohana Devi who shrugged as though it was common knowledge. Sanguine, absolutely unconcerned that she was dealing with an MP's nephew, the shrug spoke for Mohana Devi. Lakshmi hesitated for a moment, but Mohana Devi's smile challenged her. 'No,' she finally said to Selvamani. 'We must go there.'

Perspiring copiously, Selvamani protested. But Lakshmi had made up her mind. He slunk away into the crowd in search of his assistant. 'Tell them to go away,' he ordered his assistant desperately. 'This is going to be a disaster.' But his assistant, confused, could not do anything. It was already too late.

They marched to the arrack shop with Lakshmi, Mohana Devi and the still silent Mayilkannan at the head. Selvamani walked a few steps behind Lakshmi, behind the police cordon that separated the crowd from the leaders, among the Party workers, not wishing to be seen or associated with the disaster that was about to take place.

When they arrived at the shop the man behind the counter jumped up. Another man hastily emptied the till into a cloth bag and disappeared into the shop. 'See the coward run through the back door,' Mohana Devi commented with glee.

The man behind the counter came out to meet Lakshmi in the street and fell at her feet. 'I had only come to clean up the place before locking it,' he said with an ingratiating smile. 'Forever.'

'Good,' retorted Lakshmi. 'Then we'll help you lock it up.'

Mohana Devi laughed. The man directed a wrathful glance at her and Mayilkannan. Upon a cue from Lakshmi a policeman stepped up to take hold of the arrack seller. Selvamani buried himself deeper into the crowd.

Two policemen went into the store and brought out a big drum and placed it on the threshold. Lakshmi paused to allow the photographers and a couple of journalists to gather nearby. Then she opened the tap at the bottom of the drum and let the arrack run into the open gutter under the stairs that led to the store. The crowd cheered. The men then overturned the drum over the gutter, its contents sloshing and overflowing, the odour overpowering her. Next, she shut the door herself and locked it. As she turned the key the cameras clicked in unison and the crowd roared again. Even the Party workers cheered half-heartedly so as not to be faulted by Lakshmi later. Selvamani began to weep.

Later at the district collectorate, Lakshmi spoke through the megaphone, now having completely put the unnerving experience of seeing Pulcinella out of her mind. As she spoke she sensed a change in her tone and her demeanour. Buttressed and challenged at the same time by Mohana Devi's presence, she wanted to show that she was in command of the situation. The crowd wanted to hear her speak decisively. 'Congratulations to Mohana Devi, the government staff under her and the volunteers of Ezhutharivu for your courageous stand,' she said, her pitch rising in an effort to project her voice. 'This is a significant day in our fight against liquor. Your government will make sure that the law is enforced uniformly, regardless of anybody's stature. But the fight is not over until we have closed every illicit liquor shop in the state and rehabilitated all the families ruined by it. I am now in the process of setting up a fund to help the affected families. Pudupettai will soon be an arrack-free, happier district.'

She knew she didn't sound like herself. Her little speech reminded her of someone, but she couldn't quite decide whom. She waved as she stepped down. The crowd surged forward, especially the women, who shoved their babies in her face 'Ambal has come to visit us,' they cried, referring to the local deity. 'Bless our children,' they appealed to her. Lakshmi, taken aback by their reverence, obliged.

A woman pushed her way through the crowd. Untying a knot in her sari she took some money and pressed it into Lakshmi's hand. 'For the fund,' she said. 'My husband would have spent this money today on drink if you hadn't come. Please use this money to help others.'

Lakshmi looked her up and down. Her sari was torn in several places. In her ear lobes were small pieces of twigs that kept the piercings from closing up in anticipation of better times when she could wear proper earrings. Her skin was wrinkled and she looked a lot older than she must have been.

'Don't hesitate, amma,' she said, folding her hands humbly. 'It's a small amount, but that's all I can afford. There are many families that are worse off.' So saying, the woman hurried away.

When Lakshmi opened her palm she saw two rupees in it.

Mutthu laughed a lot at the breakfast table the next morning. 'This picture alone has made you a heroine, not just among the masses but also among the educated, the intellectuals, the chattering class,' he said, shoving a newspaper, neatly folded several times down to the size of the photograph, under her nose.

She nodded, but he continued to laugh for so long that she feared he was ill.

'It's about Sundarapandian, isn't it?' she finally asked, irritated.

'Yes.' Mutthu seemed somewhat relieved that the topic had finally come up. 'He's going to come here this evening from Delhi. You've made your point, so please listen to everything he has to say and do not argue or react in a bad way. We can't afford to alienate him.'

She could sense a storm brewing. Had she crossed the limits? Would her action result in a major upheaval? When she had left for Pudupettai she had no intention of closing down an arrack shop. In fact, she had assumed she would meet the collector, make a speech or two about the law and return. But she had been caught up in the events of the day. Uncharacteristically, she hadn't been in complete control of herself. Was it Pulcinella's presence? Was it his brooding silence, his molten anger that challenged her to prove that she could be just as committed to social causes? Or was it the collector's quiet confidence, her complete lack of fear?

Surprisingly, Sundarapandian smiled that evening. 'Madam,' he addressed her in English, bowing. 'I commend you on your actions. You are doing the right thing by going after rogues. But that's my nephew. He's like my son, since I have none myself. If you had warned him he would have personally accompanied you and closed the shop himself. He has very high regard for you. He'd heard of you from your days as a dancer par excellence. But now I have to intervene on his behalf and tell the police commissioner to pardon him for once.'

'She didn't know he's your nephew,' Mutthu interceded hastily. 'All she wanted to do was to make a social statement on our behalf. She simply wanted to ensure that people did not accuse us of not having fulfilled our election promises. Look how much everybody has praised us.'

'That's right, saar,' he responded evenly, still smiling. His eyes gleamed. His moustache, like his hair, was well oiled and shining. He nodded and lifted his hand as if to show there was no disagreement or rancour. Diamond and emerald rings flashed. A Rado watch peeped out of the sleeve of his white polyester shirt. 'I don't mind the bad publicity for my nephew. I don't mind what people write about me personally for what my nephew does. I don't mind that they say I'm involved in illegal trade, because I know I'm not. The fact is, even my nephew isn't. The shop doesn't belong to him. It belongs to a friend who has gone out of town, and all he was doing was to take care of it. I don't mind that I now have to explain all this to the world. The only thing I'm scared of is how I'm going to pacify his poor mother, my sister. She's so distraught! Madam, you'll agree how emotional women can sometimes get. They don't always understand the ways of the world. They don't always understand that, sometimes, innocent people have to suffer on behalf of the guilty. Her son is in jail and that's the most important issue for her. But I understand why you did that. I know you did it for the Party, for all of us. So I'll take care of my sister too. I'll be by her side for a few days and she'll cheer up.'

Lakshmi listened to his monologue stoically. Mutthu looked relieved. Perhaps he had expected worse. 'Thank you for understanding,' he said. 'You're setting a wonderful example for the Party cadres.' He got up to shake Sundarapandian's hand. Senior Party officials around them concurred and smiled. They too shook Sundarapandian's hand. The MP then turned to Lakshmi and folded his hands. 'Madam, I hope you'll pardon my nephew for his indiscretion.'

She nodded in response, forcing herself to smile at him.

Mutthu beamed. 'Now that we have settled this small misunderstanding amicably, let's move on to the next item on the agenda.' He turned to the convenor of the meeting who was seated to his right.

Lakshmi was surprised. She didn't know there was another item on the agenda; she didn't even know there was an agenda. The convenor cleared his throat and solemnly announced, 'Our MLA from Pudupettai, Selvamani, has been in poor health of late. He suffered a heart attack last night and his doctor has advised him complete rest for a while. Since he won't be able to execute his duties as the representative of Pudupettai he has decided to vacate his seat.'

Lakshmi was shocked. He seemed to be in perfect health during her visit. She looked around the room and saw grim faces nodding, understanding something she didn't. She remained silent.

'So we need to find a replacement for him,' the convenor continued. 'We can have elections for that seat held along with the other by-elections coming up soon.'

The Party officials huddled amongst themselves, murmuring animatedly. Lakshmi looked at Sundarapandian and then at Mutthu. They seemed to be already aware of this.

Presently, one of the officials broke away from the huddle and approached them. Bowing meekly, he said, 'If I may make a humble suggestion to our esteemed leaders, why not nominate Sundarapandian-saar's nephew to that seat?'

'What a wonderful idea!' Mutthu exclaimed. Lakshmi saw him give her a guilty look out of the corner of her eye.

The convenor gushed, 'After Sundarapandian himself he's the next most popular man in town. Who could make a better candidate?'

Sundarapandian made a show of protest, but the others would not hear of it. 'If that's what you all want,' the MP relented, reluctantly, 'I'll ask him. He'll do anything for his maama and for an opportunity to serve his people.' He looked at Lakshmi and hastily added, 'That is if you approve, madam.'

He caught Lakshmi off guard. All eyes were on her. She mumbled her approval and got up to leave the room.

Sundarapandian bowed to her and folded his hands once again. This time his smile appeared less fake, almost appreciative.

The significance of the meeting was not lost on Lakshmi. She recoiled from Mutthu's touch that night.

'I'm happy you averted a big fight,' Mutthu remarked, cajoling her.

'Did I have a choice?' Her voice rose.

Mutthu put his arms around her, but she pushed him away. He sighed. 'Politics is like acting in films. You play your part even when you know it's fake, even if you don't believe it. You make compromises along the way. Otherwise you're a nobody. Another nameless extra in the crowd swaying its hips to the music.'

His response infuriated her. 'You have a justification for everything. Tomorrow you'll kill me and justify your action.'

'Now come on,' he cajoled. 'Why would I do that?'

She did not respond. She didn't speak to him that night, and for several days after that she continued to shut him out. How could he have been so devious? How could he have betrayed her by handing over victory to Sundarapandian and his nephew? What else was he capable of?

One evening she sat on the floor of her dance room holding the veena in her lap. Mutthu had bought her the veena several years ago. She used to spend an hour every day playing it, for it not only helped her relax, but it also helped her dance as she contemplated the bronze statue of Shiva in the form of Nataraja and his tandava. But the instrument had lain unused for a long time. Now she plucked its strings and the twangs they produced were delicate. The notes hovered around her like wisps of smoke, permeating the room intangibly. It was then that she realized how tenuous it was, this unnamed relationship she had with Mutthu, how it could dissolve into ether, leaving echoes in its wake like these notes, until even the echoes dampened and left no reminder of their existence, of the evanescent joy they had brought to the listener. Did anybody remember Selvamani any more? How quickly he had plunged into the frightening depths of mass amnesia. She could be him: a nameless face. Featureless, powerless, with the look of quashed hopes and ideals. She would be just someone who had been Mutthu's . . . what? What was she to him?

She put away the veena and went upstairs to the veranda where she sat alone, watching the sun set over the mango tree, wondering what lay in store for her. She clutched the railing and watched the gardener hoeing, his son watering a rose bush with a watering can. The driver, leaning against the car, smoked a bidi meditatively. This house, these servants, her fame were all because of Mutthu. This was still the chinna veedu, this house that was not quite a home, perpetually reminding her of her ambiguous relationship with Mutthu. It was a sorry little house, a pretender, just a notch above a bordello, although nobody dared call it what it was to her face. And yet it elicited from people a mix of sympathy and contempt, a little less respect for it and its resident. Even from Mutthu.

She regarded it with increasing revulsion. She had to get out of it. She needed a house of her own. A proper house. A real house. A big house.

That evening when he came to visit her, she said bitterly, 'What brings you to this hut?'

Mutthu blinked at her. 'Is something the matter?'

'Everything is the matter!'

'I don't understand.'

'You understand everything that goes on outside, but you can't understand anything in here! When are you going to tell the world that we are married?'

Mutthu took a deep breath. 'Look, we've talked about this before,' he said matter-of-factly. He made no attempt to cajole. 'You know I can't. This is the best arrangement for both of us.'

'This is the best arrangement for *you*.'

'And also for you,' he said impatiently, 'in ways you don't

see sometimes.' He strode away from her. He regarded her silently for a few moments. 'Look,' he said in a softer tone. 'I know you don't like this house. I'll build you another one. A mansion. No, a palace fit for a maharani.'

Lakshmi resisted the urge to retort. 'Compromise,' Mutthu had once said to her in the voice of a teacher, 'is at the heart of politics. A good leader is one who knows when to compromise. It isn't a bad thing at all. If I don't compromise, my support will erode. And without the support of the people I can do nothing. So you tell me: isn't it better to compromise and do something for the people than to stick to your principles and do nothing?'

She had to admit he was wise. There was more wisdom in being supple and bending like a palm tree to the passing storm than in being rigid, only to snap like a proud but foolish twig.

He came towards her and touched her hand as he did whenever he wanted to test her mood. She did not resist, but neither did she completely give in to his touch. She would need time for that.

. . . And the Gadfly

Mayilkannan and Mohana Devi stood in front of the reopened arrack shop in silence. But only for a moment.

'I'll set the police on them again,' Mohana Devi said brightly.

'You'll keep sending the police and he'll keep paying the fine,' Mayilkannan responded. 'This will never end.'

'A nice little game, isn't it? Provides entertainment to our otherwise boring lives. Come on, if *you* are going to lose heart how do you expect the volunteers to carry on?'

Mayilkannan grunted. She was right, but over the years his cynicism had become too much. How else could it be when the girl in two plaits who had frolicked in the woods with him now pretended not to recognize him? 'You won't see her again till the next elections,' he had told Mohana Devi bitterly, breaking his long silence that day as Lakshmi's car had pulled out of the collector's office. 'She's different,' Mohana Devi had replied. 'Give her a chance.'

He felt vindicated now, watching the man behind the counter gleefully welcome his customers. But Mayilkannan derived no pleasure from it.

'Vaadhyare,' the man behind the counter called out. 'Welcome back! Some honey for you? It's free today! In honour of Murugesan's nomination as the Party's candidate.'

Shocked, they did not think much of the mocking tone. They had heard of Sundarapandian's nephew's release; they hadn't expected him to be in jail for more than one night. They had also heard of Selvamani's sudden resignation, but they had not heard of Murugesan's nomination.

They went to the police commissioner's office. 'Ready for an afternoon outing?' Mohana Devi asked the commissioner, having recovered her cheerfulness.

'Yes, I am. But you do realize that we won't be able to do this for too long.'

'We'll go after them as long as they keep it open.'

'Even after the by-elections?'

'Yes, even after that.'

'Even with Murugesan behind the counter?'

'*Especially* with him behind the counter.'

One evening during an adult literacy class on the government school's premises, Murugesan's campaign committee paid them a surprise visit. On the school's playground there were about a hundred adults seated on coarse cotton, jute and bamboo carpets. As the politicians approached, the surprised students got up, the teacher stopped mid-sentence and gave way to Murugesan who segued into a speech without so much as an introduction or preamble.

'Illiteracy is the darkness that envelops our country,' he declared, pausing for effect like a veteran. Murugesan, swarthy, thick-lipped, gold-toothed, luxuriantly moustached, in his uncle's trademark silk white shirt and silk veshti, smiled with the arrogance of an already crowned king. 'And these volunteers here are lighting the lamp that will defeat the dark forces of illiteracy and ignorance. I have supported their efforts right from the beginning. I remember when I first heard of Ezhutharivu. I requested its volunteers to come to our town. I helped them organize their first jatha—'

Just then Mayilkannan tore into the playground, shouting with fury. 'Dai, rascal! What do you know about illiteracy? What have you done for us? How dare you lie in front of your own family? Get out of here immediately or else I'll kick you like a dog!'

A few policemen pounced on him and dragged him away. He did not resist, but he continued screaming. The policemen locked him up in one of their vans, threatening to break his bones if he did not shut up. But he called their bluff and continued screaming throughout Murugesan's speech.

The next day, just as Murugesan padlocked one of the arrack shops in town with the solemnity of someone laying a foundation stone, Mayilkannan jumped in front of him, snarling like a wounded monkey. Policemen immediately caught hold of him and led him away, but not before he had turned his face towards Lakshmi, who had come again to Pudupettai at Mutthu's request to help with the campaign, and stared at her with such hatred that she recoiled. It was the anger of an ignored, wronged man. He didn't have to scream at her. She knew exactly what he wanted to say and it made her feel defiled and unclean.

Murugesan, in response, thundered to the police to have him locked up. But she lifted her hand and stopped them. It would only make a martyr of him. In that moment she realized the she should not underestimate the strength of this raging man. She knew that ever since he had worked in her school, when the social differences between him and everybody else around him had defined his existence, he had thrived on being the victim. She knew he must not be wounded at all cost, for it would only make him stronger.

Mayilkannan took to protesting everywhere Murugesan campaigned. Murugesan was venal, Mayilkannan proclaimed, a liar, a hypocrite. He stood at street corners with a megaphone and urged passers-by to vote for other candidates. He beat the drum all day long. It was cathartic. It helped dispel the fog of pessimism every time it surrounded him. *Thum-dum-dump-thum*, the thavil groaned under his relentless assault. It had begun sounding like anything but a thavil. The membranes on both sides had begun to fray over the bamboo rings, threatening to give way.

At a large campaign rally in the maidan, where along with all the local Party bigwigs and town councillors Lakshmi, Sundarapandian and Mutthu put in an appearance, he took to responding to Murugesan's speech. Crowds had been transported in from surrounding villages. Mayilkannan was not allowed anywhere near the maidan. Earlier in the day policemen had detained him at the Ezhutharivu office in spite of his protesting that he was a free man who could go where he wanted. Refusing to give up, he took the Ezhutharivu's public address system to the terrace and directed the speakers towards the maidan. He then locked the access door to the terrace so that nobody could stop him.

When the rally started and the speakers bellowed into the microphones, Mayilkannan launched into a harangue of his own. When Murugesan extolled the virtues of civic cleanliness and promised, if elected, to launch a campaign to beautify the town, Mayilkannan shouted into his megaphone, 'Look, the pig wants to clean everybody else's bottom when his own is dirty. I can smell the stink here!' And he beat his thavil. *Thum-thump-da-da-dum*. The crowd found it amusing, and Murugesan looked unnerved, angry, but only for a moment. He put up a brave front, pretending as though he hadn't heard Mayilkannan, and resumed his speech. Then Mayilkannan sang a song he had recently composed. It wasn't really a song; it was simply a speech he put to incoherent music. His voice, scratchy as usual, alternated between yodels and solemn depths. He was so completely out of tune that even the policemen who were supposed to prevent him from leaving the building fled with their fingers in their ears. 'Justice will be done,' he crooned, 'I've decided to rob my brothers and denude my sisters, so that I'll be made an MLA one day.' *Dum-da-da-dum-thump*.

After the rally Murugesan fumed. 'I'll have him thrown in jail! How dare he insult me!'

Sundarapandian calmed him down. 'That's exactly how he wants you to react. Why do you want to grant him victory by responding?'

Murugesan nodded doubtfully. He combed his moustache with his nails, slowly, as though he sought reassurance of his manliness and dignity from it.

'Please don't do anything foolish with him,' Lakshmi warned him before leaving. 'We don't want to make a martyr out of a gadfly.'

As expected, Murugesan won by a large margin. Mayilkannan heckled him one last time at his victory rally. And then he fell silent. He wouldn't talk to anybody except when it was unavoidable. He wouldn't talk about Murugesan even when provoked. He confined himself to organizing jathas, touring with a troupe of local volunteers to all parts of the district. He coaxed people to attend literacy classes. He initiated new volunteers and teachers in various places and put them in charge of new literacy centres.

People said the vaadhyar was going crazy, something they had suspected when he had heckled like a madman. It was all the arrack he drank, the arrack he told others not to drink. Murugesan had ridiculed him as a hypocrite in one of his speeches. But those who admired Mayilkannan thought differently. Perhaps it was his way of teaching everyone a lesson, they said, to become mad himself to cure them of their madness. This school of thought rapidly gained popularity, especially since Mayilkannan himself never responded to the criticism levelled against him. It captured people's imagination—it was a noble, sacrificial gesture. And now, like a sage, he had practically given up speaking.

Mayilkannan began to be more respected and people were patient with him when he flared up over the smallest issues. They even went to all the arrack shops in the vicinity and begged the shopkeepers not to entertain Mayilkannan. But the shopkeepers shrugged and said he never came to them. Perhaps he made it himself. Perhaps he never drank arrack at all.

Unaware of the growing veneration for him, every night that he was in Pudupettai Mayilkannan cycled to the nearby village where Thenmozhi lived and stared at her from the dark shadows of the temple, even though he sometimes feared she would stop coming because of him.

He was confused. He thought that perhaps he had misunderstood her. Perhaps she did not really make conscious attempts to avoid him. Perhaps she even wanted him to approach her. Or, worse, he feared, perhaps she just didn't care whether he was around or not. Perhaps to her he simply did not exist.

Mayilkannan spent most nights in the clearing by the stream, gazing at the stars after his kuravan friends had finished drinking and gone home. Alone, lonely, contemplating her face, her scar, sometimes the strange looks people now gave him, the look some people reserved for madmen and others for sages, till sleep overpowered him. He beat the thavil sparingly, the joy having gone out of it. It, too, had succumbed to his melancholy.

An Accident of Fate

From the time Lakshmi had taken over as the Party's spokeswoman I had stopped covering local politics in exchange for a dull desk job, occasionally writing unsigned editorials on non-controversial issues. She met the press frequently and gave them easy access to meet her during and after press conferences. I assiduously avoided these meetings. My presence would change the tone, and I wanted no part in it.

It was not entirely without envy that I listened to fellow journalists at the Press Club discuss the changing political scene in the state. In the early days, even before Mutthu had won the elections, there was something of a euphoric atmosphere at the club. Over coffee and cold drinks they sang her praises. She was articulate, trustworthy and beautiful. But what most impressed even the most cynical veteran journalists was her insistence that she was an outsider, a non-politician who did not covet power herself. She was believable, perhaps because she herself genuinely believed it to be true. 'She's a glorious misfit in politics,' a senior journalist commented.

I never told my colleagues that I had known her as a child. So I became aloof from political news, feigned disinterest during their discussions, and found excuses when asked for my opinion. Besides, K. Abdul Latheef's non-committal silence amidst the chorus of praises was a deterrent.

I'd known K. Abdul Latheef for some years now. He and I had attended college together. Unlike me, he had been a brilliant student. After college he had made it a point not to work for an English-language newspaper even though that was where the money was and reputation easier to make. He was making a political statement that I never quite understood. And, yet, he became well known fairly early on while my career remained lacklustre. He had quickly built up a reputation for his ability to smell out stories where others found none. He commanded a certain amount of respect for his dignified, hard-hitting, style. What marked him amongst investigative journalists was his integrity, which made him impervious to the fears of ordinary men. It gave him a sense of quiet self-confidence, so much so that he did not have to resort to sensationalism or shameless self-promotion to be heard.

At some level I resented his success. This was aggravated by the fact that he never appeared to take me seriously. He would discuss profound issues for hours with others, but with me he talked only trivialities.

One day a well-known editor, well advanced in age and reputation, reached out to him and asked, 'So what's your analysis of this new woman?'

Any other journalist would have been terribly flattered by the veteran's interest, but K. Abdul Latheef remained solemn as ever and said, 'Unfortunately, I haven't seen enough of her to form an opinion.'

His response distressed me. He was a man who measured his words carefully. Even when he criticized someone he was respectful. For him to be less than effusive about her was an indication that he was reserving his true opinions for later. Was there something about Lakshmi that he didn't like? Did he not trust her? Did he see something all the others did not? I wanted to burst into the conversation in her defence, and it was only with great difficulty that I stopped myself. I was taking his implicit—perhaps imagined—criticism personally. I couldn't possibly expose my Achilles' heel to him. So I held my tongue.

Now, months later, tamarind became the subject of a raging debate all over the state. Mutthu had revived the idea of giving away tamarind to the poor, and it caused a mini crisis. Some people later opined that this crisis would have led to a total collapse of the economy and of law and order had it been allowed to go on.

For weeks this scheme was a source of great satire and entertainment at the Press Club. One couldn't possibly take such a bizarre idea seriously even if the government did. Had Lakshmi not been involved in its genesis, I would have enjoyed myself too. But I stayed on the sidelines, a listener, alternately enjoying the fun secretly and feeling increasingly unsure of how many of the jokes were directed at Lakshmi.

Even before the state assembly debated the scheme there was an acute shortage of tamarind as people began to hoard it in anticipation and its price on the open market rose. Speculation was rife that those who didn't qualify for this scheme would soon have to stand in long queues to buy tamarind, if it was available at all. But on the other side of the poverty line there would be a problem of plenty. The poor would make kozhumbu and tamarind rice every day. And they would still have some tamarind left over, for which they would have to invent recipes.

This dichotomy between the poor and the not-so-poor would create an entirely new avenue for crime. The black market for tamarind would thrive. Inferior quality tamarind, liberally mixed with black stones that were indistinguishable from real tamarind stones, would make the hoarders rich. Criminal elements would accumulate fake ration cards and sell the quota they got from the government to retailers at black market rates. I could foresee that those above the poverty line would wistfully eye the mountains of tamarind all around them. They would mutter darkly about organizing protests, strikes and raids on government godowns. The more passionate ones would openly talk about organizing revolts, with hundreds of thousands of not-so-poor people marching down the beach road to the secretariat, crying for their daily sambar.

As time went by the stories became more and more bizarre. Like the one about policemen at an octroi post asking truck drivers to grease their palms with tamarind if they wanted to pass through. When the truck driver assumed they were euphemistically demanding money and handed over some he had set aside for just such a contingency, the policemen had bristled with anger. 'Dai, we asked for tamarind and you give us money!' they'd shout at the poor, confused driver. 'Do you think we're common criminals?'

There were noisy scenes in the assembly when this scheme came up for debate. The Opposition members couldn't believe that the government was even considering it. One member shouted derisively, 'Why don't you give us all a kilo of bitter gourd instead? Or why not a kilo of cow dung?' Other Opposition legislators responded by laughing and thumping their desks loudly.

I prayed, for Lakshmi's sake, that this idea be quashed before long. The absurdity of the scheme's unintended consequences was beginning to reflect even more badly on a scheme that was already flawed.

Thankfully the debate over tamarind fizzled out in the assembly and Mutthu did not insist on the scheme any more. Days later, there was talk at the Press Club that it had been Lakshmi who had convinced Mutthu to withdraw the scheme. Forgetting that it was she who had introduced the idea in the first place, my colleagues heartily approved of her role in its withdrawal. 'Only she has brains,' they said. 'The others are all nincompoops.'

K. Abdul Latheef had maintained a stoic silence throughout this episode. He preferred to sit back and watch silently, even when he could have acknowledged her contributions in getting sane legislation like the ban on arrack passed, or in killing an insane law like this one. I knew he was storing it all up for the right time, to collect enough evidence and then to swoop down hard when it was most unexpected. That was the way he was: a guerrilla journalist. Had his target been someone else, I would have applauded. But his silence with respect to Lakshmi was beginning to chafe.

★

His hands quaked uncontrollably, a seismograph's stylus during an earthquake. He spilled coffee all over himself and scalded his hand.

She got up with a start and rushed to wipe his hand, surprising even herself. The frostiness that had crept into their relationship since Mutthu had suggested Murugesan's nomination without consulting her had not thawed. In fact it was fast becoming part of their relationship. Like the frostiness between her and her grandmother. Touching his hand made her aware of it, of the absence of the old ease they had shared. A wave of anxiety swept through her, but she suppressed it and concentrated on applying ointment to his hand.

The attack shouldn't have surprised her because there had been warning signs for many months, signs she had chosen not to take seriously. He had begun to forget things. Harried by his hectic schedule and the realization that age was catching up, he did not even pretend to be a dandy any more. The drab white shirt and veshti that his chief ministership now forced him to wear made him look dowdy. Even an expensive raw silk angavastram slung over his shoulder didn't help. Deprived of sleep, his eyelids drooped further. He had become slower in his movements. A few days earlier at a meeting with industrialists from all over the state, he had fallen asleep halfway through the convenor's welcoming speech and had to be helped out of the room.

She called his doctor. After examining him for a long time the doctor shook his head in bewilderment and referred him to a neurosurgeon. The neurosurgeon didn't have much light to shed either. 'Weakness,' he pronounced, unconvincingly. 'Or alcohol.'

'But I rarely drink,' Mutthu protested.

'Then it's just weakness.'

'Quack!' Mutthu muttered angrily as the doctor walked out. 'Even my illiterate mother could have said that.'

'You need rest,' Lakshmi said. 'We should go to Kuppam for a few days.'

'How can I go now when there's so much to do here?'

But Lakshmi wouldn't listen and Mutthu relented, happy to be led away. Once in Kuppam he walked around his tamarind grove. He plucked a branch from one of the trees and popped the small leaves into his mouth. He chewed contentedly.

'I still think it was an ingenious idea to dole out tamarind to the poor,' he commented. 'Think of the possibilities. Imagine adding tamarind flavour to the stick ice cream you buy on the streets, or tamarind candies covered with Belgian chocolate, or tamarind and lime pickle, or prawns floating in tamarind and coconut gravy—'

She gently pulled him away from a low-hanging branch that he was eyeing greedily. Perhaps it was all the tamarind he ate that caused his hands to shake.

He fell silent, possibly still dreaming of tamarind prawns. But after a few hours of peace and relaxation his responsibilities caught up with him. His secretary constantly interrupted him with requests from his cabinet colleagues. An unusual lethargy came over him, and he remained sitting on the swing in the veranda for the rest of the day. 'Take care of whatever they want,' he said to Lakshmi, looking utterly disinterested in his secretary's questions.

'But how can I speak for you?'

'Just say whatever comes to mind,' he said, barely listening to her. 'They'll listen. After all, that's what I do.'

With that he nodded off and periodically rose to momentary half-wakefulness to shout his tamarind recipes to imaginary cooks around him.

One evening, a group of pilgrims returning from an old temple in the hills on the horizon passed through Kuppam. They belonged to Mutthu's fan club. Like most of his fans, they stood outside the gates, peeking in, hoping to catch a glimpse of their hero. Even though he rarely came to this house, his fans came, at least to touch the gates and the compound walls he had undoubtedly laid his hands on. Even in his absence they felt his aura. But that day, delighted to see their hero sitting on the swing in the veranda, this group scrambled over the locked gates as the watchman ineffectually tried to prevent them, and shouted, 'Mutthu vazhgai!'

Mutthu, roused from his nap by the commotion, looked bewildered as the fans rushed towards him, producing scraps of paper—receipts, old postcards, paper packets in which they had collected vibhuti from the temple—and pens for his autographs. They fell at his feet. 'Thalaivar!' they exclaimed reverentially, their pilgrimage now complete.

He obliged them, shaking hands with every one, signing autographs. One man presented his forehead. Like everyone else he was clad in a black veshti and black shirt for the pilgrimage. They had all smeared their foreheads with black ash, with sandal paste or vermilion smudges in the centre. This man cleared his forehead for Mutthu. 'It is written on my forehead that I should get your autograph,' he gushed, taking his belief in his fate literally.

In good humour now, he laughed and signed on his forehead. 'But how long will this last?'

'Forever, aiyah, I promise you. I won't wash my forehead again. I won't mess with my fate any more.'

When, finally, the watchman shooed them away, they left dancing and singing one of Mutthu's songs, badly out of tune.

Later that day the fans returned with a distinguished looking bearded man who wore several beaded necklaces made of sandalwood and ivory and carried a brass jug of water from the sacred pond by the temple. He was their spiritual leader, a holy man, apparently rapidly growing in popularity for his wisdom and prescience. As a young man he too had been Mutthu's fan till he had turned his mind to philosophical and spiritual matters. Apparently he hadn't completely overcome his former temporal preoccupations, for he hadn't been able to resist the temptation of meeting Mutthu.

Mutthu got up to receive him with exaggerated reverence as Lakshmi looked on in amusement at his changed demeanour. Mutthu always held men of religion in high esteem. He was transformed in their presence, trusting every word they said. Perhaps he even feared them. He smiled like an imbecile now, his palms still together, nodding obsequiously. Even a rogue in ochre robes could have this effect on him.

The portly man peered at Mutthu and declared, 'You're here trying to recover from some strange affliction. Something even your doctors cannot diagnose.'

Mutthu looked astounded. Uncanny, Lakshmi thought grudgingly. Or perhaps he had disciples in the Party who had told him about Mutthu's sudden absence from the City. Then Mutthu's expression changed to fear. 'How much longer do I have?'

The man enjoyed Mutthu's reaction. 'Don't worry. It's only a passing phase because Sani—Saturn—is on the ascendant. In a couple of months this phase will go away and you'll be in perfect health.'

Mutthu's head bobbed energetically with relief. 'If you say so, it must be true.'

But the man wasn't done. He leaned forward and felt Mutthu's raw silk angavastram. He sniffed at it. 'Throw this away. This is the cause of your affliction. You should wear a cotton angavastram, instead, for good health. Black.'

Mutthu immediately flung it to the far corner of the veranda. One of the disciples retrieved it and draped it over his shoulder. 'Keep it,' Mutthu said. 'It looks better on you.'

'And here,' the holy man said, dropping a packet into Mutthu's waiting hands with a flourish, 'apply this vibhuti on your forehead every morning after a bath before dawn.'

Mutthu prostrated himself before the holy man. 'I'd like to make a donation to your ashram as a token of my appreciation.'

'That's generous of you. But don't give it to me. My body burns when I touch money. My disciple here will take care of that.'

After the visitors had left with a large cheque, Mutthu turned around and asked, 'What? You think I'm a fool to believe in a half-educated fan of a film star? Go on, tell me I'm superstitious and backward.'

Lakshmi smiled. 'I'm not saying anything. But I will say this much: that man doesn't know what he's talking about.

Sani dasas are not short phases. Everyone knows Saturn is a slow mover.'

Still Mutthu ordered a set of black angavastram. When they arrived in the evening he markedly unfurled one in Lakshmi's presence and placed it on his shoulder.

'Wear ten of them if you want,' Lakshmi commented, 'as long as you allow a good rest to cure you and stay away from tamarind.'

Mutthu, Mauro Tedeschi and Surya raised their glasses and toasted universal prosperity this time. Mauro Tedeschi had come down to pitch for the modernization of the state's textile cooperative. He manufactured looms and industrial needles among other things. Surya had already had a couple of discussions with Mutthu on the subject.

'Computer controlled,' Mauro Tedeschi had said. 'For twenty-four hours of production. You can use our machines to make handkerchiefs, saris, lungis, socks, cloth for shirts and trousers, everything. In just one year the equipment will pay for itself.'

Mutthu had nodded. 'Send in your bid. I'll take care of the rest.'

Now, the deed done, Mauro Tedeschi and Surya raised their glasses triumphantly.

'You should come and visit us. I'll take you to our factory in Brescia. You'll be impressed. And how about that Ferrari you wanted to drive.'

'Did you buy it?'

'Of course. It's fantastic. You'll love it.'

That night Mutthu lay in bed speaking of building a racetrack. 'Imagine driving around it at over 250 kmph. Tell me, isn't it a shame that a large country such as ours does not send even one entry to the Paris-Dakar or the Indy 500?'

'You're not planning to buy a Ferrari, are you?'

Mutthu smiled. 'I may. But tell me, does the Testarossa only come in red?'

Lakshmi shook her head in dismay. 'Now go to sleep.'

Mutthu ignored her. 'I think we should go to Italy. Find some business to combine it with. What do you say?'

'You can go if you want. I want to go back to my dance. You know how long it's been since I danced?'

'At least tell me whether I should buy a Ferrari or a Maserati.'

'Neither,' she responded with exasperation. 'They are not toy cars.' The truth was she didn't care what he bought. She was worried about him. The rest in Kuppam had done little to improve his health and the doctors continued to be baffled. 'In any case how can you travel in this state?'

Mutthu considered her question. Then he patted the black angavastram on his shoulder. 'Why do you worry? As long as I wear this I have a weapon against the evil Saturn.'

To her dismay he closed his eyes, clutching the angavastram like a security blanket, blind in his belief that he would be fine, and fell asleep.

The phone call came at three in the morning. Mauro Tedeschi himself was on the line, his voice shaky. Mutthu had had an accident that night. He had taken the Testarossa for a drive down the hills around Turin. In the dense autumn fog, his car had shot through a red light at high speed, skidded and smashed into a lamp post on one of the bridges across the Po. He was in hospital, but was out of danger.

An hour later, Surya and Gloria showed up at the door. 'Mauro just called us,' Gloria said. 'I'm sorry to hear what happened.' She approached Lakshmi and clasped her hands. Her hands were cold and bony.

Lakshmi was surprised. There was genuine concern in Gloria's voice. 'Thanks. I'm going to make arrangements to go there right away.'

'We'll come with you.'

'No, no, there's no need. I'll be okay.'

'It's okay, madam,' Surya said. 'It's no trouble at all. How can we let you go to an unfamiliar place alone at a time like this?'

'I'll manage,' she replied weakly.

'Nonsense.'

Lakshmi wondered then why they insisted on going with her, but as soon as she saw Mutthu at the hospital a day later she understood why. Mauro Tedeschi must have told them what he hadn't told her. Mutthu was still unconscious. He had suffered head injuries and the doctors were afraid that his already weakened nervous system was damaged.

He looked ghostly against the white sheets, rigid as a cadaver, the bandage on his head a turban. But his face had acquired a serenity he had never possessed. He looked wise, not worldly-wise or cunning, but like a venerable sage. Was this the end? She clutched his hand for support. It was surprisingly warm.

Years ago, in the early days when she had been racked by doubts about him, she had imagined their relationship coming to an abrupt end. Either he would die well before her, or he would leave her for another woman, perhaps his own wife, or she would rush out of his life over some humiliation. Over time, even as she had settled comfortably into her relationship with him, that thought remained and grew in conviction, although in an impersonal, passive way. She had been sure that's how things would end sooner or later.

. Despite having prepared herself to hear the guillotine swoop down and sever the relationship in one fell swoop, she was close to panic now that she could see the end approaching. Uncharacteristically, she found herself confounded by the simplest tasks. She was unable to understand what the doctors and nurses said. She became absent-minded. For several days as the doctors struggled to get him out of the coma she stayed by his side, staring at him for long periods of time, hoping for signs of revival or not thinking anything at all.

Later she would realize how lost she had been, and had it not been for Surya and Gloria she would have probably pulled the tubes away from Mutthu in one of her moments of abstraction, just to find out if he would jerk out of his sleep. But she was never alone. Surya and Gloria were constantly by her side, taking turns staying with her at the hospital at night. It was a few days before Lakshmi realized that Gloria, usually the silent spectator, the one who spoke so little that she was sometimes mistaken for a mute, constantly talked to her like an unending recording. As though, like Scheherazade's, Mutthu's life depended on her unending talk. It was still longer before Lakshmi realized that Gloria wasn't prattling as it first appeared to her, but uttering words of encouragement.

'He'll be fine,' she heard Gloria say when she paid attention to her. 'Look, did you see his fingers twitch? Now look at the muscles on his face. They're relaxing. Don't tell me that's not a good sign. Go on, feel his cheeks, they're soft as putty. Do you want to dye his hair? He might not appreciate seeing himself in the mirror when he wakes up . . .'

And Lakshmi, comforted by the non-stop chatter, often fell asleep in her chair and woke up to find Gloria's lips still moving. 'He'll be fine. Go home now. You're going to wreck yourself by not sleeping. I'll take care of everything here. My mother just called to say she has dinner ready for you. Eat properly and sleep there tonight. Go, go . . .'

And Lakshmi, exhausted, comforted, exasperated, confused, only half aware of what she was being told, responded, 'Gloria, what would I have done without you and Surya? How can I ever thank you? Now, do leave me alone for a few moments.'

Three weeks later when the doctors became pessimistic in their prognosis, Lakshmi knew she had to take Mutthu back home. How long could they stay there?

Back in the City, the crowds waiting for them at the airport and the roads leading to the hospital surprised her. People were everywhere: on trees and telegraph poles, atop advertising billboards, on the perimeter wall of the airport, along the road for miles and miles, craning their necks. What surprised her even more was the silence. They watched in shock as the ambulance, with Mutthu strapped onto a gurney, went past, as if she were bringing him back in a coffin.

There was a bigger crowd at the hospital, and the ambulance inched its way to the entrance. The hospital staff battled to keep out visitors, and yet a constant stream of people came by to inquire after his state.

That was how it would be for the next several days at the hospital—people all around her, pushing their way towards her, commiserating, offering advice, hope and help, sometimes not saying anything at all. Their presence comforted her.

But the moment she returned home she felt like she had fallen into an empty well. The servants went about their tasks without making a noise, as if they weren't even there. Random thoughts passed by like puffs of cloud. Once she had asked Mutthu why he had not made a choice. Why had he not left his wife? Or her? He had not answered. But she knew that had he left his first wife he would have hated himself forever. Thus, he had been infinitely wiser than she had ever been by seeking a compromise and not making any harsh, unequivocal choices, for once the guilt gremlins entered you, they were impossible to shake off. She had always wondered why she had gone to him, why she had stayed with him. She had never been able to find a satisfactory answer. How could she not know?

With difficulty she lifted herself from the chair and walked out. She told the driver to take her to the hospital. Back in his room when she took his limp hand in hers, she knew exactly why. He had thrown the world open for her; she could have it all to herself. But more importantly, even while in a coma he could keep her gremlins at bay.

That this realization should dawn on her when she could not share it with him elicited tenderness in her, a tenderness that was even more ironic than the irony that caused it.

The crowd that gathered in front of the hospital periodically roused itself to activity and shouted: 'Mutthu vazhgai! Mutthu, we won't let you die!' Groups of sympathizers made their way to the hospital in processions either silently or ululating and flagellating themselves like the maatam during Muharram. Some of these groups went to temples and offered all kinds of bribes to the gods: mountains of coconuts, flowers, foods and the offer to suffer Mutthu's affliction in his stead. Similar demonstrations of sympathy occurred all over the state.

Soon crowds began gathering outside Lakshmi's house too. As the interminable line of visitors at the hospital shortened, it grew outside her house. At first she did not notice it, then one morning she woke up to the sight of the line snaking its way down the street and disappearing round the bend. The few people the guards at the gate allowed in, mainly office-bearers of the Party, had the same look of expectation as the rest of the crowd outside.

'No, no, no,' she told them all. 'I cannot deal with your issues. I'm not qualified to help you. I'm not Mutthu.'

'But, amma, to whom can we go?' they responded helplessly.

'Go to Sundarapandian. Go to Murugesan. Go to anybody else. Please leave me alone.'

But it was too late. They had already begun transferring to her the reverence they had for Mutthu. They kept coming, even the senior leaders of the Party, and spoke even when she put her hands on her ears, when she was unwilling to bear the burden of their misplaced expectations.

And yet she felt guilty. She was shooing them away like a cantankerous old hag. They who looked up to her like children. There was something touching about their faith, their loyalty, their reverence. But it also brought on the burden of responsibility and transformed it quickly to something akin to obligation. Yes, obligation. She felt obliged to them. Perhaps this was what Mutthu had felt. This was what must have driven him to politics. He could not have avoided it.

One day, the members of the Party's steering committee came to meet her. Their presence together and in full force only meant that they had something significant to say. Just as she had feared, after a long and respectful pause, they explained why they had come. They wanted her to take over the reins.

If they hadn't been this serious she would have laughed at their suggestion. After several moments of blankness, she collected her thoughts. 'I'm honoured by your request,' she said. 'But I cannot oblige you. I don't see myself actively participating in politics.'

Their expressions changed to admiration.

'Madam,' one of them said. 'What happened to thalaivar is a great tragedy. It has affected all of us. We can only imagine how much more it has affected you. Please accept our sympathies. We understand that you're very concerned and preoccupied with his health. But please reconsider your decision. We're willing to wait however long you need to make a final decision.' Everybody nodded and murmured in concurrence.

She looked at them for several moments. She became aware of their growing anticipation, and her distress deepened. 'Please,' she said. 'Please elect someone else.'

But that only convinced them that she ought to reconsider. Several of them jumped up and came over to her and bowed. 'Please think about us also,' they said. 'You're our thalaivi. You've been the one we've turned to whenever thalaivar was unavailable. The only difference now is that we want to formalize your leadership.'

They pleaded and cajoled and threatened. Some even fell to the floor in front of her. They reassured her that everything would be okay with Mutthu, that he would be cured if she took him to the best doctors. But, strangely, for all their reassuring words, they spoke in sombre tones, as if they were already writing Mutthu's obituary.

Their insistence irritated her. They'd just stopped short of giving her no choice. After the meeting she went to the hospital and sat grimly by Mutthu's bedside. 'Wake up. Look what you've done,' she said to his still body, her voice taking on overtones of resentment. She'd taken to talking to him ever since the doctors had said that that would help, aware that she had eerily taken on Gloria's characteristic of speaking even when nobody listened. 'Why have you left *me* to deal with the mess *you* jumped into?'

Only Gloria and Surya seemed to understand her. She turned to them for advice.

'If you have misgivings, be firm with them,' Gloria said. 'You have every right to ask to be left alone. It isn't easy. But you should do what your instinct tells you.'

'But nobody's willing to listen,' said Lakshmi.

Surya nodded with sympathy. 'Yes, what to do? You can tell only so many people to go away. How can you turn everybody away?'

'They're beginning to get peeved with me. But I don't mean to insult them. It's unfair, this responsibility of having to worry about everybody's sentiments.'

'Yes. You can't just ignore them either. In some ways you're expected to bear the burden. But think about it: it's only temporary. Mutthu will recover sooner or later.' Lakshmi liked Surya's optimism. He, like Gloria, was convinced that Mutthu's condition was curable. 'Also remember, once you choose the path of obscurity, it leads you to the forest of amnesia where you could be lost forever.'

'You should have been a poet,' teased Gloria. Then turning to Lakshmi she suggested, 'Since they don't want no for an answer, why don't you ask them for some time?'

'How much time? How is that going to change anything?'

'A few months at least. In the meantime either Mutthu recovers and resumes his post, or you can hope they'll forget about you.'

Lakshmi liked the idea. 'They can elect an interim leader until then. Sundarapandian wants to be their leader. Let him take over.'

'No, no, no,' Gloria responded. 'It can't be Sundarapandian. Once he's elected he'll entrench himself. And then there'll be no place for Mutthu.'

'How about Selvamani?' Lakshmi said idly.

Surya smiled broadly. 'Genius! A stroke of sheer genius! Even Machiavelli could not have come up with that. Selvamani can never be a threat to Mutthu. Besides, he's loyal to a fault.'

Lakshmi gave a small speech that she had practised before Surya and Gloria several times. She explained why she was unable to take on the responsibility although she was honoured beyond measure by the faith they had reposed in her. She was not a politician, she stressed. She knew nothing about politics or governance. 'However—' she said and paused again, shaking unsteadily. 'However, I shall always have the Party's and the state's best interests in mind. To that end, please permit me to nominate Mutthu's successor. This man has been a hard-working member of the Party for decades. He is a man of integrity, a proud son of this state, a man to whom the people of this state and the Party come before self.' She looked up at Sundarapandian. He was grinning broadly, expectantly, sure that she was referring to him. She looked away and continued. 'He has been keeping a low profile of late, but that's only at the Party's insistence. His sacrifice has not gone unnoticed. What we need is a leader like him. Someone who is only too willing to serve his fellow-members and his people. Someone who'll put his heart and soul into the development of this state.' She paused. The sense of expectation was palpable. 'I am, of course, referring to the former legislator and minister from Pudupettai, Selvamani.'

There was a stunned silence. Sundarapandian shot a wrathful look at her and stomped out of the room. The others stayed in their seats looking nervously at each other. Lakshmi had expected some surprise, but not this. With a failing heart she realized that she should have taken a few of the senior leaders into confidence to ensure smooth passage of her proposal. This was turning out to be a failure. Selvamani was a cipher in the Party now. A forgotten man.

But her anxiety turned to impatience when their silent dissent continued for several pregnant moments. If they didn't want her opinion why did they bring her here? 'I know this is not what you all expected,' she said. 'But I urge you to consider this. It's not as if he's going to be left alone. I'll always be there to help him. So will all of you. If we all come together we can help him succeed.'

Finally one of the ministers spoke. 'Yes, why not? At least the man is non-controversial. He may not be the man we all might have thought of, but, tell me, how many people dislike him?'

Sundarapandian wasn't in the room. So there was no one who disliked Selvamani. That was enough qualification for him to be elected leader of the Party.

Relieved, Lakshmi rushed out to look for Sundarapandian. She saw him huffing about in a room, looking murderously angry. 'Sundarapandian,' she began. 'I wanted to talk to you before the meeting, but I could not reach you. The first person I thought of was you. But then I realized you were far more important as our representative in Delhi. Which is why I did not suggest your name. I then thought of your nephew. But he's still young and so may not be acceptable to everyone. Selvamani is not a strong man. That's why I thought of him. Anybody else would be difficult to manage. They would not be willing to keep the seat warm for Mutthu or you or your nephew.'

Sundarapandian looked less angry and sat down.

Then, Lakshmi pressed home the advantage. 'Besides, you did not let me finish. I wanted to nominate Murugesan for the deputy CM's post.' Here she lied. Elevating Murugesan was an idea that had just occurred to her at the spur of the moment, in her eagerness to reconcile. 'To give him the experience he needs till he's ready to take the job himself.'

Sundarapandian smiled. He stood up and made way for her to sit down; now he was willing to talk.

Selvamani arrived at Lakshmi's house with his entire clan: his wife, his children, his grandchildren, his old mother who had to be carried on the sturdy shoulders of a couple of grandchildren, his brothers and sisters and their children and grandchildren. It seemed as though half of rural Pudupettai was at her doorstep, dressed in their best clothes, with garlands and sweets. They were joyous, chattering amongst themselves noisily, spilling over the lawns, children chasing each other all around the house and in the streets. In tow were musicians playing nadaswarams and molams, giving the crowd the appearance of a marriage party. Outside the compound were scores of Party workers and Selvamani's newly acquired hangers-on.

When Lakshmi appeared Selvamani garlanded her and fell at her feet. He rose with folded hands and said, 'I shall forever be grateful to you. I will always be your humble servant and do as you say.'

These were not the hollow words of a politician. Selvamani was sincere in his gratitude for being summoned out of nowhere. He had been in the Party for as long as Sundarapandian had been. He came from a family of farmers who cultivated small plots scattered all over Pudupettai district. Despite his years in politics and urban life, he had retained the earthy simplicity of those who tilled the land. He was an uncomplicated man who was openly awed by those who were superior to him in knowledge and refinement. This was the one trait that saw him rise in prominence in the Party, for not only were his superiors pleased with his wide-eyed admiration for them and his ready humility, but they also approved of his willingness to work hard. And when it was convenient to ignore him or relegate him to unimportant tasks, it was easy to do so because he obeyed their wishes.

Selvamani pointed to his clan. 'My entire family insisted on coming with me to thank you.' Turning to them, he called them out, 'Here, come and greet our thalaivi.'

They rushed towards her with garlands, piling one on top of the other till she was buried in flowers.

'Fall at her feet!' Selvamani said. 'Show your respect.' With his own people he was firm and clearly in charge. In return, they appeared proud of him.

Selvamani's wife whipped out a silk sari and presented it to Lakshmi with great humility. His old mother gestured to her grandsons to put her down so that she could hold Lakshmi's hands and mumble her thanks to her. The children, who ran excitedly all around her, screaming at each other and pointing out various objects in the house, paused from time to time to fall at her feet.

When Selvamani and his clan finally left, beating drums and cheering their family hero, Lakshmi watched them disappear down the street. Their humility had touched her. But she also felt strangely satisfied. She had held sway over a large number of people. She had successfully negotiated a political landmine all on her own, without Mutthu's help or advice.

The next time she went to the hospital, she whispered to Mutthu: 'When you wake up you'll be proud of what I did. I'm keeping the chair warm for you.'

Miraculously, a few days later, Mutthu woke up from his coma. When the nurse came to check on him in the morning, to her disbelief she found him mumbling to himself and tossing his head restlessly. By the time Lakshmi arrived it was clear that he was fully conscious. Upon seeing Lakshmi he smiled crookedly in recognition.

'You were the first person he asked for,' the nurse informed her, beaming.

There was a gasp from the far end of the room, a short, muffled cry. Lakshmi turned and, to her surprise, saw Mutthu's wife in a corner, covering her mouth with a handkerchief.

Mutthu reached out for Lakshmi and mumbled something. There was something strange about the way his lips moved. He spoke through the right corner of his mouth, which he managed to open just wide enough for words to whistle through the gap. Then she noticed that he was only moving his right hand. His left hand felt limp, inert. She looked up at the doctors.

'He's completely paralysed on the left side. He doesn't seem to be able to hear anything either.'

She took a deep breath and looked at him. A thin, imbecilic smile appeared on his lips. He had either not heard or not understood what the doctor had said. 'Can this be cured?'

The doctor shook his head. 'Not to my knowledge. He's actually lucky to even have come out of the coma.'

Mutthu beckoned her. She leaned towards him to listen. 'Is your mansion ready?' he whispered.

She was surprised that he remembered. He was referring to the house he'd wanted to build for her for a long time. They hadn't even finalized the plan. All they had was a plot of land. 'It will be in a while,' she replied.

He did not register her response. 'Is your house ready?' he asked again.

'It will be in a while,' she repeated, louder this time.

He shook his head. 'The house,' he hissed in frustration.

She gave up. She put her hand over his mouth, calming him down.

Mutthu's wife broke down upon hearing this exchange. 'He did not even recognize me,' she sobbed, addressing Lakshmi directly for the first time ever. 'He did not even look at me. But he remembers the house he wants to build for you!' Years of stoic acceptance came crumbling down. The humiliation of not being recognized by her own husband with whom she had patiently lived for over thirty years overwhelmed her. She had known him when he had been a nobody, having just graduated from an extra to minor roles in a drama troupe. She had seen him rise to dizzying heights. She had fought for many years to protect him from the preying eyes of other women. She had also witnessed his fall. Perhaps she understood it a lot better than Lakshmi did.

Lakshmi half expected his wife to abuse her, but all she did was weep. One of her relatives comforted her and ushered her out of the room. As she left, she looked back at Lakshmi and snarled, 'You have humiliated me for the last time!'

Lakshmi did not know whether that was a threat or a last-ditch effort to salvage some self-respect. Would Mutthu's wife, like Kannaki, the virtuous, wronged wife, return wrathfully and set her world on fire?

Lakshmi would never see her again. The enduring image of Mutthu's wife in her mind was one of a woman stumbling down the hallway, weakly attempting to hold her head high. She felt sorry for her, but not without a perverse, ruthless undercurrent of satisfaction, for the flip side to Mutthu's wife's humiliation meant that she, Lakshmi, meant more to Mutthu. She finally had the answer to a question that had pestered her for years, a question she'd never mustered enough courage to ask: it was clearly with her that his affections lay, and it was she who would inherit his legacy.

Starting to Dream

Devaki had started talking about getting Ragini married the proper way before she went her mother's or her grandmother's way. The odds were against her, but Devaki needn't have worried, for Ragini, aware of it, worked hard to defy her family history. She had always assumed that her grandmother or I would find her a husband. That was the only way she would have it.

Devaki knew it would be hard to get her married. There would be a lot of inconvenient questions to answer. 'Keep your eyes open for good boys,' she began telling me whenever I visited them. 'Someone broad-minded and kind-hearted. There can't be too many of them around.'

Ragini had an additional condition. 'He will have to accept my activities.' She referred to the time she spent volunteering at a home for spastic children. I did know such a man—a young journalist, bright, well read, open minded, even if a tad too radical in his politics. He was lean, hungry-looking, and sported a beard like his idol, Che Guevara. (Radical socialism hadn't become passé in our world yet.)

The day he came to meet Ragini with his parents, Devaki was a nervous wreck. She had insisted on doing everything expected of a prospective bride's family. 'I must do what is expected of me,' she explained. 'Beyond that it's not in my hands.'

When the young man, his parents and his brothers arrived, Devaki greeted them deferentially, served them coffee and snacks, and sat at the edge of the sofa next to Ragini, smiling nervously.

The visitors made polite small talk and asked Ragini a few cursory questions to interrupt the long pauses that hung between them. I could see a hint of disappointment on their faces. I could see that Ragini had noticed it too, and was uncomfortable under their critical gaze. She probably even expected the mother to request her to walk to see if she had any deformities. But, fortunately, the mother made no such requests.

Half an hour later, when they got up to leave, both Ragini and Devaki were downcast. They knew the answer. Still, Devaki brought out a silver plate on which she had placed betel leaves, a coconut, cloth for a blouse and kumkumam, and offered these to the young man's mother.

A few days later, I ran into the young man at the press club. 'Saar,' he said with deference uncharacteristic of a socialist-sympathizer, 'for us to overlook her family background at least she must be exceptionally pretty. If only she weren't so dark-skinned. How can I convince my parents to compromise on everything?'

I could not believe my ears. This was Ragini he was talking about. She wasn't even a compromise? What impertinence! 'What's wrong with her?' I replied, furious. 'I've known her since she was a baby. I tell you, she's a gem. A gem of a girl! You'd be lucky to marry someone as pretty as her.'

Taken aback at my outburst he got up and left the room. 'You only talk big,' I shouted after him. 'Like you're the most socially conscious liberal since Bharati. But you're no different from the rest.'

The others at the club turned around to watch me curiously. I fell silent, feeling foolish, wondering why I had made a scene, drawing attention to myself in the process. I smiled sheepishly and hurried out.

What was it that the young man's words broke inside me? That I should feel personally offended was reasonable. Yet what impelled me to fight when all my life I've run away from conflict?

I could not say. I could not—and still can't—say why a lot of people around me—Devaki, Lakshmi, Ragini, Nasser Sharif,

Lakshmi's grandfather, I—kept quiet when we should have spoken up, and shouted when dignified silence was called for, why we remained inactive at crucial junctures of our lives and flared up at inconsequential ones. In the event, this particular incident was quickly forgotten, and I don't understand why I've resurrected it now. Perhaps I know, but am not willing to admit it. At least not yet.

★

This was when Lakshmi's dreams intensified.

These were no ordinary dreams that everybody—even she—dreamed. These didn't come randomly during sleep and were not grainy, obscure images that were sometimes nonsensical, sometimes replays of what had happened during the day. These were not dreams that rarely remained in one's memory till the morning. The dreams—visions—that visited her now were so startlingly vivid and logical, and appeared so regularly, often repeating themselves, often continuing from where they'd left off the previous night, that she sometimes wondered if they were not scenes from an alternative existence she had just become aware of. They were always fantastic: the difference was only in whether they were phantasmagoric, exuberant images in colours that she had never seen before, swirling, tumbling, crashing into one another, zygotic fusion of forms, sometimes psychedelic ripples of light like the red glow under the cross in her room in the cloister, but always hurtling forward with the monomania of a kamikaze pilot; or they were genteel, subdued, sometimes like a chiaroscuro in monochromatic shades.

It would only be much later that she began seeing them with her eyes open, when the sorcerer, by turns Morpheus, Phantasos and Phobetor, the sons of Hypnos, and the trimurti of her sleep-world, with his ruby-red eyes and the wiggle of his long-nailed, femininely delicate little finger led her deep into the labyrinth of this mysterious world, when she succumbed in full measure to the seductive, destructive charms of these dreams, sometimes jumping headlong into them and becoming a giant moth, circling the enticing flames in the sorcerer's eyes delightedly. But for now these visions always came to her when she slept, and when she woke up she could recall them to the very last detail, for they remained etched in her consciousness.

At first they baffled her, and when she could think of no explanations for them she dismissed them just as one would dismiss ordinary dreams.

Among the first of these dreams was a scene that came to her repeatedly: a marble lattice screen bordering a corridor, looking on to a courtyard, a jasmine creeper clinging on to it, radiating like the ribs of a hand-held fan. Beyond it was a garden with flowering plants, from her vantage point all stacked up as in a flower shop: tiger-lilies, carnations, rhododendrons and hibiscus. The grass, when visible, was strewn with orange and red gulmohur blossoms, inexplicable because there was no gulmohur tree there. A stone walkway bisected the garden and led to a pergola past a marble fountain in the centre spouting water. The pitter-patter of raindrops falling from the eaves into puddles below reached her ears, and she could distinguish each raindrop as it fell, pittering and pattering at a different pitch, with a different amplitude. Mists swirled around, and from the dark featureless corner from which she viewed the scene, it had a familiar softness. She couldn't tell if it was a recreation of the cloister or the courtyard of her future home—her mansion—that Mutthu had talked about frequently before his accident with the urgency of a man looking for his final resting place.

Much later, when she visited Mauro Tedeschi at his villa in the hills in Moncalieri outside Turin, after having wandered off to admire the Bohemian chandeliers, the marble floors, the de Chiricos and Modiglianis displayed casually, she stood in one of the corridors one rainy afternoon, astonished by the similarity of the scene. The lattice screen had the same whirls, the rain a grey sheet, audible only because of the drops that fell from the roof; there was a garden beyond it, the fountain redundantly spouting water. Only some of the plants were different—there were irises, orchids, tulips, gerbera, narcissi, anemone—and the garden was strewn with multicoloured autumn leaves instead of gulmohur blossoms. And, of course, there was the mist rising from the river below.

Later still she would smile ironically and say during moments of lucidity between bouts of frightening visions, 'They foretell my past.' As though in these dreams she had managed, in celluloid fashion, to go beyond her future and look back with the wisdom of afterthought.

She did not know then how much they would control her life later on. She was happy to seek them out for now, and in those early days of Mutthu's illness, she looked forward to sleep, to re-dream her mansion, inch by square inch, both as a palliative and as a diversion.

In another of her early dreams she saw a man driving a convertible with the top down despite the chilly fog. As he drove down the hill he accelerated till he was travelling at over 140 kmph when he entered the intersection. That's when his hands began to shake uncontrollably. The brakes squealed, the car skidded and careened off the road, tore through the parapet wall and plunged into the muddy river. When they pulled him out of the icy cold water he was dead.

Every time this dream occurred she woke up when the crane lifted the red car out. And every time, to her horror, the driver in the dream wasn't really a full-fledged human, but a two-dimensional wireframe, hollow, featureless, except for the wavy outline of Mutthu's characteristic haircut.

Was that all that Mutthu meant to her? A mere outline of a person? She looked for some indication of something more substantial, something more corporeal. But she could not even tell if the driver smiled joyfully like, she imagined, Mutthu had just before he had hit the pole.

Once, just before waking up she even put her hand out to touch the driver, but her hands sliced through the wire frame. No matter how frantically she tried to grasp the figure, there was nothing tangible.

For the next several months she consulted the best doctors, took him to sanatoriums, had him immersed in bubbling mineral waters that were reputed to cure even lepers. But none of this helped. She went to fortune-tellers, but they had nothing to tell her. She had pujas and homams performed for him, but the priests who conducted them looked none the wiser. She made a pilgrimage to the temple on the hill beyond Kuppam. There she promised to donate his weight in silver if he recovered. But the gods, and Mutthu, remained unmoved.

She finally turned to the holy man from Kuppam and put back the black angavastram on Mutthu's shoulder, which he had taken off before leaving for Italy. 'It doesn't go well with suits,' Mutthu had reasoned ruefully. 'And I can't possibly wear a veshti over there.'

'It's too late for that,' the holy man pronounced, shaking his head. 'But I know a sorcerer who might be able to cure him with magic.'

As she looked at the sorcerer's brown matted hair and beard swaying wildly to the nonsense words that he uttered, his eyes blood-shot from drinking all night, she asked herself again what Mutthu had meant to her, why she was so desperately seeking a cure for him. That was when she realized for the first time that her reasons weren't entirely selfless. It dawned on her that her feelings for Mutthu had always been clinical, sanitized of unnecessary sentiments, without passion. She looked at Mutthu's withered face in the light of the magician's candle and realized that her affection for him was learned rather than felt, that there was even something oedipal and filial about it. No matter what she did, she would not be able to convince herself otherwise. But she could not give up. She had to fill up the wireframe figure of her dreams and give it form, for only then would she have a validation of what she had shared with Mutthu all these years, before it withered away, leaving no trace of itself.

They were all alike, the four Pavesi women—Gloria, her mother and her sisters—alike in their grim, mysterious expressions, their pallid, featureless faces, their scarves and oversized sunglasses: a family of wraiths. They had come on a visit. When Lakshmi had seen them all together the previous year a couple of days after Mutthu's accident, she hadn't paid much attention to them. But now, seeing them hug each other at the airport, shrouds merging into one another in a blur, she was startled, and Surya stood nearby snickering at her reaction and nodding. 'I almost wet my pants when I saw them all the first time,' he whispered to her later, chuckling.

She wouldn't have noticed Gloria's father had Gloria not embraced him. He was bald and had brawny workman arms. He had a persecuted look. 'Wouldn't you, if you lived with four women like that?' Mauro Tedeschi joked later on.

She was amused by the way the women constantly talked to each other without appearing to part their lips, the noise they made without being noisy. She was amused, too, by the father's air of detachment, by Gloria's mother's attempts to make their family sound grand. 'My husband can trace his ancestry back to the ducal family of Mantova,' she whispered to Lakshmi once.

'The royalty of Mantova!' Mauro Tedeschi guffawed when she mentioned it later. 'I love her mother like my own, but don't be fooled by her stories. They're like me: of hardy Piedmontese peasant stock.'

She noticed that Surya was always eager to please them, ready with compliments, solicitous, attentive when they spoke. But they, especially Gloria's mother, didn't seem to notice his extra efforts. When she spoke to him it was often with a dismissive tinge in her voice. He would then double up his efforts to please them, as he did once, when he mentioned how he had taken care of things at this end to ensure that Mauro Tedeschi's bid to modernize the textile cooperative went through. But Gloria's mother pursed her lips then as always, and harrumphed softly. Gloria gently herded her mother away to the far corner of the room and sat by Surya, holding his hand. He looked different then, his mother-in-law's shadow on him, the umbra of disapproval overshadowing his natural sheen. Lakshmi couldn't understand it, and Surya was unwilling to explain; he laughed hollowly when she asked him later. It was Gloria who explained everything to her, displaying unusual, heartening candour. 'My mother has never been able to accept him,' she said. 'She thinks everything he has is because of me. But he's so patient with her. He hasn't given up trying to please her. I don't think he ever will. He'll do it at least for my sake, to prove to my mother that I didn't make a mistake by marrying him.'

Gloria was clearly grateful to Surya for his efforts. Lakshmi noticed how affectionate she was with him. Juxtaposed with her mother's sniffs and snorts, her affection for everybody around her stood out. It was not the kind of affection that was obvious enough to attract attention to itself; rather, it was always present in everything she did, even when she didn't say anything at all. When she spoke Lakshmi noticed how every sentence began or ended with *amore* or *caro*. *Amore* this. *Mio caro* that. Always. Hers was not a superficial, habitual and indiscriminate usage of words of endearment, but a sincere reflection of her affection for Surya, her sisters and her parents. And every time her mother expressed her displeasure with Surya, Gloria appeared by his side, as she did that day, shielding him from her mother, touching his hand lightly, and later whispering gently, soothingly, the way Sister Cecilia used to speak to Lakshmi in the beginning. '*Mio caro*,' she would say, and the sunshine would reappear on his face.

Slowly Lakshmi came around to the view that her reserve was nothing but still, deep affection and loyalty. And that she was and would always be a blur, a shadow of whoever was near her, an amorphous—sometimes comforting—figure, one who could never be defined no matter how much one tried. She was not a mystery, only an uncertain fog, an occasional enigma.

And where Lakshmi had seen Gloria and Surya as an odd, mismatched couple, she now saw the perfect understanding between them, how they read each other's thoughts, how they complemented each other, how they adjusted to each other's forms, how they were the couple that she, Lakshmi, and Mutthu could never be, despite all appearances.

Gloria and Surya took to dropping in quite often. Surya sat beside Mutthu and chatted idly—long monologues that were part of Mutthu's talk treatment—with him, mostly about films and celebrity gossip. He was the one who brought news about the biggest break-up in films that year. A well-known actor called Gopi, who had a terrible voice and needed to be dubbed, had got into a brawl with the man who lent him his voice and had broken up their partnership some months ago. In his latest film, Gopi had used his own voice, and the effect had been so unbearable that audiences had fled theatres with their hands on their ears. And now the actor was performing pujas, pleading with the gods to help patch up differences with his erstwhile partner. Surya showed Mutthu an article in a film magazine headlined unkindly 'Gopi Brays for the Return of His Voice'. Accompanying it was a photograph of him sitting bare-chested with a few priests pouring ghee into a fire.

'What, saar,' Surya commented. 'Tell me if it was not sheer arrogance that this fellow fought with his partner. And now look at him—so pathetic. I tell you midway through the first screening of his film there was a stampede at the theatre near my house. People rushing out like there was a fire. I hear he's afraid to even talk to his wife out of fear that she too might run away.'

Mutthu looked at the magazine and nodded in recognition. 'Kobee,' he uttered slowly and his right shoulder shook as he tried to laugh.

Surya turned to Lakshmi with a bright smile. 'Look, look. He has improved so much since our last visit. Just keep up with the physiotherapy and keep him active. He'll get up from his wheelchair in a few months.'

Lakshmi liked Surya's infectious—albeit unrealistic—optimism. She'd begun to look forward to their visits. Mutthu also became unusually active and bright in Surya's presence. On the days they visited it did seem like Mutthu was making discernible progress. The nights were calmer: Mutthu slept more soundly and Lakshmi's dreams were happier, even frivolous.

But Surya had begun to confide that he had dreams, too. He could not tell what exactly they were, but Lakshmi noticed that they'd intensified since his in-laws' visit. All he knew was that he wanted to look beyond exporting some leather to Europe and helping Mauro Tedeschi sell a few crores worth of industrial looms. 'Something big,' he said repeatedly. 'Only a matter of time before I stumble upon something big.'

'Why don't you consider putting money into films?' Lakshmi suggested in jest. 'Gopi's films.'

'What, madam?' he replied with a laugh. 'Ever since Mutthu's retirement the industry has been going downhill.'

Whether Mutthu understood Surya or not she could not tell, but at that moment his shoulder shook again and she hoped Surya's prediction of cure in a few months wasn't as far-fetched at it had sounded at first.

★

The women greeted Lakshmi with garlands and applied kumkumam on her forehead. They were honouring her to celebrate the fruition of their dreams. It was her first public engagement in a long time. She had turned away all requests since Mutthu's accident, but this one she readily accepted. She was curious to find out how the women outside Pudupettai had fared.

Mohana Devi, standing beside her, whispered, 'They're very excited and honoured by your presence. Look at the pride on their faces. A couple of years ago who would have predicted this?'

In eighteen months these women who lived in the village outside Pudupettai had not only managed to learn to read and write, but had also gained skills they had never thought of acquiring before. Mayilkannan and Mohana Devi had put the money allocated to the village from the fund Lakshmi had started to rehabilitate families affected by arrack to good use. Instead of distributing the money to individual families, they had used it to train the women in embroidery, basket-weaving, and incense-making skills. Now these women had formed their own cooperative through which they sold the items they made.

The women bubbled with excitement as they proudly exhibited their wares. They gave her baskets and incense and an embroidered cloth as gifts. Fathima, the girl who had taught them to read and write, maintained their accounts. She opened the notebook for Lakshmi, pointing out the money they'd already made.

Fathima's mother, with the veil of her burqa thrown open, pushed her way through the ring of women around Lakshmi and said proudly, 'My daughter's so smart in keeping accounts. She knows where every paisa is spent.'

'That's because she's a woman,' another woman commented. 'If we had allowed men to handle this, the whole venture would have failed.' The others cackled delightedly. She had said that loudly enough for the men, who had gathered at a distance, to hear. The woman then turned to them and, with a sweep of her hand, gestured contemptuously. 'They would have spent all the money on arrack.' The men, barred from participating in the all-women's celebrations, smiled sheepishly.

'If it wasn't for your efforts we'd still be in a wretched state, and our men would still be in a stupor,' the woman who led the cooperative said to Lakshmi. She fell at Lakshmi's feet. The other women followed suit. They looked like worshippers prostrating themselves in a temple. 'Of course,' the woman continued, 'none of this would have been possible without Collector-Amma and the only sensible man around here.' She touched Mohana Devi's feet, too, and then called out, 'Aiyah! Where are you?'

Mayilkannan stepped forward. The women rushed up to him and fell at his feet as well. 'Aiyah,' they said, 'you not only gave us knowledge, but also self-respect.' The respect and reverence in which the women held him was palpable. He alone among all the men who watched silently, stood, and deserved to do so, while the others sat passively like cattle on their haunches.

Lakshmi had not noticed him in the crowd earlier. He looked different. Like the women, he was dressed for the occasion. She had never seen him in trousers. In school he had always worn shorts, even in the cold winter months. In Pudupettai she had only seen him in a lungi, hitched up, his stilt legs visible, dangling below his lungi like those of a marionette.

A group of women then danced the kummi in a circle, singing and clapping, moving sideways in synchronicity, their bare feet kicking up wisps of dust. They were dressed in brightly-coloured saris—predominantly in shades of red and purple—hitched up, almost like skirts, with peacock feathers and jasmine in their hair, their eyes darkened and elongated with kohl. Mayilkannan stood outside the circle and recited a poem, one of the rare occasions when he spoke: 'Gone are those who kept books away from women /And the strange ones who boasted, "We will lock these women in our homes"— /Today they hang their heads in shame.'

She realized then that it wasn't his clothes that made him appear different. He looked calm and mature. Perhaps it was his working with these women over the past year and a half that had brought about the change. After all he had been practically their guardian and had brought about the kind of change in their lives that few would have been able to do. If he still bore grudges against her for supporting Murugesan's candidature, he didn't show it, for he smiled at the women. She remembered his smile for a long time afterwards. It was not hideous, Quasimodo-like, as it usually was. On the contrary, it spread across his face, full of joy and fraternal pride; a smile that reflected his inner ecstasy at the fruition of one of his dreams, a smile that made her see him as a human being for the first time.

Kuravas

The innocuous marketplace disturbance caught Lakshmi's attention and she read the newspaper report with interest. A group of kuravas had got into a brawl with some locals over the price of watches they were trying to sell to a shopkeeper. What started off as a normal argument quickly flared up, with the kuravas and the shopkeepers exchanging slurs and insults. In the ensuing fist fight a local retailer was so badly beaten up that he had to be rushed to the hospital. A few others went home with broken bones and bleeding heads. The police had to intervene to maintain order.

She got up and called up the police commissioner of Pudupettai.

'Nothing to worry about, madam,' he said. 'Just a bunch of fellows fighting in the streets instead of trying to settle their differences in a civil manner.'

But Lakshmi was unconvinced. The kuravas had taken up armed struggle on their island of pearls. In recent years they had started returning to the mainland and sought refuge in the state. 'I want you to investigate this incident thoroughly,' she told him. 'There's more to it than just watches. Remember, there's trouble brewing on the island.'

A few days later the police commissioner called back. 'You were right, madam,' he began. 'Smuggled goods. Swiss and Japanese watches from Singapore and Hong Kong. Possibly stolen as well. We found hundreds of them in a shed they had rented. Pathetic fools, they didn't even have the sense to deal intelligently. They chose to fight for a few rupees when they had so many more watches in the shed. In any case it looks like these fellows are mere cogs in the giant wheel. They seem to have many chains of command, and these fellows know nothing about who's in charge, or where the profits go. But, thanks to your intuition, madam, we have uncovered something big.'

She went to meet Selvamani and some of his cabinet colleagues that evening. 'You should have them all monitored. They just cannot be trusted.'

'Of course, madam,' responded Selvamani. 'I'm sure the police commissioner of Pudupettai will agree with your assessment.'

'I don't mean just Pudupettai. This is big. Patrol the seashore. Ask for help from the central government—'

Murugesan, a lot more respectful to Lakshmi since his election, disagreed politely. 'Madam, we can prosecute the criminals, but how can we touch the innocent ones?'

'How do you know they are not all involved?'

'I don't, madam. But—'

'So until then do we allow them to run around freely in the state? Who knows what all these people are up to?'

'I agree,' interjected Selvamani. 'Today they're bringing in smuggled goods, tomorrow they'll bring in guns.'

'They already are, saar,' Murugesan said.

Lakshmi leant forward and looked at him closely. She was surprised by his nonchalance. 'Then there's even more reason to get to the bottom of this.'

'Why, madam? They're not criminals. They're fighting for their most basic rights. They're fighting for their survival.'

'Nonsense!' Murugesan's continued intransigence began to irritate her.

'Madam, we only hear of the trouble they're causing. We never hear about the reason behind it. If you'll allow me, I can arrange for all of us to meet one of their representatives to hear their side of the story.'

'I know their side of the story,' she replied curtly.

Nevertheless, a few days later she went to meet a man

claiming to represent the kuravas. He was unusually dark for a kuravan, and he wore none of the colourful clothes she remembered from her childhood. He spoke respectfully, but confidently. He told them about his people, about their current struggle.

For centuries they had migrated continuously and slowly like an inexhaustible caravan of ants and had settled down on the island of pearls their ancestors had serendipitously discovered. They lived on the coast, diving for pearls to sell and fish to eat. They learnt their trade from local pearl divers and lived among them. With time they changed: the sun and salt water made their skins dark, rough and scaly, their hair as coarse as jute, their eyes a murderous red. They now ate a different food, spoke the language of their hosts and discarded their traditional clothes for loincloths. The longer they lived on the island, the less they remembered their ancestors. It was only the constant flow of their brethren from across the narrow strait of water separating the island from the mainland that kept the memories of their ancestors from being completely obliterated.

And the newcomers disembarked from their small fishing boats excitedly at the end of their long journeys that had lasted many generations, only to be disappointed by what they saw. Their predecessors had changed beyond recognition— they looked so sallow, so emaciated and impoverished, and so dark, like the locals. They lived in tiny shacks, these kuravas who had acculturated, among refuse and utter neglect along the beach or in the interior jungles where nobody else dared venture. It was so unlike the image the newcomers had had of a paradise full of riches and happy people romping all over it.

But there was no turning back. They could not reverse a journey they had begun so many generations ago that they could not remember their home any more.

But trouble began brewing when their collective dissatisfaction boiled over with the slow recognition that they were being taken advantage of. That the pearls they dived for all day—clamping their noses for what seemed to be an eternity, during which time their lungs almost burst, diving to such depths that the weight of the water above them almost managed to keep them there—those pearls were not theirs at all. The men in silk suits who took the pearls they fished reaped the profits and built themselves large mansions in the cities, drove expensive, air-conditioned cars, and sent their children to university abroad. The bodies of the profiteers dripped with the pearls the kuravas fished for while the kuravas themselves wore none, their women's ankles and necks shamefully unadorned. How many of them had died fishing for the rich people, how many had come to the surface with collapsed lungs! How many of them had not come up in time and their bodies had washed onshore at night, their eyes popping out, their mouths open, having given up the fight and lying abandoned on the moonlit silver sands like rotting fish. How many of them had come up with digits severed by barracudas, their torsos bearing puncture wounds inflicted by sharks. Those who did survive said they had visions of their ancestors down in those depths. They said it was more difficult to bear the disappointment of their ancestors than the deaths of their fathers, brothers and sons.

It all started when they demanded more money and some pearls for themselves. They demanded fresh water to drink, schools for their children, better roads in their villages. They demanded dignity. But their words fell on deaf ears. They had been kuravas forever, they were told. At least now they had homes, ungrateful wretches. They had hitherto been uncivilized; now they had been absorbed into the island's culture.

So they protested. They refused to dive. They rioted. But the police dispersed them by beating them, by blinding them with tear gas, by arresting their leaders. And then the conflict escalated. They took the matter into their own hands. There were reprisals and counter-reprisals, lynching, kidnapping, maiming, even killing. They decided they would fight, even if it meant with guns and bombs and mines and rockets. And they always had a sanctuary to hide in, just across the straits that they could cross by hopping over the jagged rocks that appeared on the surface of the water at regular intervals like a string of pearls on the neck of the sea. Indeed, they believed these rocks were remnants of a bridge their ancestors had built for them long ago. A bridge to a paradise they were in danger of losing.

'You see,' Murugesan said later after the kuravan had gone. 'They're treated like dogs there. Do you blame them for fighting back? The least we can do is to leave them alone when they come here to hide in our hills to regroup, to fortify their spirits and bodies. Can we at least not allow them to dream here?'

Typical, Lakshmi thought. Typical of the kuravas to create a web of myth and lies to justify their existence and their aggression. What fantastic storytellers they were! They had so cleverly infiltrated the Party. Murugesan's support alone was reason enough to be suspicious.

'They cannot be trusted!' she snapped as she rose to leave. 'They're no dreamers. They're squatters. Allow them to sit at your doorstep for a moment and they'll take over your whole house and destroy your family.'

★

One evening, Mayilkannan's kuravan friends convinced him to accompany them into the forests, to a shack they'd built so deep inside the woods that they had to hack their way through bramble and thick undergrowth for a long time before they arrived there. The walls of the shack were made of mud and stones, the roof of discarded corrugated iron sheets that were so badly rusted that there were numerous holes in them. Inside it was dark, for there were no windows and the door was so small that they had to stoop low to enter. One of them flicked a cigarette lighter and lit an oil lamp in a corner of the shack. The dim light threw gloomy shadows about the room.

The shack was untidy. On the floor were a couple of unfurled mats with cotton blankets carelessly piled on them. On a jute string slung across the room hung lungis, underwear and shirts. In the far corner, camouflaging a huge sack, there were more lungis and shirts.

Mayilkannan nodded in acknowledgement. This was where they lived.

The kuravas then ushered him out once more into the forest. Less than a hundred yards away, concealed in some bushes were a few blackened pots placed on top of one another. From the side of one of the pots a thin plastic tube descended into a kerosene can. In the large copper pot at the bottom was the fermented brew—a few days' old mixture of jaggery, dates, nutmeg, ginger, poppy seeds, chillies, chalk and other ingredients that Mayilkannan could not identify—bubbling in the heat of the fire under it. One of the kuravas removed the tube and peered into the kerosene can. It was heavy with liquid. He nodded with satisfaction. He emptied the kerosene can into a larger drum of water, where the two liquids sloshed and mixed together. He then put the can back in its place and the bubbling pot continued to produce a slow trickle of arrack that arrived through the tube, dripping slowly like saline from an IV tube.

Dipping a glass into the diluted drum of arrack they offered it to Mayilkannan. He had never seen arrack being made, so he watched the set-up keenly as he sipped from his glass. The kuravas winked and chortled at his wide-eyed wonder.

They went back into the shack with their glasses and bottles full. Mayilkannan sat on the floor, leaning against a wall. One of the men pointed to the sack and said, 'Do you know what's in it? Guns and bombs!' The man waited for Mayilkannan's reaction. But there was none. 'You can have a gun, too, if you want.'

Mayilkannan did not respond. He went back to his glass.

'What's wrong? We haven't heard you speak in a long time. You haven't even recited your poetry or beaten your drum.'

Mayilkannan shrugged.

'Leave him alone,' another kuravan said to the first. 'He must be suffering from an affliction of the heart. I remember I had also lost my tongue when I fell in love.'

'So is it that woman with a scar you've told us about?'

'Be careful before you get entangled with a married woman.'

But Mayilkannan wasn't listening. He was gazing at his glass and the sack in the corner alternately. To be invited to their den was an honour. But he wondered why they trusted him so much. He had never said a word in support of their struggle; in fact he hardly knew why they were hoarding arms. All he did was to bring his gloomy presence and drink down their hospitality. What sort of naïve men were these? Or were they, on the contrary, so shrewd and subtle in their activities that they were using him to their advantage without his knowledge?

He did not know how long the chatter and the advice continued. But at some point he realized that that the topic of conversation had changed. The men around him talked about a boat that would come ashore to a tiny fishing village in the darkness of the night. It would contain guns, grenades and ammunition. All concealed beneath fish. For training, not for use on the island. They had to be careful. If discovered, their training camp would be a non-starter. 'Come with us,' they told Mayilkannan. 'Forget letters and numbers. There's a greater cause to fight for: our dignity, our ancestors.'

But Mayilkannan wasn't listening. He was thinking about Thenmozhi, the scar-face, who had taken to ignoring him, seeing through him. He nodded at his companions, more out of habit than as a sign of assent. His gaze was fixed on the glass in his hand. After every swig he studied the amount the liquid reduced by, feeling more and more sorrowful, for there were no more bottles after this. He heard the spirits of the kuravas rise; they talked about how well connected he was in case they got into trouble. But he was down to his last mouthful. As it went down his gullet he could feel the burning; his whole body was on fire. He got up and ran towards the stream. It was hardly a trickle, just about ankle-deep, summer being not far away. He lay down in it, letting the cool water flow around him and soothe him.

The perplexed men followed him to the stream and pulled

him out. 'Bathing in the middle of the night! Do you want to fall ill?'

They put him down in the middle of the shack and wiped his hair. He curled himself up and closed his eyes. The last thing he heard them talking about, before he fell asleep, was war. Bloody, ferocious war.

After the men had fallen asleep he stepped out of the shack and, even though he knew there were jackals and snakes and bears in the forest, he lay down on the ground with a sigh of relief. He hadn't slept indoors in a long time; he found it suffocating. Like a true kuravan.

A few weeks later, at night, while the kuravas and Mayilkannan slept, a posse of policemen suddenly descended upon them and pinned them to the ground even before they had a chance to open their eyes. The kuravas whimpered and shouted and pleaded their innocence, but Mayilkannan did not protest. He simply lay on his stomach as a policeman handcuffed him. The inspector who headed this team eyed each of the men and demanded that they own up without causing unnecessary delay. *Own up to what,* Mayilkannan wondered. What were the kuravas snivelling about? Then it dawned on him that the policemen were looking for the arms. He stared at the hidden sack in the corner, wondering how long it would take the policemen to discover this pathetically hidden cache. The policemen, in the meantime, had flashlights scouring every corner of the shack and found the sack almost immediately. They ripped it open and cried triumphantly as hand grenades and AK-47s spilled out. Another policeman discovered a couple of copper and clay pots the men used to distil arrack.

'Illegal arms and illegal liquor!' the inspector commented with some satisfaction. He turned around and looked at Mayilkannan. 'So this is where you get your stuff. You actually make it yourself!'

The policeman who'd discovered the pots, chimed in, 'What gall, saar! He goes around closing arrack shops by day and distils liquor by night!'

Mayilkannan still did not protest. He allowed them to escort him through the forest to the place where the dirt track that led into the forest ended abruptly. Police jeeps, flashing their blue lights, were waiting for them.

On their long journey to the police lock-up the kuravas looked at Mayilkannan accusingly. 'We trusted you,' they said bitterly, flashing their eyes at him.

Mayilkannan was taken aback at the unexpected accusation. He shook his head vigorously. 'No,' he wanted to shout. 'I know nothing about this.' But no words came out. The jeep rattled over the unpaved road loudly, its bolts and hinges loose, squeaking plaintively. Mayilkannan turned away from them. He could not bear to see the look in their eyes. They thought that he had led the policemen there. And now his silence was being interpreted as an admission of guilt. Why couldn't he simply deny being involved? Why was it so difficult for him to open his mouth and plead innocence?

Perhaps he had unwittingly led the police to the den. He wasn't sure how, but something told him he was responsible. He was not secretive enough. He possessed nothing; he hid nothing. Too many people knew he went into the forest for arrack. He had probably even played his thavil on the way there, making an infernal noise. Some even knew of his kuravan friends.

By the time he was roughly shoved into a cell by a policeman, guilt had begun to weigh heavily on him. And as if to confirm his guilt, a policeman pointed at him and said to another, 'We need to follow only a few more fools like him and the entire movement will come to a halt.'

The two men laughed. Mayilkannan turned to his companions and tried to break his silence. But still no words emerged from his lips. There was nothing he could say to explain his foolishness.

Even before Mayilkannan's arrest K. Abdul Latheef had decided to strike. Kuravas throughout the state had begun disappearing, one or two at a time. Some had returned as mysteriously as they had disappeared and had refused to talk.

In a lengthy article he called the government's case into question. He alleged that several of the kuravas had been tortured by the police and had made up wild stories of conspiracy, hoping to obtain their freedom by giving the police bigger mysteries to unravel. There certainly was a kernel of truth to the claim that the smuggling operations were tied to the insurgency efforts on the island, but far too many details were made up or exaggerated, and many innocent people remained locked up in jail without any shred of evidence of their involvement. Alongside the article were photographs of men with sallow, unshaven faces, bruised backs and blue fingernails, looking spiritless and terrified.

But it wasn't just one gadfly journalist. Of late, especially after the midnight forest raid, a lot of people had started asking questions. They questioned the motive behind Mayilkannan's arrest. His presence in the den at the time of the raid itself did not constitute proof of his involvement, they argued. Did the magnitude of the crime justify its prosecutorial zeal when much larger issues were being ignored?

K. Abdul Latheef directly accused Lakshmi of over-reacting, of fanning suspicions against the kuravas in the state, most of whom were law-abiding. How could she, a non-elected member of a political party, who was not accountable to the public, wield such influence?

What had been a virtue before the elections was now being used to question her legitimacy.

The criticism stung. Lakshmi felt humiliated by what everybody said and implied.

'How can they criticize us when they should be applauding?' she asked angrily.

'Madam,' Selvamani said, trying to placate her. 'Some people will constantly criticize no matter what we do.'

That's what Mutthu would have said as well. But it was easy to rationalize in the abstract. Here were people publicly pointing fingers at her, ridiculing her. How could she not be expected to defend herself? Wouldn't not reacting be construed as a sign of weakness, an invitation to crush her at a later date? She looked at all the cabinet members around her. 'You all may be dependent on public goodwill for your positions, but I don't have to take this lying down. I'm not going to compromise my self-respect.'

★

I heard stories of how Lakshmi had reacted publicly. My colleagues reported how icily she had begun treating journalists, how they heard her shout at K. Abdul Latheef behind closed doors after a press conference. 'How dare you accuse me of irresponsible behaviour when it was *I* who was instrumental in unearthing the whole thing? Yes, they were bringing in arms to be used not against us, but their oppressors on the island, but are you so naïve to think that all that firepower would not be as easily directed at us? And you say I'm being hysterical when you go about writing that kuravas had their nails removed, the hair in their nostrils burnt? Show me even one man who was tortured!'

I tried to verify this with K. Abdul Latheef himself. After much reluctance he nodded. 'She's a rakshasi,' he said tersely.

I must have looked unconvinced, for K. Abdul Latheef ran his fingers through his beard and said, 'A person who reacts badly to valid criticism should not be given power. But, unfortunately, Selvamani does whatever she wants him to.'

'You can't hold her responsible for everything the police does.'

But he smiled in response. A smile that wanted to tell me I was full of it, that it was my emotional attachment to her that was clouding my judgement. I got up and walked away, angry with him, and with myself.

But a few days later I saw why he had said that when I watched a video recording of one of her press conferences. With microphones arrayed in front of her, she spoke grimly, defiantly. She showed pictures of items the police had recovered from the kuravas: expensive watches piled up as casually as rice in a granary, a trunk full of foreign currency notes in large denominations, several AK-47s, a few hand grenades. The police commissioner of Pudupettai stood by, interjecting with details and confirming figures she quoted.

'There!' Lakshmi exclaimed. 'If this is not proof, I don't know what is!'

She looked around, challenging her audience to speak up. After a few moments of silence an off-camera voice spoke, 'But I don't know what all this proves.'

'You know nothing,' she snarled. 'And yet all of you make a lot of noise. Instead of appreciating the fact that we have uncovered a nexus between the insurgents and petty criminals all of you have the gall to criticize us. You who shed crocodile tears for them, will you have them for your neighbours?'

Her voice became shrill. I couldn't help thinking how foolish she had been, how instead of using the opportunity to garner praise she had wantonly wasted the goodwill that had existed between her and the press.

I took the video cassette and a photograph I had procured from one of my colleagues on my next visit to Devaki and Ragini. I showed them the photograph first. Ragini looked at it for a long time at various angles, and handed it over to Devaki. 'She's so beautiful. Can I keep it, Vasu-maama?'

'Of course. It's for your collection.'

Ragini happily pulled down a scrapbook from the shelf and flipped through its pages to find a spot for the latest addition. She had taken to cataloguing every little item related to Lakshmi that we could lay our hands on, the way I used to collect articles about my favourite cricketers when I was young. The shelf was filled with books bulging with articles and photographs, audio and video cassettes, even a mango-patterned sari that the maidservant had received from Lakshmi, wrapped in plastic with its original folds intact. These items had replaced Ragini's dance paraphernalia. Only her ankle bells still sat there, discoloured, unused since her grandfather's death.

'Actually, why don't we frame it?' I suggested.

'That's a good idea,' she replied.

'That fellow at the street corner does a very good job. Why don't you give it to him.'

Ragini left right away and I handed over the video cassette to Devaki. Devaki shook her head as she watched it. 'Why is she getting involved in all this? Why can't she take care of herself and Mutthu and leave the others to squabble?'

'It's too late,' I remarked pessimistically. 'She has allowed herself to be sucked into the muck and nobody will let her escape.'

'You journalists are being irresponsible,' she retorted angrily. 'It's all the unfair publicity that's making her fight back. Why can't you people leave her alone if you can't appreciate what she's doing?'

'How many people am I going to prevent from speaking up?'

'At least write something to counter their lies.'

I did not respond.

'Take it away, Vasu,' Devaki said eventually, popping the cassette out of the VCR. 'And don't come home if you don't have anything better to show us.'

★

Lakshmi got out of the car feeling more anxious than defiant. She'd have preferred to stay inside, but the crowd that had mobbed the car, barring her entry into Pudupettai, appeared to be in no mood to budge. She saw hands sliding over the windows and doors, seeking the handles. It was inevitable that she face them.

She had expected protestors to demand Mayilkannan's release. But that had still not prepared her for facing the crowd. It was the first time that she faced so many angry faces. She saw Mohana Devi in the crowd and her spirits rose. She smiled at the collector. But Mohana Devi did not respond.

'Brothers and sisters,' Lakshmi finally said to the crowd. 'I understand your anger. That's why I have come here. I will look into this matter and ensure that justice is done. But I can do so only if you allow me into your town.'

'Will you have him released?' someone in the crowd demanded.

'A judge from the high court is here with me. He will inquire into the circumstances of Mayilkannan's arrest. If the judge determines that Mayilkannan was wrongly arrested, he will be released immediately.'

But the crowd was not satisfied. Anything short of a direct yes meant a no. For a moment Lakshmi wished she had brought Mutthu with her; his very presence would have won over the crowd. Then Mohana Devi unexpectedly came to the head of the crowd with her hands raised, urging the protestors to let Lakshmi enter the town. Obediently, the crowd parted. Lakshmi admired the influence Mohana Devi had over them, but she also felt distinctly uncomfortable that the bureaucrat had managed to do what she herself hadn't.

Later, while talking to Mohana Devi and the police commissioner, to her utter shock, it became clear to Lakshmi that it was Murugesan who had asked his men to track Mayilkannan's movements. They had unexpectedly stumbled upon the kuravas' den and had set the police on them.

'That rat!' she muttered as she reached for the telephone and gripped it tightly so that she didn't have to clench her teeth as she listened to Murugesan.

'Madam,' his voice came through, the hiss of a viper over the crackling line. 'I was simply making sure that the police obeyed you and dealt with the kuravas with a strong hand. What can I do if that drunken poet fellow happened to be with them?'

She imagined him smiling ingratiatingly on the other end, his pearly white teeth shining against his dark, scheming face.

'Release him,' she said to the police commissioner decisively, hanging up and clenching her teeth. 'Release him right away. We have no case against him.'

But the furore did not subside. Over the next few days she kept her ears open, and everywhere she went she heard people whispering behind her back. There were voices everywhere, and with every passing day these voices only seemed to grow louder. Soon it seemed as though everyone was clamouring for her, baying for her blood.

Surya tried to pacify her. 'It's all in your head, madam,' he said gently.

But she was in no mood to be reassured. The voices were too loud and clear to be in her head. She looked at him suspiciously. Was he, too, part of the campaign to vilify her?

He unfurled a newspaper in front of her. 'See for yourself. Not one word critical of you.'

'Maybe not this one. Haven't you been reading what they've written about me? Especially that arrogant Latheef, who continues to write all those lies about me. And everybody says there's nothing we can do about him. How can that be possible? Whenever I say something everybody howls in protest. But when he defames me nobody questions him.'

'But he didn't defame you.'

'Are you deaf and blind?' she shouted, angry at his insistence that everything was okay. 'At least *you* don't have to support them.'

For the next few days she felt torn. There were times when she wanted to rush out of the house and defend herself, to shout at all her critics. She wanted to cut them down to size, all of them, especially K. Abdul Latheef, and Murugesan, the snake whose fangs bore into the very hand that had fed him. At the very next instant she would have the urge to flee farther into the darkest recesses of her house and stay there forever.

One morning she sat by Mutthu as he lay in bed. She contemplated his serene sleeping face. Only *he* could deal with all this in good humour.

'How can you continue smiling?' she had once asked him several months ago. 'Don't public criticisms bother you?'

'My dear,' he'd responded then, 'no matter what you do, out of ten people at least six will find fault with it. You should never take these things personally. You should brush them aside and move on. You need a thick skin.'

'I don't have one,' she'd said.

'Don't I know that? You must develop one.'

She missed him. She missed his self-deluding confidence that quelled any doubts in his mind. But she also realized that he was the one who had pushed her into all this. If only he'd left her alone! Resentment took root inside her and grew rapidly. She shook him angrily. 'I'm going to stay away from all of it,' she hissed. 'I'm not going to save your seat for you. You'll have to reclaim it yourself.'

He looked perplexed. For a moment she thought he understood her. 'I want to go,' he then mumbled.

'Go where? Do you want to leave me?'

'I want to go,' he repeated, this time pointing to the bathroom with a sense of urgency.

'I'm done,' she shouted in exasperation, ignoring his request. 'Do you understand? This chapter is over.'

The Birth of a Baby

One night in her sleep Lakshmi remembered the smell of her baby.

She saw herself in a strange two-storeyed house whose dilapidated walls revealed skeletal bricks underneath, reminding her of her grandmother's home. Above her was the high roof. Sunbeams fell on the floor through a couple of skylights in the ceiling. The rooms on both floors were along the periphery, forming a quadrangle in the middle. In the centre of the quadrangle was the furnace around which two men worked. One of them stoked its hot, orange flames at regular intervals, while the other, an old man, blew glass through a long tube. What emerged from the other end of the tube was something peach-coloured, ventricose and asymmetrical, and as the man rolled the tube, controlling his breath like a flautist, a molten jug took shape, changing colour to yellow, to colourless and finally to light green.

She couldn't tell how she had got there. When this dream recurred on other nights she once arrived on the prow of the boat, leaning against the railing, squinting against the cool, damp breeze that slapped her face, causing condensed vapour to trickle down her face in tiny rivulets of wintry sweat as the boat navigated a muddy brown lagoon, bobbing up and down in the waves. On another occasion she flew in on some large bird—an eagle? a griffin? Mutthu's Garuda?—that gracefully landed on the roof. On yet another occasion she simply glided through the walls as she sometimes imagined Gloria doing. Nor could she tell where she was: her grandmother's house converted to a foundry? A *fornace* in Murano? The sprawling house where Maama and Maami taught dance?

And then the old man led her past the piles of mixtures to be melted, the chemicals—chromium, lead, manganese, silica— to be mixed in, the bin of broken glass, various kinds of tools and pipes resting against the wall, and up the stairs. In a large room that had showcases lining the four walls and display cases in the centre, Lakshmi stopped to catch her breath, for all around her was glassware: vases, carafes, vials, goblets, ashtrays, paperweights shaped like dolphins and stallions and storks, crystal tumblers, oriental tea sets, rose bowls, trays, and urns. They sparkled; the colours seemed to leap out of the showcases and filled the room with rowdy enthusiasm. She had never seen so many colours, some she had never even imagined. There were all kinds of glass on display: latticino, coloured, lead crystal, opaque, sheer, plain. There were items with gold filigree, some with floral patterns, some monochromatic art deco pieces, some blown out delicately.

He then led her to the next room, which was full of mirrors of all shapes and sizes. Everywhere she turned she saw her taut face, the man's toothless grin. In some mirrors the reflection was a little distorted and the man's nose appeared larger, like a caricature. She looked away and in another mirror she noticed how withdrawn her eyes were, how mirthless the curve of her lips. Everywhere she looked she saw her own tense face, the man's nose, his impish smile, the wisps of grey hair peeking out of his cap. The longer she stared at the mirrors the more forlorn she looked, and the more impish his face became.

Finally she turned away from the mirrors and asked him, pointing to the other end of building, which was unlit, 'What's there?'

'I don't know myself,' the man said. 'Those rooms have always been locked as long as anybody can remember.'

Her interest piqued, she took the opportunity to leave the room of mirrors, relieved that she didn't have to see the reflections any more.

'According to our family legend, that part of the house is haunted,' the man explained. They stood in the corridor outside the room, leaning against the shaky wooden balustrade that looked down into the pit of the building. 'Many generations ago, the couple who occupied those rooms had a daughter who was so attached to them that she would go to nobody else. When the girl was eight, her parents left on a long voyage to far-off lands, leaving her in the care of relatives. For weeks and months the little girl cried for her parents, standing at the window, looking out towards the sea, in the direction in which they had gone. But they never came back. The little girl never left her room. She never stopped crying for her parents till she herself died young.'

The old man paused for breath. Lakshmi looked out of the window of one of the open rooms. She could only see the red tiled roofs of buildings. Some of the tiles were broken, a lot of them were blackened with moss and muck, and some had television antennae growing out of them.

'Can I see the room?'

The old man was taken aback. 'Why do you want to go there? There's nothing in there.'

But Lakshmi insisted. The old man pottered off to get a large bunch of old iron keys. As they approached the room, dust and bats flew all around them. After several minutes of trial and error the old man finally managed to unlock one of the rooms. There was nothing in the room; it was absolutely bare. Lakshmi was disappointed. She had hoped to see some evidence of the girl's life in the room: her clothes, her toys, her loss, the stains of her tears on the window sill, something to tell her that someone had lived, cried and died here long ago. But there were only generations of dust on the floor. As she walked across the room her footprints appeared in the dust. She struggled with the wooden window and pushed it open. Sunlight and dust filled the room. She sneezed. Outside, over the clutter of red tiles and antennae she could see the lagoon and the open sea. She clutched the wrought iron bars of the window and stood there for a long time. It reminded her of her days of solitude, her punishment. That was when she smelled something. She sniffed and sneezed as dust entered her nostrils. The more she sneezed the clearer her nose became and the more she could smell the scent, till she knew what it was, till she realized that the cavity in her memory had now completely filled up and there was no escaping its effects. She swiftly walked out of the room, pinching her nose between her thumb and forefinger. The glassmaker looked at her in surprise, for he had smelled nothing. When he locked the room only the scent of a baby and Lakshmi's footprints were left behind. Perhaps to be covered by more generations of dust, perhaps never to be reopened.

For several nights she remembered her daughter. Like the bout of hyperactive memory that gripped her years ago, the remembrance of milk-breath kept recurring, till she could smell it everywhere around her. She tried to distract herself by being involved with Mutthu's care. But that only exacerbated her memory till she started imagining her life defined entirely by an immobile Mutthu and a craze-inducing memory.

One morning she did what she had never thought she would do. She contacted her mother. Not directly, but through a messenger. And even then only to tell her that she would like to meet her long-abandoned daughter. Alone.

On the appointed night Lakshmi arrived alone at the beach, feeling safe and anonymous in the dark. Between the beach road and the beach, in a tiny public park with palm trees and low hedges and cement walkways, right at the spot where Lakshmi's parents had stood on a dais and celebrated Independence, there stood a bronze statue of Mahatma Gandhi, erected soon after his death. It stood tall and imposing, though Gandhi leant on a stick, on a pedestal so high that people could not touch his feet even on tiptoes. Behind it, wedged between two rows of hedges, were the busts of lesser men who deserved the honour less than either her father or grandfather, both of whom had dropped out of public memory.

When she arrived, Lakshmi was shocked by what she saw. Her daughter, now a grown woman, stood nervously by the statue that loomed over her in the moonlight like an unsculpted rock. Lakshmi caught sight of her from a distance and stopped short. In the pale light she could see her daughter's features and even though they were unlike Pulcinella's exaggerated features, Lakshmi was reminded of Pulcinella's face, of the smell of rats' guts and crushed eucalyptus leaves. She stood behind a palm tree and watched her daughter fidget with the hem of her sari and peer into the dark. The swaying palm fronds cast dancing shadows across her daughter's face, and it seemed as though she were laughing, revealing her teeth, especially her oversized canines. For the next few moments her features appeared to morph, as if she were a character in an animated cartoon, till Lakshmi saw before her Pulcinella's owl-eyes, his scaly skin, his elongated snout, his crooked mouth. Her daughter even had his loping gait, and in a woman it looked terrible. Lakshmi felt a sudden unbearable revulsion, the revulsion, she remembered, in which she had conceived her daughter. She saw in her daughter not the man who had recited poetry to the kummi dancing women, but the boy in shorts peering into a rat hole.

Lakshmi turned around and fled, abandoning her daughter for the second time. When she arrived home she was short of breath. She stood in the balcony, staring at the mango tree and the stars above it, trying hard to ignore the cacophony of accusations in her mind.

Ragini had been excited as she had never before been. All evening she had been nervous, trying on different saris, looking at the watch repeatedly. 'Do I look good in this, paati? No, no, I prefer the brown one. What do you say, paati?'

'You're behaving as though someone is coming for a bride-viewing,' Devaki had said, laughing. 'Your mother is not going to care how you look.'

But that night when Ragini had glimpsed her mother behind a palm tree and had watched her run away moments later, she had barely flinched, her face as inscrutable as ever. Devaki and I had been watching from a distance, 'Maybe she didn't see you and thought you hadn't come,' Devaki said to Ragini now.

'Yes, it was too dark.'

'That's right, dear. It was so dark I almost didn't see her myself.'

That's when Ragini snapped. She reared her head with uncharacteristic anger. 'Stop it, paati!' she shouted. 'How long are you going to fool yourself and others? Look at these miserable little lives of ours! We only watch. We do nothing. When someone slaps us we present the other cheek. We're cowards, paati. We're mere shadows of people. When are we going to take control of our lives? When are we going to assert ourselves? How horrible of amma to have left like that! Is this what a mother does? I should have run after her and demanded to know why she had left me as a baby or why she didn't want to talk to me today. Even if it meant us screaming and arguing and severing ties once and for all, it would have served a purpose. That would have been better than coming home and sobbing like this with self-pity.' Tears ran down her cheeks and she made no attempt to wipe them. 'Paati, all your life you've been so passive that you might as well have been dead. Even cows take more initiative. You're happy to have the chance to pity yourself. And that's how I have turned out. If only you'd taken some action, or allowed thatha to do something years ago we'd not be in this mess!'

She fled to her room, leaving Devaki and me aghast. But a moment later I felt so proud of her that I couldn't stop myself from banging on her door excitedly. 'Open up, Ragini!' I shouted. 'Let's go to her house.'

We never did go.

'It's not fair to get angry at your mother,' Devaki reasoned with Ragini later. 'I am the one to blame. How can a woman denied of her mother's love know to love her child in turn? How can a blind man describe the moon?'

But Devaki, despite her charitable reasoning, for once, wiped herself clean of longing and roused herself to action. She wrote a letter to Lakshmi the next day, the only one she would ever write to her daughter in all her life.

You are old enough to know how I've regretted having left you. I have not shown my face to you in all these years because I know you loathe me, and I understand why. I'm paying the price of my foolishness and it is a burden I and I alone have to bear. For a long time I had hoped that you would understand my burden since you are carrying a similar one yourself, and that in your reconciliation with your daughter we would find reconciliation ourselves. I had hoped that my foolishness would have been a lesson for you and that it would make you a wiser mother. But to my distress I realized last night that you have not only refused to benefit from my mistake, but you have also been doubly foolish in abandoning her twice. I am upset at being cheated of a chance to regain my daughter, but I'm even more upset that you have spurned your own daughter, running away like I had run away from you all those years ago. Have you not learnt anything?

How you have broken your daughter's heart! How can you not want a daughter like her back in your life? She sobbed so much last night that I was afraid she would lose her mind. Prior to last night she has not once complained that she's motherless, yet I know how all her life she has yearned for your presence. She has never wanted anything from you, but your message kindled hopes that she would get what she had never asked for. Now all she'll remember of you is your back. For once, I'm more ashamed of you than I am of myself.

She did not expect to receive a reply to the letter. And she did not receive one.

A few days later, while Mutthu lay in bed, Lakshmi again imagined what her life would be like. A pang of fear sat uneasily in her stomach and she picked up the phone and called Surya. 'Can you come now?' She spoke slowly in order to not betray her anxiety. 'I want to talk to you.'

While Selvamani continued to seek Lakshmi's advice on various policy issues, even those that she knew nothing about, she in turn had increasingly turned to Surya for his opinions. When he arrived that evening with files pertaining to a proposal she had asked him to look over a few days ago assuming that was what she wanted to talk to him about, she sat down opposite him on the sofa and let him explain his views. She listened not to his words but to the rise and fall of his voice. She paid attention not to his opinions, but to his animated expression, his bobbing Adam's apple. Throughout their meeting she did not say a word, and, finally, Surya stopped to regard her with concern.

'Are you okay?' he asked.

'Yes, I am,' she lied. 'Continue.'

But he leant forward and felt her forehead. She let him feel it and hoped he would not take his hand away. But when he did, shaking his head in confusion, she said, 'I told you I'm fine.'

The next day she called him again, as she did the following day. She prompted him to talk about issues that he knew a lot about, so that he would do all the talking, and she would be soothed by his voice. And, yet, when he was gone, after the momentary comfort that she derived from his presence waned, she felt incomplete, restless, dissatisfied. She feared she was permanently afflicted, that she would only sink deeper and deeper into the morass she imagined herself in. Finally, on the fourth day she threw herself on him and whispered hoarsely, 'Surya, give me a baby! I want another baby.'

A few weeks later when Gloria told her that she was pregnant after years of trying and almost giving up, Lakshmi was not surprised. She had seen the baby in her dreams, zygotes splitting and re-splitting innumerable times accompanied by fireworks, sparks shooting across her vision like stars, tiny lights shining and fading into the dark, a formless randomly roving cellular mass. How a human baby would emerge out of this chaos she did not know. All she knew was that it was not in her womb, because Surya had stepped back from her that night, aghast. He had been silent. Lakshmi had hoped it was only a moment of hesitation. She had hoped he would step forward and hold her close to him. But he had taken a few more steps backwards until he bumped into the glass display case where he had stood still.

'I'm worried about you,' he had finally said in a small voice. 'You have not been yourself. Look, Mutthu will be fine. I'll contact Mauro tomorrow morning. He might know some specialists in Europe who might be able to help. I'm sure they'll have a cure for him—'

'Oh, shut up!' Lakshmi had shouted. 'Go away instead of babbling. Go away!'

But, now, Lakshmi smiled. She saw the folly of the other night, the complications it could have led to, and silently thanked Surya for his wisdom. Even though in her dreams she had hissed at Gloria, 'That's my baby you're carrying,' Lakshmi felt happy for her. She felt happy for herself. It was the baby she wanted. It was the baby she had dreamed of. It mattered little whose womb it grew in.

★

Surya's brainwave was not his at all. Among the proposals that came by Lakshmi was one sent by a group of expatriate technology professionals and entrepreneurs in the United States. The group proposed setting up a high-tech centre in the state with modern facilities. There were few details in the proposal and it was unclear to her who would benefit from it. She didn't pay much attention to it till Surya returned from a business trip to the US. On the way back he had tagged along with a group of bureaucrats sent there to explore opportunities to attract investment and had met some members of this group in San Francisco. He came back star-struck.

The dark-suited executives had presented their proposal with utter self-confidence; they had used fancy multicoloured slides with attractive graphs, pie charts and animation to drive home their point. They promised to invest millions of dollars, provided conditions were right.

'This is it!' he exclaimed slapping the table so hard that he almost broke his wrist. 'These fellows only talk in millions. And that's dollars. You should look into this seriously.'

Over the next few weeks Surya worked assiduously with the expatriates to put together concrete proposals. With his soft, rounded contours, Lakshmi had not thought him capable of such hard work, such single-mindedness of purpose. With every iteration the proposal grew in ambition and scope, acquiring details and a form, like the baby in Gloria's womb, involving more and more people in its genesis. And when its composite picture was sketched out for Lakshmi, it looked like a tableau right out of her dreams, fantastic in its sweep, vivid in its details.

It was not merely a high-tech centre, but a city. A high-tech city built from scratch, visualized holistically, in a place where not even a ghost of a town existed, so that they got everything right from the beginning. Every home, every company would be built to specified standards. Every little street sign, the texture of the city's pavements, the precise angles at which its wide, tree-lined boulevards intersected would be planned meticulously. High-tech companies would coexist with suburban, red-tiled homes so that people did not have to travel far to go to work. It would be a model city, a beacon for entrepreneurs and skilled workers. It would be a world-class centre with the best amenities for everybody, the envy of the industrialized world. It would usher a new era of prosperity. Every home would have a telephone and a television (and eventually a car and a computer), every school and college equipped with the best laboratories and libraries, its teachers selected by the most stringent hiring process. It would have the most modern international airport linked to it via a high-speed highway, a commuter railway system that would be run by computers, not humans. The best brains in the country and from many other parts of the world would converge to this city, attracted by its promise of employment and riches.

But it would have to be built in a valley, preferably an isolated one where, to add drama to its existence, it would glisten like a chimera against the emptiness of the surrounding landscape. A place where the climate was just right: it had to be neither too cold nor too hot. It would be a valley of silver and gold that would make even Silicon Valley look like a poor facsimile. And, eventually, people would abandon Silicon Valley for this new centre, leaving it to the ghosts of the past like a town abandoned after a gold rush.

It was a seductive dream. A lot of people had already begun dreaming it: planners, bureaucrats, entrepreneurs, researchers, professionals and businessmen. Collectively, and with increasing passion. The romance of the dream was too hard to resist.

Later, Mayilkannan too would almost succumb to it.

One day Surya came over with a large map of the state, which he spread on a table, and pointed to a valley over the hills beyond Pudupettai. 'There's our Silicon Valley.'

She observed how he'd said 'our'. As though he already had a personal stake in it.

'But there's nothing there,' she replied.

'Exactly my point. There's plenty of land available. The few villages there can be relocated. There's plenty of water available in that lake over there. The road from here to Pudupettai can be broadened to a highway and extended over the hills to the valley.' He drew a line with his blue pen to indicate the intended path. 'And right there, on this side of the hills is a wonderful location for the new international airport.'

'But there are dozens of villages scattered around there,' Lakshmi objected.

'Yes, there are a few of them. But how difficult would it be to relocate them to the north or south of the airport?'

'Why can't the airport be built somewhere else?'

'Where else? There's a ridge right there that'll make it easy to lay a highway through the hills to the valley. Having the airport right next to the highway has its obvious advantages. Besides, think of the importance this airport and highway would bring to Pudupettai town and the entire district. Think of the number of well-paying jobs. Not to mention the riches that will fill up the valley and flow down to them from the hills.'

'But it's Sundarapandian's seat. Why play into his hands?'

'But to the whole world it's *your* idea! If anything, you'll be wresting the initiative on his own turf.'

Lakshmi studied Surya for some moments. A sense of purpose had replaced his easy-going smile. 'You've been surveying this area, haven't you?'

Surya admitted he had. She knew he had ancestral land at the foot of the hills and he often had to send his assistants there to settle disputes and collect rent from the farmers he had leased the land to. He had told her many times that leasing the farmland was a headache and that he was seriously considering selling it. She asked casually, careful to not appear interrogatory, 'What's your interest in this?'

'Lakshmi,' he coughed. 'Frankly speaking, since I'm a businessman I'm hoping to get a piece of the development project.'

'Which piece? What do you know about construction? Or city planning? Or advanced technology?'

'What's there to know? All I have to do is subcontract the work to the appropriate parties and get the work done so that the government does not have to worry about every detail.'

Selvamani, when he heard about this, nodded with admiration. 'Spoken like a true businessman.'

'Yes, a businessman with big dreams.'

'I like that, I like that.'

Lakshmi remained quiet, studying Surya. She couldn't pinpoint what had changed about him. But something had for sure. She felt uncomfortable with his sudden and avid interest in the proposal. She didn't realize then that what she had seen that day was the early stages of the change that would transform Surya, the weak flicker of avarice hidden so deep in the generous folds of his geniality as to be virtually undetectable. As events would later prove, her intuition had been right. But she made an error in not taking her feelings seriously. For his greed would consume not only Surya, but also Lakshmi herself.

★

While Surya nurtured the dream of a high-tech city, Lakshmi began dreaming Gloria's dreams. The chaos of the tableau settled down, and a form began to appear, translucent at first, with squiggly lines of red, blue and orange running through it in the form of a helix. It sometimes wiggled tadpole-like, sometimes trashed around in a colourless fluid like a fish caught in a net, but mostly it floated serenely, building up strength, biding its time for the day when it would make its presence felt with a powerful kick. And when it did kick in Gloria's womb, Lakshmi clutched her stomach and gasped.

'It always aims at the ribs, doesn't it?' Lakshmi asked a surprised Gloria. 'In the middle of the night, as if to say, "Get up, you lazy bum, walk around and lull me to sleep."' Gloria looked at her warily. Lakshmi laughed. 'Don't worry. I just have a hyperactive brain.'

But Gloria did not appear amused. 'Are you feeling all right?'

'Of course. Don't be silly. I can feel the baby inside me.' And she laughed uproariously, wickedly, at Gloria's confusion and fear.

Surya became increasingly involved with his ever-growing dream of the city in the deserted valley, leaving Gloria alone often. Gloria bore his long absences uncomplainingly, even cheerfully, and Lakshmi slid in to fill the breach with a sense of purpose. She visited Gloria often enough to supervise her diet. And her rest. She made their cook work hard, setting a standard her grandmother had established long ago, and sent back dishes that did not live up to her expectations. They had to be right: rich, hearty portions, dripping with butter and ghee and cream and cheese. Puris, bissibele bhath, vegetable and meat curries, ras malai, milk from a well-fed buffalo that had been milked under supervision to ensure that its milk was not adulterated with water, pastas of all kinds—short ones, long ones, curly ones, flat ones, tubular ones—liberally sprinkled with cheese, Indianized by the cook with ginger, spices and coriander. She made Gloria eat twice the amount she normally ate. 'Even if you don't want it, the baby does,' she reasoned, plopping an extra helping of lemon rice on Gloria's plate and her own, for she ate twice the food too. She too put on weight, matching Gloria ounce for ounce. As Gloria's stomach grew, so did hers.

While the two women accumulated fat, Surya discovered his new-found love for fallow land. Instead of selling the land he owned beyond Pudupettai town, he bought acres and acres more. While the women talked about the formless creature taking shape inside Gloria and shared stories about the jigs this creature danced, especially at night when Lakshmi could witness its talents, Surya took to driving through the empty countryside with a bag of money, stopping wherever he fancied, and asking to see the owner of the land. Regardless of whether the spot he chose was a tract of rocks or drought-hardened clay, he put a mark on it with all the enthusiasm of an explorer. The owners of these lands were usually all too eager to have someone take them off their hands, and when Surya gave them the money, they accepted it with glee. 'Poor fellow,' they said to each other, 'a bit cracked up like the land he's buying.' But the few who dawdled in selling their lands soon appreciated the wisdom in acquiescing when, clad in a suit and accompanied by a ring of assistants, Surya paid them visits and dropped names very casually.

One day, emerging from the distracting joy of impending motherhood, Gloria regarded the intense profile of Surya working at his desk with his accounts and a calculator. 'I've never seen him this obsessed,' she said to Lakshmi, and then to her husband, 'make sure you leave some money for the family.'

He looked up, puzzled for a moment, and then broke into his trademark grin, a reminder of the Surya that Lakshmi had first met. 'Don't worry, I'm not making the smallest dent in our finances. These people are giving away their land for next to nothing.' He joined them and put his hand on Gloria's stomach. 'Let me feel the baby move. Ah, you've got a football player in there!'

A moment later, his eyes inevitably glazed over and he lost interest in the budding football player. 'Besides, I'll show my uncles what fools they've been. They gave my father the most useless portion of their inheritance. I'll prove to them what a magician I am by turning those worthless stones into gold,' he said.

As he said it there was something akin to anger in his voice. Lakshmi had never seen him angry, and she frowned. But he didn't notice. He went back to his desk with knitted brows, grinning wickedly, a modern-day alchemist, spurred on by his father's moth-eaten inheritance and his mother-in-law's dismissive shrugs, in a room darkened by curtains, hunched over his cauldron of boiling land deeds and titles in a quest for the magic formula.

Gloria went back to Italy to deliver the baby. In her absence, Lakshmi's dreams about the baby increased in frequency, but they suffered from lack of clarity. The out-of-focus images she saw tantalized but did not satisfy her. And as days went by they became more and more blurred—a myopic's version of a swimming tadpole—till they became so abstract that the colours ran into one another to form dark streams that constantly gushed across her vision and yet went nowhere. She could not feel the baby any more. Moreover, she soon discovered that the surreal stationary cascades concealed bubbling boils of discontent under them, and one night these boils burst like volcanoes to spew a multi-coloured pus of fire and lava. She woke up shivering, at first thankful that the ghastly scene she had just seen had been in her head. But when she remembered how prescient some of her past dreams had been, she broke into sweat and called up Surya immediately. 'I'm going with you to Italy for the delivery,' she told him and gave him no opportunity to reply.

Gloria's family looked askance at her when she arrived, but they said nothing. She didn't care what they thought. She needed clarity; she needed to feel the kicking baby and hear its little heartbeat. She needed to feel the baby inside her. She needed to experience motherhood all over again.

The Pavesi family now lived in a house in the hills they had purchased recently with the profits from Surya's leather trade with Mauro Tedeschi. The driveway dipped down from the main road to the house, skirting past a terraced garden of lush green lawns and a variety of flowering plants. In the mornings they sat on the terrace, squinting at the scene below: the muddy Po snaking its way under bridges and curving away from them, the red roofs on old tan buildings, stacked up against each other, the distant Alps visible on clear days.

In the afternoons, after a leisurely lunch, before the evening crowds arrived, they would go to town and walk around, usually up via the Po just as the used-booksellers and African vendors of scarves and handbags and sunglasses opened up shop and displayed their wares on the arcaded sidewalk, up to Piazza Castello, which was quite peaceful at this time of day. There they would pause for a while to eat gelati and watch little children strip down to their underwear and delightedly splash about in the fountain and chase jets of water as they darted from spout to sink.

Sometimes they went farther, walking down via Roma, where all the fashionable shops were, down to Piazza San Carlo. Mauro Tedeschi owned a store there that sold expensive handmade leather items: women's shoes (some with Rajasthani mirrorwork on them), handbags and coats. Like all the other boutiques nearby, his store was brightly lit, sparsely furnished in a monotonic off-white to accentuate the contrasting shades of black and red and violet of the items on display, each of which had its own uncluttered spot on a slab of stone that jutted out of the wall, as if it were a museum piece. Lakshmi once remarked to Mauro Tedeschi, 'I admire all the things you've done with the skin of our cows. Your visit to the sewers has not been in vain.'

In a very short time the abstractions of her dreams vanished and Lakshmi regained her clarity. She held her stomach when the baby kicked Gloria, and she could hear the baby laugh when it found its mark on her ribs, the tinkling giggle resounding in her ears—and only hers—like wind chimes. She described everything she saw, heard and felt to Gloria, and the two women giggled and talked all day, rubbing their stomachs at the same time, sweating, tiring and feeling nauseous together, like sisters in their shared experiences. Gloria got over her initial misgivings and gave up questioning Lakshmi on how she knew so much about her baby. A bond that had not existed before, one that Lakshmi had not thought possible, grew between them. And in the process Lakshmi displaced Gloria's real sisters, who sat at a distance, gazing at them with envy and resentment.

When Gloria's mother and sisters watched daytime soap operas and Gloria took a nap, Lakshmi often found Surya talking on the phone or meeting people. Sometimes Mauro Tedeschi visited them with his expansive smiles and gifts, and after pleasantries, he and Surya hurried off to a room that had been converted into a temporary office. They were trying to bring together a number of companies under a consortium to put forward concrete plans to develop the valley, to build the airport, the highway and the infrastructure.

'But, Surya,' Lakshmi said. 'Why should we hand over the construction of the airport to people who built Linate, Malpensa and Fumicino? If anything, we should get the people who built Changi.'

Surya looked offended. But only for a moment. 'Why don't you see what these fellows can do with your new house? Show us the plans.'

She had been dawdling over a couple of plans for her house, dissatisfied with both, for neither conformed to the house of her dreams despite the detailed descriptions she had provided the architect. Mutthu, whom she had brought with her to Italy, had taken to looking around this large Pavesi house and mumbling, 'Your house?' She would respond, even though she knew he would not understand her, 'I'm still not done dreaming it fully.' And he would look at her impatiently, as though he were trying to say, 'Dream faster.'

Surya studied the plans Lakshmi had and shook his head. 'Think grander,' he said. 'This is not a mansion. It's just a big house. You deserve something bigger.'

'Consider marble,' Mauro suggested. 'Carrara marble. I can send you whatever quantity you need.'

Surya's world view had become grander over the last few months. He had begun thinking of everything on a large scale like Mauro Tedeschi. But he was right. The plan just didn't accommodate everything she had visualized, because the architect had circumscribed himself into a small space, just like a slum-dweller cannot visualize a palace. And Mauro Tedeschi was right, too. She'd fallen in love with the marbled interior of his villa.

So she allowed Mauro Tedeschi to introduce her to a well-known local architect, with whom she was immediately impressed. Finally, after months of indecision, while the baby grew and prepared to emerge, her dream house began to take shape, too. She spread the final draft of the plan that arrived in oversized sheets rolled into numerous tubes, from which they emerged still smelling of fresh ink and the wood of drafting tables, out on the floor of several rooms, holding the curving sheets down with paper weights, and examined them with pride. 'What do you think of this?' she asked Surya.

He nodded approvingly. 'Change my name if this doesn't mesmerize the public.'

'Change my name if it doesn't mesmerize me.' And she laughed delightedly at the thought of the luxury she would live and dream in. If she had to suffer from the effects of her memory, at least she would do so in splendour.

Lakshmi, who was born in secrecy and had given birth to a daughter in secrecy, felt at home in the curtain-darkened room of the hospital. She pushed with Gloria, feeling pangs of birthing pain sear through her body. The two of them moaned in unison, the one with a real baby, the other experiencing motherhood second-hand, and she cried with joy when the baby emerged from the dark recesses of Gloria's body. Despite exhaustion from her efforts, when the nurse handed over the baby boy to Surya, she pushed him aside and took the baby herself, swaddling it in the ample, secret folds of her sari.

She did not notice Surya's look of consternation, his sulk, his subsequent retreat from the room, as ashamed as a cuckolded husband. Her attention was focussed on the baby swimming in her sari. Watching him knit his well-formed brows and cry softly, his tiny hands and legs flailing helplessly, his face maroon with exertion, she knew why she had so desperately wanted a baby in the first place. Although she was already a mother she had not experienced motherhood before. Her daughter had been conceived in anything but love, and had hardly made her presence felt inside her and outside. She had only existed as a reminder of Lakshmi's sins, only as a notion, and even that had gradually been purged from memory to give way to an emptiness inside her. She had been too easy to discard as a baby, and too difficult to reclaim as an adult. This baby she had felt in her womb without even having conceived it, and here he was in her arms, a real baby, a baby that should have been hers in the first place. 'My baby!' she whispered joyfully and smothered him, while Gloria cried in confusion. But Lakshmi did not hear Gloria either, for she was busy hiding him, fleeing with him into the secret absurd world of vicarious motherhood.

★

I went to the airport on a lark. I did not see Lakshmi; I only saw a commotion, a babble of voices rising, a crowd moving through the airport lobby like tumbleweed, flashbulbs of bright light aimed at its centre. The crowd paused for some moments, the noise died down as cameras and microphones converged.

I could still not see or hear anything. Impulsively I fished out a pair of oversized sunglasses that I rarely used to cover part of my face, pushed my way past the crowd, flashed my press pass at the securitymen at the door and slipped into the press enclosure. I made no attempt to get to the front. I had clear visibility from my vantage point behind the cameramen and harried reporters as she paused, with Mutthu beside her in his wheelchair, to greet those waiting for her.

I was struck by the change I saw in her. She looked rejuvenated. She smiled cheerfully, and was at ease with herself and the world around her. She even posed obligingly for several pictures. She appeared to have made her peace with the press.

Selvamani and several of the cabinet members had come to receive her. 'Mutthu-saar,' Selvamani sputtered as he garlanded Mutthu, you look strong enough to resume your duties. And, madam, Italian weather has made you and Mutthu-saar so rosy-cheeked and healthy.'

Watching the fawning crowd and their reverence, I could understand why our leaders bloat with self-importance; this was how the world must have appeared to Lakshmi too, as if she were a giant in the world of Lilliputians. Even her chattering-class critics must appear like inconsequential dwarfs to her.

When I met Devaki and Ragini later, I reported that Lakshmi had never looked happier.

'Did you see the baby?' Ragini asked.

I had not. It had not even crossed my mind to look for the baby in the crowd.

'What kind of a journalist are you, Vasu-maama? Everybody is curious about the baby and only you didn't look. It was probably right under your nose. Anyway, here, look at the pictures.' She showed me a newspaper photograph.

'Cute little fellow, isn't he?' I remarked. 'Looks like you, your little brother.'

Ragini yanked the paper away from me angrily. 'You should write gossip columns with your ability to make up stories.'

'A bit of sibling jealousy, I see,' I teased.

And Devaki, happy whenever Lakshmi looked happy, said light-heartedly, 'Lakshmi is carrying on this family's grand tradition of our women not raising their own children.'

'But Ragini will break this tradition.'

'She'd better. She has no choice. I'll be too old by then, and her mother has just acquired a brand new baby and will not be ready for a new one for a long time.'

A City Conceived

Surya—who in pursuit of modern-day alchemy did not notice Gloria's postpartum rivalry with Lakshmi over the baby, and had quickly forgotten his own consternation—managed to suck Lakshmi into his dreams. It was not very difficult. His dreams permeated the air wherever he went, his enthusiasm too infectious to fight off. 'This is an opportunity of a lifetime,' he'd say with passion, over and over again. 'Think of the difference we can make! We can do what nobody else in the country has managed to do. We can put this place finally on the world map.'

At first the idea of putting the place on the map did not appeal to her. 'Think of the legacy you will leave,' he pitched to her. 'You won't be remembered simply because of Mutthu.'

A legacy was not something she'd had the space in her mind to consider. But, with the baby as her talisman, an antidote to her past, and her demons fleeing at the sound of the baby gurgling, she now had space for such thoughts.

In the meantime, the plan was gaining momentum and it began to take on a life of its own. Multinational high-tech companies had already begun petitioning for land and special incentives to start subsidiaries there. They wanted the valley to be declared an export zone—they would export software, designs for new chips, computer systems, telecommunications equipment, even people. Other companies with expertise in city planning and construction sent in their proposals to design the infrastructure. The consortium of companies floated by Surya and Mauro Tedeschi wanted to construct the airport and highway.

But there was still a lot to be done, a lot of people to convince before it could come to fruition. A committee appointed by the central government was studying the feasibility of such a city and airport, and she expected their initial findings to be not entirely encouraging. There would be issues with water supply and power, with the relocation of villages to accommodate the airport and super-fast highway. There would be the usual bickering, the alternative proposals put forward by those afraid of losing out, and allegations of corruption and favouritism. It was now that she received her first real confirmation of her wisdom in elevating Selvamani, for only he would work tirelessly and loyally to surmount the hurdles along the way. And Surya worked with him day and night looking after details for which she never had the patience. She admired the way in which he marshalled his resources and roused people around him with his enthusiasm, the meticulous planning that went into it, the way he evangelized his grand vision.

'This is it,' Surya said one day. 'If we weren't meant to do something big why would we be put in such a position?'

She began to be seduced by his vision, by his almost-religious fervour. She began to see that through his eyes the world was indeed limitless.

The day she and Surya delivered the final blueprint to Selvamani, she sat by Mutthu and held his hand. She too had taken to talking to him often. He was her sounding board. She now showed him the blueprint.

'We're going to transform this state,' she said.

He smiled at her. 'I'm proud of you,' he would have said if he were able to understand. 'You're doing more for my people than I ever could have.'

She felt reassured. His mere presence was support enough. Now that she was alone, without his shadow to take refuge in, without his cheerful cynicism to take potshots at, she had to acknowledge that his worldly wisdom had seeped into her by stealthy osmosis, that his efforts had not gone in vain. She had to admit that his approval mattered to her now, when, ironically, he could not express it, more than ever.

'Get up and implement it, Mutthu,' she whispered. 'They're waiting for you.'

★

The silence Mayilkannan had adopted after Murugesan's election had become a habit, and he decided one day that there was no need to talk, ever again. Silence could be empowering. It could be used as an effective weapon of protest. And he had been protesting ever since. He was like a mute sage now, communicating only with gestures and by writing.

But every morning he woke up with the sun and started his day by gargling with salt water. No matter where he spent the night, he went looking for water the first thing in the morning and filled his large brass pitcher to the brim, warmed it, added salt to it, looked up at the sky open-mouthed and gargled with all his energy. *Gluglugluglugluglug.* The noise could be heard a furlong away, and it heralded the new day. Nobody knew where the noise would come from the next morning since Mayilkannan rarely slept in the same place more than once: one day in the heart of the town, another day in the outskirts, and yet another day in the woods, accompanied by the startled cries of birds and animals. Like the noise he used to make with his now-deceased thavil, his gargling was dissonant. But he derived a lot of pleasure from it. Dissonance went well with his personality. He competed with crowing cocks for pre-eminence till they gave up and retreated to their roosts in shame. He varied his pitch and tempo according to his mood, sometimes rumbling like a train, sometimes crying like a peacock, sometimes braying like a foolish donkey, sometimes creating out-of-tune music that was his gargling suprabhatam to salute the rising sun.

'Why do you do this?' people would ask, amused at the care he took of the one part of his body he had vowed to never use again.

'I need to keep my throat in shape,' he would respond

patiently with gestures. 'Who knows when I might have to use it again.'

Sometimes people would not understand his gestures and would look at each other in bewilderment. One group of men had a particularly hard time understanding him once. 'Are you going to sing one day?' one of them asked fearfully.

Mayilkannan shook his head vigorously. He repeated his gestures.

'You mean your voice is a divine gift that should not be used for chit-chat?'

'No, no,' another man interjected. 'What divine gift? Haven't you heard his voice? He's saying his throat is like a car engine and it has to be oiled regularly.'

Mayilkannan shook his head irritably this time. He picked up a pen and wrote his response down, as he sometimes had to: *Yo, what is all this talk of cars and motor oil? I said I might have to use my voice one day.*

He almost used it the day he found out that Thenmozhi was pregnant with her husband's child, when even arrack could not console him. At night, when the urge to scream became unbearable, he rushed to Mohana Devi's bungalow and rang the doorbell continuously till the servant woke up and opened the door. Behind her Mohana Devi, without a trace of irritation, came out to sit with him in the veranda and listened to his anguished gestures. This was the first time he tried to talk to her about Thenmozhi. What gesture could he use to represent Thenmozhi? How does one express a word as beautiful as Thenmozhi with hands and facial expressions? All he could do then was to mime honey and bring his fingers to his lips. He expected her to think he was talking about arrack, but to his surprise she understood him immediately. Why, he asked her, encouraged, why did Thenmozhi go back to her husband?

Mohana Devi let him shout with his hands, and when he paused, she touched them, calming him down, and said in a gentle tone, as if addressing a traumatized child, 'She did what most women would have done. You despair not because she went back to her husband, but because you want her so badly for yourself.'

Mayilkannan was jolted by her words. How did she know? He had never said a word about Thenmozhi to anybody before. How easily Mohana Devi had seen through his anguish! How perceptive she was. Would he have been as outraged had some other woman gone back to her husband?

He poured his heart out to Mohana Devi that night. He expressed feelings he had never clarified to himself before. And in the end, when he was done, she said in the same gentle tone, 'There's not much you can do for Thenmozhi. What's the point of despairing for her when she herself has made peace with her husband and has come to terms with her life? We all make compromises. She has made hers. Who are we to say whether she is right or wrong?'

He felt ashamed that he had not been capable of such understanding, that his despair for himself was greater than his despair for Thenmozhi. He understood Thenmozhi's action a little better that night. It was a matter of making difficult choices, of making compromises. Otherwise life could be too burdensome, too dark, too harsh.

One day he stopped mid-gargle when one of his Ezhutharivu associates waved a newspaper over his upturned face. The article said that the committee that had recently been constituted to study the feasibility of the proposed high-tech city and airport had released its recommendations. Aside from a few superficial changes to the original plan, it had been approved wholeheartedly.

This was what he had feared. Some time earlier a university professor from the city had warned the people of Pudupettai about the proposal and what it really meant. He had said that urban planners and environmentalists vehemently opposed it. The valley was drought prone, they said. The lake at the foot of the hills outside town had just about enough water to support the current population of Pudupettai district. Diverting the water to the new city would mean dry taps in Pudupettai town and ruined farmlands over vast swathes of the surrounding countryside. Besides, a city like that would attract a lot more people than planned for, and in a few years this would lead to haphazard and unplanned growth that would further strain the infrastructure.

The airport, too, was a bad idea, the professor had said. The airport and its satellite structures would occupy the most arable tracts of land in the district and would displace too many farmers.

As he held the newspaper in his hands he knew what his next battle was going to be. He went straight to Mohana Devi, as he always did for advice, and waved the newspaper at her.

'It has to be stopped,' he said to her with his hands. 'Otherwise the poor of this district will be doomed.'

Mohana Devi looked over the article and shrugged. 'Officially, it's not under my control,' she said to him. 'But I'm willing to help you in a personal capacity.'

He must have looked disappointed at her less than effusive reply, for Mohana Devi smiled, as if making amends for her lack of interest. 'I'll help as much as I can, but you have got to break your vow of silence. How are you going to organize people against this proposal if you're not going to talk?'

But Mayilkannan was adamant. 'I can communicate without speaking,' he retorted in gestures. 'I have fingers, I have hands. And I have you to interpret me for everybody.'

Mohana Devi sighed. 'Be careful. Those in power can tolerate a loose tongue but not a powerful hand.'

'Don't I know the power of silence?' he replied, and smiled.

And, so, once again they galvanized the volunteers into action, to spread the word around at literacy camps, roadside meetings, jathas and through their newsletter. A group of them, with Mayilkannan at the head, went to the Party's district headquarters to express their opinions. Both Murugesan and Selvamani were in the capital, but a functionary came out of the building to meet them. When he saw Mayilkannan, his demeanour changed.

'Oh, you!' he said in a surly voice. 'What do you want?'

Mayilkannan wasted no time in telling the man what he had on his mind. But the Party functionary did not understand his gestures and regarded him with increasing impatience. Finally, he snapped: 'Yo, what's all this drama? Open your mouth and speak if you have something to say. Otherwise get lost!'

One of the volunteers interceded. 'We want to tell our leaders that the people of this district will not allow their plan to be implemented, even if we have to physically stop the bulldozers and cranes—.'

But the Party functionary interrupted him. 'Don't waste my time! Protesting against everything we do has become a habit for you people. What's there to protest I don't understand. You'll bark even at the person who feeds you. Go on, clear out of the office. I have no time for your constant complaints.' And he slammed the door shut on their faces.

That was as good as a declaration of war. A few weeks later they rallied in the open area between the Party's headquarters and the collector's office. Hundreds of people turned up, enough to make the police nervous. If the noise the protestors made at the rally did not reach the ears of the leaders in the capital, what happened afterwards caught their attention. After the rally ended with promises to keep up the fight and to involve more people in it, a group of young hot-heads, who had found the speeches rousing, threw stones at the Party's office on their way back, shattering several windows and wounding the Party functionary who had earlier refused to listen to Mayilkannan. Mayilkannan and Mohana Devi publicly distanced themselves from the miscreants, but they were not wholly unhappy with the outcome, for the wounded functionary went to the capital the next day with a bandaged head and a mouthful of complaints.

Mayilkannan was particularly satisfied with the number of people who had come to the rally. More importantly, he was happy to see their collective concern. His task was not so much of rousing their passions as it was of simply giving them the facts. It was their land, after all, their water, their livelihoods. When all that was taken away from them what would they have left?

The protests in Pudupettai annoyed Lakshmi like the buzzing of a persistent mosquito. 'They're complaining like children,' she said, feeling remarkably clear-headed. 'Give them some toffees and they'll stop crying.'

Surya raised his eyebrows. 'We all know they're being silly to protest our economic development plan. But it's in our best interests to pacify him and Mohana Devi. What you need to do is to explain to them that their fears are unfounded. Once the area is developed Pudupettai can only gain from it. You have to try and bring them round to our point of view. Otherwise we'll have larger problems to tackle in the future.'

So Lakshmi left for Pudupettai once more—reluctantly this time, but Surya had insisted—with an assortment of assistants, advisors, political leaders and bureaucrats. This time her convoy comprised of a number of vehicles, many with flashing neon-blue lights on their roofs and their sirens screeching.

Protestors waited for her in Pudupettai behind barricades erected by the police on either side of the road. They crowded around her, raising their banners and posters that bobbed over their heads like paper boats in a pond. Mayilkannan held many of them as if to make up for his lack of spoken words. His posters were different. Lakshmi could tell that he had personally written all of them in his self-taught hand. One said: *Take our farmland, take our water, take our lives away.* Another one said: *An airport cannot satisfy our hunger, a new city cannot quench our thirst.*

He was his usual silent self, glaring at her from the depths of whichever world he had retreated to. What a contrast he was to Mohana Devi. Yet they stood by each other every time she came to Pudupettai, comrades in arms, always opposing someone, something, or digging up an issue when one wasn't readily available. They're Marxist sympathizers even if they don't want to admit it, she thought to herself as they went into the Party's district office to talk things over.

Lakshmi decided she would not look at him lest he be encouraged to speak. But he spoke anyway. Through Mohana Devi, that is. How many farmers would be displaced, he asked and Mohana Devi began interpreting his gestures. Lakshmi stopped her. She, the dancer, who knew the most complex of gestures in the art of abhinaya, could surely understand his limited repertoire of unlettered, uneducated hand movements and frowns. Where will they be relocated? he continued. Where will the new city get its electricity? How can the government prevent the over-crowding of the valley and the eventual spilling over of the population this side of the hills, along the highway, devouring more farmland and villages along the way? What will happen to the already scant forest cover in the district? The rains that year were poor and there was barely enough water to support the current population. So how would the additional population be supported?

With every question the frown on his face became deeper. With increasing annoyance she listened to him and when it was time for her to respond she said nothing at all to him. She addressed Mohana Devi, instead, regurgitating the line of reasoning Surya had coached her in, sticking to generalities and avoiding every question that Mayilkannan had raised. Even though she did not look at him, she could feel his glare piercing her.

Then, suddenly, he stood up, pushing the steel chair on which he was sitting with such force that it slid across the mosaic floor, toppling behind him along the way, and struck the wall on the far side. He stormed out, flashing his livid eyes at her, leaving everybody gathered around them aghast.

It did not take Lakshmi long to react with equal anger. 'I did not come here to be insulted like this by an illiterate man.'

'How dare he!' exclaimed Selvamani rising from his seat. 'Go and bring the rascal back.'

But Lakshmi stopped them. She waved at Mohana Devi to signal the end of their meeting. As the bureaucrat was about to step out of the room Lakshmi called out to her, 'Associating with a man like him will not do your career any good.'

Mohana Devi stopped. Her usually smiling face turned grave. 'Is that a threat, madam?'

Lakshmi did not respond, but waved her out instead.

It was all because of Mayilkannan, his utter lack of respect for her, his insolence, his frigid silence. How had he known that silence terrified her? And she had sensed that terror coming back, and had to counter it. It was he who had clouded her judgement and had made her utter words that sounded like a threat in retrospect. He must hate her too much to care for the consequences of his actions. How dare he, a mere fly on the wall, the absurd-looking Pulcinella who smelt of rat's breath, insult her in front of others? The memory of his walking out of the room speared through her like a harpoon through a whale's belly.

Later that day, on the way back to the city, she was quiet—she could see in her mind's eye the waters of the sea turn red with the blood spouting from the whale's belly. The blood of her honour spilled by a vagabond. She reached under her sari and felt her stomach just to make sure there was no wound there. But she continued seeing blood all around. Whether it was the miscarriage of the new city or simply a clot forming over a gash, she could not tell.

'What should I do?' she asked Mutthu that evening. He sat in a wheelchair, wheeled into the bedroom by his nurse.

He stretched his right hand out, touched her chin lightly, as if admiring it. When she was young her chin had been prominent and she had used it to great effect in her dance. But now it was lost in the gathering fat around it. Keep your chin up, he seemed to say.

He was right. She stood up. She was determined to quell any hesitation in her mind. She could not allow Mayilkannan to emerge victorious over her yet again. Especially not after his very public challenge. Another defeat would seal her fate.

Puppets

The baby was chubby, active, perpetually curious and happy in general. Puppy fat made his cheeks jiggle like jelly. Gloria was good at keeping him entertained. It was amusing to see her constantly running after him without seeming to move, chattering to him without parting her lips, making him throw his head back and laugh delightedly despite her hooded eyes, all of which belied quiet, incessant activity that the baby recognized easily. He flourished in her presence. He became active, unusually expressive, and enjoyed himself thoroughly. Even during bad bouts of colic when everything else failed, her very touch calmed him down, and the unattractive, unclear voice with which she sang lullabies, as if into a pillow, soothed him further. *O mio bambino caro,* she would sing in the middle of the night and soothe him right back to sleep.

Lakshmi, on the other hand, could hold the baby only when he slept. When awake he wanted to be with Gloria or his ayah. In Lakshmi's arms he became bad-tempered or simply bored no matter what she did to amuse him. Once, he wriggled out of her lap and crawled back to Gloria in a marked rejection of her affections. For a moment she suspected that Gloria was behind it, whispering poisonous words into his ears as he fell asleep, feeding him the wily ways of the world. For Gloria had begun to show her displeasure with Lakshmi. When Lakshmi battled to calm the baby she would reclaim him with icy stares. The sisterhood that had grown out of their shared experience of his birth had vanished.

But the suspicion stayed in Lakshmi's head. It stayed with

her till, to her horror, she realized that she had begun believing it to be true, when she shuddered, shook herself up and sat down next to Gloria, hoping to recapture the companionship they had once shared.

When he slept and she held him in her arms she gazed into this face and glowed, for in the slight fluttering of his tiny eyelids, in the way he clenched his fist, in the way he parted his lips and smiled (what kind of dreams made babies smile, even laugh like tinkling bells in their sleep?), she forgot the rest of the world. He was innocence distilled to its purest form, and some of that innocence reflected on her, making her feel purer, suffusing her with a kind of joy she had hoped to find all her life, but had not until then. What would she not do for his smiles when awake. What would she not do to see him come to her for comfort. What would she not do to have him babble contentedly in her arms. 'Everything I have is for you,' she whispered once.

And later that day she overheard a vexed Gloria ask Surya, 'Why is she always competing with me?'

She did not hear Surya's response. He might not have responded at all.

Lakshmi stopped reading newspapers and magazines. She never turned on the television. She ignored the growing criticism of the government's plan. She redirected petitions from critics to Selvamani and other government officials.

'The best way to respond to critics is to be happy in their presence to let them know that their opinions have not had the least effect on you,' Mutthu had once said to her. And she was determined to show her happiness and optimism no matter what the cost. She immersed herself in overseeing the construction of her mansion, adding last-minute embellishments and fancy accoutrements. Money was not an issue at all. It poured in from all directions, for there were those with a lot of money who supported her.

The edifice rose slowly, brick by brick, marble slab by marble slab, built with the utmost care, overseen by the best contractors, built from the best materials procured from around the world. From the street it loomed over the high compound walls that would be topped with jagged glass and electrified barbed wire. It rose behind the trees whose branches unfurled into vast canopies, its red Andalusian tiles specially ordered, its walls sparkling white to lend it majesty. From the street, through the ornate grilles of the huge iron gate, one could see the white marble columns of the portico—sent from Italy in shipping cases in its component blocks—rise two storeys high, the tiled roof sloping over them, ending in eaves that dropped down over their entablatures like a veil. Beside the gate was a kiosk for the sentries who would guard the house day and night. The cobbled driveway from the gate curved through the landscaped grounds, bordered by manicured bushes and fountains, to a parking area from where a trellised walkway, overhanging with wisteria, led to the house.

The L-shaped mansion had over twenty-five rooms. The interior had been as meticulously planned as the exterior. With Lakshmi's involvement at every stage interior designers with the help of the architect planned every detail: the corners of rooms had to be rounded just so; the wood work, made predominantly of teak imported from Burma, had to be polished to silken smoothness; the lighting in the bathroom needed to blend the sharpness of gold-plated taps with the dreamy milkiness of the marble countertop; the vaulted ceiling in the reception room was to be at just the right angle for the chandelier to be reflected in its full glory. Soon all the rooms would be decorated with furniture and knick-knacks. The chandeliers, the gilt-edged full-length mirrors, the vases, the urns, the rose bowls, the antique figurines, the tapestries, the statuettes and the paintings she had purchased during her travels or received as gifts were everywhere. A bonsai expert placed plants in various rooms to balance the overwhelming assault of the expensive furnishings on the senses.

Everyone who saw it from the outside was awed by it. Those who were fortunate enough to enter it would insist afterwards that they had been to another world. Everybody referred to it as an aranmanai, a palace. And from repeated usage, the word stuck as a proper name.

At the grihapravesh when, accompanied by Mutthu wheeled in by his nurse, she formally stepped over the threshold to the welcoming chants of a group of eager priests, she turned around and grabbed the baby, now a year old, from Gloria's arms before she put her first foot in. She noticed Gloria's expression harden, the resisting tug when she took the baby. Distracted momentarily, to her horror she realized that she had inauspiciously put her left foot in first. Rattled that the baby should have also taken this inauspicious step with her— for she was willing to believe in superstitions when it came to things that were dear to her—she paused, went back, and re-entered the house. Once inside Lakshmi turned back, smiled, and allowed Gloria to reclaim her child.

But Gloria was not amused. She took the baby away in a huff and stayed outside the house for a good part of the ceremony. Lakshmi feared that she had gone too far. She went out to where Gloria stood, and despite the latter's cold stares, she said, 'Come in. It's too hot here.' And after a pause, 'I didn't mean to take him away from you.'

To her relief Gloria relented and blinked, but Lakshmi resisted the urge to reach out for the baby again. She didn't want to test the limits of Gloria's willingness to forgive.

★

One by one the farmers around Pudupettai town received visits from the land and revenue department officials with documents and challans to sign or put their thumb imprints on, to transfer their lands to the government, for the sake of development. They were told that there would soon be tall glass buildings that touched the sky, roads so wide they wouldn't be able to see the other side, so much money that they'd all be rich enough to not have to work again. But only if they exchanged their land for what the government gave them. 'It's more fertile than the bed of rocks you now have,' the officials told them. 'All you have to do is throw seeds around and very soon you'll have a harvest.'

The farmers didn't believe them, of course. They went to Mayilkannan, who knew that dry scrub land eighty kilometres away, far away from the proposed highway in the interior, was being cleared to make way for new farms. The rains had failed that winter, so the scrubland, already dry and thirsty, burned quite easily. There had been a fight in the legislature not long ago. The Opposition had threatened to walk out if the relocation plan was approved. During a particularly heated debate one legislator tore off his shirt and threw it at the Speaker. 'Take my shirt away!' he shouted and walked out of the chamber, hitching up his veshti. Inspired by Mayilkannan in the art of protest, he had given up wearing shirts and came to work proudly baring the lush springy black and grey hair on his chest.

When they received court-ordered eviction notices, the farmers organized a protest march. They and their families, smelling of freshly threshed grain and urea, went to Pudupettai and assembled in the maidan with their motley implements of protest: placards, banners, drums, pipes, dung, sickles, hoes, bullocks, bales of hay, and tractors. They marched through town slowly, beating drums and chanting slogans, making detours to the homes of Murugesan and Selvamani, in front of which they shouted vociferously. Next, they went to the collector's office. Mohana Devi, as the government's representative, was involved in implementing the relocation plan. When she came out of her office to meet them, they surrounded her and demanded that their farms not be confiscated from them. Mayilkannan stood at the far end of the compound, pressed against the wall, observing the goings-on with an air of detachment. He was the one who had recommended to the farmers the means of protest although he himself took no part in it since he wanted them to feel they were in charge of the struggle themselves. He caught her eye and stared back, challenging her.

Mohana Devi looked uncertain for a few moments. Then

she raised her hands to calm the agitators. 'My friends,' she addressed them, 'I fully support your cause. But as the district collector I'm forced to follow all orders. Even those that I don't agree with. But I'll do my best to resist implementing this one. Go back to your homes in peace. I will fight on your behalf and ensure that you don't get thrown out of your homes.'

'How do we know this is not another empty promise?' someone in the crowd shouted. 'Swear on your children!'

Mohana Devi looked around, searching for the person who had shouted. She looked uncomfortable and cleared her throat. Finally she said, 'I swear on my children, I'll do all I can to keep you from being evicted.'

That mollified the farmers somewhat. Mayilkannan broke into a smile. After the farmers dispersed he approached Mohana Devi. 'I was happy to hear that,' he said with his hands.

She smiled weakly in response. A crease of worry streaked across her face.

'That was brave of you to promise to stand up to authority,' Mayilkannan continued. 'We'll all be behind you.'

Mohana Devi nodded. 'I'm sure you will,' she said distractedly. 'But, tell me, have you ever thought of the consequences of our activities?'

Mayilkannan shrugged. He never thought of the consequences of what he did. He was happier that way. Worrying about the future was an unnecessary burden that interfered with the struggles of today. 'Why do you ask?'

She did not respond. It was her turn to shrug.

Mayilkannan did not drink that day out of respect for Mohana Devi. He didn't know what to say. She had received her transfer orders a few days earlier. They wanted her back in the city, at the secretariat, where they could keep an eye on troublesome, meddlesome bureaucrats who behaved like potentates in rural areas and decided which laws to implement and which ones to flout. 'You kept saying she would do what's good for the people,' he said in gestures. His expression was neither accusing nor admonishing. 'She's turned out to be just like everybody else. Worse, in fact, because she's not accountable.'

Mohana Devi smiled. Despite what had happened there was no trace of bitterness in her. 'There are consequences to every action. Whether it was her or somebody else, I'd have received the same punishment. At least because of her they're sending me to the capital to be with my family. Somebody else would have banished me farther away.'

Mayilkannan spat in disgust. 'You're a simpleton,' he said, supplanting his gestures with words he wrote down on a piece of paper. 'I knew then, the first time I saw her when she was a girl in her dorai school, that she had the arrogance of royalty. Now it's only worse, because she doesn't have to pretend to be royalty any more. People treat her like a queen. She does exactly what she pleases. Such arrogance is dangerous in a leader. Things will only get worse from now on.'

He didn't tell her that earlier that morning, before dawn, men wielding axes and bamboo sticks had knocked on the doors of the farmers who had protested and had warned them that if they did not move out within a week they would be forcibly thrown out. He knew one or two had already started packing and others would follow suit. He didn't tell her because he didn't want to dampen her spirits further on her last evening in Pudupettai.

'You're a good man, Mayilkannan,' Mohana Devi said. He was surprised to hear that. She had never said anything so overtly complimentary before. 'But you must learn to forgive.'

Mayilkannan looked at Mohana Devi closely. She wasn't being critical. On the contrary, she was now looking at him with compassion.

'I've learnt a lot from you,' she continued. 'I've learnt to be passionate. I've learnt that there is hope for everyone. I've learnt how flawed we all are despite our good intentions.'

Mayilkannan wondered if she was referring to his dependence on arrack. She had never questioned his drinking before, not even in the most oblique manner. He hung his head, feeling his throat itch. It was he who had forced her, by staring at her that day, to take a stand in public, to prove to the farmers that she cared. He had coerced her into participating in his fights. Left alone she might have done her duty, helped a few causes and moved on to her next posting with dignity. He was alone, a vagabond; he didn't have to worry about the consequences of his actions. But it was different with her. She had a family, an incredibly supportive husband who stayed back in the city to raise their two daughters. For her to be publicly seen revolting against government decisions was a much riskier act. It was a much bigger sacrifice. And, yet, there was no rancour in her voice.

What would he do without her? She, the person he went to when communication with everyone else failed, the woman who indulged his silence and learnt to interpret his gestures, the woman to whom he went for advice and, sometimes, for comfort when he despaired.

He now felt an overwhelming urge to speak. He did not know how to communicate through gestures what he wanted to say. For a moment he refused to consider the possibility of breaking his vow of silence. But then he realized she was right. He must learn to be more forgiving. Before he could forgive others he had to learn to forgive himself and he would get such an opportunity if he broke his vow. 'I'm sorry,' he finally blurted out, uttering words after such a long time that his voice was gravelly. 'How can you ever forgive me?'

Mohana Devi looked shocked. Then she smiled. 'What's there to forgive? I did what I did on my own accord.'

'No,' he insisted. 'It was all my fault.'

She put her hand over his. Her hands felt soft and fleshy over his calluses. He looked around furtively to make sure nobody was watching them. He did not want to get her into more trouble. But it was already dark. The bougainvillea, climbing around the pillar in the veranda obscured the moon and cast a shadow on them.

'I didn't think I'd have the honour of making you break your vow,' she said, smiling.

Mayilkannan withdrew his hands and reverted to

communicating with gestures, 'But only temporarily.'

Mohana Devi laughed. 'Who will interpret your gestures now?'

'What's there to interpret? I have nothing to say to anyone.' He hung his head despondently.

'Will you promise me something?' she said. Mayilkannan nodded uncertainly. 'Please do not protest against my transfer. I'm only a speck in the larger scheme of things. It's too late to reverse that decision. Instead, focus on the real battle. Don't let the people down. My transfer was meant to distract attention. Don't let them have the pleasure of succeeding in their strategy.'

Mayilkannan did not respond. He had in fact been planning to protest. A hunger strike. And he wanted to bar the new collector from entering the building.

'Please,' she said. 'For my sake, forget about my transfer.'

He eased back into his chair thoughtfully, neither refusing, nor agreeing. They sat in silence. He traced the edges of the umbra of the shadow of some leaves. He could almost see the edges move as the moon traced its arc across the sky. At long last he got up. She had to leave early in the morning.

As he stepped down from the veranda, Mohana Devi stood holding the pillar. 'You should be careful,' she said. Her voice was urgent and anxious like that of someone bidding farewell to a lover. 'Please focus on the real struggle. And don't alienate anybody.'

He did not look back. He wondered if she was aware of the contradiction in her words. How could he struggle for the rights of the people without alienating anybody? But he knew why she had said that. He, too, was nervous. If a well-educated, respected woman like her could be swept out of the way so easily, how much time would it take to get him out?

★

Mutthu had always thought of himself as a street fighter who never shirked from rolling up his sleeves and hitching up his

lungi to wrestle his opponents. 'I don't like to fight,' he had
said often to his followers, 'but if someone flings mud on me,
I'm going to fling it right back. Otherwise I become weak and
emasculated. So keep your arms exercised and healthy. I don't
want to see you all running away from a fight like cowards.'

Lakshmi decided to take her case to the people, to fight
back as Mutthu would have. Ignoring the chattering class
hadn't worked. They had only stepped up their protests. If she
did nothing about it, their accusations would become the truth.

'I'll arrange your tour, madam,' Murugesan offered. He
and his uncle had already thrown their weight whole-heartedly
behind the proposal. It was their district after all. 'It has to
be like an election campaign. I'll take care of everything. In
no time the tide will turn in our favour.'

The blitzkrieg tour around the state did turn out to be like
a campaign. Murugesan marshalled all the resources available
to him and every public meeting was a success. When she
took Mutthu with her they touched his feet and wept. At other
times they scrambled towards her and Selvamani graciously
stepped aside. At one reception a man recited a poem he had
composed in her honour. He repeated every line with increasing
gusto, pausing and gesticulating for dramatic effect. His manner
reminded her of district office-bearers of the Party who tried
to outdo each other with their flowery and sycophantic
introductions of Mutthu and her, but there was no artifice in
this man. He believed every word he said. He referred to her
as his people's thalaivi. 'Thalaivi, thalaivi, thalaivi!' he
concluded, shouting into the microphone at the top of his
voice, like a judge handing down a sentence, breaking into
rivulets of sweat from his exertion. The crowd cheered
approvingly and he retreated to his seat, wiping his face with
a handkerchief and grinning broadly.

Women, especially, had not forgotten what she had done
for them. 'You're a goddess,' they said. 'You bear your
misfortunes with such fortitude. You saved our families from
being ruined by arrack. How can god not see that and cure
Mutthu?'

But after one public meeting she found herself unexpectedly in the midst of a contentious impromptu press conference where journalists dropped all pretences and made insinuations about her role in Mohana Devi's transfer. She kept cool, answered their questions the way her advisors had coached her for just such an eventuality, but she left the room steaming.

On the way back to the city, she stared dully out of the tinted windows at passing trees, somnolent cows by the wayside and villagers driving goats down dusty paths. There was a large poster—perhaps from the days of the elections—of her and Mutthu on a billboard by the road. She could see it from afar, her face a smudge next to Mutthu's exaggeratedly rosy cheeks, and as she got closer she could see that her entire face had been blackened. It could have been the work of someone like Mayilkannan.

'But you assured me nobody will make a big issue of this,' she said accusingly, turning to the advisors. 'You were sure nobody would care if one bureaucrat was transferred.'

'Don't worry, madam,' Selvamani said. 'These newspaper fellows will make a little noise for a day or two to show they're doing their work, and then they'll keep quiet. Don't worry too much about what they say.'

'But it's my reputation that's at stake.'

'Don't worry, madam.' It was Murugesan's turn to speak. 'We're here to take care of things for you. Now, look all around you. Look at the number of people who come to see you. Why worry about a few fools when so many people worship you?'

She closed her eyes and took a deep breath. The accelerated heartbeat couldn't possibly be good for her.

She had begun to jealously guard the adulation she received. She tried to capture that feeling of utter bliss she felt in a secret vault deep inside her, so that she could dip into it during moments of doubt and need and scarcity such as this. She dipped into it now and willed her heartbeat back to normal.

They were driving past a hamlet that sprouted out of the surrounding barren landscape when a small wooden structure with a strip of worn awning fluttering in the breeze caught her attention. There was a small crowd in front of the structure. She leaned forward and commanded the driver to stop. Without waiting for her companions to get down, she ran down the embankment and made her way towards the crowd. She had recognized the wooden structure. It was a stage, a smaller version of the kind travelling theatres puppeteers performed in, a castlet, as Sister Cecilia would have called it, although that was too grand a name for this rickety, unpainted structure. Her hunch had been right—a puppet show was in progress. The distracted audience turned around in surprise. Some of the men and women in the back got up, having recognized her, but Lakshmi sternly waved them down and put her finger on her lips.

The play was an episode from the Ramayana. The puppeteer used four simple wooden puppets: Rama, Sita and a deer transforming itself into a rakshasa as Sita crossed the Lakshman-rekha when Rama was away. The puppets looked sorry and indigent. Their clothes were old and faded, their noses and ears chipped, their hair jute-coloured with dirt. The voice of the puppets was obviously that of a young boy, but neither the puppeteer nor the boy was visible. Lakshmi was instantly drawn into the play, for despite the worn-out puppets and the absence of bright props, there was charm in the simplicity of the setting and the tone of the play, in the way the puppets moved awkwardly around the stage, in the way the boy tried to emulate the deep-throated laughter of the villain Ravana or Sita's high-pitched shriek as she was whisked away by him, in the way the cloth covering Rama's torso accidentally fell off while he was bemoaning Sita's disappearance, revealing, much to the amusement of the audience, the bare featureless body of the puppet. The unintentional comedy of the situation worked well on the audience, and she noticed how engrossed they had quickly become after the brief interruption of their attention. Even the adults, impressionable and lost like children in the wonders of the puppet show, quickly forgot her presence.

When the play was over the adults approached her with folded hands. But for once she was not interested in their worshipful gestures. She went behind the stage and parted the curtain that covered it. From behind it a young boy, not more than eleven, holding the puppets, emerged, blinking at her and the bright light in confusion. There was nobody else with him; in fact there was no space for anybody else behind that cramped stage.

Lakshmi was astonished. 'Were you the puppeteer?' she asked.

The boy nodded.

'And the voices?'

He nodded again.

'Show me how you do it,' she commanded him.

The boy wiped his nose on his soiled sleeve and obediently put his puppets in position and made them come alive as he spoke for them in different voices. His hands and nimble fingers flew all over the place in a blur, malleable to the point of being formless, as if made of putty. Even Sister Cecilia, whom she remembered as being the best puppeteer she had ever seen, could have been no match for this small boy.

When he stopped, he put his puppets away in a jute sack and started dismantling the stage all by himself, oblivious to everybody around him. The villagers, who had gathered around them, beamed with pride and enjoyed Lakshmi's astonishment. 'He lives here,' they said, pointing to the clump of mud houses with thatched roofs. 'And here are his parents.' A bare-chested man in a torn lungi tried to cover his body with a towel out of deference to Lakshmi and stepped forward with his wife. They both fell at her feet and folded their hands when they got up.

Lakshmi, uncharacteristically, remained tongue-tied. 'Your son,' she blurted out finally, 'is a very good puppeteer. Who taught him?'

'I did,' the father said, nodding humbly, smiling in ecstasy as though the village goddess was talking to him.

She took out some money from her purse and gave it to him.

Rage

'No, amma,' he replied, recoiling. 'He does that for fun. He never gets paid for his shows.'

'Take it,' Lakshmi insisted. 'He's worth a lot more than this.'

The father held his hands out and accepted the money with his head bowed. Then both he and his wife touched her feet again. The rest of the villagers followed suit. The boy, who had by now dismantled the stage completely, stood by and watched, perplexed.

For the rest of her way back to the city Lakshmi was deep in thought. Upon reaching home, she knew she had found her answer. That puppeteer-boy could do wonders. She had her weapon to combat criticism, to shield her from the pointed arrows whizzing towards her. And an eleven-year-old would lead the fight with his innocuous but powerful wooden messengers. It was so laughably simple that even the most perceptive and critical of people would have a hard time resisting its charms.

She was finally prepared for the street fight.

★

At first the travelling puppet shows were a curiosity. It was a new kind of theatre, a modern one, of immediate relevance, of high pedigree. It had star power even before it became a crowd puller. A couple of playwrights who had been close associates of Mutthu during his acting days wrote plays for the puppeteer. Shiny new puppets were carefully designed and carved of ivory. Their dresses were made of raw silk and brocade; their jewels were made of pure gold and precious stones. A man who designed sets for movies made a new portable stage with colourful curtains and realistic backgrounds. The boy received a handsome salary to travel with his parents around the state to perform in towns and villages.

As the news of the puppeteer boy and his shiny puppets spread, larger audiences turned up to watch the shows. Lakshmi the deity was a revelation. The pale white skin of the puppet, the shining jewels, the benign smile played on the audience's imagination. The carefully scripted dialogues were dramatic and flamboyant. 'My people,' a monologue in one of the plays went, 'I have come to deliver you from the scourge of poverty and disease. Like the goddess Durga I have come to vanquish the demon amongst us. Follow me to the land of bliss, of green fields and large factories. Lend me your hand in our march to the future. Prosperity shall be ours!'

While Lakshmi could only be envisioned as a deity, Mutthu came in various forms. He was by turns a hero, a leader, a demigod, a victim of cruel fate. And Lakshmi the goddess was always with him in his different avatars, bestowing success, popularity and riches upon him, finding joy in his success, utterly disconsolate when he is felled.

The puppet shows quickly became popular. They also became more elaborate. Coloured strobe lights enhanced the visual effect, with different colours for different moods. They were accompanied by live music, with pipes and drums playing beside the stage. Then there were sophisticated backdrops, tableaux of bright colours and idealized scenes that changed at appropriate times.

Audiences started coming in larger numbers. In rural areas villagers walked for miles to the show, making it a grand outing for the entire family. They were impressed with the razzmatazz, the show of light and sound, the grand orations. It was better than going to the movies because this was live and more colourful. Young and old were entranced; they sang and danced before and after the shows.

Devaki, Ragini and I went to watch one of the plays when the troupe performed in a tenement colony teeming with people. We came away impressed, blinking at each other as if we'd just watched a film extravaganza. 'That was just super,' Devaki gushed. 'The puppets were so alive I kept thinking that that was Lakshmi out there.'

Soon, recognizing the opportunity, vendors set up shop wherever the troupe camped. They sold roasted groundnuts, ice cream on sticks, tender coconut, cheap bottled soda, bidis, betel leaves, and crude plastic replicas of the puppets. Then there were fortune-tellers and their parrots with clipped wings that could barely walk; holy men who went around with small braziers of coal and camphor and incense; men with performing monkeys in funny fezzes and jackets; beggars, some with no limbs or noses or eyes, milled about, pleading for alms. Some of these hangers-on began travelling with the troupe: a train of camp followers that kept growing as the troupe traversed the state, adding to the pomp and carnival atmosphere.

It was a while before anybody criticized the puppet shows. It was a while before K. Abdul Latheef reared his head again. *It's a travelling circus*, he wrote one day in disgust. *The puppeteer boy, who should be the ringmaster and run his show exactly the way he wants, is now a puppet himself. And that is the saddest part of this charade.*

But nobody paid attention to him this time.

It was around this time that I travelled through Pudupettai and its neighbouring districts and what I saw was a revelation to me. What had started as a clever move by Lakshmi had now taken on a form and life of its own, a juggernaut that propelled itself on the energy it generated, growing like a monster. The tiny myth that originated from Lakshmi had found a willing audience, willing co-conspirators, willing actors who played their parts to perfection, and willing retellers who carried it farther and wider than perhaps even she had envisioned. It was like a cult, the cult of a goddess, raging across the countryside. The dazzling jewels blinded the audience, the benign smile seduced them, the light and sound and the grand tableaux mesmerized them. And behind all this lurked a collective awe at the grandeur, at the perfectly orchestrated spectacle, even a fear of the powerful and the omnipotent. Sometimes it all seemed unreal, surreal.

In one village, ahead of the local legislator's visit, the local branch of the state-run literacy mission organized a jatha. Only this time it was not to extol the benefits of literacy to the rural community, but to stage one of the puppet troupe's plays with human actors. In another village, in the next block, school children were taught songs from the plays. At the district headquarters of a neighbouring district, the collector, upon learning that I was a journalist, not only ushered me into his office with great deference, but also spoke of the wondrous deeds their thalaivi had done for the village. When I pointed out that his district still had the largest number of illegal arrack shops, he hastened to rebuke me. 'Chee-chee-chee, saar, what are you saying? Our leader herself came here just a month ago and closed down a dozen of them in front of my own eyes.'

I became increasingly distressed as I travelled around. I wasn't sure why I was travelling. Perhaps I did so in the hope that I might find a legitimate reason, however tiny, to explain the sudden rise in reverence for her, and to quell my growing disenchantment. But I didn't. I finally understood what K. Abdul Latheef had foreseen before anybody else. I had not known this facet of her personality. I tried to think of a parallel situation from our childhood, but I found none, for although she always fought back—savagely, sometimes—she did so without deviousness.

But no matter how much I tried to rationalize, I did not believe my own rationalizations. Devaki grew annoyed at me. My change of heart offended her. 'I don't know what's happened to you,' she once said angrily. 'You're becoming a cynic. Questioning for the sake of testing the other person's knowledge, arguing for the sake of making noise, doubting because you don't want to believe. Why can't you accept that people genuinely like her?'

I looked at Ragini. She pursed her lips. 'What's there not to like about her?'

I searched her face. I found no traces of sarcasm. Nothing to indicate that she was playing along.

I went away quietly in search of K. Abdul Latheef. *He* was the only one who made sense any more.

When the cranes and bulldozers and concrete mixers arrived, Mayilkannan was stunned. For, although the propaganda blitz had worked elsewhere in the state, the residents of Pudupettai had remained opposed to the plan, which had made him think that the government would at least delay the start of the project if not reconsider its viability. But the heavy equipment rolled on, rumbling darkly past Pudupettai, to the abandoned farmlands that had been cleared out only a few weeks before. The land where rice once grew, standing serenely in calf-deep water, now lay empty, with clumps of dry ochre earth in place of the soft, dark clay. These farms had been the pride of Pudupettai district. The emerald paddy fields irrigated by numerous wells and the lake was an oasis in the semi-arid district. One didn't have to stretch one's imagination: the brown, barren hills in the background provided an easy contrast. These farms had produced enough rice to feed all of Pudupettai district. Now the bulldozers trampled on them, flattening and crushing them.

Before their very eyes, with vengeful energy, even before the final approval for the plan had been granted by the central government, construction began. Trenches were dug where raised earth had once demarcated one field from another. Concrete was poured into the skeletal frame of iron rods that jutted upwards from the ground like the limbs of a dead animal lying on its back in rigor mortis.

Before long, arrangements were made to lay the foundation stone in a formal ceremony. All the leaders were expected to attend: Lakshmi, Selvamani, Murugesan, Sundarapandian, Mutthu wheeled in his chair, and a couple of ministers from Delhi. Billboards and posters went up all over the district to announce the ceremony.

After the initial shock, Mayilkannan watched all this activity quietly, smiling enigmatically, refusing to tell anybody what was bubbling in his head. The night before the ceremony, he and several activists sneaked past the guards at the construction site and went through the bamboo barricades erected to keep those who came to witness the ceremony at a safe distance from the VIPs. There was a red carpet inside the pandal, placed on the walkway that led to the foundation stone. There was a rough rectangular section in the wall where a plaque commemorating the laying of the foundation would be cemented into the wall. The black marble slab, with white letters carved on it lay on the ground near the wall. As part of the ceremony, Lakshmi would apply cement to its back and all around it with a mason's spatula and put it in its place in the wall.

Mayilkannan and his companions climbed over the low foundation wall and dropped into a trench. Silently, pressed against the wall that smelt of fresh concrete, they spent the night in vigil, awaiting the break of dawn.

The next morning a buzz of activity broke out in preparation for the ceremony. Policemen and bomb squads combed the area to ensure that there were no strange objects lying around. Electricians tested the sound system. A few lorries carrying construction materials wandered to and fro. But nobody thought to look behind the foundation wall where Mayilkannan and his companions strained their ears to interpret the various sounds they heard and hissed to each other whenever something sounded like a cue. They had to be careful; timing was of utmost importance. Making their presence known at the wrong time would render their plan ineffective. They could hear the cacophonous and self-important voices of the organizers overseeing the preparations. They could hear the audience come in early to get the best places to sit behind the bamboo barricades. They could hear policemen blowing their whistles, more frantically as the hour progressed, physically examining visitors before allowing them in. They were taking extra precautions, but clearly their efforts were misplaced. Mayilkannan's companions exchanged sneers.

Finally, when everybody on the other side of the wall began babbling at the same time, they knew it was time to act. They climbed over the wall and, before the security guards could react, they rushed to the carpeted walkway leading to the foundation stone and lay down on the carpet shoulder to shoulder across its breadth, holding on to each others' arms tightly, forming a human chain.

Over two dozen policemen descended on the protestors and yelled at them to clear out. But they lay still, tightening their grip, looking resolutely at the policemen looming over them. The policemen tried to physically move them out of the way, but every time they lifted one protestor, the others pulled him down.

Television cameras now captured the drama unfolding in front of the black stone and flashes from several cameras lit up the pandal.

'She'll have to walk over us to lay the foundation stone,' the protestors—except Mayilkannan in the centre, still and grave—yelled into the cameras.

The audience, both in the VIP section and in the general section, surged forward, craning their necks, pushing against the bamboo barricades that threatened to give way. The policemen swung their lathis in an effort to get the protestors out of the way quickly and managed to dislodge a few protestors. But, to everybody's surprise, replacements arrived. Members of the audience spontaneously broke through the cordon of policemen to take the place of the protestors who were being manhandled and led away. When a few policemen aimed their lathis at Mayilkannan, fellow protestors instinctively shielded him, taking the blows on their backs instead. With every blow they received they cried in pain and defiance, 'You will have to crack our skulls before you break open a coconut. We'll wash the stone with our blood before you pour coconut water over it.'

Eventually, the policemen managed to keep the crowds at bay by firing a couple of tear gas shells. They rounded up all the protestors by forcibly lifting them one by one and shoving them into waiting vans. Mayilkannan found himself in one that had a particularly low roof and he sat crouched on the hard bench, his hands tied behind his back, his head pressed against the roof. There was only a small ventilator in the cabin, but it was covered with a dirt-filled gauze that effectively kept the air out. Five other protestors were loaded into the van before it drove off. As the van bounced and rattled over the potholes Mayilkannan remembered his first trip to the police station in a similar van. Lakshmi had intervened then, out of fear, and freed him. But this time he knew she would do no such thing. He had seen that wrathful look in her eyes as he was being led away. She was there at the far end of the red carpet with her bodyguards (whom she had acquired recently), the other leaders, Mutthu looking with unseeing eyes, Surya, Gloria and the child in her arms. He had responded to her fiery stare with a laugh, for the protest had achieved its purpose. But before he had climbed into the van he had turned around to throw his head back in a bold challenge, and he had seen her flinch and put her hand on the gun of one of her bodyguards, searching for the trigger. This had made him want to spit at her, but he had remembered Mohana Devi's parting words. She would not have approved of it.

'I wanted to shoot him!' Lakshmi screamed all through the labyrinthine corridors of the Aranmanai, as her house was now called. A mild echo spoke back to her in dampened tones. She found herself overpowered by rage. As always, it started with pain, a mere pinprick, but soon it tore through her flesh, leaving her writhing. Sometimes it was like poisoned arrows or swords flying out of their scabbards and glinting in the afternoon sun or harpoons that covered great distances noiselessly. These could devour her insides, leaving her empty, palpitating, reaching out for support, and anger would fill her up to counter the draining sensation. Anger so deep that sometimes that was all that she had, layers and layers of it, regurgitating old, unrelated wounds and finding hitherto unknown connections between them. Anger that made everything so frighteningly clear that it removed all doubt. Anger that made her want to pounce on her target like a wounded tigress and decimate it so that there was no trace of it; nothing to remind her ever again of the emptiness it caused in her, for often the memory of a wound hurt more than the wound itself.

She now rushed from room to room, up and down the stairs, along the length of every corridor, Surya and her advisors trying hard to keep up with her. She wasn't looking for anything; she just couldn't bear staying in one spot for more than a moment, for everything maddened her: every room, every piece of furnishing, even the faces of the people around her. 'He had that trademark smirk on his face when he looked at me, as if to tell me I can't do anything to him. Doesn't he know who I am? Doesn't he know that I can finish him off in an instant?'

Surya interjected: 'But Lakshmi—'

'Don't interrupt me!' she snarled back at him. 'If he doesn't know what fear is I'll teach him what it is. Bring him to me! I'll teach him to fear me! If he thinks he's courageous, I'll show him who's stronger. Bring him to me! Bring the bastard here! Bring the bast—'

She stopped suddenly and looked at them. Surya looked pale. He looked like he wanted to say something but didn't dare to. What did he want to say? That she should calm down? That everybody respected and loved her? Or that she of all people had no right to question the legitimacy of Mayilkannan's birth?

She cringed, stepping back from them slowly, staring at them, waiting for them to react, to say something, to reach out and touch and hold her. But they stood still, staring back implacably. She ran towards her suite, her body breaking into sobs, with the men following her closely. As soon as she entered her suite she bolted the door behind her and threw herself on the bed. 'The bastard!' she cried into the pillow, her brittle voice cracking. 'The bastard!'

She was aware of her body trembling. This had never happened before. The rage had gripped her like an ogre; its accompanying clarity had allowed her to see herself tremble helplessly.

She realized that every successive bout of anger over the years had become progressively larger in amplitude. Of late she could sense the difference herself. Was there a limit to the amount of anger one could feel? How far was she from the limit? And what would happen when she reached and crossed it? Did such concentrated doses of anger burn one up just the way sunlight focussed through a magnifying glass burned paper? Or were the destructive effects gradual, imperceptible till it was too late?

Lakshmi allowed Surya in to calm her down. He sat on the bed beside her for a long time without uttering a word. The Aranmanai was silent.

'Don't worry,' Surya said finally. 'We'll just have to step up the campaign and in a month nobody will remember the incident.'

'Surya,' she said, instead. 'Come with your family and stay here.' A look of incredulity crossed his face. 'I'm afraid of being here alone. I don't want to be here by myself.'

A Famine and a Feast

I became a father the day Ragini got married. I gave her away.

The groom was a paediatrician who came three times a week to the home for spastic children where Ragini volunteered her time. He was handsome and had a presence. They were drawn to each other from the moment they had met. He admired her compassion and she his intelligence. He matched her stoicism with his dignity. They looked wonderful together. Devaki could not have asked for a better man for Ragini to marry.

Ragini had insisted on sending an invitation to her mother ('Whether she comes or not, we should fulfil our duty and invite her,' she had argued with her grandmother), but she had had the good sense to not expect her. But her mother did come. In the form of a large wooden cut-out, larger than life, a full-size image of her, hands folded, greeting invitees with a smile at the entrance to the marriage hall. Posters, billboards and cut-outs had been going up all over the state as if in preparation for an election, and someone had had the foreknowledge to install a cut-out next to the marriage hall the day before the wedding. Ragini and Devaki were pleased with its presence. But I kept quiet, not wanting to start a quarrel on an important day.

As Ragini sat on my lap dressed in bridal finery in the mandapam while the priests chanted verses that sanctified the marriage, I couldn't help thinking that I was too young to be her father, even a substitute one, that this culmination of the responsibility I had felt ever since Nasser Sharif's death sat uncomfortably on my shoulders.

Afterwards, in the privacy of one of the back rooms of the marriage hall she fell into her grandmother's arms and wept. It was odd to see tears on such a joyful occasion, even if hers were tears of joy for having her family around her, a family that had been cobbled together, joy at having broken the two-generation-old cycle in the family. She fell into my arms next, and as I held her, her joy permeated into me.

It was only later that I found out another reason for her joy. Among the gifts she had received was one that was unaccounted for. It was a diamond necklace. The card on the gift had Ragini's name written on it and nothing else. I recognized the handwriting, and evidently so had Ragini.

★

When Mayilkannan was released from jail he had no rabble-rousing ideas. That summer, as the sun scorched the earth dry, construction commenced in many parts of the district. Foundations for large buildings were laid in the valley. The pass in the hills between Pudupettai town and the valley had been blasted with dynamite for the new highway. The foundation for the airport terminal and other buildings expanded like a spider's web. All these projects began quietly, without fanfare, often starting in isolated areas with unimportant, auxiliary structures before encroaching stealthily on to the main site, taking nearby residents by surprise. The strategy worked, for protestors often arrived at new construction sites too late to prevent the bulldozers and cranes and the earth movers from doing their jobs.

Instead, Mayilkannan left the town of Pudupettai and headed for the relocated farms. In this part of the district the sun was merciless; along the way, as he rode the bus, he noticed how rocky and dry the landscape was, how large the crevices that had formed in the bed of a dried river were. For miles and miles there was nothing but ochre wasteland of brown scrub and dark rocks dotting it like warts. The harshness of the land and the sun made Mayilkannan wonder how the farmers were able to grow anything at all. So he rubbed his eyes in disbelief when he saw fields of standing crops appear before him suddenly, quite like the oasis they had cultivated at the foothills near Pudupettai town. These were not fields of rice, which the farmers were used to growing, but barley, millet and maize because the land was poor and water scarce. But when he came closer he noticed that the plants were stunted and their leaves were drying. There were no irrigation pipes or canals from distant rivers as the government had promised. All they had was well water.

He immediately set to work and roused the farmers to dig wells. Every morning before dawn they would gather at the digging site, wearing only loin cloths and towels on their heads like turbans, and they would dig, all of them, with pickaxes, shovels, anything they could get their hands on. The earth was hard, so progress was excruciatingly slow. They could dig only a couple of feet in the forenoon, after which the sun blistered their sweat-soaked skins and made them light-headed. They had to dig deep to find any water, and even then they only found muddy, brackish water; often they found nothing. The water diviner they had consulted had been particularly poor in his predictions—only a couple of wells yielded water in worthwhile quantities.

Soon there were so many holes in the ground that the crater-scarred land must have looked like a battle zone from the air. The little water they did find was used to irrigate their fields. But no sooner had they watered the fields than the earth sucked it all back in, cracking and breaking up with a vengeance under the continued onslaught of the sun.

Finally, the farmers gave up but still Mayilkannan persisted. He suggested that they dig up the dry river bed to look for possible underground streams. They could build a canal to redirect the water to their fields. He even took them to the river bed and asked them to put their ears to the ground.

'We don't hear anything,' they said.

'But I hear it,' he gesticulated frantically. 'I hear a lot of water down there.'

But the farmers were morose. 'It's in your ears, aiyah,' they said and led him away.

Mayilkannan refused to believe them. He stayed with them for a few more days and dug the river bed all by himself. He worked through the night in the light of an oil lamp, for the days were now unbearably hot. He dug deeper and deeper into the river bed, but found nothing. Finally his conviction crumbled. He emerged from the hole one morning when he realized that there was more moisture on his body than in the ground and acknowledged that he had been defeated. With crumpled shoulders he returned to Pudupettai, promising to get them famine assistance. The fields were brown now, covered in acres and acres of hay yet to be harvested.

It was around this time that K. Abdul Latheef and I happened to meet outside the Aranmanai. He was standing across the street and peering into the grounds through the iron gate under the suspicious stares of the guards. I joined him and peered, too, without exchanging a word with him. Presently the guards walked over to us and told us to clear out before they called the police. They lifted their rifles to drive home their point. As the two of us walked away to the end of the street where we had been forced to leave our scooters—since unauthorized vehicles were not allowed into the street any more—he looked pained.

'What's the matter?' I asked him, breaking the silence.

'I wonder where she gets all that water for those large fountains when those farmers don't have water even to make kanji.'

'Everybody knows that those in power get special treatment when it comes to municipal services,' I responded, eager to prove that I wasn't blind to Lakshmi's flaws.

'But still. At least for the sake of public perception she could have turned it off.'

Soon, at the Press Club, someone decided to hang a framed

photograph of the fountain on the wall. A close-up, taken at night, multicoloured lights playing on its various jets. One could have mistaken it for a fountain at the Brindavan Gardens. We sat under the photograph and exchanged news and gossip, mostly the latter, and mostly about the Aranmanai and its occupants. My colleagues were a fount of information. But I wondered how much of what I heard from them was true and how much was cynical exaggeration.

Of the Aranmanai itself, they were only able to tell what they'd seen during the house-warming festivities.

'Where did she get all that money?' I asked, for the descriptions I heard from them sounded too fantastic and incredible.

'All of Mutthu's money went into this.'

'How much money could he have had?'

'Saar, you know how it is with even the most honest of our leaders. For every rupee they take over the table, there are a thousand waiting underneath.' There was general laughter.

'A lot of it has come from those people around her, especially Surya and Tedeschi,' somebody else commented. 'How much this Surya has made selling all his land back to the government! They say the land was assessed at a value even higher than he had expected.'

'Yes, yes, in her name he's making crores. Everybody around her is making money. We have to wonder how much of this she knows.'

'How can she not know about it? She's not a fool.'

'One has to wonder how much of that money is going to her.'

'Even if she's not getting the money directly, at least some of it eventually finds its way to her indirectly. And now with Surya and his family staying with her, is there any reason to doubt it?'

'Yes, what's this arrangement all about? The two women don't even look at each other, and yet they live under the same roof.'

'Yes, it is odd, isn't it? Must be all about money. But you

can't blame Gloria for getting upset. Wouldn't you be if someone else tried to take your child away from you?'

It was distressing to hear such talk. I hoped this was nothing but idle gossip, but I was no fool. And such stories only increased as time went by. Stories of how a lot of decisions were made in the bowels of the dimly lit, mysterious hallways of the Aranmanai to which very few people had access. Of the coterie of businessmen and leaders of the Party that had formed around her, jealously protecting its turf and holding secret meetings in the dark rooms. The members of the coterie alone knew what transpired in them. They made, or at least influenced, most of the decisions Selvamani made.

'It's not a kitchen cabinet,' someone remarked. 'It's a secret society.'

Indeed, it did not take them long to become a cabal to which membership was likely preceded by an unspoken oath of lifelong secrecy. As criticism directed against her and the government grew, she retreated further inside, and now she was rarely seen in public.

That my colleagues disliked Surya was clear to me. But it was for Gloria that they reserved special criticism. Although she didn't seem to do anything at all most of the time, they didn't trust her because her presence was everywhere in the Aranmanai. They hated the way in which she darkened a beautiful place like that with her heavy curtains and drapes and dim lights.

But Lakshmi seemed to derive strength from this darkness and secrecy. She wrapped herself up in her coterie as though it were a cloak, and seemed perfectly happy to meet no one else for days on end.

What they told me was reflected in her actions. When she appeared publicly she was not only surrounded by security men, but also increasingly by select Party officials with well-oiled hair and businessmen in drab safari suits and beringed fingers. Even cabinet members who were not part of this group had a hard time getting access to her and were reduced to ineffectually grumbling amongst themselves and to journalists off the record.

And at the club we continued to sit around the card table, sometimes late into the evening, past dinner time. I mostly listened, having very little to contribute. It seemed appropriate that we should drink bottle after bottle of chilled soda and beer under the photograph of the fountain, dawdling at the club to put off facing the heat outside and the worries about water scarcity. Those days Lakshmi wasn't alone in trying to escape reality.

'Do you know anything about this family?' Devaki asked me once. 'Are they good people?'

'I think so,' I replied without conviction.

'I don't get a good feeling about them. Someone should tell her to be careful. Please send a message to her.'

Before I could answer, Ragini said, 'Why should he or someone else communicate with her on your behalf, paati? Why can't you do so yourself?'

Devaki sighed. 'It's too late to change things, ma. You're still young. You won't understand.'

'I do, paati. And that's why I've decided not to be helpless any more. Amma is right. If you can't have something, it is best to let go of it completely. She's smarter than all of us.'

I knew her comment was directed as much at me as at her grandmother. But I couldn't help worrying. I couldn't help being helpless. I sometimes daydreamed of storming the dark interiors of the Aranmanai and rescuing her, fleeing to a timeless dimension with her. But, later, I would wonder what I wanted to rescue her from. From her present and her past? Or did I want to rescue myself from the guilt I still bore?

Only Ragini was in the process of coming to terms with her mother. And I envied her for that.

★

That year summer extended well into the months when the weather usually cooled down somewhat in anticipation of rain-bearing clouds from the sea. Lakes and reservoirs had dangerously low levels of water. Rivers that had never ran dry were reduced to scrawny, muddy streams. Taps ran dry too, as did irrigation canals. But the drier the state became the larger the posters and the wooden cut-outs of the leaders grew.

Mayilkannan kept returning to the displaced farmers even after it was too late to save their crops. With every trip he noticed how the farmers and their families had changed a little, how they were a little closer to destitution. At first they wept when they saw him, and he was encouraged by it, for people weep only when they think there's some hope of redress. He told them he was trying to get aid from the government, loans to see the rest of the year through and to buy seeds for the next season. He told them he was trying to get the government to build irrigation canals to bring in water from afar. He took them to every government office he could possibly think of and filed petition after petition on their behalf.

The first sign that the farmers and their families were losing hope was when the adults stopped weeping. They followed Mayilkannan impassively and did what he asked them to do. Then mothers stopped trying to calm their crying children. Instead of cajoling them with words of encouragement, they simply let their children cry themselves to sleep. The adults spent all their time sitting on their haunches with their heads in their hands, staring at their ruined fields. No matter what Mayilkannan promised them they would not look up. Not a smile broke through their lips. Not even a sigh of resignation.

And yet, when he discovered one day that several homes had been abandoned, he was shocked.

'They went away, aiyah,' the ones who had stayed behind said with no emotion at all. 'Who knows where they went? Anywhere would be better than here. What is left for them here? A worthless piece of land and the ghosts of their dying crops.'

Beyond, he saw a woman wearing one of the free mango-patterned saris drawing water from a well. She tilted her bucket gingerly over a sieve and drained the water into a copper kitchen urn. A mound of mud collected in the sieve. Picking up the urn and placing it on her hip she carried the muddy water to her house.

The villagers who had gathered around him said, 'They were smart to leave. All we have left is shit and mud.'

They appeared to have made up their minds and Mayilkannan did not wish to stop them.

★

The fountain at the Aranmanai, hewn from one large solid block of Carrarra marble, had always been a novelty. Not only could it dance to music, it could also sing. Lakshmi spent many hours lounging on a chair beside it in the evenings when the cool sea breeze blew in, calmed by the soft music she heard in the streams of water hissing at different pitches as they emerged from the spouts. The fountain had an endless repertoire and never repeated a tune.

Gloria's—*her*—son loved it, too. He was a water baby. He took to water the way a newly hatched turtle seeks the ocean. He was particularly happy at bathtime and refused to get out of the tub, surrounded as he was with soap suds, his rubber duck, his boats and other water toys. When Lakshmi sat by the fountain, he usually played by her feet, watched over by the ayah, squealing periodically with delight at the sight of the water. He often asked to be put down in the fountain where he splashed around naked. Sometimes he stood by the fountain and beat the parapet wall with his two tiny hands as if keeping rhythm to the music. Lakshmi could watch him for hours on end, captivated by his joy, enjoying his drum-beating more than the music the fountain produced.

Of late the fountain had begun attracting a lot of birds and squirrels. In the evenings, when the heat was more bearable, the fountain looked like a watering hole in a forest, with crows, mynahs, sparrows, pigeons, and sometimes less common birds like cuckoos, weaverbirds and woodpeckers. Once in a while she saw what looked like warblers and teals. She liked the racket the birds made, sometimes loud enough to drown the music.

But one day she regarded the fountain for a long time and summoned one of the servants. 'Shut it off,' she said, regretfully. 'People don't have water to drink, and here we are playing with it.'

But that evening Gloria's son stood beside the fountain and bawled as he never had. He smacked and kicked the parapet wall. He screamed when Lakshmi tried to pick him up. His ayah took him inside and filled his tub with water, but he refused to get in. Gloria sang to him to no avail.

That night he cried himself to sleep and Lakshmi sat by his bed for a long time and watched the tears dry on his cheeks. She left him alone only when she was satisfied that he had fallen fast asleep.

The next day as Lakshmi sat down in one of the darkened chambers in the Aranmanai, where she usually met Selvamani, Murugesan and others once or twice a week, she was surprised to see a picture of the fountain in a newspaper.

'It's nothing, madam,' Selvamani said. 'It's that Abdul Latheef fellow. What other work does he have other than to find fault with us?'

She looked at the caption. She expected an excoriating line or two. But, oddly, it only said 'The Fountain'. She noticed that it used the definitive article, as if there were only one fountain in the world.

'The mischief-maker is being insidious as usual,' she said.

'Don't worry, madam. It's the hot season.'

It was true that tempers had become short and insults long. Every day they heard stories about people pouncing on each other like beasts. The heat was driving them crazy. The government was doing everything it could to ease the situation. It had opened up its granaries and had requested more aid from the central government. It had granted financial relief of all kinds to those most affected by the drought. But unless the rains came, all forms of redress would fall short.

'These fellows need something to find fault with,' explained

Murugesan. 'After a long time they have something to write about.'

'I agree,' Selvamani said. 'Is it our fault that we have had two successive years of drought?'

'How are people surviving the water shortage?' Lakshmi asked.

'Actually the situation isn't as bad as people make it out to be,' Murugesan insisted. 'The drought of 1975 was much worse. Simply to cause trouble people spread misinformation. They have to keep needling the government for something or the other.'

'People will read this and blame us. They'll ask, "How come you don't control the winds and the clouds?"'

'Especially that troublemaker Mayilkannan. He'll compose poems about it and go around gargling them.'

'For a man who has sworn not to speak, he does make a lot of noise.'

As the conversation proceeded, Lakshmi's eyes strayed back to the newspaper. The accompanying article was titled less subtly: 'Royal Decadence'. She did not read the article. She didn't have to. The title said it all.

'The one indulgence I have and he has to pounce on it,' she remarked, hurt. 'And even that I've already stopped. Turn the fountain on again. I don't want people thinking he's the reason behind my turning it off.'

She looked at the article again. The more she considered the title, the angrier she felt. 'Royal decadence? What is royal or decadent around here? I'll show him what royal decadence is.'

'What are you going to do?' Surya asked with concern.

'I don't know yet. But I do know that I'm not going to take this lying down. I'm going to show him what little effect his views have on me. I'm going to make sure he knows I'm happy. Very happy. And that I indeed live like royalty.'

One of Surya's investments even before his son's affinity for water became apparent was in an amusement park an acquaintance of his had started constructing by the seashore.

This park was either eclectic or kitschy, depending on one's point of view. It had gut-inverting and nausea-inducing roller coaster rides in a fantasy land that had toy bullet trains, model skyscrapers, a recreation of the world of dinosaurs, sprawling lawns and wooded areas, and a portion devoted to an aquatic theme with dancing fountains, water slides, artificial lakes and waterfalls. This last part of the park was added to the original plan after the park's developer had had the epiphany one day to defy nature by celebrating with an excess what the city lacked even in the best of times.

But, ironically and as expected, for many months large areas of the park had not operated owing to lack of water. But it was here that Lakshmi said they should celebrate the completion of the first phase of development of their city in the valley.

There was a sense of exaggeration to everything that happened that day. It was hard to say how much of it was real and how much fantasy. Or how much a magic trick, an illusion conjured by potent chants, played on an unsuspecting audience by the wizard with the light and sound show.

But this much is true: celebrations of the kind the city had never seen before took place at the park. Many parts of the city were given a facelift, like a child well scrubbed for an admission interview at a prestigious school. The airport and the road leading to the city were spruced up in anticipation of the guests who came from around the country and abroad. The park itself was given a makeover: lush green lawns, manicured bushes, a red carpet covering the main walkway, bordered by potted bonsais and dwarfed varieties of unheard-of trees, freshly cleaned and chlorinated pools. Its sluice gates were opened and water magically rushed through every orifice and channel in such abundance that Gloria's son went delirious with joy.

All day, thousands of guests partook of the fun, splashing in the pools, riding dragons, trains, teacups, sliding down water chutes, standing under the artificial waterfall, slaking their thirst in the absurd abundance of water.

In the evening, attired in their best clothes, they gathered on the banks of the long artificial Venetian canal, at one end of which on the podium was a huge cake, a model of the city they were constructing in the valley. Beside the podium technicians operated large, impressive sound and light equipment. The tables where the guests were to be seated were placed all around the canal.

The evening's entertainment was lavish. In the gathering dusk, after Lakshmi had cut the cake to the accompaniment of a live orchestra, scores of waiters in turbans and cummerbunds brought in an unending train of food and drink. A dizzying array of vegetable and rice dishes seasoned with saffron and spices, garnished with fruit and nuts, fowl with their little feet sticking out, slabs of meat floating in gravy and seafood went by sizzling, hissing, leaving behind aromas and flavours so heady that the guests would remember them for days afterwards.

At the head table, tucking into avial and truffles, pulao and caviar, surrounded by Mutthu, Surya, Gloria, their child, the Pavesis, the Tedeschis and Selvamani, Lakshmi temporarily forgot her worries. Everybody was having a good time. The sight of so much water made them thirsty, and they drank in abundance. All evening, whenever the orchestra played a lively tune they got up and danced in the aisles. Even Mutthu recognized a few of the songs and nodded happily.

The main attraction of the evening's entertainment, however, was the laser show. Heavy with rich food, tired after all the dancing and excitement, the guests eased into their reclining seats after dinner to watch the show. It was spectacular. The explosion of light and colour, the splashes, the sparkles, the thundering cascades, the rivers overflowing from the bubbling brew in the centre of it all—they were enthralled. The figures and patterns the light created in the dark new-moon sky were astonishingly realistic. They were not meaningless figures dancing across the sky to the music. Like a symphony they contained a story, an abstraction of expressions conceived by the most precise of actors in the sky. The climax of the show was the special effect that the creator, who was an illusionist and a high-tech magician as well, had worked very hard on. A gigantic, abstract figure that changed forms, morphing from one into another smoothly, loomed over them. Some said it was a goddess, descending down upon them from heaven. Others swore it was Lakshmi. Still others thought it was the new city that was being built. The effect was so realistic that the guests braced themselves to be crushed under its weight as it came bearing down on them. But when they realized it was only an illusion they laughed sheepishly relief.

By the time the entertainment was over and the guests started leaving, it was past midnight. Alcohol had flowed continuously all evening. Several guests had to be helped out of the park to their cars. As they streamed out, they were all quiet, stupefied by drink and dazed from the evening's relentless assault on their senses.

The lavishness of the evening had not sunk in yet, nor had its recklessness.

While the guests were being entertained at the park, Mayilkannan and a large group of men silently made their way to the Aranmanai after dark. The men Mayilkannan led were armed with bamboo sticks. The guards at the Aranmanai grew nervous when the crowd arrived. They locked the gates and waved their guns in the air. But the men stood their ground, demanding that they be let in. When it was clear that the guards would not oblige, Mayilkannan stepped forward and climbed up the gate.

'Get down!' the guards yelled. 'We'll turn on the current and you'll be roasted in no time.'

But Mayilkannan did not listen. His companions now followed him. Over the sharp arrows at the top of the gate they went and down the other side. There was no electricity in those arrows.

'We'll turn it on now!' the guards shouted.

One of the guards placed his finger on a switch inside the kiosk, looking determined. Mayilkannan expected him to turn it on. So he stood on top of the gates, straddling the arrows, directing those who were already on the gate to jump down inside the Aranmanai and stopped the others from climbing up. He looked back at the guard who had his finger on the switch, challenging him to turn it on. The two glared at each other for several moments, each waiting for the other to make the first move. Finally the guard's determination gave way. Nervously he stepped out of the kiosk. 'Please go away,' he pleaded. 'We won't call the police if you go away right now. You don't know the kind of trouble you'll get into for doing this.'

Mayilkannan did not respond. He gestured to the rest of the crowd outside to climb over the gates. Only when the last of them had jumped over did he himself climb down. The guard who had not switched on the electricity came running to him. 'Aiyah,' he pleaded again, clearly recognizing him. 'Please go away. You know we can't do anything to so many of you. But please don't do anything foolish.'

Mayilkannan and his companions walked past the guards. They went straight to the fountain that was lit up by coloured lights. The high arcs the various streams of water made in the air were easily visible in the light. Water also flowed from the open mouth of the gargoyle that stood on a pedestal at the centre. The sound of flowing water excited the intruders. Mayilkannan, clad in shorts and a homespun vest, felt gloriously naked in the sybaritic mansion. Wasting no time, he searched for the controls. It was not difficult to find; his informant had been precise in his directions. He turned off the water supply and the fountain sputtered for a few seconds before dying. The gargoyle in the centre looked ghastly without water flowing out of its mouth.

With great efficiency, Mayilkannan and his companions mixed the cement and sand they had brought with them and some water from the fountain in shallow pans. When the mixture was ready they poured it into every spout. Then Mayilkannan climbed on to the pedestal in the centre and filled the gargoyle's mouth with the remaining mixture. His companions let out a cheer as he climbed down. One of them then took pictures of the sealed gargoyle and the empty fountain.

Satisfied, the men retraced their steps. They ordered the guards to open the gates. With great relief the guards jumped up to open them. One of Mayilkannan's companions warned the guards, 'If you try to remove the cement we'll be forced to use our sticks.' But the guards were only too happy to oblige as long as the intruders left.

Before he left, Mayilkannan turned back to look at the fountain. The sound of flowing water had been annoying, even maddening. Now, in the silence, the fountain looked tolerable, harmless, nondescript as it always should have been—an expensive non-functioning toy of the rich and powerful.

He knew it would rain now.

Mayhem

The next day the park looked like a site a particularly vicious tornado had touched down on. The City's corporation would be busy cleaning it up for several days. For a couple of days afterwards, the hungry lined up patiently outside the park for their share of the leftovers, which they received on plantain leaves. For once in their lives they ate the food of the rich, and for many it was the first proper meal they had had in several weeks. For many days after that some of these people pretended they were rich themselves: you are defined by the food you eat.

But at the end of it all there was silence. Not the silence of sleepy guests walking back to their cars, but the silence of bewilderment. There had been something unearthly about the evening. The spectacle could only have been created by creatures who did not inhabit the world—the world as they knew it.

But bewilderment does not last long—it turns to hope or despair soon. Perhaps all this was done to propitiate the gods, people said, to coax them into giving us rain. So they waited. Waited for something to happen. If they deserved it, the heavens would open up. Or else, the sun would scorch them with renewed vigour, while they, like fish, would flap furiously one last time in search of water.

Something was bound to happen. And they waited.

'What were you idiots doing?' Lakshmi thundered at the guards. 'I leave the house under your care for one evening and you open the gates to bandits! Those guns are meant to keep robbers away, not to escort them in! Ungrateful wretches! Is this what I pay you for?'

The guard who had not turned on the switch, stepped forward, quaking in his boots. 'But, amma, there were too many of them.'

This incensed her further. 'Cowards, all of you! Did they have guns and bombs to frighten you? Then why didn't you shoot them down? You should have shot every one of them and presented a heap of bodies to me as a sign of your loyalty and courage. But what did you all do? Cowered like frightened mice and allowed them to enter my house. I should have hired women instead. Every one of you should shave off your moustaches. You don't deserve them!'

When she went inside, the servants quickly got out of her way. Even Gloria scurried down the hallway, shepherding her parents and sisters, who had come a few days ago for the celebrations. Lakshmi locked herself up in her suite, shuddering at the certainty of her thoughts, aware of the hot blood rising within her, her face flushing, yet unable to calm herself down. That was always the case. She was a mere pawn in this game, a mute spectator who observed with remarkably rational fear as this ogre overpowered her, the ogre her mind and her memory had created for their amusement.

He had already violated her, all those years ago in the forest of eucalyptus trees, and repeatedly after that in numerous ways. Why had she foolishly followed him in the dark to the rat holes and allowed him to touch her? What power did he possess over her?

She did not sleep all night. The next morning in the room downstairs where she met her advisors every day, she looked at Selvamani accusingly. 'The law and order situation has become so bad that even my house is not safe any more.'

Selvamani smiled sheepishly. 'Madam, the superintendent says the entire police force was at the park. But I'll reprimand him for not posting policemen at the street corner as you had requested. I'll make sure this doesn't happen again.'

Should she trust him, the man she had trusted completely not too long ago? Was this part of a plan he and Murugesan were hatching to embarrass and humiliate her? 'You've given me similar assurances in the past. How do I know you'll do what you promise?'

Her tone cut through Selvamani. 'What, madam . . .,' he began and then fell silent, looking hurt.

'Anyway, I've given him enough chances,' she continued. 'If I keep pardoning him he'll only sit on my head and continue to cause trouble. I want him to be taught a lesson. Once and for all!'

Murugesan smiled with some satisfaction. 'I told you, madam, long ago, that he's a rascal. But you were too kind to him then. Don't worry about him now. We'll take care of him.'

After everybody else left she turned her attention to Surya. He got up to leave, too. He didn't appear to be aware of what was happening to her. Or perhaps he didn't care? Didn't he know how much criticism she was facing because of him? None of this would have happened if it hadn't been for his ambitions, if he hadn't infected her with his dream. Her resentment seethed for a few moments. 'Why didn't you tell me your buying all that land would get me into so much trouble?' she demanded.

Surya turned around, surprised.

Before he could respond, she continued belligerently. She *had* to confront him. Perhaps he too was in league with everybody else. 'Why didn't you tell me this consortium of yours would make me the villain?'

'Lakshmi,' he said, trying to soothe her, 'what has that got to do this? In any case it should have been obvious to all of us that some questions will be asked. But that's normal. Everything will be okay.'

'That's what you and the others keep saying. But, look, everybody is asking questions.' She flung a newspaper at him.

Surya leant forward with concern. 'You're tired. You need rest.'

'I don't need rest. I want answers!'

'I understand what you feel. But just ignore that Mayilkannan fellow. Ignore the newspaper. Ignore everybody. Why do you want to unnecessarily increase your blood pressure?'

'You don't understand anything,' she snapped. 'Nobody does.'

She stormed out of the room. She wanted to be alone. Alone with her boiling thoughts, to allow them to simmer down. Alone, because she was scared. Scared of the force inside her goading her to hack away at another relationship.

★

The morning after he had turned off Lakshmi's fountains, Mayilkannan appeared at Mohana Devi's house unannounced. Mohana Devi was surprised to see him. She welcomed him a touch too effusively, as if over-compensating for some discomfort. She looked distracted, and surprisingly she had trouble understanding his gestures.

'Is the secretariat as bad as you thought it would be?' Mayilkannan asked.

'No,' she replied after frowning at him for a moment as she tried to understand him. 'It's quite good to work there. I don't see any difference.' But her answer was far from convincing. The smile that followed it was clearly forced.

When he told her what he and his companions had done the previous night the expression on her face changed to something he could only describe as fear.

'What are you doing here then?' she asked anxiously. 'You should be hiding. If they find you she'll show no mercy this time. Why did you do such a foolish thing? Didn't I tell you to not cross the limits? Go away, Mayilkannan. Go and hide in some deep forest, preferably outside the state. Go to a place where they can't find you.'

Mayilkannan was disappointed and hurt by her response. What limit had he crossed? It wasn't as if he'd indulged in mayhem. He had expected her to be more supportive, even happy with what he had done, to commend him for his highly symbolic and effective means of protest. 'If I knew I was unwelcome I would not have come to visit,' his eyes seemed to say as he left in a huff.

'Wait,' Mohana Devi called after him. 'I'm not afraid for myself. I'm afraid for you.'

But he did not look back as he walked down the path to the compound gate. Without stopping anywhere else he took a bus back to Pudupettai. All the way he mulled over the change he had noticed in Mohana Devi. The company of scores of other fawning bureaucrats seemed to have sapped her of her individuality and even instilled fear in her heart. Her transfer to the City had already achieved its purpose.

He felt angry and betrayed. The more he replayed her words in his mind the more he resolved not to fall victim to her fears. He had done nothing wrong. He would not lie low or hide from anybody. They may have rattled Mohana Devi, but he would not let them scare him.

It was in a defiant mood that he got off at Pudupettai. He took his bicycle from the kiosk owner at the bus stop with whom he had left it. He did not go home but headed out of town, past the highway where tractors and rollers were laying the road, into the woods where he used to meet his kuravan friends. He left his bicycle leaning against a tree at the edge of the clearing where he had spent many a night, and walked over the dry, stony bed of the stream, past the shack in the heart of the woods where he and the others had been arrested; it was now in ruins, having been abandoned after the police raid. When he came to a wall of thorny bushes he crouched and parted the branches carefully. The brambles had grown over the opening and he had to cut off some branches to make it wide enough for him to go through. He squeezed past the thorns, scratching himself in the process, and dug the earth with a stick till he hit a buried brass container. He cleared the area of dirt with his hands and the rim of the container revealed itself. He lifted it gently; it was heavy with sloshing liquid. He had remembered right. Nobody had come for the buried arrack in all this time. He tore open the plastic wrapping that held the copper plate cover in place. He lifted the plate and sniffed at the liquid inside. It was obviously in an advanced state of fermentation. Perhaps it had even gone bad. Does arrack go bad like milk or fruit juice? He didn't know. But he lifted the container to his lips and sipped. He grimaced, for he had never tasted anything this bitter. After a few moments he lifted the container again to his lips and drank more. It tasted better this time and he gulped another mouthful before putting the container down.

Dusk was fast approaching. He could hear only a few chattering monkeys far away, perhaps in Thenmozhi's husband's village. He noticed how he could still not think of it as Thenmozhi's village; it was only her husband's village. He was convinced she did not belong there despite her claims to the contrary. Her husband had never accepted her, nor had the villagers.

He took another big swig from the container. The arrack was beginning to taste good.

He looked down at the container. It was still half full. He kicked it with his foot and followed it with his eyes as it rolled in an arc on its circular side until it hit a large stone and stopped. A trail of wet, smelly earth marked its trajectory. His anger persisted, but its target became even more undefined than before. Earlier he thought he was angry with Lakshmi. But now he wasn't so sure. He felt angry with everybody and everything in general: Thenmozhi, her husband, Lakshmi, Sundarapandian, Selvamani, Murugesan, Mohana Devi, her husband, her children. His misanthropy festered in his mind like the wound on Thenmozhi's face. This indiscriminate anger began hurting his head. He lay down on the ground with his fingers interlocked behind his head and closed his eyes, trying hard to expunge all thoughts from his mind.

When he woke up it was dark and the woods were full of insect noises. His head still hurt badly, but he remembered where he was and staggered to his feet. He retraced his steps to the clearing where he had left his bicycle. It was so dark that he had to switch on the bicycle light and heard the dynamo whirr against the rear wheel. As he rode past Thenmozhi's husband's village, along an embankment above dry fields on either side, he heard someone scrambling up the slope ahead of him. He slowed down to peer into the darkness. Suddenly he could see several pairs of eyes glinting in the light of his bicycle lamp. Then a torch appeared and shone directly into his eyes, blinding him. He put his hands over his eyes. The men now advanced towards him, the torchlight still focussed on his eyes so that he could not see them.

'Schoolmaster-saar!' one of the men called out to him. The tone was not respectful. 'The village bard! The mute saint! Ah, the peacock-eyed one! We knew we would find you here.'

Mayilkannan calmly stood his ground. He remembered Mohana Devi's words—perhaps she was right, after all. He waited as the men surrounded him. One of them caught him by the scruff of his neck and tackled him. He fell on the gravel. The man fell on top of him and pinned him down. Mayilkannan did not struggle; there was no point in doing so.

The mocker continued. 'You claim to be mute, but you talk a lot. Too much, some would say. Your hands are wonderful and meddlesome things. You write with them, you work with them, and, worst of all, you speak with them. We have a very easy and effective cure for your overactive hands.'

Another man leaped forward and pulled Mayilkannan's hands from under his torso. He held them both tightly. Mayilkannan could now see the flash of metal, the glint of a sharp edge. The mocker crouched in front of him, holding an axe. Mayilkannan braced himself. In a flash the axe rose before his eyes and swooped down on his pinned hands. Once. Twice. Each time he could feel his breath leaving him, his lungs collapse, blood rush out of his body. He could feel himself dying. And in that moment of extreme pain he chose to break his vow of silence, a vow he had successfully maintained for so many months. Later, when he looked back on that night, he would not be able to explain why he had chosen that moment to speak. He would sometimes think it was because of the pain, for deathly pain can make a person momentarily mad. But sometimes he would think of the potent arrack he had drunk earlier and would be convinced it was the alcohol that had made him lose sanity. Whatever the reason was, he cried out, unfortunately not having forgotten how to speak in all his time of forced silence. 'You can take my hands away,' he screamed, 'but you can't take my words from me!'

As soon as uttered those words he regretted them. He wished they had not heard him, that he had only been hallucinating, that he could somehow pluck them back from the air and stuff them down his larynx.

But he could hear the mocker laugh villainously. 'We can fix that too!'

One of the men forced his mouth open and held his jaw down. 'No!' Mayilkannan screamed despite himself, for he knew this was worse than death. He fought savagely to close his mouth, but the blood that spouted out of the stubs of his hands left him weakened. The mocker put his fingers into Mayilkannan's mouth and pulled his tongue out. He stretched it as far as he could. Mayilkannan thought the man would yank out his guts. The man produced a knife and whipped it across his tongue. Mayilkannan could feel something give way and fly out towards the fields. He wished it was his life and not his tongue. He screamed, but his lungs were giving way and he could hear no sound at all.

The men then vanished into the darkness. Mayilkannan did not remember much of what happened after that. But he did remember looking up and seeing a scarred face staring fearfully at him. The last thing he remembered seeing before he lost consciousness was Thenmozhi covering her face, screeching like a banshee, and slumping on top of him.

★

Gloria sat down beside Lakshmi, having forgotten, at least temporarily, the resentment that had built up over the months.

She looked deeply concerned. That was what Lakshmi liked about her: the ability to leave her personal complaints aside when the situation so required.

'Is that what you really wanted them to do?'

Lakshmi had not heard Gloria speak to her directly in a while, and she had to refamiliarize herself with Gloria's voice. 'I wanted him to be taught a lesson,' Lakshmi insisted, unrepentant.

Gloria looked like she was in despair.

'But, still,' Surya said, looking equally concerned. 'Don't you think they went too far?'

Lakshmi hesitated. He had this way of making everything sound very reasonable. She could feel her anger crack against his reason. 'I just wanted him to be roughed up a bit.'

Surya and Gloria sighed. They appeared relieved, as though they had expected her to say that she had sent instructions right down to the last detail. As though she were the ogre that now possessed her. How little they knew her even after all these years! How little they must think of her! But, still, she was happy to have them around her. They genuinely tried, and cared.

'But you can't say this to the public,' Surya said.

'Of course, not. I'm not an imbecile.'

'No, no, that's not what I meant.' He put his hands out gingerly, hesitated and then pulled them back. Gloria completed his gesture for him. She put her hand on Lakshmi shoulder. 'What I meant is you need to stand firm. Any sign of weakness will now be viewed as guilt. They won't see that these ruffians took matters into their own hands.'

'We're here for you,' added Gloria.

Lakshmi nodded. 'Let me play with the child for a little while,' she said instead, and got up to go look for him.

Later, as she sat in the inner corner of the building behind the lattice screen, an old vision came back to her, this time even with her eyes open. She saw a formless figure in the darkened corner rise and float in the air behind the screen, its two large eyes its only recognizable feature, appearing like eggs above it, the yellow yolks like jaundiced eyeballs. The eyeballs darted to and fro, impatient with the nagging rain on the other side of the screen. When she looked more closely, to her amazement, she noticed that what she had always thought to be the fountain was not a fountain at all, but a flame, crackling and spitting at the drops of water, its white plumes peeling away to reveal orange and red fingers performing a bizarre martial dance with the rain. Then another finger appeared, a severed digit, from under the formless figure's cloak, and beckoned her towards the fountain of fire, slowly, its long, glossy, garishly painted nail swaying back and forth. She held back. It floated away through the lattice screen like smoke in an attempt to convince her, to entice her, and circled the flame. It dipped its dainty finger into the flame and held it there long enough for even the least inflammable material to catch fire. Then it retracted its unscathed finger and raised it in the air. A deep, gurgling laughter filled the courtyard, and the form swooped into the flame and disappeared.

She shook as she stood up. She went to the screen and peered through it. With relief she found that it was hot and bright outside, the fountain in the centre of the garden silent, sealed up with concrete. She should have someone fix it soon, she reminded herself; otherwise it might actually start spitting fire, and she might not be able to resist it for long.

★

The day after K. Abdul Latheef named Lakshmi as being directly responsible for the attack on Mayilkannan with pictures of the bard's hands that now ended at his wrists and a tongue that was barely there, the editorial office of the newspaper he worked for was ransacked by workers belonging to the Party. The horde came carrying cricket bats, and smashed everything they could get their hands on: windows, bookshelves, photocopying machines, telephones, typewriters, furniture. The employees were not hurt only because they managed to flee the office through a back door. The proprietor of the newspaper gave in. He lodged a police complaint only because he didn't want to appear to have capitulated without a fight. He terminated K. Abdul Latheef's employment with immediate effect and gave no reasons for it.

When I caught up with K. Abdul Latheef and declared how he had my support and sympathy, he listened gravely and nodded. I then asked him about Mayilkannan, for I knew he knew more than he had written about. He regarded me uncertainly for a moment and said, 'Why don't you go there and meet him yourself? It would mean a lot to him and his cause for people to meet him. Besides, journalists should get around.'

Whether that was his way of gently rebuking me I could not tell. But I ended up in Pudupettai a couple of days later. Thenmozhi had gone back to her father's house because her husband had thrown her out of his house again. It was there that she had taken Mayilkannan after a doctor had dressed his wounds. A large group of young men stood guard all around the house and refused entry to visitors. Despite identifying myself as a journalist they did not allow me in.

'Saar, we won't let even the prime minister in,' one of the men said exasperatedly. 'Please go away.'

His words were unequivocal. Disappointed, I made my way back to town.

In my anxiety to meet Mayilkannan I had not noticed the lack of activity in Pudupettai when I had arrived in the morning. But now on my way back it grabbed my attention like a misplaced painting would a museum curator's. The town wore a deserted look. Shops were closed; children who should have been in school were playing in the side streets; at intersections groups of youths stood outside kiosks drinking coffee and smoking bidis as if they were waiting for someone to show up. An unusually large number of policemen strolled about the town's major intersections, looking casual, idle. Only the district collector's office was open, but even that was not crowded.

I waited for a few hours: something was bound to happen

soon. But by evening I got tired of waiting, and when I left the town it wore the same look of uncertainty as it had when I had arrived. Without Mayilkannan it was a town waiting idly for something to happen.

But after I left, the town roused itself finally and mobs came together spontaneously and rioted late into the night, ransacking the district headquarters of the Party and the local office of the consortium from which all construction activities were overseen, breaking windows, hacking open desks, burning blueprints, plans, memos and invoices and lobbing a firebomb when they were done. Indefinite curfew was imposed that night for the first time ever in Pudupettai.

A couple of days after the riots in Pudupettai I attended a government press conference, which was a crowded affair. The conference room was already crowded. Television crews and press photographers mobbed the podium. I found myself in the doorway, sweating profusely, squished between two other reporters who had shown up at the last minute.

I was going to see her in the flesh after a long time. The last time I had seen her at close range was when she had returned with the child. But at that time I hadn't been able to see her well. I remembered her mainly from the photographs. I recalled some of them when she was young, when she was a dancer. I could see images of her flash before my eyes, the young Lakshmi, so devastatingly beautiful, so shy and vulnerable, the Lakshmi who could sometimes look like a hunted deer and leave me painfully sorry for her. There was an innocence in those images, a pathos that could break one's heart. It was an older version of that Lakshmi that I expected to see that day. When she arrived with Selvamani and Murugesan, I had to stand on tiptoe and crane my neck over the shoulders and cameras of those standing ahead of me. I was shocked when she came into view. None of the photographs or television images had prepared me for this. Sunken-eyed, her features hardened by a kind of stern worldliness, she looked like a schoolteacher getting ready to punish an errant pupil.

The three of them looked grim as they took their seats. 'My enemies are carrying out a smear campaign against me,' she announced without much prompting. 'They first spread rumours about me. I ignored them as much as humanly possible. But these same people are now making such libellous charges against me that I cannot ignore them any more. This is now becoming a vendetta against me. I have personally asked Selvamani to institute an inquiry into this incident. The truth will soon be known to all.'

'What about the riots in Pudupettai?' asked a reporter. 'Who is responsible?'

'The same goons who want to see me and my colleagues finished.'

'Who are these enemies?'

'All those people who do not have the welfare of the people in their hearts. Those who do not want to see our state progress, those who do not want our people to emerge from poverty, and those who foment trouble under the guise of educating our people. And those to whom we refused to give refuge for terrorist activities in our state and elsewhere. It is those terrorists with the support of certain NGOs who threw the bomb into our district headquarters.'

There were murmurs in the room. 'Do you have any proof of their involvement?'

'I know what I'm talking about!' she snapped. 'You'll be shown adequate proof when the time is right.'

There was a pause. The discomfort of the assembled media persons was palpable. They knew better than to ask any more questions. But one man, standing against the wall in the back of the room, raised his hand, and without waiting to be given the cue, commented, 'But, madam, don't you think it's incorrect to characterize all your critics as enemies of the Party and the people? Don't you think there are valid criticisms against you and the government? Take the celebrations, for instance—'

'What mistakes have the government and I made?' she interrupted him, raising her voice. 'Is developing this state into a world-class technology centre a mistake? Is it our fault that the rains have failed? Is it wrong to snuff out terrorists who—'

'Madam,' the reporter interjected. There was a growing sense that he was being reckless. 'It is not your fault that the rains have failed. But don't you think at a time when everybody is hungry and thirsty, flaunting your wealth like that was in bad taste?'

Lakshmi stared at him as though she could not believe her ears. The tension in the room increased several notches. I wasn't sure what I was hoping for, but at that moment I felt bad for her. What could she say?

'I don't have to answer every fool who walks into this room,' she finally said shrilly. 'I don't have to explain every personal action. In any case, what you see as bad taste, I see as my contribution to the many people who earned money by being directly or indirectly involved in the celebrations! How many hungry people we fed!'

Two men sidled up to the reporter and quietly escorted him out of the room. As they passed by me I could see that the reporter was livid. 'What have you to say about your Italian connections?' he shouted. 'What about the allegations of corruption against you and those close to you?'

There was a sense of relief in the room after his voice trailed down the corridor. It was easier to carry on without the gadfly.

'I'm late for my next appointment,' Lakshmi announced abruptly just as it seemed as though the conference would go on. 'Thank you.' With that she walked off just like that, with her colleagues just as taken aback as the assembled press people.

But this time she walked away alone, and I couldn't help wondering where that defiance—now jaded and frayed from all the battles—sprang from, what made her assert herself even to the point of risking losing her friends. I shook my head and stood outside, wondering what I would tell her mother and daughter when I saw them. I don't know how long I stood there, but at some point someone tapped me on the shoulder and said, 'Move along. We're closing this place for the day.'

And I moved along, as I had for all these years, an impotent observer. There was nothing I could do for her even in her moment of need.

After days of isolated strikes, the Opposition finally called for a general state-wide strike. On the day of the strike a massive demonstration was held in the City. Various organizations gathered at the beach, on the hot sands stretching for miles from the statues of past leaders to the point where the ancient church that jutted into the sea abruptly broke the shoreline. At the head were the leaders of the various organizations who carried clay statues of Lakshmi as a rakshasi, with large enraged eyes, long bloodthirsty tongue sticking out, her hair a mess around her cruel face. She looked ghoulish. Intellectuals and artists marched just behind the leaders, chanting slogans and carrying banners. Then came the farmers, with tractors flying banners, their emaciated cattle painted over with slogans. Then there were students, teachers and members of Opposition parties wearing black headbands, driving donkeys that carried the effigies of Lakshmi, Selvamani, Sundarapandian, Murugesan, Surya and Gloria. And behind them were thousands upon thousands of ordinary people, those who belonged to small organizations and those who belonged to none. Some had come from far, enduring hunger and thirst, their clothes soaked in sweat, their legs covered with dust.

Several people made fiery speeches. The echo of their anger resounded with the crowd. Roused by the speeches they started their long, slow, noisy march through the City. The police had barricaded the entire route of the march. Into the wide beach road they poured slowly, like sand in an hourglass. By the time the last of the marchers joined in, the head of the procession was miles ahead.

From the beach road they turned into the City's streets, the procession lengthening as the roads narrowed, shortening when they broadened. All along the way crowds had gathered to greet them and wave encouragingly. It appeared as though all of humanity had showed up to witness the event. Children on the shoulders of adults, babies in their mothers' arms, the elderly squatting on the footpath, shielding themselves from the blistering sun with towels and rags. People leaned out of balconies and roofs. They climbed trees and electric poles. Every inch of available space, horizontal as well as vertical, was occupied all along the route.

The police and thousands of volunteers wove in and out of the crowd ensuring that nobody got too excited. Yet I was nervous. If the crowds got out of control there would be disaster, and the City could go up in flames in a matter of moments. But fortunately nothing of that sort happened. Other than minor fistfights over premium viewing or marching space, nothing untoward happened that day.

The procession slithered slowly like an anaconda, winding itself around large parts of the City. One square mile around the Aranmanai had been cordoned off, patrolled by platoons of paramilitary personnel. The organizers prominently marked the closest point the procession could get to the Aranmanai by hanging a grotesque effigy of Lakshmi and the others from a tree. As they walked past this point, the marchers paused to hurl abuses at the effigies with renewed strength before moving on. It was here that the students took down the effigy of Lakshmi they were escorting and burnt it, dancing a macabre dance around it as it burned.

Filing past the legislature the procession re-entered the beach road at the point where the Shakadai flowed into the sea as a large sewage canal. Pregnant with the City's refuse and effluents from the industries and tanneries further upstream, nobody would believe that it was really a river, so much so that its real name was forgotten and everybody called it Shakadai-Sewer. Layer upon layer of refuse had built up at the mouth of the river and had become so deeply entrenched that even high tide could not dislodge it.

The day's protests came to a climax on the bridge that spanned the Shakadai. It was here that the leaders of the procession stopped and waited for all the important people to gather around and for the television cameras to get ready. Then they leaned over the railing, facing inland, covering their noses against the unbearable stench and ceremoniously threw the clay statues into the sludge. As the statues tumbled down and broke apart, hitting the water, a deafening cheer rose from the crowd. The marchers beat drums and danced with joy. A sense of accomplishment pervaded the air, for in throwing the statues they had symbolically rid themselves of Lakshmi and the other leaders, consigning them to where they believed they came from.

I witnessed the event from a raised platform specifically set up for the media at the end of the bridge. It was a photographer's dream moment, and cameras clicked away joyously. The sense of relief and joy of the protestors was real and unrestrained. To feel such exhilaration after such a tortuous walk through the City spoke of the power of collective determination, of a catharsis, a communal exorcism of the demons that had plagued them for too long. At that moment they seemed to have forgotten all their worries. They didn't care that they were dangerously close to being struck down by the sun or that they were faint from dehydration. They didn't care that their act was meaningless, that they hadn't actually got rid of Lakshmi, or given back Mayilkannan his tongue, or reinstated K. Abdul Latheef, or given back the land the farmers had lost. They didn't care that they still lacked food and that there was not a cloud in sight. It was a moment of pure innocence, childish naïveté, something they did for the sheer joy of it without being concerned about the utility of their act.

Heartbreaking as their actions were to me, I couldn't help rejoicing briefly with them, for in their act of dumping the statues they had banished cynicism in favour of hope. In the process they had shattered the myth of Lakshmi's popularity, and had proven that those who could follow her puppets devoutly could also, in an act of iconoclastic fury, destroy them. But my joy was short-lived. Because in shattering one myth they had created another one. I wished I could cling on to that moment forever, to capture it and take it to Lakshmi, to tell her that these people, too, like her, had resorted to creating an illusory world for themselves, a world in which they were so powerful that they could destroy their opponents with such a simple, symbolic act. This myth—not unlike the one she had created—was ultimately an act of desperation, for it was better to imagine joy than to live in the steadfast disappointment of reality. It was for this reason that, despite the veneer of hope by the end of the day, I felt so oppressively burdened that I could not share their joy.

I returned home in the bleakest of moods.

The bridge became a shrine of sorts. People came there to look down at the sludge and try to identify the spots where the clay statues had fallen. They looked like masked bandits covering their noses with cloth. Some threw flower petals in mock homage. Others broke coconuts and offered them to the river. This continued for several days till policemen started patrolling the footpath on the bridge and chased people away when they approached.

If that was their way of praying for deliverance, their prayers were partially answered one day not long after that when winds from the northeast began to howl through most of the state. In the City, residents came out of their houses and stared expectantly at the eastern sky. Those more impatient assembled at the beach. I was one of them. I spent an entire evening under a statue basking in the cool wind. A man who, like me, had come to pass his time, sat down beside me. He broke a murukku in half and offered me a piece. 'Heh, heh, saar,' he said grinning broadly. 'Such breeze can only mean that rain is not far behind. At least now I can take a bath.'

I noticed that a jagged circle of sweat under his armpit had stained his shirt. I nodded. I was privileged enough to have the luxury of anticipating the rain for different reasons. With the coming rains, I was sure Lakshmi's troubles would ease up as people turned to true rejoicing.

But the rains were farther away than we thought. The sky

did not reveal any signs of clouds. Only the wind blew, with unusual enthusiasm, picking up force slowly, penetrating well inland, tantalizing everyone with the smell of rain. A day or two later a few wisps of clouds did appear high in the sky, but they disappeared just as quickly. The weather toyed with our emotions and I became increasingly desperate.

Then, one day, winds buffeted the shoreline with the force of a gale, darkening the sky with ripened clouds. And when the clouds tore open to dump the truant rains, the wind howled with laughter, as though it had enjoyed the joke enormously, blowing off roofs, electricity poles and old trees on the way. For three full days there was no reprieve. The City received more rain in those three days than it had in the three previous years. In low-lying areas people waded through chest-deep water. The lawns of the Aranmanai lay submerged in pools of muddy water. But nobody complained—even those who had lost their roofs—for their thirst had not yet been slaked.

And then, at the end of the downpour, there was a tremendous, ear-splitting boom, louder than the strongest monsoon thunder. It sounded as if scores of cannons had been fired simultaneously. The echoes continued to buffet the City for several minutes. Then the wind calmed down, the rain let up, and all was quiet.

It took a long time for me to realize that the noise had came from the direction of the Aranmanai. I rushed out of my house, well aware that submerged manholes had been opened up to ease the clogged sewage drains, and that one false step would mean getting sucked into a whirlpool of shit and scum. But before I had gone far I realized that I had lost my bearings. Passers-by pointed the way in all directions and each had a different theory as well. The City's hundred-and-fifty-year-old banyan tree had fallen, one man said. It was a lightning strike, another said. A lightning strike does not make so much noise, countered another, it's a bomb. That was what I had been afraid of. *A bomb.*

I made many frantic phone calls to whoever I could connect to, and it was only upon learning the truth that I was relieved.

Relieved that it wasn't a bomb or a missile, and that it wasn't at the Aranmanai. The largest wooden cut-out of Lakshmi that had risen like a sky-scraper at the entrance to a colony called Gandhinagar, and visible from miles around, had fallen. The sturdy wooden props holding it up had collapsed under the sustained force of the wind. 'But don't sound so happy,' my informant, who lived not far from there, told me. 'It has flattened out a large section of the slums. God knows how many people have died.'

'Oh, nobody would have died,' I said, relieved to the point of recklessness. 'How can cardboard kill?'

'You must be crazy,' my informant retorted. 'It was made of wood. You know how many weeks it took to put it up? It was like constructing a building. Just think: how could a cardboard cut-out of that size even have been erected?'

He was right, as I was to find out later. Dozens of people had been crushed under Lakshmi's weight. Thirty-five of them had died. Hundreds had lost their shanties. When I arrived at the scene the next day I found them huddled together, marooned on raised ground, dazed.

The area over which the cut-out had fallen, precisely tracing the contours of Lakshmi's body, was completely flattened and submerged under water. The roofs of the neighbouring shacks around the perimeter had been blown away by the impact. It was a miracle that only thirty-five people had died. On the surface, turned upwards, was Lakshmi's face, smiling cheerfully back at the homeless. Bits of wood and household items were floating in the water around the cut-out.

An old man, sitting on the roof of one of the shacks with his head in his hands, bawled, 'After ages of wandering we decided to settle down. And this is what happens to us. It is our fate to be wanderers forever. Serves us right for defying our fate.'

A few residents gathered around me. 'Write in the newspaper that it was that amma who killed so many people,' a kurava said. Over the last few years kuravas who had lost hope of ever receiving the land that had been promised to them had started moving into this slum. There were twenty-five of them among the dead. 'Even a bomb would not have killed so many people.'

'They erected it at that spot on purpose,' another young kurava said. 'They know there were plenty of us living near the entrance. They're trying to finish us in every way they can.'

Their attitude became increasingly hostile. I knew they would be in an ugly mood by that evening when Lakshmi was scheduled to pay a visit. I needed no further confirmation of this. As I slunk away one of the men shouted, 'Tell that amma that if she cannot bring back our dead she needn't bother coming here. We're not beggars. We don't need her charity.'

★

Lakshmi was surprised and pleased when Gloria said she'd come too. Lakshmi had expected only Surya to turn up, and even that she wasn't sure of. Whether Gloria's presence added any real value or not, it at least rekindled her hopes that the ice between them had melted.

So Lakshmi arrived at Gandhinagar surrounded by Gloria, Surya, Selvamani, Murugesan, the local MLA and an assortment of police personnel. A platform had been hastily raised on a dry patch for her to stand on and address the residents. The police had cordoned off the area so that she would be at a safe distance. Behind them were the slum-dwellers, packed tightly into a small area. Babies, crushed in their mother's arms, bawled. Those who had lost somebody or their home ululated. The others were clearly restive or stared sullenly into space.

The moment Lakshmi appeared in sight there was pandemonium. The crowd surged forward, straining the cordon of policemen, each linked to his neighbour by a lathi. The mass heaved this way and that, threatening to break out at any moment. And that's exactly what happened when a small boy managed to sneak through the cordon and the policemen pounced on him. At this point the crowd went berserk. It poured out like water from a breach in a dam, and the policemen helplessly watched the onslaught.

What happened next was like a surreal scene from a film. Through the tight circle around her Lakshmi could see men, women and children running towards her. Like an avalanche they came in slow motion, their strength and determination concealed by their deceptive pace. The kuravas were in the forefront. On the way, some of them bent to pick up some mud, and when they got closer, they flung it in her direction. As they came closer, she could clearly see their mouths contort, their eyes dilate, their fists clench. The black skirts of the women fluttered behind them like flags, their arms covered with bangles that clanked angrily. The men, their turbans coming undone, their thick moustaches upturned to give them the ferocious look of ancient warriors, looked savagely determined.

Despite the protective ring of policemen and her companions around her she saw only kuravas all around her. They were swarming like angry cobras, hissing and spitting and slithering over one another in their attempts to reach her. It was only a matter of minutes before the ring gave way and they fell upon her like ravenous beasts. She remembered, after so many decades, the words of abuse the kuravas had hurled at her when she had accused them of stealing her Charlie. They were vile, spiteful, more hurtful than the rocks they threw at her. She heard those words again, loud and clear, as though somebody were bellowing them into her ears.

In desperation the policemen raised their guns and fired into the air. Over the noise the crowd made she could hear the guns pop like balloons bursting. But the kuravas remained unafraid. Provoked by this display of firepower, someone pushed a policeman and he stumbled backwards, his finger still clenched around the trigger. She heard another pop, and a thin voice cry out for just a moment. Then there was complete silence. The residents stared, horror-struck, frozen like a city caught unawares in the path of a volcano. Then the statues suddenly came alive, screaming and scattering in all directions. She could now see a kuravan boy with a wound on his head, lifeless, sprawled on a wooden plank submerged in the water below, his warm blood oozing out and flowing with the flood water towards the Shakadai.

Someone pushed her towards her car, and she went, involuntarily, hurriedly, lest the crowd turn around and pounce on her. And in her mind's eye she could see the water closing over the boy.

The Fountain of Fire

Surya came to her suite and announced that he was taking his family to Italy.

She wasn't surprised. She had seen the look on Gloria's face when they had fled the slum. For once Gloria's features had come alive and there had been an expression of horror and fright on her face. Then blood had drained away from her face, leaving it even more ashen, withering, her newly animated features crumpling.

'They want a vacation,' he said.

Lakshmi looked up, surprised that he would use such a lame excuse.

'Well, she wants to go,' he stuttered.

'Will you be taking the child also?'

'Of course. How can we leave him behind?'

'Why can't you? There are so many people to take care of him here. I'm here.'

Surya did not respond, and Lakshmi suddenly became aware of the absurdity of her suggestion.

'When will you be back?'

'As soon as I drop them off.'

'Will you be back?'

He shuffled uncomfortably. He didn't look at her while he spoke. 'Gloria doesn't feel safe here any more.'

'I don't either,' she responded. She reached out and held his hand. 'That's why I want you.'

Surya's eyes roved into the distance. He eased himself out of Lakshmi's grip and began to move towards the door. He waited at the threshold for a few moments fidgeting with the cuff of his shirt. When Lakshmi went to look for a handkerchief to blow her nose into, he quietly slipped away before she could look up.

The next day when he and Gloria knocked on her door to say goodbye, she did not open it. 'I don't believe in goodbyes,' she told them from behind the door, 'just go away.' She paused as a faint ray of hope appeared to her. 'Unless you've changed your mind about going.'

There was no response. A moment later she heard footsteps make their way softly down the corridor.

Nobody called on her any more. Not even Selvamani. Only groups of protestors who stood at the end of the street, which had been cordoned off by policemen, shouting slogans. She could hear them every now and then, their voices carrying through the closed windows. Her secretary came dutifully every day. It was from him that she got all the news of the outside world. She suspected though that he edited out certain portions, and sometimes even concealed certain things from her. But he was her best source of information.

Mutthu remained in the Aranmanai, wheelchair-bound, isolated from the rest of the world in the deepest recesses of the building, his nurses his only companions. The man who had once been so vain that he had commissioned his statue to be installed after his death on the beach alongside those of Gandhi and other leaders was now unaware of himself. Lakshmi felt a stab of pity for him, a sympathetic reaction to her own abandonment. She went to his room, but found him asleep in his wheelchair, his face lolled to one side, his chin buried in his black angavastram, serene in his ignorance. The nurse sitting beside him got up and put her finger on her lips. Would the nurse have dared to shush her a few days ago? Her sympathy for him vanished immediately. At least he had someone by his side. The longer she looked at him the angrier she felt. How could he have escaped all the torment, the tumult in her life? How could he have washed himself of all responsibility so easily? How could he be so serene at a time like this? She shook him out of his sleep just to spite the nurse. He woke up with a bewildered look.

'Look what you've done to me,' she said to him. 'You're the cause of all this. Why didn't you leave me alone to my dance? Why did you drag me into this muck? All those promises of how you had to serve your people. *Your* people. That's right. They're not my people as you can see. You promised to do everything for them and then left me to fulfil them. What a smart move! Everybody still thinks you're god. They're still breaking coconuts in your name, those fools! And I? A rakshasi. Surpanakha, Puthana. Can you not hear their vile abuses? Can you not see that I've already died a thousand times at their hands?

'I'm done, I tell you. This time for good. I tried my best. But nobody cares. Not even you. So I'm going to stop trying. Let it all be laid to waste, all this work that I've done for others. I don't care. I don't care what people think. I'm tired of trying to make everyone happy. I'm tired of people. They're all ungrateful. Every one of them. Even you!'

As she walked back to her suite, her resolve began to crumble. She noticed how empty the Aranmanai felt even though the servants were supposed to be carrying out their duties as usual. At the far end of one of the corridors she could see a maid scurrying in and out of rooms. Lakshmi summoned her and asked, 'Where are the rest of the servants?'

'They're all here, amma,' the woman responded.

The response was too earnest, and Lakshmi looked at her suspiciously to see if there was any hint of mockery. 'What are they doing?' she demanded.

'They're doing their work, amma.'

'Then why do I not hear any sound? Why is it so quiet?'

'They're working quietly. So that they don't disturb you.'

'Why should they not disturb me? Why, what's happened to me? Tell them to assemble downstairs immediately. I want to see who has come to work and who's missing.'

A few moments later she came down the broad stairs,

eyeing the bewildered servants who had assembled in the landing. They were all there. She grunted in dissatisfaction. 'Palani,' she said, addressing the gardener. 'You look like you have been dozing. Have you trimmed the hedges?'

'No, amma, I wasn't dozing. Yes, I have trimmed the hedges. You can see for yourself.' He lowered his head.

'Valar, have you dusted all the furniture on this floor?'

A thin woman nodded. She did not dare look up at her.

At this Lakshmi flared up. 'I don't believe any of you,' she shouted shrilly. 'You were all whiling away your time, gossiping amongst yourselves. Talking viciously behind my back, like everybody else. You mock me when I'm not around. Don't any of you have any gratitude?'

She paused for breath. 'I don't want any of you to leave today, do you understand?' she continued. 'I don't want any of you to leave me at any time. I want you all here day and night!'

The servants gaped at her and nodded slowly. 'Where would we go, amma?' one of them ventured to say. 'We've been with you for years. You think we'll leave you just like that?'

Lakshmi looked at the servant. He was an elderly man who did odd jobs. He had been with her for years. He did not talk much, but she knew he possessed a certain knowledge about the world that made him appear wise. He looked kindly at her now, as though he knew, as though he understood, as though he would say more if he were not a mere servant. 'Talk to me,' she wanted to tell him. 'Say whatever is on your mind.' But she turned around and swiftly went up the stairs without looking back at them.

★

'Vasu,' Devaki said softly, hiding her desperation. 'I want to see her. Take me there.'

'There's no point. You won't be allowed anywhere close to her house.'

'They'll allow me!' she said sharply. 'How do you know in any case?'

I knew because I'd tried several times, despite the few privileges that my press pass gave me, despite the connections I had and the recommendations they were willing to make on my behalf to get through to her. None of it had worked. 'She has gone underground,' an influential member of the Party explained. 'Even I can't talk to her. But this is only to be expected after all that has happened.'

'I'll take you there if you want,' I replied to Devaki. 'But, trust me, it will be useless.'

Devaki gave me a withering look. 'I've never asked for your help. The one time I do, is this how you respond? Go, I don't need your help.'

She brushed past me with surprising strength and energy.

When she arrived near the Aranmanai, the policemen at the street corner regarded Devaki with pity.

'Let me in,' she shouted, trying to get past them. 'I tell you I'm her mother.'

'Amma,' the harried inspector said. 'Everybody is her mother.'

Devaki looked at the policeman angrily. 'Don't patronize me, you understand! Let me go. I'm not a mad woman. I'm her mother.'

'I know, I know. But she's not at home now. Why don't you come back tomorrow?'

A few university students around her snickered. Crowds usually stood at the street corner to shout slogans every day. Today it was the students' turn. Devaki looked at them and shook with rage. 'What are you all doing here? Instead of studying is this what you do all day? Loitering around? What are you protesting against? If you have a complaint to make about her come to me. What's happened to your tongues now?'

Some of them continued smiling. Devaki rushed towards one of the students and raised her hand. The inspector caught her and steered her away. 'Yo!' he shouted at a rickshaw driver nearby. 'Take this amma home.' Even as Devaki protested, he pushed her into the rickshaw. 'Yes, amma, come back tomorrow. I promise you we'll let you in. Now go home and lie down.'

As the rickshaw sputtered and lurched forward Devaki leaned against the side and promised herself that she would come again the next day, and every day after that, till they let her in.

★

For several days Lakshmi did not emerge from her suite. She did not part the curtains even once; she opened the door only after ascertaining that the person on the other side was someone she wanted to see. Food was brought to her. She made the cook eat a portion of her meals and watched him closely for any signs of discomfort before she accepted the plate.

The rest of the time she spent with her visions. She sought refuge in them, for they crowded out the memories that rapped at the window, shouting to be let in. Before her she saw an assortment of still images stitched at odd angles into a virtual quilt. She could choose whichever image she wanted to animate. She reached out for one that was grey and a little obscure, and touched it with her finger. It sprang to life, filled up her vision. She saw the abandoned room over the glassmaker's factory. She was the girl who lived in that room, standing at the window, clutching the iron grille, looking over the tiles and the gargoyles and the griffins out into the fog-shrouded sea. She waited for the fog to lift, for a ship to appear and cast anchor at the edge of the lagoon, for a boat to be lowered from its aft, to be rowed towards her, for her parents to scramble ashore excitedly upon seeing her. But for years the fog lay brooding over the lagoon, thickening and obscuring the sea when it rained, with no sign of a ship.

Then, one day, after a week of persistent drizzle, the mist began to clear, as though a large cherubic face in the sky was blowing it away, and she could see a ship on the horizon, at first as a minuscule dot, but later as a large galleon as it neared the lagoon. With pounding heart she waited as the boat was lowered. The oarsmen, doubling up, rowed furiously towards land. As the boat came nearer she could see her parents in it standing at the prow, looking fresh and beautiful, as though they had never undertaken the arduous journey. She jumped up and down in her room, stretching her hands through the grilles towards her parents. But just as the boat was about to pull up to the quay, to her horror, her mother shoved her father into the water, screeching with laughter and jumped into the arms of a band of kuravas waiting on the shore. Before anybody could react, she was gone, having evaporated like the fog, her villainous laughter echoing through the alleys.

But her memories did manage to intrude into her celluloid, fictional preoccupations, sneaking in at moments when she wasn't vigilant enough. They insisted on replaying her life, especially moments of regret, when she could have uncomplicated the excessive complications of her life, but had not, for she had always wanted to be vicious with herself, a viciousness that was both a form of punishment and an escape.

As the revue of her follies played before her eyes, mocking her, it clarified something that had never been clear to her: the utter pointlessness of her battles, the waste of all the energies she spent on battles she could have easily avoided. She had been—and was still, especially now—a moth attracted to a flame.

All day Lakshmi remained indoors, trying to distract herself in vain. She went to Mutthu's room and flipped through old albums for him. He looked at the photographs and nodded at every one of them, clearly not recognizing any of them. And she went through every album she could find, looking but not registering the photographs, for all she could see was the quilt.

Finally, in desperation she went to bed, hoping sleep would clear her mind and soothe her frayed nerves. But it only brought more frightening dreams. First she dreamt of Pulcinella appearing without any limbs, his face scarred, a piece of flesh flapping over where his left eye should be. Then she saw him with his kurava relatives, whom he had never acknowledged to her. Her mother, too, was with them, lying motionless before them on the floor. Pulcinella picked up a large carving knife in his mouth and in a flash slit open her mother's gut. He then said something that she could not understand, and in a flash they were all running towards her, the limbless Pulcinella leading the charge, floating through the air like a vampire. She ran for her life, but could not go fast enough, for the air was turgid, like sheets of thick liquid. No matter how much she exerted she could not go faster and the kuravas, now multiplying like amoebae, were catching up fast, their fingers like the talons of an eagle, poised to rip her apart. Just as they were about to get her, all went black, as though she and everybody else had fallen into a deep abyss where nothing existed.

She woke up quivering like a leaf. It was getting dark outside. She pulled the curtains tightly together so that she could not see the dark.

She finally admitted that she was afraid. Afraid of the world, but even more afraid of herself.

One day she brought out items that she had saved from her childhood. There was the rag doll and Hari the wooden rocking horse among other things. Moths had eaten into the doll's cheeks where there had once been rouge. The horse was rickety, with peeling paint and slivers of wood like the quills on a porcupine. She placed it in the centre of her room and sat on it. Gently she rocked as it creaked under her weight, but, surprisingly, it did not fall apart. She remembered rocking on it in the courtyard, sucking her thumb as she watched her grandmother cooking in the kitchen.

It was then, as she rocked herself to quietude that she saw the formless figure from behind the lattice screen rise, revealing itself for the first time, feature by feature, till a sorcerer, a kurava, emerged from under the cloak, smiling enticingly at her, wiggling his finger. He was long-necked like a swan, graceful in his sinister seduction, his ruby-red eyes, twin flames of charm that she willed herself to resist.

He appeared to her repeatedly, his wiggling finger whittling away at her resolve, till she finally went to him one day, convinced that she had truly had enough, convinced that everybody exulted in her misfortunes. He spread his striated cloak on his back like a magic carpet and she sat on it. He then rose and floated towards the fountain of fire in the middle of the garden. She felt as though she were riding a giant moth, and they circled the fountain, getting closer and closer, accelerating with every revolution, till with a rush of blood she found herself plunging into the all-encompassing hands of the fire, and there she was, in an abyss of perpetual dreams.

Epilogue

When Devaki, Ragini and I arrived at the Aranmanai it was empty. There were no guards outside, only the usual posse of policemen at the street corner. The doors and windows were open, and the wind whistled through, causing the drapes to billow. Every now and then the doors and the windows rattled or creaked at their hinges, breaking the silence the mansion was enveloped in. It had the forlorn look of a place hastily abandoned by its residents, like an empty ship washed ashore by a storm. And yet, it seemed to revel in its newfound freedom, opened at last after constantly being closed and watched over by zealous guards, suffocated and made to feel small despite its grandness.

Lakshmi's secretary was in her suite, silently contemplating her body. Lakshmi was curled up in a ball on the floor in the foetal position, rigid, on her side. Beside her was the weapon: a small, stubby, narrow-barrelled pistol. All over the room items from the past were strewn: her rag doll, a well-chewed plastic bone that belonged to Charlie the Dog, a red embroidered skirt that she had been particularly fond of, a eucalyptus leaf that had been pressed between the pages of a book, a wooden puppet that Sister Cecilia had given her, photographs of her early years as a dancer, clippings of reviews of her recitals . . . I wandered into the large closet. It was similarly strewn with articles. What caught my eye was a pile of notebooks in the corner. They were books of all sizes and shapes, many of them frayed or torn, others relatively new. I pounced upon them ravenously, for I knew at once that they were her diaries in which she meticulously wrote down everything that happened to her ever since Sister Cecilia had introduced her to the habit. These were a treasure trove of information on her, a chronicle of everything she had experienced, even though they were all written in the distant third person as events taking place in someone else's life, a protagonist whom she had even given a name to. She had gone to great lengths in creating a personality that was quite different from hers, and indeed quite her opposite on many occasions.

As I rifled through her belongings, I came across a disc-shaped stone on the floor, smooth, black, clean after years of handling. It was odd that it should be in the midst of her mementoes. But then, suddenly, I remembered that the day we had run away from the kuravas after she had accused them of stealing Charlie the Dog, she had bent down to pick up the stone that they had thrown at her. I picked it up and examined it again. It was definitely that stone. I had even asked her what she was going to do with it. 'Keep it,' she had said simply and I hadn't given the matter another thought. But now I was unnerved. It wasn't because of childish acquisitiveness that she had picked it up. She knew even then what she was doing. I shuddered at the thought of her having jealously held on to it all these years, to have carried such an insignificant item from her past wherever she had gone, to have preserved and taken it out to examine during her last moments.

We carried her on a stretcher, straining under her weight, stumbling down the stairs, almost tipping her over several times. As we left Devaki asked Lakshmi's secretary, 'What did she tell you about us?' Even at this time she had not given up hope of redemption.

To her disappointment, the secretary shrugged. 'Just that you were relatives.'

Outside, the streets were empty as though curfew had been imposed. The whole world appeared dead. It was dank and gloomy. The wind had ceased. It was so still that it felt as though we were in a vacuum. I was beginning to wonder if I was dreaming the whole thing, for it was, after all, a time of intemperance.

Whether she had wanted us at her funeral or not, I didn't know, but in death she didn't have the choices she had in life. As the priest chanted shlokas, the pyre burned and the fire leapt up and danced. Through the shimmer and the haze I could see Devaki and Ragini, their heads bent towards each other, watching the flames consume Lakshmi's body.

Then it started to drizzle. The priest poured more ghee into the pyre, and it continued to burn—absurdly—through the rain.

A few days later, Ragini saw her father for the first time. Mayilkannan and Thenmozhi were at the gates, Thenmozhi heaving under the weight of her unborn baby and Mayilkannan gesticulating and babbling at the top of his voice. 'Aeh, aeh, aeh!' he said, his voice deep and grating. He made incoherent sounds, a mute struggling to communicate, and waved the stumps of his hands. He faced the gates of the Aranmanai and spat, unable to direct his spit without a tongue. Again and again he spat, writhing in agony, and spraying spit all over the place.

Ragini, unable to bear the sight, turned to her grandmother. 'Tell that man to stop, paati,' she cried. 'Please tell him to stop. She was my mother!'

But like the hideous gargoyles of the Aranmanai that spouted rain water below, Mayilkannan continued spitting and spraying, and finally when he left shouting like a madman it wasn't clear to me any more who was the more unforgiving.

Acknowledgements

I would like to thank:

Jaideep Varma, for the shared journey as writers and for his generous help and opinions at all times;

The Mahoneys (Sean and Pervin), Pratibha Kelapure, Raji Pillai and Moazzam Sheikh, for reading various versions of the manuscript, for sharing their views and for helping in numerous other ways;

Lynn Franklin, my agent, for her patience and help;

Bill Contardi, for putting me in touch with her in the first place;

Leyla Selmi, for early encouragement;

The Penguin team, particularly V.K. Karthika and Poulomi Chatterjee;

Amulya Malladi, for being so generous with her experiences as a writer;

The Cilentos (Andrea, Giorgio and Matilde), Sumana Srinivasan and T. Ramakrishnan, for sharing their knowledge;

Marc Ferrié, for giving me the time to complete the first draft;

And, more than anybody else, my wife Karuna, for giving me the space and the time, and for learning to live with my absences even when I was physically at home.